Irresistible

It was the way Lily refused to see him, as if she could pretend she didn't feel the pull as long as she didn't look directly at him. He took two steps closer, stopping near enough that her scent welcomed him, even if the rest of her did not. The jump of his heartbeat warned him to make this quick.

"Yes, we'll go," he said. "But first . . ." And he leaned in to plant a kiss on her frowning mouth.

He expected a punch, and not just from the kiss. He'd already decided to let her connect. But he didn't expect to land on his butt in the dirt.

Rule stared up at her, astonished. She'd hooked her leg behind his knee, pulled—and down he went, before his mouth even touched hers.

"Ask, don't assume." She opened the car door. "Oh, and you can give me that explanation," she said, climbing in, "on the way back." And she slammed the door shut.

TEMPTING DANGER

EILEEN WILKS

BERKLEY SENSATION, NEW YORK

THE BERKLEY PUBLISHING GROUP
Published by the Penguin Group
Penguin Group (USA) Inc.
375 Hudson Street, New York, New York 10014, USA
Penguin Group (Canada), 90 Eglinton Avenue East, Suite 700, Toronto, Ontario M4P 2Y3, Canada
(a division of Pearson Penguin Canada Inc.)
Penguin Books Ltd., 80 Strand, London WC2R 0RL, England
Penguin Group Ireland, 25 St. Stephen's Green, Dublin 2, Ireland (a division of Penguin Books Ltd.)
Penguin Group (Australia), 250 Camberwell Road, Camberwell, Victoria 3124, Australia
(a division of Pearson Australia Group Pty. Ltd.)
Penguin Books India Pvt. Ltd., 11 Community Centre, Panchsheel Park, New Delhi—110 017, India
Penguin Group (NZ), 67 Apollo Drive, Rosedale, North Shore 0745, Auckland, New Zealand
(a division of Pearson New Zealand Ltd.)
Penguin Books (South Africa) (Pty.) Ltd., 24 Sturdee Avenue, Rosebank, Johannesburg 2196,
South Africa

Penguin Books Ltd., Registered Offices: 80 Strand, London WC2R 0RL, England

This is a work of fiction. Names, characters, places, and incidents either are the product of the author's imagination or are used fictitiously, and any resemblance to actual persons, living or dead, business establishments, events, or locales is entirely coincidental. The publisher does not have any control over and does not assume any responsibility for author or third-party websites or their content.

TEMPTING DANGER

A Berkley Sensation Book / published by arrangement with the author

PRINTING HISTORY
Berkley Sensation mass-market edition / October 2004

Copyright © 2004 by Eileen Wilks.
Excerpt from *Mortal Danger* copyright © 2004 by Eileen Wilks.
Cover art by John Blackford.
Jewelry design by Ann Biederman, courtesy of Meryl Messineo.
Interior text design by Kristin del Rosario.

ISBN: 978-0-425-19878-0

BERKLEY SENSATION®
Berkley Sensation Books are published by The Berkley Publishing Group,
a division of Penguin Group (USA) Inc.,
375 Hudson Street, New York, New York 10014.
BERKLEY SENSATION is a trademark belonging to Penguin Group (USA) Inc.

PRINTED IN THE UNITED STATES OF AMERICA

13   12   11   10   9   8

This book is dedicated to my agent, Eileen Fallon, who hung in there through thick, through thin, through writer phone calls. Just want to say, "Hi, Eileen—this is Eileen. It wouldn't have happened without you."

ONE

❧

HE didn't have much face left. Lily stood well back, keeping her new black heels out of the pool of blood that was dry at the edges, still gummy near the body. She'd seen worse when she worked Traffic Division, she reminded herself.

But it was different when the mangling had been done on purpose.

Mist hung in the warm air, visible in front of the police spotlights, clammy against her face. The smell of blood was thick in her nostrils. Flashes went off in a crisp one-two as the photographer recorded the scene.

"Hey, Yu," the officer behind the camera called. He was a short man with chipmunk cheeks and red hair cut so short it looked like the fuzz on a peach.

She grimaced. O'Brien never tired of a joke, no matter how stale. If they both lived to be a hundred and ran into each other in the nursing home, the first thing he'd say to her would be, "Hey, Yu!"

That is, assuming she kept her maiden name for the next seventy-two years. Considering the giddy whirl she laughingly called a social life, that seemed possible. "Yeah, Irish?"

"Looks like you had a hot date tonight."

"No, me and my cat always dress for dinner. Dirty Harry looks great in a tux."

O'Brien snorted and moved to get another angle. Lily tuned him out along with the other S.O.C. officer, the curious behind the chain-link fence, and the uniforms keeping them there.

Spilled blood draws a crowd as easily as spilled sugar draws flies. The members of the public attending this particular crime scene probably didn't come from this neighborhood, though. Here, people assumed that curiosity came with a price tag. They knew what a drive-by sounded like, and the look of a drug deal going down. The members of the public craning their necks for a glimpse of gore were probably customers of the nightclub up the street. Club Hell did attract a distinctive clientele.

The victim didn't look as if he came from around here, either.

He lay on his back on the dirty pavement. There was a Big Gulp cup, smashed flat, by his feet, a scrap of newspaper under his butt, and a broken beer bottle by his foot. Whatever had torn out his throat and made a mess of his face had left the eye and cheekbone on the right side intact. One startled brown eye stared up at nothing from smooth skin the color of the wicker chair on her mother's porch. Name-brand jeans, she noted, the kind you find in pricey department stores. Black athletic shoes, again an expensive brand. A red silk shirt.

The silk of the right sleeve of that shirt was shredded over the forearm. Three deep gouges there—defensive wounds. That arm was out-flung, the hand lying palm up with the fingers curled inward the way a child's will when it sleeps.

His other hand lay about twelve feet away, up against one of the poles of the swing set.

A playground. Someone had ripped this guy's face off in a playground, for God's sake. There was a hard ache in Lily's throat, a tightness across her shoulders. She'd seen death often enough since she was promoted to Homicide. Her stomach no longer turned over, but the regret, the sorrow over the waste, never went away.

He wasn't young enough to have enjoyed those swings recently—mid-twenties, maybe. She put him at about five ten, weight one eighty. Weight lifter's shoulders and arms, powerful thighs. He'd been strong, perhaps cocky in his strength.

Strength hadn't done him much good tonight. Neither had the .22 pistol he'd apparently brought with him. It rested near the severed hand, as if it had fallen from those fingers once death relaxed them.

"Careful, Detective. Don't get your pretty dress dirty."

Lily didn't look away from the body. She knew the voice, having taken the man's report when she first arrived. "More crime scenes are contaminated by police officers than civilians. You have a reason for bringing your big feet over here, Phillips?"

"I'm ten feet from the body, for Chrissake."

Now she looked at him. Officer Larry Phillips was one-half of the responding unit. Lily hadn't run across him before, but she knew the type. He was over forty, still on the streets and sour about it. She was female, twenty-eight, and already a detective.

He didn't like her. "Believe it or not, evidence has been found more than ten feet from the victim. What do you want?"

"Came to let you know none of the helpful citizens over by the fence admits to having seen anything. They were partying at the club, left together, and saw the pretty lights flashing on the squad cars. Came over to see what was going on."

"Club Hell, you mean?"

"That's where you'll need to look for your killer. The lab won't learn squat about this one."

"There are other types of evidence."

He snorted. "Yeah, maybe he dropped a calling card. Or maybe you agree with my partner. He thinks a puppy dog did it."

She glanced at the gap in the chain-link fence that served as an entry, where Phillips's partner—a young Hispanic officer—was one of the officers handling crowd control, taking names and addresses. "Your partner's a rookie?"

"Yeah." Phillips took a wrapped toothpick out of his pocket, peeled the cellophane off, and stuck it in his mouth. "I explained about puppy dogs and how they don't usually bite a hand off in one chomp."

Phillips wasn't stupid, she acknowledged. Just annoying. She nodded. "A fit man can usually fight a dog off. Not much sign of a fight, and there's that pistol. . . ." Which the victim had probably been carrying, though it was just possible there'd been a third person at the scene. She shook her head. "The beast must have hit him quick."

"They're fast, all right. Poor bastard probably didn't have time to know his hand was gone."

"He had good instincts, though. He tried to pull his head down, protect his neck. That's when he lost some of his face. Then it ripped out his throat."

"Now, now. You're not supposed to say 'it.' We have to say 'he' now, treat 'em like people. Full rights under the law."

"I know the law." She glanced up at Phillips. Way up—he was a long, stringy man, well over six feet. Of course, Lily had to look up to meet almost anyone's eyes. She'd almost persuaded herself that didn't irritate her anymore. "This is your turf, Officer. Can you ID the victim?"

"He's not from the hood."

"Yeah, I got that much. Maybe came here for a little action—dope, sex, maybe the slightly more legal entertainment of Club Hell. If he's a regular, you could have seen him around."

He shook his head. The toothpick seemed glued to his bottom lip. "This wasn't a drug killing, or pimp punishing a john who didn't pay. Not even murder, really."

Three years ago a case like this would have been handled by the X-Squad. Now it went to Homicide. "The courts say otherwise."

"And we know how smart those bleeding heart judges are. According to them, we're supposed to treat the beasts like they're human now. That mess at your feet proves what a great idea that is."

"I've seen uglier things done by men to other men. And to women. And the scene still has to be kept clear."

"Sure thing, Detective." Phillips gave her a mocking grin, turned, then paused and took the toothpick out of his mouth. When he met her eyes, the mockery and anger had faded from his. "A word of advice from someone who put in fifteen years on the X-Squad. Call them whatever you like, but don't mistake the lupi for human. They're hard to hurt, they're faster than us, they're stronger, and they like the way we taste."

"This one doesn't seem to have done much tasting."

He shrugged. "Something interrupted him. Don't forget that they're only legally human when they're on two legs. You run into one when it's four-footed, don't arrest it. Shoot it." He flicked the toothpick to the ground. "And aim for the brain."

"I'll bear that in mind. Pick up your toothpick."

"What?'

"The toothpick. It's not part of the crime scene. Pick it up."

He scowled, bent, snatched it from the ground, and went away muttering about brass-balled bitches.

"Don't think you made a friend there," O'Brien said cheerfully.

"I'm all torn up about it, too." She paused. The car pulling up behind the ambulance was from the coroner's office.

Better get it done. "Looks like our victim will be declared legally dead soon. You finished with the pictures?"

"You need to get a closer look?"

The words were innocuous, the tone of voice casual, but she knew what he meant. O'Brien had worked with her enough to know it wasn't a closer look she was after. He wouldn't say anything, though. It wasn't illegal to be a sensitive, but it could be complicated. The department's official policy about such things was, "Don't ask, don't tell."

This wasn't pure prejudice. Irreproducible data was not admissible in court, and a good defense attorney could rip an officer's testimony to shreds if there was a whiff of the paranormal about the investigation.

But cops tend to be pragmatic. The unofficial policy was to use whatever it took to catch the bad guys, even if you had to do it under the table. Which was why Lily was in a slum studying a corpse instead of fending off Henry Chen at her sister's engagement party.

Which just proved there was a bright side to everything. Lily met O'Brien's eyes and nodded.

"Go ahead," he said and shifted to stand between her and the crowd by the fence, fussing with his camera.

He wasn't big enough to completely block anyone's view, but he'd made it hard for them to see exactly what she did. Lily appreciated it. She set her backpack on the ground and moved closer to the corpse, then knelt, careful of the way her skirt rode up. And reached for the dead man's hand.

It was limp. No rigor mortis yet. Skin waxy. His hand looked blue, and his face had a purplish cast. Lividity minimal. None of it was conclusive, but it did suggest he hadn't been dead long when dispatch received the anonymous tip at 11:04.

He'd kept his nails short and clean. They were square, the fingers short for the size of the palm, which was broad and flat. Partially healed scrapes across the knuckles . . . he'd been in a fight a few days ago. Pale nail beds. No rings on the fingers.

And no response in her own flesh.

Blood had run into his palm to dry in a blackish brown patch that cracked slightly when she tilted the hand to catch the light better. That blood had trapped a tuft of mottled hair. Lily touched it.

It was like touching the concrete after the sun had set and finding the lingering heat. Or like the moment after releasing a drill, when the flesh still held the memory of vibration.

Though it wasn't really heat or vibration she felt. Lily had never found a word to describe the sensation of touching something that had been touched by magic, but it was unmistakable. She'd tried to explain that to her sister once—the younger one, Beth, not her perfect older sister. If everything you touched all day, every day, was smooth, the second you touched roughness you would *know*. Even if it was only a tiny bit rough, as was the case tonight.

No, Lily thought, setting the hand down gently. The lab crew wouldn't learn much about this killer. No more than she'd learned from touching the hairs he'd left behind in his victim's blood. She stood.

"So, was the beast chaser right?" O'Brien asked. "Am I wasting my time collecting samples?"

She gave him a sharp look. "You'll do things by the book."

He rolled his eyes. "Yeah, I need you to tell me how to do my job."

"Sorry." She exhaled, pushing her emotions away with the breath. "Yes, Phillips was right. The victim was human, but the killer's a werewolf."

"Lupus, you mean." He waggled his eyebrows at her. "We got a memo about that. Lupi is plural, lupus is singular."

"A killer by any other name . . ." She shrugged, impatient

with PC-speak, and glanced at the onlookers by the fence.
"Looks like I'll be paying a visit to Club Hell tonight."

FIFTEEN minutes later, the coroner's assistant had declared
the victim dead, and Lily had an ID: Carlos Fuentes, age
twenty-five. The address on the driver's license was 4419
West Thomason, Apartment 33C. Phillips was running the license. Lily went to talk to the helpful citizens.

There were six of them, four women and two men. Leather
and body piercings seemed to be the dominant fashion theme
for both sexes. And skin.

The one currently looking at the driver's license she held
in a plastic baggie wore leather pants dyed lime green and
inch-wide leather straps crisscrossing her chest: X marks the
spots. Her hair was blonde where it wasn't purple. She had
seven earrings in her left ear, three in her right, a ruby stud in
one nostril, and a tiny hoop in her navel.

Her name was Stacy Farquhar. Her voice was as soft and
high as a little girl's. "I know I've seen him before, but driver's
licenses, you know, they never look like the person."

A skeletally thin man in a black leather body suit was looking over her shoulder. His dark brown hair, glossy and well
kept, hung past his shoulders. He wore a single earring in his
left ear, either a diamond or a good imitation. "Looks like
Carlos Fuentes."

"Carlos?" That came from the other woman, a chubby
Caucasian with dyed black hair twisted into dozens of braids.
She crowded closer and peered at the license in Lily's hand.
"Oh, God. It's him. Poor Carlos."

"You know Carlos Fuentes, ma'am?" Lily asked.

"We all do. That is . . . he hangs out at the club sometimes." She exchanged an uneasy look with the other woman.

"Oh, for God's sake," the thin man said. "It's not like it's a
secret. They're going to find out anyway."

"You know what you are, Theo?" the chubby woman said.
"Jealous. You're just jealous as hell."

"Me, jealous? You're the one who—"

"I can't believe you'd rat him out!" Stacy cried. "You know
what kind of deal he'll get from the cops!"

The chubby woman nodded. "They've always persecuted the lupi. Centuries of—"

". . . in a lather . . . everything but dope Rachel's drink to give you a shot at him."

"Police brutality isn't a myth, you know. Just last year in New Hampshire—"

". . . rubbing all over him last Tuesday. Too, too obvious . . ."

"Used to shoot them on sight, so if you think any lupi would get a fair hearing—"

"But he didn't want any part of what you were offering, did he?"

"You just wish he swung your way!"

"Who's *he*?" Lily asked mildly.

They fell silent, exchanging guilty glances.

One of the men—Franklin Booth, medium build, shaved head, leather vest the color of his skin worn over a black shirt and jeans with silvery studs up the seams—tossed aside the cigarette he'd been smoking. "Poor Rachel."

Lily turned to him. "Rachel?"

"Carlos's wife." He sighed. "She's at the club now with—"

"Franklin!" the chubby one exclaimed.

"Sugar, it's no good," he said gently. "Theo is right. They're going to find out. And maybe he's alibied. I mean, we all saw him there, didn't we?"

There was a relieved murmur, with Stacy asserting loudly that "he" had been there for hours. Lily spoke to Booth again. "Rachel Fuentes is at Club Hell now?"

"She was when we left."

"Who was she with?"

The thin man laughed. "Why, who else would put the ladies in such a flutter? Some of us gentlemen, too, I'll admit," he added with a little bow to the chubby woman, conceding her point. "For all the good it does us. Lupi are religiously hetero."

"I could use a name."

"Rule Turner, of course. The prince graces the club with his presence now and then." He smirked. "Recently he's been gracing Rachel with a good deal more."

* * *

LILY had orders to call Captain Randall once she'd finished the preliminaries. She did this on her way to Club Hell.

The click-click from her heels on the sidewalk made her feel isolated, though she could hear the bustle at the crime scene behind her. She blamed the feeling on the odd mist, so unlike San Diego. It hung in the air like a cold sweat. She was glad she didn't wear glasses. She just wished she wasn't wearing heels. They'd be hell to run in.

Of course, she was supposed to have been off duty tonight. She punched in the captain's number.

She couldn't remember the last confirmed case of a human killed by a lupus. Certainly there hadn't been one in San Diego since the Supreme Court's ruling rendered the lupi subject to the penalties and protections of the law instead of a bullet. It didn't take a precog to picture tomorrow's headlines. This one was going to generate a lot of heat.

Lily's years in Vice and Homicide prior to making detective had rubbed the green off, but her shield was still shiny. She figured she could be philosophical about handing this one off to one of the senior detectives . . . *after* she conducted the initial interviews at Club Hell.

Randall was waiting for her call. It didn't take long to summarize her progress. "After speaking with the bystanders, I followed the tracks left by the perp Visible traces petered out near the west end of the playground, but I was able to continue beyond that." She'd taken off her shoes and stockings, actually, letting her bare feet find traces where magic had passed. Her feet were filthy now, but it had worked. "The trail ended in an alley between Humstead Avenue and North Lee."

"You couldn't track him beyond that?"

"No, sir. I believe he Changed there, between two Dumpsters." The magic imprinted on the dirty concrete had been strong—unfamiliar but distinctive. "In human form, he wouldn't leave the kind of traces he does in wolf form."

"Hmm. You've secured the alley?"

"Yes, sir. The S.O.C. crew will get to it when they can. I left O'Brien in charge at the scene."

"What the hell do you mean, you left him in charge? Where are you?"

"Outside Club Hell," she said, exaggerating a trifle, since it was still half a block away. "The victim's wife should be there. I need to notify her. I also need to talk to Rule Turner."

The raspy sound in her ear was only recognizable as a chuckle because she'd heard it before. "Think you're stealing a march on me, Yu? Relax. I didn't have you yanked out of your sister's fancy party because I wanted someone else in charge."

"Then it's still my case?"

"You're lead. Unless you think you can't handle it."

"No, sir, I do not think that. But I don't have as much experience as some of the others."

"Your, uh, particular skills may be useful. And the last thing I need is some prejudiced asshole making like a tough guy with the Nokolai prince. He's good at playing the press, and they're going to be breathing down our necks on this one. So it's yours. But unless you get a confession right off the bat, you're going to need help."

Still swimming in surprise, Lily agreed automatically.

"I can let you have Meckle or Brady."

"Mech. Sergeant Meckle, I mean." Both were good cops, but Brady didn't play well with others—especially young, female others. "Tell him to pick up an evidence vac and some paper from O'Brien. If the lupi at the club cooperate, I'll get their shoes for the lab. Mech can vacuum their clothes."

"The killer wasn't wearing clothes when he ripped out Fuentes's throat."

"No, sir. We won't be able to tie him to the scene, but we might be able to connect him to the alley where he Changed. He'll have had a lot of Fuentes's blood on him. Even if the Change removed all traces from his body, it wouldn't clean up any drops that fell. Might be some of that blood got on his shoes after he dressed, or something else from the alley that connects him. Or maybe a few of his own hairs got in his clothes—wolf hairs, I mean."

"Good thinking. It's worth a try. I'll roust Mech out of bed and send him to you. In the meantime, handle Turner carefully. Call if by some chance you make an arrest. Otherwise, I'll expect to see you in my office at nine." There was a click, followed by the dial tone.

Lily frowned as she jammed the phone into its pocket in

her backpack. She didn't suffer from false modesty. She was a good cop, a good detective—but she wasn't the only good detective in Homicide. The only sensitive, yes, but the captain could have had the use of her ability without putting her in charge. She'd never been lead on a case this big.

He must think she was up for the challenge. She meant to prove him right.

TWO

THE mist had thickened. The smallest breath of wind would have chased the tiny droplets together, turning dampness to drizzle, but the air remained still. Blurry halos hung around streetlamps, stoplights, and neon signs.

Like the one Lily was looking up at now. Neon red devils danced at either end of the sign, jabbing tiny pitchforks into the glowing letters that read Club Hell.

"Kitschy," she murmured. The sign suggested a fifties sort of naughtiness, innocent compared to the real nastiness of the neighborhood. How long had the club been around, anyway? "I wonder if that's on purpose?"

"Pardon?"

She glanced at the young man who'd spoken—Officer Arturo Gonzales, Phillips's partner. He was about five inches taller than her and husky in a fit, just-out-of-the-service way, but with the kind of round cheeks old ladies like to pinch. She'd sent him to keep an eye on the club's entrance until she could get here. "The club must do a pretty good business if they can afford a parking lot and guard. You ever been inside, Officer?"

"No, ma'am."

A smile tugged at her mouth. "You're Southern, I take it."

"No, ma'am. I'm from west Texas."

"Sounds Southern to me."

He nodded seriously. "Funny how people who aren't from Texas think that. I guess it's like with folks from Los Angeles. They never say they're from the West Coast or California— just L.A."

"I guess that says it all. What do you know about Club Hell?"

His lips twisted. "It's a werewolf hangout. Them and their groupies."

"Don't forget adventurous tourists. They like to check it out, too." She studied him a moment. Lupus sexual mores being what they were, the nightclub was considered seriously depraved. Naturally this made it a popular spot. "Texas was one of the shoot-on-sight states, wasn't it?"

"Yes, ma'am, it was. Till the courts changed things."

"Well, California wasn't. So it's always been legal to be a lupus here, as long as you were registered." That's who originally hung out at Club Hell—the registered lupi, the ones who'd been given shots that prevented the Change. The ones people thought were safe.

"Your X-Squads killed them."

"Only if they violently resisted registration or if a court determined there was a clear and present danger." That was the theory, at least. Federal law used to call for all lupi to be registered—forcibly, if necessary—and given the shots. But "forcibly" covers a lot of territory when you're dealing with creatures who can absorb a couple of rounds without slowing down on their way to rip out your throat.

Lupi had been notoriously averse to the registration process.

"I'm going to talk to the people inside now," Lily said. "Some of them will be lupi. They're citizens now, entitled to the same rights as other citizens. You okay with that, or do I need to get someone else to assist?"

He thought it over. Lily didn't know whether to be appalled at how much thought it took, or impressed by his honesty. At last he nodded. "Guess we're around to enforce the law, not decide on right and wrong."

"Guess we are." She started down. The entrance to Club Hell was, appropriately, located below ground level. Wide, shallow steps led underneath the building, down a tunnel faced with stone. It gave the descent a nice dungeon ambiance, she thought, though the cold blue lighting made Gonzales look like the walking dead.

At the bottom was a plain metal door, painted black and leaking music. It swung open easily.

Scent, sound, color—all smacked her in the face at once. Colored lights strobed a cavernous room crowded with tables, people, voices, and music. The ceiling was high and lost in darkness, the music was loud, and she smelled smoke.

Not tobacco or pot. Not woodsmoke, or anything else she could name. More of a scent than actual smoke . . . someone's idea of brimstone, maybe?

The song crashed to an end. Belatedly she identified it and grinned: "Hotel California." Management obviously believed in staying true to its theme.

"Welcome to Hell," a deep bass voice rumbled on her left. "Now you must pay the price for crossing the portal."

She turned her head. A little man with a big head and burly shoulders sat on a high stool beside a table holding an old-fashioned cash register. His suit could have come straight from an old black-and-white movie, but that wasn't what made Lily stare. He possessed ugliness the way a few rare souls possess beauty, an ugliness that fascinated.

His nose was long and thin. It stretched toward his mouth like a cartoon witch's, as if it had melted, then re-formed in mid-drip. He had no hair, not much in the way of chin or lips, and skin the color of mushrooms. His feet were the size of Lily's hands and dangled well off the ground.

She blinked. "Ah—there's a door fee?"

"Twenty a head."

"Not this time. I'm Detective Yu," she said, taking her shield from a side pocket of the backpack and holding it out. "And you are . . . ?"

"Call me Max." He squinted at her shield suspiciously. "So what do you want?"

"To speak with some of your customers. I understand Rachel Fuentes and Rule Turner are here."

"And I should care?"

"You should cooperate. Are they here?"

He shrugged. "I guess."

"How long has Mr. Turner been in the club?"

"Why?"

"Because I'm a cop and I get to ask questions. Have you been at the door all evening?"

"Since nine."

"Do you know how long Turner's been here?"

"Maybe."

He didn't add to that, just stared at her. He had a disconcerting stare, unblinking as a reptile's. Lily's lips thinned. "Maybe I should speak to the owner or manager."

"No manager, and I'm the owner." He sighed. "All right, all right. His Big-Deal Highness arrived at nine-fifteen, nine-thirty, something like that. Fuentes was already here."

Nine-thirty. That was within her best-guess window for when Fuentes had been killed, but she was hardly an expert. "Where's your exits?"

"This one and the fire exit at the back." He sighed heavily. "I hate cops."

"And I should care?"

"Maybe you aren't as stupid as you look." He spoke pessimistically, as if he held out little hope of the possibility. "Nice boobs, though. I like 'em little. Want to fuck?"

Her mouth fell open. Her hands twitched with the urge to strangle the little creep. "Want to spend the next couple weeks locked up in a teensy, tiny cell?"

"Hey, I just asked."

"Take me to Rachel Fuentes." Popcorn? Did she smell popcorn? Surely not.

"She's with Turner."

"Then take me to Turner."

"You don't read the papers? Everyone knows what he looks like."

"I've seen pictures." The prince of the Nokolai Clan was something of a celebrity, appearing in gossip columns and magazines, getting his picture snapped with actresses, models, and the odd politician or business tycoon. He lobbied Sacramento and Washington for his people and partied with the Hollywood crowd. "I'd still like him pointed out. And Rachel Fuentes."

"All right, all right. You!" He hopped off his stool as he yelled at a bare-chested young man distributing drinks. "Dip-shit! Come take the door." He scowled up at Lily. "You coming or not?" And started off.

Lily followed him into the crowded room, Gonzales trailing behind.

Her stomach was starting to hurt. In a few minutes she'd be telling Rachel Fuentes that her husband had been murdered. Maybe the woman had been getting some exotic extramarital nooky. Didn't mean she'd take news of her husband's death calmly. Experience had taught Lily that love took many forms, not all of them obvious or even healthy.

At least this time she wouldn't have to treat the new widow as a murder suspect. Accessory, maybe, but whoever had killed Carlos Fuentes, it hadn't been his wife. There was no such thing as a female werewolf.

Her short, surly escort had paused to deal with a couple of customers who wanted to know when the floor show would begin. When he started moving, Lily asked again for his name. She'd need it for her report.

"Don't listen well, do you? Max."

"You have a last name?"

"Smith."

Smith? That shrunken blob of malevolence was named Smith?

Gonzales moved closer and whispered, "He looks like a gnome."

"Too big. Too mean. And who ever heard of a gnome hanging around humans?"

"A crazy gnome, then. On steroids."

Her lips twitched. "I guess so, in a psycho sort of way. But gnomes can't own property." Though that would change, if the Species Citizenship Bill went through.

The place was busy. They threaded their way through a maze of small, black tables and their chattering occupants. The overhead lights had stopped playing rainbows and were stuck on a less-than-hellish rosy pink. A glance overhead told her the lights came from spots fixed on scaffolding that criss-crossed the gloomy upper regions.

Red candles flickered on most of the tables. A circular

stage, currently empty, held down the center of the big room, while neon flames climbed the stone walls. So did two circular staircases, fading into darkness after the first story.

She saw a lot of odd hair and look-at-me clothes, but many of the customers looked like club hoppers anywhere. Gonzales's uniform drew a lot of attention as they reached the dance floor, which was emptying now that the music had stopped.

Through the thinning crowd she saw where Max Smith was taking them. In the farthest right corner of the room three larger tables floated in their own little island of space, set apart from the rest. There were five men at those tables . . . and a lot of women.

All of the men were dark-haired, probably Anglos. One of them looked naked, though the table hid his lower half. Maybe he was one of the servers, who were all young, male, and bare from the belly button up. The women were more of a melting pot. She counted three redheads, two African Americans, three blondes, and four women with brown or black hair.

Lily had reached the edge of the dance floor when two of the women stood. The shorter one looked Hispanic, though it was hard to be sure. The pink lighting was flattering but not very bright. She had butt-length hair and large breasts fighting to escape the bodice of her tight red dress. She bent over the man closest to her, the one in the table's center. He had one of the redheads snuggled up on his other side.

He turned his head. Lily got a glimpse of his face before the woman's hair fell forward, curtaining what looked like an enthusiastic kiss.

Rule Turner. Even in the dim light, he was easy to ID.

She'd already guessed that the power at that table rested with the man at its center. Bodies tilted subtly his way. Chairs were arranged so the others could see him. And he was the very picture of elegant debauchery, wasn't he? Sprawled in his chair so comfortably, loose-limbed, his black shirt unbuttoned nearly to the waist. Kissing one woman while he held on to another.

Lily's lip curled. "Mr. Smith," she said. He didn't pause or acknowledge her, so she took a quick step to catch up and put a hand on his shoulder to stop him.

And snatched it back immediately, amazed. The buzz had

been strong enough to come through his suit. *I guess some gnomes really are hostile little perverts, and not shy at all. . . .*

"What?" he snapped, turning.

"Is that Rachel Fuentes?" She resisted the urge to rub her palm and nodded at the woman who, having finished kissing Turner, was leaving the table with her friend.

"Yeah."

She turned to Gonzales. "Keep an eye on her. She's probably headed for the ladies' room, but we don't want to take any chances. If she tries to leave, stop her. Don't tell her why, don't answer questions. Bring her to me."

He nodded and moved away.

"The men at those tables—are they all lupi?"

"They're the draw, aren't they? Not that I don't put on a good show, too. Stay around, and you'll see." He winked.

"I'm going to need a place to conduct interviews."

"I won't have you hassling my customers."

She considered the unpleasant little man—if that's what she should call him. Did male gnomes think of themselves as men? "Are we going to argue about every request I make?"

"Probably." He turned and walked off.

Lily followed, and got her first close-up look at Rule Turner. *Mixed European heritage,* she thought, looking at sculpted cheekbones and a strong, slightly crooked nose. *Great teeth,* she added when he grinned at something said by the man across from him—a man whose hair halfway hid the silvery numbers of a tattoo, indicating he'd once been registered. *Not to mention wicked eyebrows.* Lily noticed eyebrows the way some people paid attention to shoulders or lips, and Turner's were distinctive—dark slashes that mirrored the angle of his cheekbones.

The eyebrows in question lifted quizzically when he noticed them approaching. Then dark eyes met hers, and she stopped thinking altogether.

. . . what? she thought a second later. *What the hell was that?*

". . . tongue back in your mouth," Max was saying. "Got a woman for you, but this one claims to be a detective." He added something in a language Lily didn't recognize. One of the men laughed.

Some kind of blood sugar thing, maybe? But she hadn't gone dizzy or fainted. Just . . . blank.

"Ignore Max," the bare-chested man said. "He doesn't have to practice obnoxious—he's got it down pat."

Lily gave him a closer look. He was lean, with tousled hair the color of cinnamon and the most stunningly perfect face she'd ever seen on a man or woman. Not to mention an incredible body . . . which she could see a great deal of, though a few details were concealed by the table.

She blinked. "You're naked."

"Not quite, darling. G-string. Must keep Max legal."

It said something about Turner's presence that she'd noticed this nearly nude Adonis second. "And your name is?"

"Cullen. Come have a seat, love." He patted his thigh as if he expected her to plop down in his lap. "Rule doesn't need any more women."

"And you do?" Turner retorted mildly. His voice was rich and nuanced, like melted chocolate. No registration tattoo, she noted. "But I suspect it's a moot point. Is this an official visit?"

"I need to ask some questions, Mr. Turner. I'm Detective Yu," she said, once more holding out her shield.

He barely glanced at it. "I'll be happy to help," he murmured, making it sound as if the help he offered was highly personal. "Call me Rule."

Not in this lifetime. "Do you know Carlos Fuentes?"

One of the women started to laugh but turned it into a cough. Others grinned. "We're acquainted," Turner said, unperturbed. "I've been seeing his wife, Rachel."

Candid fellow, wasn't he? "Are they separated?"

"No, they're quite happy together."

"Well, to use 'seeing' in a less ambiguous sense, have you seen Carlos tonight?"

"No." The eyebrows lifted. He glanced at the others. "Anyone?" It appeared, from the murmurs and headshakes, that no one had seen Fuentes. Max went so far as to state that Fuentes hadn't been in the club.

Turner faced her. "What's going on?"

"How long have you been here?"

His fingers thrummed once on the table. "I'll play along a

little longer. Then I want some answers. I arrived shortly after nine."

"And you haven't left the club since then?"

"No. I believe I can find witnesses to confirm that, if necessary."

Three of the women spoke at once. "Hold on a second," Lily said, setting down her backpack so she could get her notebook from it. "I'll need your names. You first," she said to the tall, dark-skinned woman closest to her.

She looked alarmed. "Is this really necessary? I don't want my name in the papers."

"I don't have any control over what the papers print, and yes, it is necessary."

The redhead draped against Turner's side chuckled. "Come on, Bet, you're always saying you don't care what that husband of yours thinks."

"Ex-husband, as of tomorrow," the black woman snapped, "and he can eat worms. It's not him I'm worried about, it's the partners. They aren't exactly liberals."

"All law firms are conservative. It's the nature of the beast." The redhead straightened. She had a piquant little face shaped like a cat's—wide through the forehead and temples, narrowing to a pointy chin. Her hair was cropped extremely short, and gold dangled from her ears. No leather, but her snug white top showed off plenty of creamy skin that suggested she was a natural redhead. "I'll be happy to testify that Rule's been here since nine-twenty or so, Detective Yu."

The slight stress on Lily's last name caught her attention. "And your name is?"

"Ginger." A small smile played over her lips. "Ginger Harris."

Lily froze.

"Didn't recognize me, did you? Well, it's been a long time. Imagine you growing up to be a cop. While I . . ." she laughed, high and tinkling. "I became a slut."

Turner said something. Lily didn't take it in.

How could she have failed to recognize Ginger's eyes? The color, the size, the shape . . . they were set wide and so deep that the upper lid almost disappeared. The pupils were a dark amber, like a beer bottle held up to the sun. Her eyebrows were skimpy, like her lashes.

But it had been so long. Lily hadn't seen those eyes since shortly before her seventh birthday . . . except in the occasional nightmare. Ginger's eyes were just like her sister's. "You're wearing contacts," she said stupidly.

"Lasix surgery, actually. You haven't changed much, aside from growing a few inches. Still the same sweet, serious little prig you were back then."

Lily wanted to ask Ginger if her world was divided into prigs and sluts. She wanted to ask about Ginger's parents, her brother. But there was a dead man on his way to the morgue. She had to be Detective Yu now, not Lily. "I'll need a current address."

"If you want to do lunch, sugar, I'll give you my cell number. Hard to catch me at home."

"I need your address for my report."

Ginger made a little moue of distaste. "All work, aren't you? Oh, all right. I'm at 22129 Thornton, Apartment 133."

"And now," Turner said, "we have demonstrated our willingness to cooperate with the police. I'd like to know what investigation we're cooperating in."

Lily met his eyes. Nothing happened.

Idiot. Had she really been afraid that something would? Blood sugar, that's all it had been. She held his gaze for a moment to prove that she could . . . and felt a tug deep in her belly, the liquid roll of desire. Unmistakable. Infuriating.

"Homicide," she said, and hoped her face was as hard to read as his. "This is a homicide investigation."

Everyone else reacted. Not Turner. He didn't shift position by so much as a finger. Rather, he seemed to gather stillness around him like a force field, a quiet whose power lapped out over the others, gradually silencing them. He spoke two words: "Who died?"

"Carlos Fuentes."

"Jesus!" one of the men exclaimed. "Oh, no, poor Rachel," came from one of the women. And the naked Adonis— Cullen—looked briefly, intensely relieved.

Turner's gaze suddenly shifted to behind Lily. "You'll be

kind to Rachel," he told her, then stood and started around the table.

She turned. Rachel Fuentes was returning.

From a distance, all Lily had seen of the woman were big breasts and magnificent hair. Up close . . . Lily blinked, startled.

According to the gossip columns, Turner had dated some of the most beautiful women in the country. Rachel Fuentes wasn't one of them.

She was young, not much over twenty. And her hair was indeed lovely, her breasts large, but everything else was average. She carried fifteen extra pounds, and not in the right places. Her face was narrow, her nose large, with a high bridge that made her eyes look too closely set. Still, those eyes were her best feature—large, dark and luminous.

She looked happy. "What, you missed me?" she said when Turner reached her, and looped her arms around his neck.

"There's a police officer to see you," he said gently. "She has bad news, *querida*."

The happiness drained out, along with much of her color. Lily stepped forward. There was no good way to deliver news like this. "I'm very sorry, Ms. Fuentes. Your husband was killed tonight."

"Killed?" She shook her head. "No, you must be wrong. He's at church. There was a rehearsal. He's a singer. Did you know that? He has a beautiful voice. He . . ." Her face crumpled. "Y-you're wrong."

As gently as she could, Lily gave her the basics—the place and manner of death, the identification based on the driver's license and what was left of the victim's face.

The fact that he'd been killed by a wolf.

Rachel Fuentes shuddered once. She began to wail. Briefly, Lily met Turner's eyes. Rachel seemed oblivious to the irony of being comforted by her lover for her husband's death. Rule Turner wasn't.

THREE

FOUR hours later, Club Hell was empty of customers and cops. Scents hung heavy in the air, a blurred bouquet impossible to sort when Rule was two-legged—alcohol, fruit, smoke, sweat, humanity. And that damned incense Max was so fond of, that was supposed to represent brimstone.

And *her.* She'd left an hour ago, but her scent lingered.

Or maybe he was imagining that. Rule sighed, sat in the same chair he'd occupied earlier, and punched in a number he knew better than his own. Max and Cullen were at the bar on the west wall, making busy with drinks to grant him privacy.

After nine rings, a sleepy female voice said, "This had better be important."

"I need to talk to the Rho, Nettie."

"I'll have him call you—*after* he wakes up. He's in natural sleep now, but he needs that, too."

"You misunderstand. I did not ask to speak to my father. Your Lu Nuncio needs to speak to his Rho."

There was a moment's silence. "God, you do that well. Too well for my peace of mind. All right, I'll take the phone to him. But if he has a setback, I'm taking it out of your hide."

"I hope to have a hide for you to take it out of."

She muttered something about lupus politics. He heard her movements, then his oldest brother's voice. Benedict had come down from his mountain in time to save their father's life, and stayed to guard him.

A moment later his father came on. "Yes?" Isen's gravelly bass was strong in spite of his condition. But then, he did still have both lungs.

"The husband of a woman I'm involved with was killed tonight. The police believe a lupus did it."

There was a long pause. "You aren't under arrest?"

"I'm a suspect, of course. So is every other lupus who was here. I was very cooperative." He glanced wryly at his bare feet. "They had us strip."

"What?"

"It was all very respectful." And it had been fun to see the look on the lovely detective's face when, complying rather more instantly with her request than she'd intended, he'd started to unzip his pants. She'd stopped him, of course . . . but part of her hadn't wanted to.

She hadn't liked that. "I was escorted to the men's room, where I stood on a sheet of white paper to disrobe. A male sergeant went through my things thoroughly."

"What were they after?"

"Evidence, I suppose. Though if the killer was in wolf form, I can't see what they hoped to find. But Detective Yu is no fool. There must be something they thought could link one of us to the scene. Which, by the way, was a playground very near here."

"What's he like?"

"She." Rule took a moment to order his thoughts, filtering out the personal. "Bright. Determined. Probably ambitious. Doesn't like me much, but she hasn't made up her mind I'm guilty, either. I have the impression my alibi doesn't cover the time Fuentes was killed."

"What alibi?"

"I have numerous witnesses to my whereabouts from nine-thirty on, including several humans, which helps. But I was alone from late afternoon until I left for the club."

"Hmph. I can get you witnesses for that period easily enough, but they'll be lupi. Cops and juries don't trust a lupus's testimony."

Rule's lips twitched. "Maybe they have reason."

Isen chuckled. "Maybe they do. Okay, here's what you do. First, find out if it really was a lupus who killed the man. Wouldn't be the first time someone tried to pin his sins on one of us."

"That had occurred to me. I've spoken to a reporter who's willing to exchange information, but he doesn't have anything yet. Given what Cullen told us, though—"

"Which may or may not be true."

"He was right about the attack on you."

"But his warning came too late, didn't it? If he was trying to convince me of his bona fides—calm down, boy. I can practically smell you bristling over the phone. I know he's your friend, and I'm not discounting what he said. But I'm not swallowing it whole, either. He's clanless."

"But not outlaw."

"A rogue is, by definition, insane."

There was nothing Rule could say to that. "We know something is cooking."

"But not what, or who the cooks are." Isen sounded weary. "Guesses, that's all we have. I need facts. The cops may stumble across some. I need to know what they find out, and you need to stay out of jail. The obvious solution is for you to seduce that pretty detective."

Rule felt sucker-punched. It took him a second to get his breath back, and all he could think of to say was, "What makes you think she's pretty?"

Another deep, rumbling chuckle. "You can hide a lot of things from a lot of people, but I'm not just your Rho, I'm your father. Think I can't tell when you're attracted to a woman?"

Isen had more questions and instructions. Rule answered with half his mind. The other half was screaming at him to tell his father he couldn't seduce Lily Yu for such a reason, that she was . . . she might be . . . *might be,* he reminded himself. He didn't know. One whiff wasn't proof.

"Attraction aside," he said, "it would help if I could tell her some of our suspicions."

"Don't tell her anything," Isen snapped. "She won't believe you. It would interfere with gaining her trust."

"You sound as if Nettie let you out of Sleep too soon."

"You all think you know more about my body than I do . . . yes, dammit," he said to Nettie, whose voice Rule could hear in the background. "I know you've got a piece of paper saying you do. Think I'm impressed?"

Rule could picture Nettie standing near her patient's bed, arms crossed. He heard her saying that she did know a lot more about Isen's body than he did, and he ought to be glad of that, since he was an idiot.

"We think you have no idea of your limits," Rule told him soothingly, worried by the querulous note in Isen's voice. His father was not a querulous man. "Besides, I'm scared of Nettie. She's already threatened me."

That brought a chuckle, but it lacked strength. "You should be. Damned tyrant . . . no, you will not," he said, but the last was addressed to Nettie, not his son.

Rule heard both sides of the argument that followed. Nettie won. A few minutes later, she came on the line. "I've put him back into Sleep. This time he's staying under for twenty-four hours."

He ran a hand over his head. "He'll be fuzzy after so long in Sleep. Of course, if he needs it—"

"Rule, you saw his wounds. There's nothing he can't heal, but until he grows some of those bits back, his condition is *not* going to be stable. Unless you covet your father's job—"

He growled.

"Don't be so touchy. The plain fact is that you're heir. If the Rho dies, you take over. And some will wonder if you wanted it that way."

"You're giving me gristle—lots of chew, not much meat. How is he, really?"

"Hardheaded. Worried. And older than he wants to accept. The pain's too much for him, and he doesn't heal as fast as he once did. He won't go to a hospital—no, don't bother to explain. I understand his reasons. But if he can't use technology to keep him going while he heals, he'll have to spend a lot of time in Sleep."

Rule swallowed his fear. He couldn't be a child now. There was bloody little room to be a son. "If he must, he must."

"I shouldn't have let him out of Sleep as soon as I did," she admitted. "He faked me out. Got his vitals under control long enough to . . . well, never mind. Don't worry about things here. Your father will heal, and the Council can handle things while he does."

He wanted to be at Clanhome, too, dammit. Tradition banned him from his father's presence while he healed, but not from Clanhome itself. That was his big brother's doing. Benedict's authority to bar the Lu Nuncio from Clanhome was shaky in theory, firm enough in practice. No one argued with Benedict about security. Most people didn't argue with Benedict, period.

At least he knew the Rho was safe. Barring a strike by the U.S. Air Force, nothing and no one was getting to their father when Benedict was there. "Give Toby a hug for me," he said. "I'll be in touch." He disconnected and tucked his phone in his jacket pocket.

Then he just sat for a moment. He was scared. For his father, his people, and himself. This was a hell of a time for the Nokolai leader to be incapacitated.

Which, of course, was exactly what Isen's attackers had wanted. Rule stood and headed for the bar and the one scent that drew him right now. "Ah. My coffee's ready."

"Don't see how you can drink that crap," Max said.

Cullen grinned and slid a mug across the bar. It held coffee made from Rule's private stock of beans.

"It requires a palate." He could keep his shoulders loose. He could control his expression, his voice, and to some extent his smell. But he couldn't keep the nerves from crawling across his belly, making it as jumpy as a Chihuahua on caffeine. "This place looks like hell with the lights up," he observed, sliding onto a stool.

Max set his own mug—which would hold Irish whiskey, not coffee—on the bar and hopped up on the stool next to Rule's. "That's the point."

"But this is the morning-after kind of hell. Like a carnival before night falls and the lights and music turn tacky into mystery."

"It's five o'clock in the goddamned morning, what do you

expect? Anyway, I don't want to hear about carnivals. Makes me think of the years I spent in the sideshow."

"You were in a sideshow?" That was Cullen, who'd stayed on the other side of the bar. He was in one of his restless moods, fiddling with first one thing then another. "Was this before the war, or after?"

"Which war? Humans are assholes." He tilted his mug, downed half of the contents, and belched contentedly. "Leave the damned glasses alone."

Cullen continued polishing the glass he'd picked up. "World War Two. That's the one you always lie about."

"Jealousy." Max shook his head sadly. "This younger generation is sick with it. Lacks respect, too."

Cullen paused. "You calling me a member of the younger generation?"

"You're all younger. Children, every one of you, running around like crazy so you won't notice how soon you're gonna die." Max took a silver case out of his jacket, opened it, and selected one of the cheap cigars he liked to poison the air with. "Take the way you idealize truth—telling it, finding it." He snorted. "Finding it! As if it were lying around somewhere, waiting for you to pick up. Childish. People live by stories, not truth. What you really want are answers so you won't have to figure things out for yourselves." He pulled out his lighter. "I admit, thinking takes time."

"Don't," Rule said wearily.

Max paused, squinting at Rule for a moment. He put the lighter down. "Your father?"

"The Rho is healing. Sorry. Didn't mean to make you think something was wrong." Rule grimaced. "That something *more* was wrong, anyway."

"You're shook," Cullen said, surprised.

Rule took a moment to sort out what to say. Max and Cullen were his friends. At the moment they were colleagues, too, of sorts. But they weren't Nokolai. "None of us expected them to act this soon. And I didn't expect it to be this personal." He thought of Rachel, her eyes red and swollen, empty of everything but grief. "Perhaps I should have."

"Regrets are the most useless form of guilt," Cullen said. "They always arrive too late to do any good."

"That's their nature, isn't it?" He pushed that aside and spoke formally. "The Rho extends Nokolai's gratitude, and offers you the aid and comfort of the clan for a moon cycle."

"I thank the Rho," Cullen said, his voice light, his fingers tight on the glass he'd been polishing. "Canny old bastard that he is. I'm surprised he didn't offer me money."

"The Rho has a great respect for money—and an understanding of what it can and can't buy. The offer wasn't meant as an insult, Cullen."

The other man shrugged and slid the glass back in its overhead rack. "Perhaps not. I'm tempted to show up at Clanhome for a month just to make his hackles rise."

"You need a bodyguard," Max said suddenly. "We knew they'd targeted Isen. Why wouldn't they try to get rid of you, too?"

"Killing Carlos is an uncertain means to that end. Besides . . ." Rule paused, frowning. "It doesn't fit. Why risk an investigation?"

Max shrugged. "Might be cocksure."

"Might have reason." Cullen was messing with the wine bottles now, rearranging them to suit some arcane sense of composition. "So far they're batting a thousand."

"Not even five hundred. They tried to kill Isen and failed. Now they've tried to get Rule put away, but the frame's sloppy. Quit that," Max snapped when Cullen moved another bottle. "My bartender won't be able to find anything."

"You're assuming we know their goals," Rule said slowly. "Isen isn't dead, but he's out of the picture for awhile. That may serve their purpose just as well. And we don't know why Fuentes was killed—or that I'll manage to stay out of jail."

"You're not going to jail," Max insisted.

Cullen turned. "Stop playing Pollyanna. The role doesn't suit you. Rule is right. Our opponents are subtle, and we can't afford to underestimate them."

Max snorted. "You been tuning in *Mission Impossible* on your crystal ball? Subtle's another way of saying convoluted. In real life, the fancier the scheme, the more likely it is to fall apart."

"Some do." Cullen picked up Max's lighter, flicked it, and

studied the flame. "There's a rumor of a banshee sighting in Texas."

"Is that what this is about? Signs and portents?" Max cackled. "The big, bad werewolf has his panties in a twist because some idiot can't tell marsh gas from a banshee. And in *Texas!*" That, apparently, was the best part of the joke, for Max slapped his knee and nearly fell off his stool laughing.

Cullen didn't say a word, but his face tightened, his pupils contracted—and the lighter's flame suddenly shot up a foot and darted toward Max.

"Hey!" Max did fall off the stool this time, landing on his butt. "Are you crazy? You want to set off the smoke alarms? Burn the place down? Like I really need to explain to the fire department and the insurance company about my crazy were friend who has this little problem with anger management." He stood up, muttering and rubbing one hip.

"Cullen," Rule said.

The other man looked at him. After a moment his eyes went back to normal, and the fire died.

"I'm not laughing," Rule said. "What are you suggesting?"

"I tossed the bones after the cops left."

Max rolled his eyes. "Teenage tricks."

Rule knew little about divination, but everyone tried tossing the bones at some point—usually, as Max had said, as a teenager, when the lure of the forbidden was strong and common sense was short. The results were unreliable, at best. Or so he'd always thought.

But done by a sorcerer of the Blood? His eyebrows went up. "And . . . ?"

"I asked for information about your enemy. And got . . . this." He pulled a handful of dice out of his pocket and tumbled them onto the bar.

Snake eyes. All of them. All six dice had a single dot on every side.

There was silence for a moment, then Max breathed, "Jesus."

Rule's mouth was dry. "I don't suppose there's a chance you did that yourself? Accidentally?"

"About the same chance you have of turning into a kitty cat at the next full moon."

"Another sorcerer?"

Cullen's lip curled. "I don't think so."

"There's some of the Fae could do it," Max said. "Don't know why they would, but who knows why a Fae does anything?"

"Or we can consider the obvious." Cullen looked at Rule.

"Yes." Rule drew a deep breath. "Maybe one of the Old Ones has woken, and is stirring this pot."

FOUR

THE low ceilings and twisty ramps of the subbasement parking at headquarters always made Lily feel as if she were traveling through the guts of a concrete behemoth. Her cell phone rang as she pointed her old Toyota down yet another rigid intestine.

She glanced at the Caller ID, grimaced, and answered anyway. "Hello, Mother. I'm a bit pressed for time. I'm due in the captain's office at nine."

"The captain's office? Are you in trouble?"

Why did her mother assume that? It's not as if Lily had been in trouble all the time as a kid. Just the opposite. "It's a briefing. Kind of like a meeting, you know? Like people with real jobs have."

Dead silence on the other end. Lily's breath huffed out. Her mother could cram more reproach into silence than most people managed by screaming curses. "Sorry. I'm short on sleep."

"This will just take a moment. You left last night before I got a firm date from you for the fitting."

"I'm being digested by the parking garage at the moment. I don't have my planner handy."

"Then you will call me once you do. Really, Lily, my cousin's friend is a very busy woman, and she's given us a handsome discount. You must show some courtesy. You've already missed one appointment, and your bridsesmaid gown simply has to be altered. The bodice looked terrible on you."

Lily wanted to say that no amount of alteration would make her look good in puke green, but she was already in trouble. "I'll check my schedule and E-mail you, okay? That will be quicker for me than calling."

Her mother wasn't fond of E-mail but grudgingly accepted the compromise and launched into a detailed description of the newest wedding crisis. Lily's older sister was going to be married in grand style if it killed their mother.

Lily pulled into her parking place deep in the belly of the garage, most of her attention on the report she'd pulled together before leaving her apartment. "Mm-hmm," she said as she grabbed her backpack, shut and locked her car door. Then what her mother had just said sank in.

It seemed the menu for the rehearsal dinner had to be changed. The groom's sister was allergic to ginger.

"Lily? What is it?"

She realized she'd made some small noise. "You mentioned ginger, and it reminded me. I saw Ginger Harris last night."

Her mother made one of those very Chinese exclamations, sort of a short *eh!* It was a sure sign of distress. Normally Julia Yu sounded as Californian as The Beach Boys. "Ginger Harris? Why would you want to see her? What's going on?"

"I didn't want to see her, I just did. It was in connection with a case. Do you know what happened to the Harrises, where they moved?"

"This is not healthy. I thought you'd put all that behind."

"I have." Except for the nightmares, but they were rare. "This is for the job, Mother."

"I don't know where they went. I don't remember. I suppose I could ask Doris Beaton." The offer was obviously dragged out. "I believe she kept in touch."

"I'd appreciate it if you would." Lily punched the button for the elevator.

"I don't understand why you need to know about the Harrises."

"I'm not sure yet. Police work would be a lot easier if we

knew ahead of time which leads were important." Was it intuition or the past crawling across Lily's shoulders? She rolled them, trying to dislodge the sensation. "Thanks, though, for offering to check with Mrs. Beaton. I know the subject distresses you."

"This isn't about my feelings. I worry about you."

"I know. I'm fine." But it had always seemed to Lily that it *was* about her mother as much as herself. So many threads spinning out from that one event . . . no matter how she tugged, clipped, or tried to untangle them, the knots remained. "The elevator's here. I'd better go."

Julia reminded her to check her planner and said good-bye. Lily slid her phone in her backpack and stepped into the little metal box.

It was a relief to return her mind to the case, the facts and the possibilities. Threads. That's what she had—a confusing tangle of threads, and not much in the way of hard facts to tell her where to tug. She'd taken a lot of statements, but there would be lies twisted in with the truth, and all sorts of evasions, omissions, and simple mistakes.

Time of death was likely to be critical with this one. Maybe the lab would have a preliminary report soon. Not that they'd be able to tell much, but they should at least be able to confirm that the killer was one of the Blood.

Science depended on things happening a certain way without fail. Water boiled at 100 degrees C at sea level no matter who did the boiling. Mix potassium nitrate, sulfur, and charcoal together in the right proportions, and you ended up with gunpowder every time, no random batches of gold dust or baking soda to confuse matters.

But magic was capricious. Individual. The cells and body fluids of those of the Blood—inherently magical beings— didn't perform the same way every time they were tested. Which could make it possible to identify the traces magic left in its wake, but played hell with lab results.

The elevator creaked to a halt on the first floor, where two people got on. Lily glanced at her watch. Maybe she should have taken the stairs.

If the parking garage was the beast's guts, the elevators were its circulatory system. Which meant the building was often in shock due to circulatory failure, because the elevators were notoriously slow and cranky. This one did eventually deposit Lily on the third floor. She checked her watch again as she shoved open the door to Homicide. If she hurried, she could grab a cup of coffee.

"Hey, Lauren," she said to the chunky blonde woman at the first desk. Three of the five desks in the bullpen were occupied. Mech's wasn't. "Is Mech here?"

"Do I look like a receptionist?" Lauren squinted at her computer screen and kept typing. "Why does everyone mistake me for the goddamned receptionist?"

"It's your charming manner. Makes us feel all warm and welcome." Mech was probably around. He would know she'd want to talk to him before reporting to Randall. She headed for the coffeepot.

Sean Brady looked up from the folder he'd been studying, grinned, and howled like a wolf.

"For crying out loud," the woman at the desk next to his muttered, "turn it down, will you? No one, but no one, is going to mistake you for a lupus."

T.J. poked his head out of his office. "Hey, has anyone seen my—oh, hi, Lily." He grinned and exchanged a glance with Brady.

T.J. had been a cop since God was young, and a detective almost as long. He had Santa Claus hair, gold-rimmed glasses, a face with more droops and folds than a basset hound's, and an appalling sense of humor. Lily wondered if she should check her desk for booby traps.

"Anyone seen Mech?" she asked. The pot was nearly empty. It was always nearly empty. The rule was that whoever emptied it had to make the next pot, so everyone tried to leave a little liquid in the bottom. Lily poured a few swallows of black sludge into a mug that read, UFOs Are Real. The Air Force Doesn't Exist.

"You talking to us peons?" Brady asked. "Should we tug our forelocks when we answer?"

Lily rolled her eyes. "Heaven help us. Brady's been reading his vocabulary list again."

"I just wondered. You're consorting with royalty now. The prince." He made another howling sound.

"Someone put a muzzle on him, will you?" Lily headed for what she liked to call her office. It was really just a small ell off one end of the main room, lacking the dignity of a door or windows. But it was a private nook and had room for her desk, some filing cabinets, an extra chair, a struggling philoden-dron, and a pot of ivy out to conquer the world.

"You know, Brady," Lauren said, "I bet you have no idea what a forelock is."

"I'm sure I could find one. Hey, maybe this—"

"You go tugging on *that* in here, I'm arresting you for in-decent exposure."

"Mech's guarding your domain," T.J. said as she passed him.

She paused. "Your eyes are twinkling, T.J. I don't like it when your eyes twinkle."

He shook his head. "So young and so cynical." Then he smiled. "Hope you enjoy our little present."

Oh, crap. Lily was on guard as she approached her office, though she couldn't imagine what they'd cooked up. If Mech was there, she ought to be safe from practical jokes. Mech was the polar opposite of Brady and T.J., serious to a fault. He'd tell her if they'd rigged her chair to collapse.

So what kind of "present" had they left for her?

She rounded the corner and found out.

"Detective Yu," Rule Turner said, rising politely from the battered wooden chair to the left of her desk. "Your col-leagues assured me it was all right to wait for you here." His smile was crooked and charming. "I think I've been used."

"Um," she said cleverly. He was wearing black again—an open-necked black shirt with a black jacket and slacks. Very Hollywood. The jacket looked as if it had cost as much as her car was worth. "I'm afraid so. The joke is strictly on me, how-ever." It was a backhanded jibe at her lack of a social life. She sighed. "Cop humor has a lot in common with kindergarten humor, only more R-rated."

"The chief sent him to see you," Mech said. He was sitting on Lily's desk, trying to look relaxed.

Mech was ten years older than Lily, five inches taller, and eighty pounds heavier, with every ounce muscle. He was a quiet, methodical man with Job's patience, skin the color of her favorite caramel latte, and a strong streak of the puritan.

Mech didn't do relaxed well. "He—uh, His Highness wants to assist in the investigation."

Turner shook his head. "I'm not a highness. The press likes to call me prince, but the press likes to sell magazines and newspapers."

"I've noticed that about them." Lily slung her backpack onto her desk. "Thanks, Mech. You can tell T.J. he's on my list. Brady, too."

Mech hesitated, as if he weren't sure he should leave her alone with Turner. She flicked him a glance as she unzipped her backpack. He nodded reluctantly and left.

She pulled out her laptop. "While we always appreciate civic-minded citizens, there's something of a problem with one of the suspects in an investigation assisting in that investigation."

Turner's straight slashes of eyebrows lifted. "You're blunt."

"But I did use my polite face. Chief Delgado sent you to me?"

"He did. I called him this morning, offering my help. If you want to catch a lupus, you need to know something about us, and I doubt you do. That's not a criticism. There's very little real information available."

"You mean Hollywood didn't get it right with *Witches Sabbat?*" She shook her head. "Next you'll be telling me Charlie Chan wasn't really Chinese."

He chuckled. "Point taken. He was played by an Occidental actor, wasn't he?"

"Sydney Toler, among others." Lily would never admit she had a sneaking fondness for the old Charlie Chan movies, chock-full as they were of cliché and stereotyping. But they were so much more fun than James Bond or Bruce Lee. Chan had relied on brains, not technology or kung fu, to defeat the bad guys. "Your information might be difficult for me to verify."

"And you have no intention of trusting me. Understood. But I've a strong interest in seeing this case solved quickly. I want to see only one lupus blamed for the killing, not all of us. And I don't want that one to be me. I didn't do it, but you'll need proof to believe that."

Taking a sip of the cooling sludge in her mug, she studied him. It wasn't unheard of for a lupus leader to cooperate with the police. If a werewolf went on a rampage and wasn't caught, the repercussions for all lupi could be severe. People tended to panic about that sort of thing. And there was a bill coming up in Congress—the Species Citizenship Bill—that could be affected by adverse public reaction to the case.

But the lupi version of cooperating with the police didn't necessarily involve niceties like testimony or evidence. They'd been known to deposit a body at a police station with a note saying that the problem had been taken care of.

She set her mug down. "Last night you said you didn't have any idea who killed Carlos Fuentes."

"I don't."

"I won't tolerate any form of vigilantism. Murder is murder in my book."

"An admirable attitude. Of course, the law only considers it murder if we are killed while two-footed." He waved that aside. His hands were graceful and long-fingered, like a pianist's. It was hard to imagine them turning into paws. "But you misunderstand. I'm not offering to find your killer for you. I'm offering to brief you on lupus culture and habits."

If he was dealing straight, this was a first. On the candid and forthcoming scale, the lupi ranked about even with the Mob or the CIA. "I do want to talk with you," she said, reaching for the printer cable and plugging it into her laptop. "But I'm due in the captain's office in . . . damn," she muttered when she glanced at her watch. "Two minutes. If you wouldn't mind waiting in the other room, Sergeant Meckle could get you a cup of coffee."

He winced. "Are you referring to whatever is in your mug?"

She smiled. "Too strong for you?"

"You give it to suspects to soften them up, right?"

"Only works on the wimps."

He shook his head. "I'm in trouble. Already you've discovered my weakness. I'm a coffee snob."

It wasn't what he said so much as the way he said it. She burst out laughing. "Don't let anyone tell you you do humble well. You don't."

"We can't expect to master every skill." He smiled, and his gaze flickered over her—too briefly to be insulting, but his appreciation was obvious. "I have the feeling you don't do humble well, either, Detective."

"My grandmother claims that humility is the public face of envy." And why was she talking about Grandmother to this man?

The little ping that had landed with a tug in her belly might be a clue. He'd probably picked up on her response, too, dammit. He'd been winning at boy-girl games for a long time. She shook her head. "You're good, I'll give you that. But I'm not playing."

"And you're direct. I like that." He moved closer, smiling, and brushed his fingertips over the ends of her hair. "Your hair smells of oranges."

She leveled a stare at him and ignored the flutter of pleasure. "You're beginning to annoy me."

"You'd like to keep this impersonal." He nodded and let his hand drop. "Reasonable, from your point of view. But you should know I'm not good at treating a woman I'm attracted to impersonally."

"Another of those skills you haven't mastered, I take it. Cheer up. It's never too late. You can start working on it right away."

His lips twitched. "I have a ten-thirty appointment, and you're late for your meeting. Do you work on Saturdays, Detective?"

"I will be. Why?"

"Why don't we have a nice, businesslike lunch tomorrow and discuss things? Somewhere public, to encourage me to behave myself."

She'd seen him in public last night at Club Hell, and he hadn't been behaving himself. But so what if she couldn't trust him? She trusted herself. "That works. You know Bishop's, on Eighth?"

"I'll find it." His eyes laughed at her as he held out his hand. "One o'clock?"

"Okay." He might have meant the handshake as a dare. She accepted it for her own reasons—mostly to get a feel for his brand of magic. His hand closed around hers, large and warm and solid.

Her stomach hollowed. Her breath went shallow, her head light, as if she'd lost oxygen. The muscles in her inner thighs quivered, and she stared at his mouth—at the neat, white teeth revealed by lips that had parted, like hers. Lips that looked soft. She wanted to touch them.

Her eyes flew to his. She saw flecks of gold in the dark irises, and the way his pupils had swollen. The pink triangles at the inner corners of his eyes. The dark, thick eyelashes. And the way his lids had pulled back in shock.

He dropped her hand. For a moment they stared at each other. Her heart pounded. His nostrils were flared, his breathing fast.

Dear God. What did she say? How did she put that moment away, unmake it?

He broke the silence. "I won't be behaving myself," he told her grimly. And turned and left.

FIVE

THE hall leading to the captain's corner office was beige—beige walls, beige woodwork, beige carpet. No windows. Lily headed down that beige tunnel with her heartbeat still unsettled, her report in her hand, and her mind in a whirl.

Popular fiction was full of stories about the supposed sexual power of lupi, their ability to entrance helpless females. Most experts believed those were self-perpetuating myths. Wickedness has always possessed a certain glamour, and mystery casts its own spell.

Until a few moments ago, Lily had agreed with the experts.

Now . . . well, whatever had just happened between her and Turner shouldn't have. No question about that. What's more, it shouldn't have been possible. Even if lupi did possess some arcane sexual power, she was supposed to be immune. Magic slid over her surface, prickling along her skin. It didn't get inside and affect her.

Yet she couldn't accept what had happened as normal sexual attraction—it had hit too fast, too hard. And he'd looked so shocked. As if he, too, had been blindsided . . .

Lily shook her head, trying to physically throw off confusion. None of that mattered as much as what *hadn't* happened. She'd shaken the hand of a lupi prince—and felt not one tingle of magic. For that, she had no explanation at all.

She rapped once on the captain's door, then opened it.

"Glad you could join us, Detective," Captain Randall said dryly.

Lily checked on the threshold. The room held three men, not one.

Frederick Randall sat behind his desk. The captain was a short, bald man on the shady side of sixty with all of his features crowded together in the bottom half of his face. He looked like a bureaucrat—well-fed, not too bright. It was a misleading impression.

The other two men wore suits and professionally grave expressions.

Uh-oh, Lily thought. *Feds.* "Yes, sir. Sorry I'm late."

"These are Special Agents Karonski and Croft from the FBI. They're interested in the Fuentes case."

Got it in one. Lily nodded a greeting, but doubt tugged at her. Randall wouldn't have told them about her—would he?

The two men started to stand. Randall waved. "Sit, sit."

It was a corner office, but it wasn't large or fancy. The only empty chair was plain wood and sat on the right of the captain's desk, which put her sideways to him and to the men sitting across from him.

The agent closest to her had good teeth, skin several shades darker than Mech's, and a pleasant smile. He was growing more forehead than hair these days. "I'm Martin Croft," he said. "As I explained to your captain, we're not claiming jurisdiction—"

"We could." The other one didn't smile. "Karonski," he said to Lily.

The captain snorted. "You don't have a leg to stand on."

"Murder by magical means is a federal offense."

Lily tried to be tactful. "Um . . . magical means? Fuentes was killed by teeth, not a death spell."

"According to the captain, he was killed by a magical creature," Karonski said. "That's murder by magical means."

Her eyebrows rose. Her captain's response was more direct. "Bullshit. Even if you convinced a jury that murder done by one of the Blood constitutes murder by magic, the courts would throw out any conviction."

"Maybe." Karonski was eyeing Lily with disapproval. "She's young."

"Not as young as she looks, and she's fully qualified. In addition, she has contacts in the, ah, paranormal community that may be useful. Is that your report you're clutching, Yu?"

Okay, he hadn't told them. She hadn't really thought he would. "Yes, sir." She leaned forward and handed it to him.

Croft said wryly, "There's some disagreement here, obviously. Since this is the first murder purported to have been committed by a lupus in wolf form since the Supreme Court's ruling—"

"The first?" Lily said, surprised. "In the country?"

"The first when the killer's identity is unknown," he amended. "There was a murder in Connecticut, but the case was, ah . . . solved by the lupus community."

He meant that the killer had been killed by his own people. She remembered reading about it. His body—in wolf form—and a signed confession had been left at the courthouse. "And that business in Texas last year was ruled self-defense."

His eyes widened slightly. "Yes. An interesting case, from a legal standpoint."

She nodded. The lupus involved had been in man form when attacked by a dozen gang members. He'd Changed. Three of the gang members had survived. "The ACLU was involved."

"It's a landmark, the first judicial recognition that the right of self-defense can apply to a lupus in wolf form. Limited in its application, of course, because of the way the judgment was worded."

The defense had argued that, under the circumstances, Changing was no different than loosing a trained guard dog. That the defendant's wolf form had protected his human form, which was legally entitled to self-defense. The appeals court had agreed, but . . . "The judges waffled around about what constitutes sufficient 'clear and present danger' to justify turning wolf. So it's a precedent, but not a clear one."

He smiled. "I begin to see why your captain wanted you on this case. I don't often encounter officers with such a good grasp of my turf. Ah . . . I don't think Captain Randall mentioned it, but we're MCD."

Magical Crimes Division. Well, that made some sense, but calling this a federal case was a stretch. But they weren't claiming it officially, were they? Just putting the captain on notice that they could make things difficult if he didn't cooperate.

Cooperate how? What did they want? She glanced at Randall, who spoke without looking up from her report. "Your written reports will be copied to these gentlemen after I've seen them. Go ahead and hit the high points for them."

"Thank you, Captain," Croft said. "But we can wait and read the report. Between your briefing and what's in the papers, we have the basics, I think. Except for one thing. I need to know how sure you are, Detective, that the murder was committed by a lupus."

"For proof, you'll have to speak with the coroner's office. But I'm pretty sure of it." She couldn't tell them why she was so certain, and it would be inadmissible, anyway. But there were plenty of of other indicators.

Lily reconstructed the attack, describing the wounds, blood splatter, and severed hand. "One of the first-on-scene officers used to be X-Squad," she finished. "Fifteen years' service. He believes the attacker was a werewolf."

"Lupus," Croft corrected her absently. "It is consistent with a lupus attack."

Karonski scowled. "Consistent isn't conclusive. Now and then someone who wants to get away with murder tries to make it look like a lupus kill. Though most attempts are crude," he admitted. "This isn't."

She studied him. Average height, bad suit, built like a barrel. A little younger than Croft, and a wedding ring on his left hand, which Croft lacked. "The killer almost certainly left saliva in the wounds. The lab may not be able to run a DNA match on it, but they can tell if it came from one of the Blood. Someone clever enough to fake those wounds—which I do not think were faked—would know that."

"Magic can create some great fakes."

That jolted her. "Is that possible? I mean . . . I suppose the wounds themselves could be faked, but could magic duplicate the kind of weird results typical of body fluids from a lupus?"

"I don't know," he said gloomily. "Do you?"

It was a disquieting thought. Magic on that level was illegal, of course—but so was murder. "If such a thing were possible, it would constitute murder by magical means. Is that why you're here?"

Croft shrugged. "Partly. We need to confirm or deny the possibility. There's also a concern that this will have political repercussions."

Lily frowned. "The Species Citizenship Bill?" Congress had almost managed to duck its responsibility by losing the bill in committee, but its sponsors were pushing for a vote.

"Politics." Randall spat out the word, putting down Lily's report. "Not my job, thank God. When you talk about magically faking things, you're talking sorcery."

True. Witchcraft couldn't change the basic nature of things, and she'd know if sorcery were involved . . . wouldn't she?

Croft was unmoved. "It's a possibility."

"It's a dead art," the captain said impatiently. "Sure, we run across a dabbler now and then, someone who thinks he's found a fragment of the Codex Arcanum. But no one's been capable of transformative magic since the Purge."

"Which was a European phenomenon," Croft pointed out. "There are African sorcerers, and rumors of sorcerers who escaped the Communist cleansing of the sixties."

Randall shrugged. "There are always rumors, and African sorcery is more like witchcraft than true sorcery. Or so I've read. You saying different?"

Croft and Karonski exchanged one of those impenetrable looks shared by longtime partners and married couples. Croft spoke. "We're not suggesting you should doubt your laboratory results."

"That's good, because I don't intend to. You two are supposed to be hoodoo experts, not stringers for the *Rational Inquirer*."

That irritated Croft. "The only real experts in magic are its practitioners. Abel and I can advise you about investigative procedures and apprehension, and we know a few things about lupi that aren't common knowledge. This case is likely to set precedents. The agency feels our experience could be valuable to you."

Oh, my. Lily's lips twitched.

Captain Randall's gaze swung to her. "Something funny, Yu?"

Her sense of humor was going to get her in trouble yet. "I just realized that these gentlemen are offering to be expert consultants."

"That's right." Croft smiled at her.

He really did have a nice smile. "It, ah, struck me as funny. You see, I ran late because Rule Turner made me the same offer. We have a meet set up. He wants to instruct me about lupus customs."

Croft tensed, as if he were coming to attention sitting down. "Rule Turner? The Nokolai heir?"

Could there be two people with that name? "Yes."

Croft and Karonski exchanged another of those looks. Captain Randall said, "Turner's a suspect."

"Yes, sir. It generally pays to let suspects talk as much as they like."

Karonski looked irritated—but that seemed to be his normal expression. "Turner didn't kill Fuentes."

She decided to let her eyebrows do the talking for her.

"I suppose you have to consider him a suspect," Croft conceded. "But it's unlikely he's guilty. First, lupi are not sexually possessive, so the motive doesn't work. Second, if he'd killed Fuentes, you'd never have found the body."

"You know him?"

"We have a dossier on him that you might want to look at."

"That would be useful. Thanks."

"You want to read it before you talk to him." Karonski had a way of leaning his upper body toward her as if he wanted to grab her and make her agree. "You need to know what you're dealing with."

Randall looked at him with open dislike. "Maybe the two of you could leave that file with us and make an appointment to brief Detective Yu later. Right now, I need to talk to her about her caseload."

They didn't look happy about the dismissal, but there wasn't much they could do except leave. Lily wondered what lay behind Randall's antagonism—it seemed like more than the usual territorial wariness. Maybe he had a history with one of them, some old case where they'd clashed? Or maybe

Karonski just rubbed him the wrong way. The man was intense.

Both men stood. Croft dug into a leather briefcase and pulled out a fat folder. "These are copies, so you can keep them."

She stood, to be polite, and accepted the file. "Thanks. I'm likely to be tied up until midafternoon, I'm afraid. Three o'clock okay?"

"That works." Croft held out his hand. "We'll meet you here."

They shook hands, then she held her hand out to Karonski . . . and got her next big surprise of the day. This one didn't send her into a sexual trance, but it sure did raise questions.

A witch. Karonski was a practicing witch.

The door shut behind the two agents. "What's your case load?" Randall asked. "You ready to close on anything?"

She jerked her attention back. "The Meyers case. Valencia, too, I think. I'm waiting on lab results on two others. The rest," she admitted, "are pretty cold."

"Keep the cold cases. They won't distract you. Pass the others on. Give the Meyers case to Lauren. She wants to make detective, so she needs the experience—and something more to complain about," he said with the ghost of a smile.

"But . . ." But they were *her* cases.

He leaned back in his chair, folding his hands over the little potbelly that never got bigger or smaller. "You're ambitious. That's not a bad thing. But you're part of a team here. You've got a good record. Letting someone else get the credit for closing a couple of your cases won't hurt you. You'll get plenty of shine if you nail Fuentes's killer, and that's where I want you focused. Got it?"

"Yes, sir." But he was wrong. She didn't want to keep the cases so she could hog the credit. Well, yes, she did want credit for her work, but . . . but that wasn't the main reason. With the Meyers case, she wanted to be the one who clapped the cuffs on the slime who had offed his ex-wife. With the others, she wanted to finish them. To connect the dots herself.

"Good. What are you pursuing yourself? What's Mech doing?"

"As you saw in the report, two of the five lupi at Club Hell are alibied. Mech's checking those alibis, then he'll talk to

Fuentes's boss and coworkers. The beat cops are handling the door-to-door near the scene. I'll be in touch with them. This afternoon I'll talk to the widow. She was too distraught to get much from her last night. I plan to speak with the neighbors, too. And Turner's neighbors. The timing's going to be important on this one."

He nodded. "If Turner's guilty, you'll want to make sure he can't wiggle out with some trumped-up alibi. The closer you can pin down Fuentes's and Turner's movements, the better."

"Yes, sir. I also want to check out the church where Fuentes was supposed to have been rehearsing with the choir. The Church of the Faithful, it's called."

Randall raised his eyebrows.

"Yes, sir. Bit ironic, under the circumstances. It sounds like more of a cult. They worship some goddess, call themselves the Azá."

"The Azá. I've heard of them. Got a temple or something like that up in L.A. There was some kind of trouble with a group of fundamentalists, can't remember the details."

Lily nodded, making a mental note to find out more.

"What about this morning?"

"I'll be using my contacts in the paranormal community," she said, straight-faced.

Humor flickered in Randall's eyes. "You do that, Detective." He picked up her report and tapped the pages into tidiness, signaling the end of the discussion. "Reporters'll be all over you like fleas on a dog with this one. Refer them upstairs. Don't give any interviews yourself."

"I . . . wasn't planning to."

"Good. Your report's thin," he said. "But it will do, under the circumstances. Keep in mind that all your reports will be shared with the Feds."

Was he warning her not to put everything in writing? But she never referred to her less respectable abilities in a report. She never quite mentioned them out loud. Neither did he. *Don't ask, don't tell.* So what did he mean?

There was something here she wasn't getting. "Yes, sir. Ah, is there something I should know about the MCD agents?"

"Pair of glory hounds. Especially Croft. He's the kind who likes to go in with guns blazing. He'll try to pump you for information. Don't let him. Here," he said, passing her a form. "You'll need to requisition special rounds and restraints. The pencil pushers insist I sign off on them—pretty pricey, with the amount of silver required. Now go make Lauren's day." He waved her out.

LILY frowned at the folder she'd just closed. Lots of interest in the dossier the MCD agents had given her, but one fact clung to her mind like a burr.

Rule Turner had a child. An eight-year-old son. Technically the boy's mother had custody, but the woman was a reporter, off on assignment all the time. Years ago she'd dumped him with her mother to raise.

It wasn't an unusual story these days. Mom's too busy to be a mom, and dad has better things to do, too. Like attend Hollywood parties and hang out at Club Hell.

Ridiculous to be upset, she told herself as she stood and moved to the tallest file cabinet. What was it to her if Turner's interests didn't include his son? She might think that made him a scumbag, but he was hardly the only man with serious failings in that area. He'd taken some responsibility, she admitted as she yanked open a drawer. He paid support, and the boy spent summers at the Nokolai enclave, where presumably he got to see his father now and then.

It wasn't enough.

She shook her head, impatient with herself. She had better things to do than waste time deploring Turner's flaws. She had to pull the files on every case that stood a good chance of being solved, and pass them out. Better not forget to check her planner, either. Somehow she had to make room for a fitting.

But as she removed files, her mind wasn't on weddings, or on what Lauren would do with the Meyers case. She was trying to decide if she was being set up.

She tapped one finger on the folders she'd pulled, unhappy with her thoughts. She'd always thought Captain Randall was a fair man as well as a good cop. Dammit, she trusted him. Some of that trust came from their history, true. He'd been a brand-new detective, and kind; she'd been eight years old, and traumatized. But he'd earned her respect as an adult, too.

Still, Grandmother always said that the canard about death and taxes left out another inevitability: politics. Two people will fight, play cards, or make love. Three, and someone's going to start playing the angles.

If this case blew up on her, she'd be left with one huge failure on her record . . . and a handful of cold cases. No recent successes.

Lily's finger tapped a little faster. Was that why she hadn't told Randall about Karonski? She didn't tell him every time she ran across someone with a Gift or a touch of the Blood, true. But he'd want to know about an FBI agent who was a practicing witch.

She didn't want to tell him. Was that instinct or hurt feelings?

The captain was going out on a limb, making his newest detective lead on a case this big. It made sense for him to limit the damages. If she solved it, everyone looked good. If she screwed up, or if the case dragged on too long and someone had to be sacrificed to the media sharks . . . well, she could see that it might seem best to risk a fledgling rather than someone with fifteen or more years on the force. It might be easy to risk losing a woman . . . a Chinese woman.

Or maybe she'd turned paranoid.

She grimaced and dealt with the simplest problem on her list, opening her planner. Brief study confirmed her suspicions: no time was good for fittings. She supposed she'd have to give up a meal. Probably wouldn't be the only one she missed with this investigation.

But not tomorrow. Tomorrow she was having lunch with Rule Turner. Today, she'd eat on her way to check with her "contacts in the paranormal community."

She turned to her computer and sent a quick E-mail to her mother. Then she picked up the phone and called Grandmother.

TWELVE years ago, Grandmother had shocked the family by moving out of the Chinese neighborhood where she'd lived since coming to the U.S. as a war bride. Her home sat on the five acres she'd kept out of a larger tract she'd bought over forty years ago, long before the city grew out this far. She'd had it built to her specifications, and she'd paid cash.

The house didn't exactly blend with its neighbors. It was a square stone building gabled with a lilting roofline more suited to the snows of northern China than the heat of southern California. The windows in the exterior walls were high, horizontal slits, giving it the look of a fortress wearing a fancy hat. There was no driveway. Grandmother didn't like driveways. She wasn't crazy about cars, either, though she owned one. The aging second cousin who lived with her was allowed to pilot it occasionally.

Lily parked in the street and headed up the wandering gravel path to the bright red door flanked by snarling stone lions. She rang the bell.

"Lily. So good to see you." Age had softened the square of Li Qin's face and blurred the angular body into something more androgynous than feminine. Her voice was her one beauty—low and soft and clear as bells. "Come in. Your grandmother is in the garden."

"Thank you. You're looking well." Something about the older woman's gentle courtesy always made Lily feel clumsy, as if she might accidentally bruise some tender petal with a hasty word. Which didn't make much sense. The woman lived with Grandmother. She had to be tough as nails, or she would have cracked years ago.

"Thank you. I'm feeling well." Li Qin moved aside. Lily stepped out of her shoes and into a small slice of China . . . or Grandmother's version of it.

The entry was small and almost bare. An intricately carved stone fountain tinkled on a shiny black table, and a plain wooden rack held outdoor shoes and several pairs of slippers. Lily slipped on a turquoise pair and followed Li Qin.

They passed through what Lily and her cousins called the Trophy Room, filled as it was with Grandmother's collections—jade, pottery, lacquer. New pieces were mixed with old. A handful were museum quality, and a few were just plain odd. Grandmother's tastes were unpredictable.

The door to the garden stood open. Passing through it, Lily moved from China to an exuberant mix of the Mediterranean and the tropics. A flagstone courtyard shaped like a lifesaver left a circle of grass open at the very center and rounded off the square courtyard. In the four corners, sticks on fire mixed with hibiscus, lavender bloomed, and bamboo thrived, while Santa Barbara daisies frothed around the feet of a small orange tree.

Dead center in the courtyard, a tiny woman sat at a round table. Her face showed signs of age, but her bones were limber, for she sat tailor fashion. The black hair with its dramatic white wings was pulled into an unforgiving bun. She wore tailored black slacks and a collarless red shirt, both silk. Her face was turned up to the sun.

Lily walked out to her. "Grandmother," she said reproachfully as she bent to kiss a soft, powdered cheek, "the lavender is blooming."

"I like the scent." Grandmother spoke in Chinese. This was a rebuke.

Reluctantly, Lily switched to Chinese. She understood it better than she spoke it. "It's the wrong time of year for lavender to bloom. That's hard on the plant."

Penciled-in eyebrows lifted. "You are here to ask me a favor?"

And hadn't yet been invited to sit. She was not off to a good start—yet she laughed, suddenly rushed with affection for the old woman. *"Wo ai ni, Dzu-mu."*

The old woman reached up and patted Lily's cheek. "I am fond of you, too. Though I don't know why. You are impertinent, and your accent is barbaric." The small hand waved regally. "You may sit. Li Qin will bring tea."

Which meant they would not be getting down to business right away. Lily sat and managed not to squirm with impatience. For the next twenty minutes they sipped oolong in delicate, handleless cups and discussed The Wedding—it was beginning to appear in Lily's mind in capitals—and California politics, which amused Grandmother vastly. And baseball.

Grandmother was a passionate Padres fan. No number of lackluster seasons could dim her ardor. After making pronouncements about several of the players, she added, "I have had the team's horoscope cast. This will be their best season yet, if they can avoid injuries."

"That would be a first. They had, what—five players out last year?"

"So many injuries can't be natural." Grandmother brooded

on that a moment. "I will send the manager the name of a good antihex firm." She cast Lily a sly look. "I hear Chang's company is looking for a sensitive. They pay very well."

"Not you, too!"

Grandmother chuckled. "It would please your mother. But not, I think, me."

Lily had never wanted to work for any of the private firms that employed sensitives. Or for the government in that capacity, for that matter. For centuries, sensitives—and some who claimed to be, but probably weren't—had been used to sniff out otherness. It had been worst during the Purge, but it continued to this day. There was still so much prejudice, and sensitives could be used to "out" someone who had good reason to keep his Gift or bloodlines a secret.

"Actually, I came here to ask you about that. Being a sensitive, I mean. And about lupi."

"I read about this in the paper. You are with this killing, are you? No." Grandmother switched to English, which she spoke perfectly well, though with an accent every bit as bad as Lily's was in Chinese. "I mean—on the case. You are on the case."

"I'm lead. And I need to know more about lupi than I do."

Grandmother tapped the rim of her cup with one long, painted fingernail. "This is your favor? You wish to ask me about lupi?"

Lily answered carefully. Some things were not to be spoken of directly. "I know a little, of course. But there are so many stories. I need help sorting story from truth. Lupi are grouped by families or clans—"

"Eh! I know little about lupus clans. They are a secretive people."

"Yes, but . . . you can help me understand what they're capable of, what their weaknesses are. They're fast. I know that. But how fast? The report I read estimated that they could run a hundred miles an hour in wolf form."

That sent Grandmother into peals of laughter. "This is experts? Experts believe this? Cheetahs run this fast! Wolves do not."

"But they aren't regular wolves."

"No, but they aren't cheetah, either." Her eyes were shiny and damp with mirth. She dabbed at one with her fingertip.

"What they have—you know this!—is very quick response. Two times as fast as human? Three times? I don't know. I don't put a number to it, but very much faster than humans. When they try," she added, still amused. "They don't go around speeded up all the time."

Two times faster would be plenty quick, Lily thought. "Weaknesses?"

"They don't like small, closed-up places. Putting them in jail is bad idea. They go crazy sometimes."

A race of claustrophobes? "They can regenerate limbs, right? That's why registered lupi were tattooed on their fore-heads. When they tried tattooing their hands, the lupi cut them off and grew them back without the tattoos."

Grandmother shrugged. "Sometimes experts are right."

"What about the rumors about their, ah, sexual potency? Is there anything to the idea that they bespell women?"

Grandmother snorted. "They are potent, yes, but there's no magic to it. Unless you call it magic when a man pays atten-tion to what a woman wants." That amused her. "Maybe it is. You have a lupus's attention, child?"

"I'm meeting with one today, about the case." She frowned and pushed her hair behind her ear. She hadn't really thought she'd been bespelled . . . but what *had* happened? "Is there any way for a lupus to lose his magic? A curse, or some kind of magical accident? Can a lupus *be* a lupus without magic?"

"What?" She drew herself up, stern as a cat presented with the wrong food for dinner. "You will explain."

"I shook his hand. The Nokolai prince. I shook his hand, and I felt nothing." That wasn't quite accurate. She flushed. "No magic, that is. I have to know why. If my ability is fading—"

"You know better. You can lose an arm or leg. You cannot lose what you are."

"Then what happened?" she cried, frustrated. "He's sup-posed to be the heir, the number-two muckety-muck in his clan. He must be lupus, yet I didn't touch magic! I have to know why. I have to know if it's him or me. If I read him right, then he can't Change, so he can't be the killer. Which I won't be able to explain to anyone or prove, but it's a starting point. *If* I'm right. I have to—"

"Enough! You are overwrought. Be quiet. I must think."

With difficulty, Lily subsided. Grandmother's fingernail tapped the rim of her cup—*ting, ting, ting*. She sat very still, very straight. There was a distant look in her eyes and a worried tuck to her thin lips that made the wrinkles show more than usual.

Of course Grandmother saw the implications, and a good deal more. That's why Lily was here. A lupus's magic was innate, like Lily's ability to sense it. If one could be reft away, so could the other. As could other things.

"You were right to bring this to me," she said at last, reverting to Chinese. She gave a sharp nod. "But I do not know the meaning. I will have to inquire of . . . another."

"Who?" Lily asked, startled. "Someone who knows—"

"You will not ask," Grandmother told her firmly. "This is not someone I go to lightly, but a favor is owed . . . has been owed for a long time. A very long time now."

Alarming possibilities skittered through Lily's mind. She leaned forward, touching Grandmother's hand. Magic purred from the wrinkled skin into hers. "Don't put yourself at risk."

The thin lips twitched, and the dark old eyes softened. She patted Lily's hand. "I am very fond of you, it is true. But I do not do this for you. Not *just* for you. And now," she said, settling back in her chair, "I will tell you what else I know about lupi."

SIX

THE Fuentes apartment was in La Mesa. The bland, two-story buildings formed a square with a swimming pool and parking filling the center. Some poet wanna-be had named the complex The Oasis—a name it failed to live up to. There were two royal palms street side. No gardens, porches, or balconies. No green.

At least the exterior wasn't pink. Lily sighed as she hunted for a parking spot, thinking of her own tiny apartment. She put up with the Pepto-Bismol paint job and lack of space because the place was three blocks from the beach, but sometimes she suffered dwelling envy.

She had to park two blocks away, but the walk was pleasant. It was one of those clear, perfect days that hit the city sometimes in the fall, the kind of day people move to California for. It made Lily want to get her hands in the dirt. Not that she had a garden of her own, except for a few pots, but she had free rein in the naturalized area around Grandmother's place. Maybe she could squeeze out an hour later.

Lily buzzed Rachel's unit; after a long wait, the girl told her to come up.

The Fuentes apartment was a corner unit, second floor. The staircase was enclosed, and the stairs themselves were cement and led to a landing that served two apartments. Lily would talk to the residents of 41-C later, see what they knew about Rachel and Carlos Fuentes.

She rang the bell and waited. She was debating whether to ring it again when it opened.

Rachel Fuentes looked like hell. Her face was splotchy, and the big eyes that had glowed last night were dull and red today and hidden behind a pair of rimless glasses. She wore shapeless sweats that had been washed with something red at some point; they were a funny shade of purple. That luxuriant mass of hair was tied in a rough knot at her nape. "I guess I have to talk to you."

"This is a difficult time, I know. I'm sorry to intrude."

"Come in."

Despite the pleasant weather, Rachel had the air conditioning on. The apartment was downright chilly. It was larger than Lily's, but whose wasn't? It was also more cluttered—not out of control, but not the place of a neatnik, either. And a lot more colorful.

All the color that tragedy had sucked out of Rachel still lived in her apartment. The walls glowed a rich, multihued gold. The couch was slipcovered in red and strewn with throw pillows in orange, yellow, and lime green. The chairs in the dining area were each painted a different color. There were paintings on the walls, not prints but actual oils—a bright, slightly surreal landscape, a grinning blue dog surrounded by colorful shapes.

"Did you do the room yourself?" Lily asked.

"What?" Rachel paused in the middle of her pretty room, blinking. "Oh. Yes. Carlos likes bright colors, too, but he isn't . . . he wasn't interested in decorating."

"I'm impressed." And she was. Too bright for her tastes, but it had taken an artist's eye to put so many vivid colors in a small space and make it work. There was passion here, Lily thought. That didn't surprise her. The sense of balance and harmony did.

She wasn't sure Rachel had heard her. The young woman stood near the couch, hugging her elbows to her body and frowning around at the room as if the sofa or table could tell her what she was supposed to do. How do you treat the detective investigating your husband's death?

Lily tried to help. "Your sister isn't here?"

"She had to work."

"Would you rather do this when she can be with you?"

"I want to get it over with. And there are some things . . . it will be easier to talk about it without her. She's protective." Rachel shrugged. "My big sister, you know?"

"I've got one of those. She's okay, but she never forgets that she's the big sister. Can't quite get it that I know how to tie my own shoes these days."

A glimmer of humor appeared in Rachel's dark eyes. "Sounds familiar. Della, she wants to help, but she didn't think much of Carlos. And she really hated Rule—oh, not him, exactly, but that I was involved with him. It's hard to be around her right now."

"Your parents don't live here, I understand."

"No. Mama moved back to Tucson after Daddy left, and none of us knows where he is. She . . ." Her grimace held pain and guilt. "She's praying over me. I hate that. I hate it that she thinks I'm some sort of adulteress. It wasn't like that."

"What was it like?"

Rachel gave her a long, hard look, but Lily saw her throat work when she swallowed. "I guess I have to tell you. I want you to catch him. I want him punished, whoever it was. Carlos . . . he was a mess." She gave a short, harsh laugh. "More of a mess than me, believe it or not. But he didn't deserve this. He didn't deserve to have all his chances taken away."

"No, he didn't. Maybe we could sit down, and you can tell me about it."

"Oh. Sure." She dropped onto the couch. "I should have . . . I'm not thinking right."

The chair opposite Rachel was striped in yellow and lime green. Lily moved a newspaper to the floor and sat down. "You won't be, for awhile."

"I guess not." A long strand had worked loose from the knot. Rachel shoved it behind her ear and leaned forward, her hands gripping each other between her spread knees. "You want to know who did it, who killed him. I can't tell you that, but it wasn't Rule."

"You sound pretty sure."

"He didn't . . . he couldn't . . ." She had to stop and swallow.

"I could tell you that he couldn't have sat there with me at the club and talked and smiled if he'd just killed my husband, but that's just my opinion, isn't it? And you're thinking that of course I'd say that. Otherwise Carlos's death would be my fault. But it is anyway, isn't it?"

Lily's throat ached with pity. "Why do you say that?"

"It was a lupus who killed him." She shot to her feet and began pacing. "It wasn't Rule, but it was a lupus, so it has to have something to do with Rule, or with the club. Something to do with me. Only I can't figure out what it could be."

"I'd say you're thinking pretty clearly."

Rachel paused, shot Lily a bitter look. "And maybe that's not a compliment. Maybe I should be falling apart."

"We all deal with grief differently." And there was no doubt in Lily's mind this woman was grieving. "Did your husband own a gun, Ms. Fuentes?"

"Yeah, he . . ." She rubbed her forehead. "Did you say something about that last night?"

"I did." But Rachel had been incoherent then. "We found a gun nearby. We're running the serial number, but it would help if you could tell me what kind of gun your husband had."

"It's a pistol. A twenty-two."

"Did he often carry it with him?"

"No, but when we went to Club Hell, he did. It's not a safe neighborhood."

Lily's eyebrows rose. "He went to the club with you?"

"Not . . . not lately." She stood very still, hugging her arms to her, looking down—or into the past. "I'm going to tell you how it happened, how Rule and I got together. I don't want to. I don't want it to be any of your business, but I want you to catch him. Whoever did it, I want him to pay."

"Catching him is my job. Making him pay is up to the DA."

"Good enough." But she didn't move or speak, just stood there, her arms wrapped tight around herself.

Lily tried to give her a place to start. "I understand you met Rule Turner at the club." That much she'd learned from Turner. He'd been closemouthed about most everything else about his relationship with Rachel, though he had admitted to knowing Carlos.

"Yeah." A small, sad smile played over Rachel's mouth.

Her eyes softened as if she was looking back at memories that comforted. "I never thought it would work. Most men are easy—they think they have a chance at sex, they take it, you know? But Rule . . . he could have pretty much anyone, and I'm nothing special. Not ugly, but not beautiful, either. But he made me feel beautiful."

Heady stuff, Lily thought. *And all related in the past tense.* "You fell for him."

"Not the way you mean. I was dazzled, I guess. But not in love or anything, no more than he was." She woke from her memories to give Lily a sharp look. "He liked me. He was kind to me, too, the sort of kindness that's hooked to respect, not pity. But he wasn't jealous, not at all. You might say he was born with what Carlos wanted, or thought he wanted."

"What do you mean?"

Her mouth thinned, though whether from pain or anger or some combination of the two, Lily couldn't tell. "You must have guessed that Carlos and I didn't have a picture-book marriage. More like a roller coaster. Things were really good, or really bad. He'd be super sweet for awhile, then he'd twist off, and I'd be the one trying to hold steady so we could put things back together." She took a shaky breath. "I got tired of being the steady one."

Lily took a guess. "He had affairs."

"He screwed around." She'd held still as long as she could, apparently. Her legs pushed into motion. "He loved me. I knew that, even when I was crazy with hurt. But he had to prove something to himself, over and over. See, he had mumps when he was sixteen." The words stopped; her legs kept moving.

"He was sterile?"

She nodded, reached the wall, and turned back. "We've been together ever since I was a sophomore, got married right out of high school. He was the only one for me. The only one I wanted, the only one I'd ever been with. I needed him to feel the same way. I needed to be the only one he wanted, too, but he couldn't give me that. Time came when I couldn't deal with it anymore. So finally I gave in. This last time, when he started in about how jealousy's the big evil, not infidelity, I said, okay. Let's see who's right."

"You decided to have an affair."

"I *agreed* to have an affair." She stopped, chin up, mouth in a bitter twist. "Does that shock you? It was Carlos's idea. He wanted me to unlearn my jealousy, he said. He talked about equating sex with love, said it was a childish attachment to a romantic ideal that messed up people." Her eyes blazed. Her fists clenched at her sides. "Only it was all *their* words. Not his. He was just mouthing what they'd taught him."

"Who taught him to say that?"

"That stupid church he went to. The Azá."

AT eleven-thirty on Friday night, Lily was curled up in the chair and a half that constituted one-third of the furnishings in her living room. The other two-thirds were the teak coffee table by the window and the red floor cushion next to it. What she lacked in furniture, she made up for in plants—ivy on the kitchen pass-through, an ambitious azalea in one corner, and eleven terra-cotta pots sharing space beneath the single large window.

Lily had a pint of Ben and Jerry's in one hand, a pen in the other, a yellow pad on the arm of the chair, and a nineteen-pound gray tabby with one and a half ears curled up on her feet.

Much as she appreciated her laptop, it didn't help her think the way a yellow pad did. She'd turned the pad sideways so she could make columns. The names of the lupi who'd been at the club last night topped four of them; the others were Carlos, Rachel, Azá, and Lupi.

She couldn't assume the killer was a lupus who'd been at Club Hell that night, but the club was tied in somehow. Someone had killed Fuentes less than a block away. That couldn't be coincidence. Two of the lupi who'd been there last night were solidly alibied; no known motive for the others, except Turner.

Her pencil tapped the second name. Cullen Seabourne. He stood out in one way: he wasn't Nokolai. The other three were. When she'd asked the name of his clan, he'd smiled sweetly and told her he didn't have one.

Back when registration was being enforced, every lupus

who'd been caught had claimed to be clanless to keep the authorities from using them to flush out others. But there was no reason for a lupus to insist on that fiction anymore.

What did it mean to a lupus to be clanless? Why would it happen? Was he outlawed, or had he never been brought into a clan for some reason? She'd tried calling him around supper, but no one answered. Not even an answering machine or voice mail. She'd left a message with the surly gnome who owned the club, since presumably Seabourne would show up for work tonight.

She jotted "Outlaw?" under Seabourne's name and moved on to the next column: the Azá.

Her pencil began tapping again, this time with irritation. Mech had left a message on her voice mail. He'd interviewed a couple of elders at the Church of the Faithful . . . which would have been okay if he'd checked with her first. She was lead. He wasn't supposed to hare off on his own.

Not that he'd done a bad job. Mech was methodical, and he'd covered the obvious questions about Fuentes. But the message he'd left raised other questions for her. Tomorrow, she told herself, she'd read his report, then check out the church. And have a little talk with Mech.

Her pencil moved on, stopping at *Lupi*. Under it she'd written, "Promiscuous. Species Bill/prejudice. Pack (Clan): the priority, messy internal politics. Hierarchical. Jealousy?"

Rachel said that lupi weren't jealous. But Grandmother said the apparent lack of jealousy was nurture, not nature, in action. They were taught not to be sexually possessive, just as children are taught to share their toys.

But childhood greed often lives on into adulthood. Lily had arrested plenty of people who wanted what they wanted, when they wanted it, and didn't see anything wrong with taking it—as long as they weren't caught. "Play nice" training didn't guarantee results.

Had Turner burned with a jealousy all the more powerful for being prohibited, hidden?

Her foot was falling asleep and her hip was throbbing. Lily frowned at the cat. "I am going to have to move soon."

Dirty Harry's eyelids lifted just enough for him to glare at her out of baleful yellow slits. He punctuated his nonverbal comment with a flex of one paw, digging the claws into the cloth of her *gi*.

"Quit that," she told him. "I'm in no mood for a demanding male." In fact, if she didn't know better, she'd have thought she was getting her period. She felt restless and grouchy, and she'd apparently moved into klutz territory.

She'd landed badly tonight. A simple shoulder throw, and she'd gone down hard, like a beginner afraid of the mat. Hugely embarrassing. John had looked at her so reproachfully. But then, her *sensai* had never really forgiven her for not pursuing the art more diligently. He'd wanted her to compete, but judo had never been about trophies for her. At first it had been a way to feel safe. Now . . . she wasn't sure. Habit? An unwillingness to lose her skills . . . or maybe she still needed to feel safe.

Her frown deepened. "Okay, Harry, move it. I may need to use that foot again someday." She reached for him, knowing he'd jump down before he'd let her pick him up and move him.

He did. Then he sat there glaring at her like a fuzzy, malevolent demon, tail twitching. When he was sure he had her attention, he stalked into the kitchen.

"Oh, all right." She got up and followed him.

He wasn't supposed to be fed again till morning, but Harry didn't agree with the vet about his proper weight. She supposed if she'd lived on sparrows and garbage for awhile the way he obviously had, she'd have some food issues, too.

Lily got out the dry food. He looked disgusted and stalked over to the refrigerator. "Just a little bit," she told him, put the dry food back, and got out some milk. The vet said cow's milk wasn't good for cats, especially overweight cats, but Harry adored it, and she hated to deny him his treat. She poured a stingy amount into a saucer and set it down.

Lily wasn't at all sure she was doing things right with Dirty Harry. He was her first cat—if she bowed to convention and called him hers. Most of the time she thought it was the other way around. She'd found him on the beach about a year ago, half-starved, with one leg swollen and useless and killing him with infection. It was the only time he'd ever let her pick him up.

"So what do you think, Harry?" She leaned against the

refrigerator, arms crossed, and watched him lap up his treat. "The animal world—excuse me, I mean nonhuman-type animals—isn't free of sexual possessiveness. Chances are that's what happened to your ear, back before we met."

Harry ignored her.

"And wolves do fight over females. But lupi aren't exactly wolves, are they? They have rules about fighting, ritualizing it, Grandmother says—though it's not supposed to happen over a woman."

Harry polished off the last drop and began cleaning his face. Lily rubbed her hip absently. Something was nagging at her, some sense that things didn't add up. "Either Turner killed him in a jealous rage, or . . . what?"

She pushed away from the refrigerator and started pacing. It didn't take many steps to be back in her living room. "Unless Turner is besotted or wildly territorial about Rachel, he didn't have a reason to kill Fuentes. Maybe he did it. But if not . . . if not, what's the motive?"

Lily stopped by the window, scowling at the closed drapes. Who benefited by Fuentes's death? That was always a good question. Half the time, the answer involved money. Maybe not this time, though. There was a small insurance policy through his job, according to Rachel, but it wouldn't do much more than get him buried.

Passion? He'd played around, again according to Rachel. But it hadn't been an angry husband or boyfriend who'd killed him. It had been a wolf.

Well, what was the most obvious result of his death?

"Me," Lily said slowly. "Investigating his murder." And focusing on Turner because he'd been involved with Rachel, and he was a lupus. And the one thing they were sure of was that Fuentes had been killed by a lupus.

Wait a minute. Maybe the question really was, why had Fuentes been killed by a wolf? Not just by a lupus. A lupus who'd Changed. A lupus who might as well have left her a note telling her one of his kind had done this.

The lupi were most deadly when they were furry, but they were fast and scary-strong in human form, too. He could have killed Fuentes without Changing.

Harry stopped against her leg once, purring. "You're right,"

Lily said. "It's late. I'd better get to bed." But as she went through her bedtime routine, one question kept circling around in her head.

Why had Fuentes's killer Changed?

SEVEN

A scrappy little road wound up into the mountains northeast of the city. About twenty miles up that road some forgotten county planner had stationed a scenic overlook boasting a cement picnic table and a metal trash drum. At eleven o'clock Rule was waiting there, leaning against his car with his arms crossed and his nose lifted.

The sun was a glaring disk in an empty sky, but there was wind—a sharp, dusty wind smelling of sage and creosote and rabbit. Before him the folded earth descended in irregular humps to the city, satisfyingly distant. A mile up the road, hidden by scruffy oaks and the curve of the little road, lay the entrance to Nokolai lands.

Rule closed his eyes and wished for time. He needed to be in two places at once right now—and neither was where he wanted to be. He'd been trying to reach Cullen all morning. He needed to find him, or at least find out if his friend had pulled one of his disappearing acts. Every so often Cullen dropped out of sight, telling no one where he was going or when he'd be back. It was annoying at the best of times.

This was not the best of times.

Rule held himself in quietness, trying to settle. It had been too long since he'd run these hills in his other form. Too long since he'd even walked them in this one. He needed to absorb and be absorbed by the land, and there was no time . . . yet he was here now.

He looked upwind, searching out the source of the rabbit scent, and found it beneath a scrubby bush, where a dun-colored patch of fur quivered, barely distinguishable from the dirt. Rule watched, motionless himself, and breathed deeply. It helped.

Her face floated across the surface of his mind . . . a heart-shaped face with a strong, straight nose and eyes like black almonds. When she smiled, her mouth made a pretty triangle, and her cheeks rounded. He thought of her skin—thick cream, with honey stirred in. And her scent. A touch spicy. Wholly human. Unique.

The memory aroused him, turned him restless. He wanted to see her now, not two hours from now.

And that, he thought, was not a good sign. Not good at all.

A few minutes later, tires crunched on gravel. The rabbit bolted from its hiding spot. Rule turned to watch a dirty gray Jeep pull up behind his convertible. Two men got out instead of the single man he'd been expecting. Both wore jeans and athletic shoes. Both were bare from the waist up. One—the Jeep's driver—had three long scars across his chest, remnants of the attack two days ago.

He was a big man, with the build of a fullback and a basketball player's hands. Unusually dark for a lupus, he had his mother's coppery skin. His silver-shot hair was black and very short. The leather sheath on his back held a machete; the one at his waist was for his knife. The blades of both would be sharp, Rule knew, in spite of the softness of the metal. There was too much silver in the alloy for it to hold an edge well.

The Jeep's passenger was built like the blade the first man carried—long and slim, with broad, bony shoulders standing in for the hilt. His face was narrow, his skin and eyes pale, and his light brown hair was long enough to tie back. Most people would have guessed him to be about Rule's age.

They would have been right. But then, most people didn't know Rule's real age. "Mick." Rule straightened, a familiar wariness stealing the bit of ease he'd snatched. "I didn't know you were here."

"Drove down," the slighter of the two men said as he

approached. "The vineyard can toddle along without me for a few days. Toby sends his love," he added. "Along with a request for Sweet Tarts or anything else to rot his teeth. You know how Nettie is about a healthy diet."

Rule's heart jumped. "You saw him?"

"For a few minutes, before the slave drivers carted him off to his lessons. You're overreacting there," Mick commented. "No need to yank the boy clear across the country. No lupus would harm a child."

Rule just shook his head. Mick didn't know about Cullen or what he'd discovered. For now, that's how Rule wanted it. He held out his hand, and the two of them clasped forearms in formal greeting—then Mick grinned and pounded Rule's back hard enough to have staggered a human.

It wasn't the mock-friendly blow that had Rule pulling back, his lip lifting in a snarl, knees flexed, and arms ready at his sides. It was the scent.

The big man gripped Mick's shoulder. His voice was cavern-deep. "Cry pax."

"For the Lady's sake, I just slapped him on the back!"

Benedict snorted. "You stink of so much *seru* even a human would react. I've no time to waste on this foolishness. Cry pax."

Mick looked sullen, but he muttered the word. Rule eased his stance, but it would take a while for the chemicals flooding his body to disperse. The stink of his brother's hostility hung heavy in the air.

"And you," Benedict told him, "had better learn control. The Lu Nuncio can't afford to react like a challenge-crazed adolescent."

Rule's lips tightened. He didn't react that way anymore—except with Mick. The two of them had always been competitive. Mick had envied Rule for living at Clanhome. When they were children, Rule had envied Mick for having a mother who wanted him. But the relationship hadn't turned bitter until Isen named his youngest son his heir. "I know. I'm on edge."

"All the more need for control." Benedict released Mick's shoulder. "We need to get straight to business. I don't want to be away from the Rho for long."

"Your choice," Rule said. "We could have met closer to

him." Why had Benedict brought Mick to their meeting? He must know there were things Rule couldn't discuss with anyone else present.

"I argued with him about that, believe it or not," Mick said, rubbing his shoulder. "Not that it did any good. But I don't see any reason to ban you from Clanhome."

Benedict favored him with one of those expressionless looks that used to make Rule squirm, back when Benedict was training him. "You're very tender about your brother's rights."

"I suppose you expected me to rejoice that he's banned." One side of Mick's mouth tucked down. He looked away. "I've got a problem with my little brother being Lu Nuncio. You know it, he knows it, everyone knows it. Maybe that makes me all the more angry when someone else shows disrespect."

"The ban is customary. Wait." He slashed a hand through the air, cutting Mick off. "I'm aware that custom bars him from the Rho's presence, not Clanhome. But Isen agreed with my decision."

Mick looked shocked. Rule wasn't. He'd guessed as much. Isen hadn't been asleep or in Sleep the whole time. He could have countermanded Benedict's orders . . . if he'd wanted to.

"Rule," Mick said, "I—I don't know what to say. Our father *can't* suspect you."

Rule shrugged, ignoring the ugly tangle in his gut as best he could. "Isen always has reasons for what he does."

"If it makes you feel any better," Mick said, "I'm not allowed to see him yet, either." He gave Benedict a sour look.

Benedict was unmoved. "I let you tag along so I wouldn't have to say everything twice. So listen."

Anger flashed in Mick's eyes. "So speak."

"It looks as if Nokolai has a traitor. That's the main reason Rule is banned from Clanhome while our father heals."

Rule felt sick. "The attack. They didn't know you planned to meet Isen on his return, but they knew you hadn't accompanied him."

"Wait a minute," Mick said. "First, Benedict is good, but his mere presence doesn't magically ward off attack."

"There were five of them," Rule said. "Would you be willing to go against Benedict and our father with only four at your back?"

"Okay, you have a point. But we know who did it. Leidolf. Three of the attackers were definitely theirs. The two who got away probably were, too."

"Clan Leidolf has been contacted," Benedict said. "The Council issued a formal complaint and demand. Their Rho disavowed the attackers."

"The Council?" Rule frowned. "If the complaint didn't come from Isen, they'll know he's badly injured."

"That's how he wanted it."

Rule chewed that over. Apparently Isen wanted to present the appearance of weakness—make it seem he didn't trust his heir, let their enemies know he was badly hurt. But what did that gain them when the pretense was at least half true? He looked at Benedict, worried, and got back the smallest of shrugs.

So Benedict didn't know what their father was up to, either. "I don't suppose Leidolf offered reparation."

"No, though they must realize they'll have to, eventually. For now the Council is willing to let them drag things out. Both sides are growling. No one is challenging."

Rule nodded. Leidolf and Nokolai were enemies from way back but had managed to avoid Clan Challenge for the better part of the last sixty years.

War was too wasteful; Isen preferred more devious means to his ends. Leidolf, being more numerous, might think the all-or-nothing justice of war favored them, but Nokolai had too many friends. They wouldn't fight alone. Even Leidolf could see what a disaster a widespread conflict would be.

"The point is," Benedict said, "the attack was timed too well. Very few knew about the meeting between Nokolai and Kyffin. On our side, just the three of us and the Council. I told no one other than the guard I sent with Isen, and he's dead."

"Leidolf is notoriously sloppy about their word," Rule said, "so it's conceivable they'd kill their tool to keep him from talking—"

"Rule," Mick said, shocked. "You're talking about Frederick."

Rule shook his head. "I know. Instinct rebels at the idea, but I'd still like Benedict's opinion. He was there."

"Frederick died defending his Rho," Benedict said flatly.

"There is no room for doubt. Did you mention the meeting to anyone, Mick?"

"Of course not."

"Rule?"

One person outside the clan had learned about the meeting, though not from Rule. Cullen. Rule phrased his answer carefully. "I spoke to no one about it before it took place."

"I've spoken with the Councilors," Benedict said. "None of them admits to having told anyone."

Mick snorted. "Which proves nothing, since you won't let Rule into Clanhome to put the question to them."

Rule lifted his brows. "You'd have me put the question to *Council* members? Without the Rho's orders?"

Mick grimaced. "All right, all right. I wasn't thinking. But we're getting sidetracked. Even if the Councilors kept their mouths shut, there were two clans at that meeting. What about Kyffin?"

"Jasper's a hothead," Rule said, "but an honest one."

"I'm not accusing their Rho of anything except talking to the wrong person."

Benedict shook his head. "Jasper kept the meeting even more secret than we did. He says only he and his Lu Nuncio knew about it in advance—and he is willing to back his word. He has agreed to submit to Nokolai in formal ceremony."

"Merde!" Rule exclaimed. He shook his head in rueful admiration. "Isen manages to land on his feet even when they've been bitten off. This isn't the way he'd planned to obtain Kyffin's support, but I'll wager he'll be pleased. Restrictions?"

"Nothing unusual. Year-and-a-day term."

"You'll have to let Rule into Clanhome, then," Mick said. "Unless you plan to keep Jasper kicking his heels until our father is well enough to participate."

"The Lu Nuncio must accept for Nokolai, of course. Jasper arrived an hour ago with seven from Kyffin plus two from other clans to bear witness. The ceremony is set for two o'clock. Rule will return to Clanhome with us."

"Now?" Rule said, startled. "Was there some reason you needed to arrange this without contacting me?"

"You've a peculiar idea of my authority. I didn't arrange it. The Council did."

Of course. Rule felt foolish. Had his desire to see Lily addled his thinking? He'd have to call her, postpone their date. Not that she was thinking of it as a date. . . . "It's lousy timing, but I suppose that can't be helped."

"You had something more important to do than accept Kyffin's submission to Nokolai?"

"If I were sure it was more important, I'd ask the Council to reschedule," he snapped. "But I am trying to avoid being arrested for murder. Aside from my own feelings on the matter, California is a death penalty state. It wouldn't be good for the clan for the heir to be executed."

A flicker of emotion disturbed Benedict's face. "Who did you kill?"

"No one lately. Bloody hell. You don't know, do you? Does no one at Clanhome ever listen to the news?"

"We've been a little preoccupied," Benedict said dryly.

Rule ran a hand through his hair. His question had been largely rhetorical. Many of those lucky enough to live at Clanhome did shut out the human world. The Council couldn't afford to, but, as Benedict said, they'd had other things on their minds. "It looks like I've been set up," he said, and hit the high points.

"So they're after you, too." Mick scowled. "They want to destroy Nokolai. And we know why, don't we? Isen's damned political maneuvering! Why can't he see that meddling in human politics never pays off for us?"

Rule said nothing. As Lu Nuncio, he wasn't allowed the luxury of opinions.

Benedict didn't comment either, but that was typical. He would have made a perfect Lu Nuncio, had things been different. "You need bodyguards," he told Rule.

"Killing me would disarrange their plans."

"They may prefer getting you arrested to killing you, but what happens if you aren't arrested?"

Rule nodded, conceding the point. If they couldn't get rid of him one way, they might try something more direct. "Understood. But I can't do what I need to do while trailing bodyguards. And it's not as if I would be easy to kill."

Benedict gave him a hard look but dropped the subject. He might rule over security within Clanhome, but he couldn't force Rule to accept bodyguards outside its boundaries. He dug in his pocket and tossed a set of keys to Mick. "I need to talk to Rule. Take my Jeep back."

Mick's expression darkened with temper, but there wasn't much point in arguing with Benedict. After a moment he shrugged one shoulder and nodded at Rule. "See you shortly," he said and headed for the Jeep.

Benedict waited until Mick pulled away. "All right. What's going on? That cryptic warning you gave me this morning needs explaining."

"That's why we're here." Benedict was responsible for protecting the Rho. He had to know what he might be up against. "Do you remember Cullen Seabourne?"

"Seabourne . . ." Benedict paused, frowning. "You used to hang out with him, back when you were younger and dumber. But that one . . . wasn't he clanless?"

"Yes. And also my friend."

"You have some peculiar friends." Something like bafflement overtook his dour expression. "I remember now. He had a cat."

That made Rule smile, if fleetingly. Lupi and cats generally avoided each other. "So he did. What I'm going to tell you is for your ears only, Benedict. Isen knows about this. The Council doesn't."

Benedict nodded. "You're itchy," he observed.

"Moonchange is close, and it's been awhile. And . . ." He thrust a hand through his hair. "There's a lot to be itchy about right now."

"You need a workout, but there isn't time. We'll walk." He started for the road.

One of the annoying things about Benedict was how often he was right. It did feel better to move. "Cullen is only one of those I've kept in touch with from my younger and dumber days. Not just lupi, either. Too often, those of us of the Blood operate like little islands in the sea of humanity. We don't talk to each other, much less cooperate."

"I'll assume you're not suggesting we make common cause with banshees."

"I think that was a joke."

"Let me know when you're sure."

They turned together just short of the road, automatically moving against the wind. The ground along the shoulder was hard and dusty. Rule's footfalls were soft; Benedict's were all but silent, even to Rule's ears.

"We're used to hiding," Benedict said. "All of us. Plus there's a few centuries of dislike and distrust involved in some cases. There are reasons for that."

"Some of those reasons should have stopped mattering after the Sundering. Most of the rest have been asleep for centuries."

"You'd have me believe that's no longer true."

Rule nodded. "Not that I'm certain, but Cullen is."

"You have some reason other than friendship to believe him?"

"You remembered his cat. She was his familiar."

"He's not a witch. He can't be. He's of the Blood."

"Not a witch, no. A sorcerer."

Benedict's breath sucked in. "I take it you mean a real one, not some idiot dabbler. But . . . how? That path is closed to us."

"I don't know, except that his mother was a witch."

"Which also shouldn't be possible. A lone wolf sorcerer . . ." He shook his head. "You're scaring me."

"I haven't gotten to the scary part yet," he said grimly. "Cullen came to me a few weeks ago. He'd noticed some odd things about the energies he uses—turbulence, he called it. I won't go into detail. Well, I can't, because I didn't understand the half of it. But basically he suspects a conflict between forces in other realms is being reflected here, and Nokolai is somehow involved—or our enemies are, with the same result."

Benedict shook his head. "There's not enough congruence between the realms for that. Not anymore."

"That's what we've believed. But there have been rumors of things sighted that shouldn't have been able to cross—a banshee in Texas, a gryphon in Wales."

"Rumors," Benedict said dismissively.

"I know, I know—rumors don't prove anything. But Cullen came to me because . . . damn. I almost forgot to tell you." Rule inhaled slowly, trying to calm himself. Movement had only helped for a few moments. The restlessness was back, and getting worse. There was an odd crawling sensation in his belly. "In return for Cullen's warning, Isen extended him the aid and comfort of the clan for a month. I doubt he'll show up, but if he does—"

"I'll see he gets in. Finish explaining."

"Right." *Keep moving,* he told himself. But he was going the wrong way. He was headed for Clanhome, and he wanted . . . needed . . . "Cullen came to me after an elemental took up residence in his scrying flame. It was frightened."

Benedict made a scoffing sound. "Isn't that how scrying works? In return for the flame—or water, or whatever is used—the elemental shows pictures. Mostly lies," he added. "Or useless. Elementals are too simple to sustain a thought or much of an emotion."

"Normally, yes. But this was a very old, very *large* elemental. And, according to Cullen, it was not from our earth."

"You're right," Benedict said after a moment. "That's scarier."

Rule's head was growing light, as if he weren't getting enough air. His feet drifted to a halt. "Last night Cullen cast the bones. I saw them afterward, Benedict. Snake eyes, every one, on every side."

Benedict never cursed, but his expression suggested he wanted to. "I'm not swallowing his story whole, understand, but if even half of it—what's wrong?"

"I can't . . ." *Breathe. Can't . . .* "I have to go back." He turned—and wobbled so badly he might have fallen if Benedict's hand hadn't closed over his arm, steadying him. "I have to get back." He started walking. Yes, this was right—this was the right direction. The dizziness eased, but the urgency increased. He picked up his pace until he was running, with Benedict running silently beside him.

He must think I'm crazy. He'd be about half right. But Rule didn't stop to explain. Seconds later he reached his car and stopped, bending over with his hands on his thighs, dragging in air in gulps.

Such a brief run shouldn't have elevated his heart rate, much less winded him. *Damn, damn, damn . . .*

Benedict scowled. "You're going to tell me what's wrong. Now. Right now."

"Sorry." Rule straightened. He had to call Lily—to change the time for their lunch, for one thing. And to make sure she was okay. If she'd been driving just now . . . "I can't enter Clanhome. You'll have to bring Jasper here. No, maybe he'd better come to my apartment in the city. We have to settle how we'll handle the ritual."

"What are you talking about?"

"I wasn't sure until now, but . . . it seems the Lady has chosen for me."

Benedict's eyes widened. "Who?"

He took one more breath and held it, letting it out slowly as his heartbeat settled. "The police detective investigating the murder I'm supposed to have committed."

"Bloody hell," said the man who never cursed.

EIGHT

THE neighborhood where Carlos Fuentes had been shot looked just as seedy by day, but Lily noticed that the area immediately surrounding Club Hell was a wobbly notch above the rest.

Most businesses had bars on the windows, true, but at least they were open, not abandoned. The usual clutter of sullen young men dotted the sidewalks, but there were women out, too, and not just the working girls. Ahead of Lily two old women moved slowly, casting baleful glances at the young men and chattering at each other in fierce Spanish.

Today Lily's feet were silent on the sidewalk, no awkward clicking of heels. No ugly cop shoes, either. Running shoes were one of the perks of moving out of uniform.

She was glad to have them. She felt itchy, on edge. As if she might need to run. "Did you pull her sheet?" she asked.

"No sheet." Officer Larry Phillips sauntered along at her side, still tall, skinny, and sarcastic. "Juvie might have something, but it'd be sealed. She's been on the street awhile, but not as an adult. According to her ID, she just turned nineteen." He snorted. "Gonzales thinks she's clean."

"Mmm." It was theoretically possible for a prostitute from this neighborhood to avoid using drugs. Just not likely. "You did good finding her."

He shrugged. "She's not exactly ironclad, but who else was I gonna find who'd been out at night around here? Pimps, whores, pushers, and users. That's about it."

"You left out gang members." There was a tugging beneath the itchiness, as if she needed to go somewhere, fast. What was the matter with her? She knew very well she wasn't a pre-cog, so it wasn't some kind of psychic shit.

"The gangs mostly stay away. It's that one on the end," he added, nodding at a run-down brick building at the west end of the street. "Third floor. You seem awfully damned pleased about this. Doesn't her story mess up things with your prime suspect?"

"It fits with other testimony. We have Fuentes leaving a church in La Mesa around eight-thirty."

"That's thirty minutes away, tops. So what else did he do between then and nine-fifty?"

"Don't know yet." Lily walked on a moment before adding, "Tell me something, Phillips. You've got experience with lupi. Why would one of them change to wolf to kill?"

"I dunno." He sounded surprised. "Instinct, maybe. Fuentes had a gun."

"From what you've told me, and what I've read, a .22 pistol isn't much of a threat to a lupus."

"If he'd been shot, it would have fingered him pretty clearly for us. They heal quick, but not so fast you wouldn't have seen the wound when you went to Club Hell."

"I wouldn't have gone to Club Hell right away if we hadn't known a lupus was responsible. It's like he posted a sign for us: Killer lupus on the loose."

"Or else he just wanted to get his teeth into Fuentes. Hell, could be all kinds of reasons no human would think of."

"Maybe." Or maybe she was being steered. Why had the killer turned wolf to attack Fuentes? Had it been deliberate or instinctual? The instinct argument didn't hold up unless there was something unusual about the circumstances she didn't know. Other lupi hadn't been driven by instinct to Change and kill, not in the last eleven months.

But killing in wolf form would have been necessary if the killer wanted the lupi blamed for it. Or one lupus in particular.

The one she'd see at lunch.

A weird little spasm in her gut left her feeling hollow. She rubbed it absently. Had she eaten breakfast?

"This it?" she asked when they reached the dilapidated brick building on the corner.

"Yeah." He reached over her shoulder and pushed open the door. The vestibule was tiny and dirty. She started up the stairs ahead of him. "What did you mean about the gangs staying away?"

"The wolves," he admitted grudgingly. "Word is they put the fear into a couple gang leaders so customers at the club wouldn't get hassled. Or maybe that weird little guy that owns it has 'em spooked. For whatever reason, none of them claim the immediate—hey! What is it?"

She'd stopped, her hand tight on the rail. Trying to keep from tumbling back down the stairs. "I . . . give me a second." But the dizziness that had hit so quickly wasn't easing. It seemed to be squeezing the air out of her chest.

"You don't look good."

"Dizzy." She put her hand on her chest, as if she could push more air in that way. And breath by breath, the spell began to pass, until she was standing there feeling foolish. "Whew. I don't know what that was, but . . ." She caught a glimpse of Phillips's expression. "I am not on anything," she said sharply.

"You're a little young for a heart attack. Low blood sugar?" He sounded skeptical as only a cop can.

"Maybe. I forgot to eat breakfast." She'd never had a problem before, though. She thought of the way she'd bruised her hip last night and frowned. Maybe she was coming down with something. "Never mind. I'm fine now, and we've got a witness to talk to."

THE witness's room was tiny and crowded with dolls.

Baby dolls, Barbies, porcelain-headed dolls with lacy dresses and shining, perfect hair. They filled two bookcases, cuddled into corners, sat on the coffee table, and lay on the pillow on the twin-size bed. And every one was blonde.

In addition to dolls, the room also held an ancient refrigerator, a two-burner stove, a chest of drawers, and a lumpy blue love seat without legs. Therese Martin had waved them to the love seat. She sat on the bed, a skinny little waif in an oversize blue T-shirt and nothing else—no pants or bra, certainly. Lily didn't know about panties.

Therese had shiny blonde hair like her dolls, though the color was a result of better living through chemistry. If Phillips hadn't sworn the girl's ID was valid, Lily would never have taken her for legal. "I oughta be sleeping, you know," Therese said, eyeing her hostilely. "This is the middle of the night for me."

"I appreciate your willingness to help us out." Lily took the photo of Carlos Fuentes from her purse.

"Don't know why you're here. I already told him everythin'." She jerked her chin in Phillips's direction.

"He didn't have a photograph to show you. I do." Lily didn't have any illusions about the girls and women on the game. Prostitution was survival at its grimiest, a life based on using and being used. It didn't allow much room for morals or standards. But those dolls . . . the hard ache of pity had Lily clearing her throat. "Is this the man you spoke to last night?"

Therese took the photo Lily held out, looked it over, and handed it back. "Yeah, that's him."

"Officer Phillips said you knew him."

She shrugged one thin shoulder. "Not by name. I've seen him around. Helps to have an eye for faces in my business."

"I can see where it might. What time did you talk to him?"

"I already told him. Oh, all right. I'll show you."

She scrambled off the bed, which answered the underwear question. She wasn't wearing any. She snagged a cell phone from the lap of a doll on the coffee table and handed it to Lily. "See? I've got Caller ID. It records when I get calls. Last night, I was headed for my spot when Lisa called. I wasn't workin' yet, see? So we were talking when I saw this guy pull up by the playground."

Lily looked at the phone, which did indeed show that a call had come in at 9:49 P.M. the night before. She made a note of the number. "You say he pulled up. Was he alone?"

"Yeah."

"What kind of car?" They'd found Fuentes's car parked just down from the playground—a big, dark blue Ford, several years old.

"Dunno. Big, ugly car, four doors. Dark color." She went back to the bed, this time sitting with her feet dangling. "So anyway, I was talking to Lisa an' I watched him for a minute. You can ask her about that, 'cause I told her. Then I thought, why not give him a try? So I told Lisa bye and went to see if he was, you know, lonely or something."

"He arrived at the playground shortly after nine-forty-nine, then." Which meant he'd still been alive between nine-fifteen and nine-thirty, which was when seven witnesses had Turner arriving at the club.

Therese rolled her eyes. "That's what I *said.*"

"You talked to him for how long?"

"Hardly any time at all." She grimaced. "He wasn't buying, an' I got a living to make, don't I? I headed for Proctor—that's my regular spot."

"You didn't see anyone else approach him?"

The girl shook her head.

"Was anyone else in the area?"

"Maybe some people got out up at the club." She squinched her face up. "Yeah, I think so. They parked in that lot."

"They? How many were there?"

"I dunno. They were women, see, so I didn't pay attention. Didn't see no one else till I got to Proctor."

"All right. What about this man?" Lily took out a picture of Turner. "Did you see him that night?"

"Not then. Seen him around a few times, talked to him once." She sighed. "Just talked. His kind, they don't pay for it. He's okay, though. Real respectful."

"What about this man?" The photo Lily offered this time was of the dancer, Cullen Seabourne.

Therese's tongue darted over her lip. She looked greedy. "Course I've seen him. He dances there, you know. Takes off all his clothes. Just like me." She giggled. "Told him that once, that he and I had sorta the same job, only mine was more hands on. He laughed."

"Did you see him last night?"

"I told you who I saw—that first guy, and some women. That's it."

"One more thing, Ms. Martin. Have you spoken to anyone about seeing that man arrive at the playground?"

She snorted. "Hell, no. Think I'm an idiot? Around here, you shoot off your mouth, you get in trouble."

"That's good. Just keep thinking that way. What about your friend—the one who called you? Did you tell her?"

"Just said I might have some business, then hung up. She don't know who it was."

Lily stood. "Thank you for your cooperation. Officer Phillips will bring you a statement to sign so you don't have to go to the station house. I'm sure you don't want anyone to know you've spoken with us. I don't, either."

Lily gave Phillips a few instructions—he'd follow up with the friend, get that confirmed, and make sure she didn't know anything. Then she left.

She checked her watch as she started back down the stairs. Twelve-oh-five. Plenty of time to make it to Bishop's. She was looking forward to the look on Turner's face when—

Her cell phone rang. She fished it out. "Detective Yu."

"This is Rule."

Oh, she wished her heartbeat hadn't done that skip-jump thing. She spoke sharply. "Yes?"

"I deeply regret this, but I can't make lunch. Some clan business requires my attention. Can we get together about two-thirty?"

"I've an appointment at three." Lily stepped onto the sidewalk. Dammit, she was not disappointed.

"What about dinner, then?"

"What about four-thirty? We don't have to eat while you tell me about lupi."

"Why not, though? We both eat. You can ask questions about lupi pertinent to your investigation, and I'll have the opportunity to hit on you again."

The laugh was out before she could stop it. Oh, he was dangerous, all right. "This isn't social."

"You're free to continue thinking that." He hesitated. "There's a chance I can get you into Clanhome, if you're interested. There would be conditions."

"I'm interested." For years, most people had thought the Nokolai enclave outside the city belonged to a nutty, pseudo-religious group who didn't allow outsiders on their land. Though the clan had come out of the closet after the Supreme

Court ruling, they remained unwelcoming—and outside the city limits. A city cop didn't stand much chance of getting a toe across their boundaries without a warrant.

"We can discuss it over dinner."

"All right. I'll be working late. Eight-thirty okay?"

"Dum alius hora, delicia."

"What does that mean?"

He chuckled. "So suspicious. Eight-thirty is fine."

"At Bishop's," she reminded him.

"At Bishop's. Be safe," he said and disconnected.

Be safe? She frowned at the phone in her hand. One of her instructors at the academy had ended every lesson with a similar phrase, but she'd never heard a civilian use it. They used to say it on that cop show, too. . . . What was the name of it? Maybe Turner had been a fan.

The idea of a lupus prince hooked on a television cop show had her grinning as she finished descending the stairs. Enough about Turner, she told herself as she headed for her car. There was another man she needed to know better: Carlos Fuentes. He'd arrived at the playground shortly after 9:49. But why had he gone there? Who had he met? And how had he really felt about his wife's affair?

One of the last people to speak with Fuentes before he died was the Most Reverend Patrick Harlowe. So her next stop was the Church of the Faithful. She could eat on the way.

"WHAT do you mean, he can't talk to me?"

The pudgy little man was upset. "I didn't say that. Oh, no. The Most Reverend will certainly talk to you, Detective, but he isn't here right now. He had to go to our Mother Temple in Los Angeles. He should be back tomorrow." He smiled at her hopefully.

"Tomorrow." Lily frowned. When was Turner planning to get her into Clanhome? Her gut was telling her she might find some answers there. This was beginning to look like some kind of lupi-against-lupi deal, for all that the victim had been human. "What time?"

"In the evening, I think. Father Hidalgo will be handling the morning services."

"You have two fathers?"

"Two priests," he corrected her. "There are several degrees of priesthood—father, reverend father, most reverend, holy, and the most holy, who's rather like our Pope." He beamed at her. "He's in England normally, but he's been visiting our new Mother Temple. That's why the Most Reverend Patrick had to be away."

"That's a lot of structure for such a new religion." And were all the priests male? In a religion centered around a female deity, that seemed odd.

"No, no, the church isn't new. Well, it's new to America, but the faith has been around a long time, a very long time. It originated in Egypt in . . . oh, my, I'm not good with dates. The Second Dynasty? We were dreadfully persecuted during the Middle Ages." He shook his head. "We had to go underground. That's why you won't have heard about us, but the rituals weren't lost. Not entirely. Many of them can be traced back for thousands of years."

The battier the cult, Lily thought, the more they liked to claim an ancient lineage. And there was nothing like a little persecution—preferably in the past—to lend their beliefs a certain cachet. "You seem pretty knowledgeable. Maybe you could help me out, answer a few questions."

His smile faltered. "I don't see what I could tell you. I knew Carlos, but not well."

"You spoke to him Thursday night."

"Briefly." He was unhappy. "I told your officer that."

"I just need to confirm a few things, get some background." She gave him a trust-me smile. "You know how it is. I have to be able to answer anything my superior might throw at me."

He nodded, but doubtfully. "I suppose we could use the secretary's office."

They were in what she assumed was the sanctuary, though it looked rather like the bank lobby it used to be, only with pews. "You don't have an office?"

"Oh, no." He shook his head, smiling again as he started toward the back of the building. "I'm just a lay brother. A carpenter—or was. Retired now, you know, so I help out, but I've no official status."

"Did you do some of the work here?"

"I did." His face shone.

"Used to be a bank, right?"

"That's right." He glanced around with proprietorial pride. "Built in 1932, but it was empty for years. We take pride in the restoration we've done here. The building was in dreadful shape, truly dreadful."

"Mmm." Took a lot of money to restore an old building. This one was small, as banks go, but it still seemed an odd choice for a church. But apparently the Church of the Faithful wasn't hurting for money.

As it turned out, the chubby lay brother and retired carpenter really didn't have much to tell her. He confirmed that Fuentes had been at the church Thursday night—he'd seen him arrive— but not to rehearse with the choir. He'd been closeted with the most reverend fellow, receiving some private counseling.

Tomorrow, she promised herself as she unlocked her car, she'd talk to the Most Reverend Patrick Harlowe. Tonight . . . her lips curved up. Tonight she'd have dinner with Rule Turner. She was looking forward to seeing his face when he walked into Bishop's.

NINE

RULE knew he'd been set up before he'd been in the place ten seconds.

Bishop's was more bar than restaurant, with all the ambiance of a locker room. Photographs in cheap plastic frames hung on paneling from the seventies. The wooden booths lining the narrow room looked as if they'd been through a couple of minor wars and would still be around after the next one. The place smelled of fried fish, hamburgers, and hostility.

As Rule made his way to the back of the room, heads turned. Conversations paused. Being watched was nothing new, but the expressionless gazes that tracked him weren't the reaction he usually received.

Bishop's was a cop hangout.

Lily Yu sat at the next-to-last booth on the left. She wore an icy yellow jacket with a black tee and slacks. The jacket, he knew, hid a shoulder holster. No jewelry. Her hair—shoulder-length, lustrous, as black as the inside of his eyelids on a moonless night—hung loose.

He wanted to run his fingers through it. To nuzzle her neck beneath that shining curtain and soak up her scent.

Fat chance. That didn't keep his heart from pounding as he slid into the booth across from her. He could feel the wanting in his fingertips, a tactile need for her. He smiled crookedly.

"Maybe I will behave. There are a lot of guns in this room."

Amusement lit her eyes, that fugitive humor he'd glimpsed before. It gave him hope. The Lady knew he needed some.

"You guessing about the guns?" she asked.

"Gun oil has a distinctive scent."

She nodded. "It's weird to think you're getting information all the time that's not available to me. Just how sensitive is your sense of smell when you're . . . well, like you are now?"

"Not as good as when I'm four-footed. Then, the air has weight and texture, and scent moves through me like a shifting tapestry."

"You miss it."

"Yes. It's been awhile."

It was the sort of place where the flatware comes wrapped in a skimpy paper napkin. Lily unwrapped hers, giving the task more attention than it rated. "I've heard that lupi *have* to Change every so often. That you can only put it off so long, and the full moon . . . damn."

The young woman who'd glided up to their booth wore baggy jeans that hung low, showing off her belly button ring. Her hair was short, as was her T-shirt. Her nipples were hard. She held an order pad, and she smelled excited—and frightened. "I'm Sharon," she said, her voice slightly breathless. "What can I get you?"

Automatically his smile gentled. "Hamburger, rare, made with two patties. Serve it dry, please. Is your coffee any good?"

"It's okay. I'll make some fresh," she promised.

"Thank you. Lily?" He quirked a brow at her.

"I think you mean 'Detective Yu.' " She looked at the waitress. "I'll have a hamburger, too, but make mine well done with extra pickles. Lots of extra pickles. And coffee, blond."

"Sure thing. I'll be right back." She stared at Rule a moment longer before giving a little sigh and hurrying off.

"You feeling more welcome now?" Lily asked dryly.

"As welcome as a man can be when he's having dinner with a lovely woman under the eyes of a couple dozen of her big brothers."

She chuckled. "Testosterone practically drips off the wall in this place, doesn't it? But you're from a male-dominated culture. Ought to feel normal."

"Lupi are male, yes. But our culture isn't male-centric. We treasure women."

"Funny, that's what the men say who lock their women up in purdah."

"It's not like that." He studied her a moment. There was something different about her tonight. More relaxed. That was exactly what he wanted, but he'd expected to have to work for it. "It must have been difficult for you, succeeding in a field that, ah, drips testosterone. You would have had to prove yourself over and over."

"They want to know you've got their backs, that's all. You know what it takes to really join the gang? Get in a fight." She shook her head, amused. "One good knock-down-drag-out, and you're one of the guys."

He went still. "You've fought? Hand-to-hand?"

"You can't always avoid it, though I . . . you've got a funny look on your face."

She was so small. Tough in spirit, physically fit, but no match for nine out of ten men. "I've a strong protective instinct. All lupi do. We see Deity as essentially female."

Her eyebrows lifted. "The Great Mother, you mean?"

"Something like that."

"Who probably doesn't need big, strong males to protect her."

His lips twitched. "Point taken."

"I've been talking to some other people who worship a female deity. Supposedly her name is too sacred to be spoken except by priests consecrated to her service."

"Talking in connection with your investigation?"

She ignored that. "They're the Church of the Faithful, officially, but like to call themselves the Azá. It's supposedly from some ancient language—Babylonian or something. Ever hear of them?"

"Can't say that I have." He spread his own napkin in his lap. "You said you were interested in seeing Clanhome."

"I am."

"There will be a ceremony tomorrow that I must attend. I believe I can arrange for you to accompany me." She had to be there, of course. At least, she had to be close to Clanhome, or he wouldn't be able to attend, either.

"You're the heir, the crown prince. How much arranging does it take?"

He shook his head. "My position is . . . you'd call it high-status. And that counts among lupi, certainly. But I've no real authority. That rests with the Rho."

"Your father."

"Yes. Can you give your word to hold confidential everything you observe that isn't directly applicable to your case?"

"I've never heard of an outsider being allowed, much less invited, to attend a lupi ceremony. Why me?"

Rule gave her the truth—or part of it. "I want you to trust me."

Her index finger tapped the table as she thought it over. Not much given to impulse, his *nadia*. Finally she gave a brisk nod. "All right. You have my word. What time?"

"I'll pick you up at eleven."

"No, I'll pick you up. Where will I find you?"

"I prefer to drive myself."

"So do I."

Why did that not surprise him? "We don't always get what we want, do we? You won't—ah, thank you." The waitress was back with their coffee and water. She'd spritzed herself with a musky scent. Long practice kept him from wrinkling his nose in distaste. "Sharon, I think you forgot my companion's cream."

She blinked. "Oh. Oh, right." She dug into a pocket on her thigh and pulled out two containers of a substance that had never been within shouting distance of a cow. "Here. Be right back with your burgers," she told Rule with a smile and started to move away.

A man in the table nearest their booth grabbed her arm. He was young, with buzz-cut brown hair. The two other men at the table were slightly older. "Sharon, if that guy gives you any trouble," he said loudly, "you let me know."

She blinked, confused. "Uh, sure. But he isn't—"

"I know what he is." The young cop gave Rule a hard look, then turned it on Lily, though he still pretended to be talking to the waitress. "I also know you've got too much self-respect to hang out with his kind."

Rule tensed. Lily wouldn't thank him for smashing the pup's face in, but—

"Hey, Crowder," Lily said loudly. "Got a tissue?"

One of the older men at the table looked taken aback but recovered quickly. "Nah. Didn't bring my purse." The other man snickered.

Lily shook her head sadly. "You ought to be better prepared." She pulled her purse onto the table and ostentatiously dug inside it. "Here," she said—and tossed him a packet of tissues. "Wipe behind your trainee's ears, Crowder. He's dripping."

That brought a round of laughter—and not just from the three men at the table. The young cop flushed and released Sharon's elbow.

"You handled that well," Rule said.

She grimaced, broke open the coffee creamer packet, and emptied it into her coffee. "I didn't realize it would be this bad. I wonder if this is how a white woman felt in Alabama thirty years ago if she ate with a black man."

"Not quite that bad, I hope. Our fellow customers aren't likely to drag me into the alley and beat me up."

"I don't suppose they could, unless they drew on you. There are parallels, though, aren't there?" She sipped her coffee, eyeing him over the rim of the mug. "The civil rights movement opened doors for lupi that would have remained closed otherwise."

"True. If people hadn't started refusing to sit in the back of the bus, measures like the Species Citizenship Bill wouldn't be possible now. I need to talk to you about that. First, though, have you given any thought to going out with me?"

She sputtered into laughter. "Does the head-on approach usually work for you?" She shook her head, amusement fading. "It's not going to happen, Turner. You're lovely to look at. Charming, too, if a bit cocky."

"Cocky is for puppies."

"Did I mention arrogant? Never mind. It doesn't matter how pretty or charming you are—you're not worth tossing my career out the window."

"Is that what would happen?" He paused, then nodded. "I see. That makes things difficult for both of us."

"There is no 'us.' I'd like to ask you some questions."

"I hope they're personal."

"About lupi. Does the full moon force a lupus to Change?"

The temptation to keep pushing her was almost irresistible, but he wasn't here to indulge himself. He sighed. "To business, then. The full moon affects all of us, but only forces Change on young lupi. Like most adolescents, they have to learn control."

"So the Change is volitional?"

"Generally."

The pucker between her brows suggested she'd marked his evasion, but she didn't pursue it. "What about very young lupi? Children lack control."

"The Change arrives with puberty, not before." *That startled her. Good.* "I hope you won't put that in your report. It's not exactly general knowledge."

"I'm aware of that," she said slowly. "Why did you tell me?"

"I'm cooperating. Would it be possible for me to see Fuentes's body?"

"Good grief. Why?"

"There's an outside chance I might be able to scent his killer. If not, I could still pick up information that wouldn't be obvious to others."

Her finger began tapping the table again. "What sort of information?"

"The wounds might give me some idea of the nature of the killer—first, whether he really was a lupus, as you are assuming. Also whether he was an adolescent or a berserker."

"Berserker. That sounds ominous. Is that a certain type of lupus?"

"More like a condition. Rare, fortunately."

"Speaking of rare, here comes your burger. Hope she remembered mine."

Sharon wafted up on a cloud of musk, smiling shyly, and delivered two enormous hamburgers on plates piled high with french fries. She lingered a moment, fussing with the condiments, asking if Rule wanted anything else. More coffee, maybe? Another customer called to her to bring the coffeepot his way. Sharon sighed and departed.

Rule waited until she was out of earshot to say, "I've often wondered why human men like women to smell like the musk gland of a male deer."

"I take it you're not fond of perfume." Lily spread

mayonnaise on the bun. "Hey. I've misjudged Sharon. She remembered my pickles."

"She's just a little starstruck. I'm probably the only lupus she'll ever meet. Knowingly, at least."

"Hmm." The pickles were thick wedges, not slices. There were six of them. She cut them neatly to fit, then began layering them on top of the meat. "In every picture of you I've seen, you're wearing black. You wore black last night. You're wearing it today. That's on purpose, isn't it? You want people to recognize you. You want them to know they're meeting a lupus."

"Black is good theater," he admitted. "Are you really going to eat that?"

"You like raw meat. I like pickles." She set the top of the bun on her pickle mountain. "You do the mystery bit well—sex, sophistication, the allure of the forbidden or the dangerous. It's on purpose, isn't it? That's the image you want people to associate with lupi. Glamour, not bestiality. You've made yourself into a poster boy for your people."

His lip curled. "Why, thank you."

She grinned. "Starting to believe your image?"

"Maybe I really am sexy, sophisticated and—how did you put it? Full of the allure of the forbidden."

"Full of something, anyway."

He grinned back, enjoying her, and reached for the ketchup. "What about you, Lily? Do you believe your image?"

"I don't have an image."

"Sure you do. The tough, cynical cop."

"No, that's the real me. No secrets . . . well, maybe one or two." Suddenly all the fun leaked out of her expression. "But not on your scale. I don't keep any kids tucked out of sight so they won't spoil the image."

TEN

~

LILY thought he was going to jump her. The fury that leaped into his eyes looked like violence about to happen.

For a long moment he didn't move, didn't speak. At last he asked, low and silky, "How do you know about my son?"

Her mouth was dry. It infuriated her. "You don't want the police to be aware of him?"

"I forgot I was talking to the police. Foolish of me. No, I don't want the police to know about him. I don't want anyone outside the clan to know about him—though not for the reason you suggested." His lip curled. "What an interesting opinion you have of me."

She'd hurt him. The notion shocked her, and immediately she tried to reason it away.

He wasn't a serious suspect now. Too many witnesses placed him at Club Hell at 9:30, and Therese and her cell phone proved Fuentes was still alive at 9:50. So maybe she'd relaxed too much. She'd let things get too casual, too friendly. Maybe, for some ungodly reason, she actually liked this man. She'd felt bad for him, talking about how he missed the Change. What had happened to wrest his magic from him? Could he get it back? She couldn't ask.

But she didn't know him, not really, nor did he know her.

Her opinion couldn't matter. And yet . . . "I crossed a line," she said quietly. "I'm sorry."

"My son isn't part of your investigation." He tossed his napkin on the table, slid out of the booth, and pulled out his wallet.

She slid out and stood, too. "You don't have to—"

"I invited you. I'll pay." He threw a couple bills on the table. "*Bon appétit,* Detective. If you wish to see Clanhome, be at your headquarters building at ten-thirty tomorrow morning. I'll pick you up."

He left to the same silent chorus of stares that had greeted his arrival.

Okay, Lily thought, picking up her hamburger and trying to take some interest in eating it. *Looks like I blew that one.* She was chewing a tasteless bite when Crowder came up.

"Lost your date?" He slid in across from her without asking.

"I'm trying to have supper here."

"You go right ahead," he said, and dragged one of the fries on Rule's plate through the ketchup. "Got any mustard?"

"No." She deliberately took another bite.

"Oh, there it is." He pulled the squeeze bottle over and squirted a thick yellow stream on the bun. "Be better with some onion," he said, fitting the bun on top, "but I'm not picky."

"The meat's rare."

"Like I said, I'm not picky." He took a huge bite.

She sighed and put her hamburger down. "You aren't going away, are you?"

"Nope." He chewed, then wiped his mouth. "Wanted to apologize for Tucker. Kid's wet behind the ears, just like you said. Thing is . . . well, I thought you ought to know. Someone's been shooting his mouth off. Tucker's too green to take what he hears with a grain of salt."

"Talking?" Her stomach felt tight. "About me?"

He nodded and disposed of another fourth of the burger in one bite, chewed, and swallowed. "Nothing that bad, just . . . you know. Talk. About you and Turner, the effect his kind have on women. That sort of thing."

"Who?" she demanded. Dammit, she'd only been on the case since last night. "Who's talking me down?"

Crowder shook his head. "I don't like to say. You know how it is."

Yeah, she knew. You were one of the guys—right up until you weren't. Locker room talk was still governed by the high school code: don't repeat it to the girls. Probably just as well, a lot of the time, or none of the women on the force would be able to stand working with a lot of the men.

Crowder had bent those unspoken rules by coming over here. "Thanks for the warning."

"No problem." He polished off the burger. "Would've been better with onions," he said, and pushed to his feet. "You take care, now."

"Yeah. Stay safe."

Crowder ambled back to his table, leaving Lily thinking furiously. Crowder worked the same shift she did. Who knew about her case that might have been in the locker room at the end of shift, shooting his mouth off?

She grimaced. Too many possibilities. But she couldn't help remembering the way Mech had tried to protect her from being alone with Turner. *Don't jump to conclusions,* she warned herself.

But the ugly thought had destroyed any hope of forcing more of her meal down. She grabbed her purse and scooted out of the booth.

"The food wasn't good?" The starstruck waitress stood in front of Lily, her eyes dark with anger and disappointment.

It wasn't the food she was worried about. Lily sighed. "The food was fine, but he had to leave. And so do I."

Sharon shook her head. "Take my advice, and don't go running after him. Make him come to you. Not that I blame you." She sighed. "That man just radiates sex. Like a stove. I'll bet he—okay, okay!" she called to someone else wanting her attention. "Be right there." She smiled kindly at Lily. "My momma always said, if you can't play hard to get, then just play. Have fun." She patted Lily on the arm and hurried off.

Lily stared after her. She had definitely misjudged Sharon. She forced her mind back to business.

PAIN was a dull, sullen presence, hardly compelling. But something else pushed at Cullen, telling him it was time. Time to wake up.

He stirred. Something hard beneath him . . . hard, it was so hard, to wake up. Shouldn't be. He'd been . . . he was . . .

For a moment the knowledge simply wasn't there. The spurt of panic pushed him the rest of the way to the surface. He opened his eyes.

Raw wood overhead. Wood beneath him, too. The cabin. *Yes,* he thought, relieved. *That's right.* He was at the cabin. He'd come here to . . . the thought slid away.

His ribs hurt. He sat up carefully, letting the blanket that had covered him slide to his lap. He blinked. He'd been lying on the floor, fully clothed. And there was a large hole in the north wall.

Oh, yeah. He'd gone sailing through it when he got into a little disagreement with Molly's friend. He touched his side, grimaced. Hadn't won that argument, had he?

The memory was oddly fuzzy. He must have been slightly concussed, though his head didn't hurt. Healed it while he was out, he supposed, and pushed to his feet. He'd had time for that. The light streaming in through the damaged wall told him it was early morning. He'd come to the cabin with Molly and her sorcerer friend yesterday about noon. They'd talked about exchanging spells, and then . . .

Had it been yesterday? He frowned. Must have been, he decided. If he'd been out for more than a night, his ribs wouldn't still be this sore. And he'd be a lot hungrier.

Not that he wasn't hungry. First things first, though. He touched his wards mentally, found everything secure, then went to check the damage to his ramshackle *pied-à-terre*.

He wasn't much of a carpenter, but the repair seemed to lie within his skills. He'd have to get to it pretty quickly, though—the roof was sagging. Someone had wedged a couple of the broken two-by-fours across the top beam, temporarily reinforcing it, but a good wind could take it down.

Considerate of them, he thought, ambling over to the ice chest he'd brought. They'd knocked him out, cracked a rib or two, but at least they'd kept the roof from falling in on him while he was unconscious. They'd tossed a blanket over him, too, before departing.

That had probably been Molly's idea. She had a soft heart. But he didn't think she was strong enough to have made the temporary repairs to his roof. That must have been . . . what was the man's name?

Frowning, he took out the carton of eggs, then paused, trying to identify the mechanical *whup-whup* sound his ears picked up. A helicopter, he decided. Off to the south. Not a common sound up here—he was pretty remote. But not alarming, either.

He headed for the little propane-powered stove. He'd have to give Rule a call. There was some serious stuff going on, weird energies moving between the realms that he didn't understand. Though he had an idea, from something the other man had said . . . something to do with the realms shifting?

Dammit, he really needed to remember. He turned on the burner and poured oil into the cast-iron skillet, scowling. What was his last clear memory?

The encounter with that pretty little detective at Club Hell was clear enough. Cullen grinned. Rule had a definite interest there. Should he tell his friend that his newest inamorata was a sensitive?

Maybe, but never mind for now. That memory was clear enough. So was the next morning, when Molly's phone call had dragged him out of sleep far too early—and seriously aroused his curiosity. A few hours later, he'd gone to the airport to pick up Molly and her current lover, who was a sorcerer, like him.

Only not like him. Cullen frowned. That's where things got fuzzy. He couldn't call up the man's face or much about what happened after Molly and what's his name arrived. They'd argued, him and the other sorcerer. He remembered that much. He'd wanted more than the other man . . . Michael. Yes, he thought, relieved to have retrieved that much. The man's name was Michael.

The one he'd used, anyway. Sorcerers were a secretive bunch, so it probably wasn't his real name. Normally Cullen wouldn't have invited another student of the *sorcéri* to his retreat. There was a small, untapped node beside the cabin, one he didn't intend to share. But Molly had vouched for the man.

And Cullen had ended up unconscious for about twenty-four hours. Well, he thought, absently rubbing his side, maybe he'd deserved that. He and Michael had swapped a couple of basic spells—nice stuff, but nothing really new. When they started talking theory, though, it had been obvious the man was holding back. Cullen couldn't recall exactly what had happened, but he had the notion he'd pulled something a bit underhanded.

It had worked, too. He grinned, elated, the two eggs in his hand forgotten as at last one memory kicked in, clear and sharp.

What was a cracked rib or an unplanned nap on the floor? He had a dandy new illusion spell, elegant and powerful. Far more sophisticated than anything he'd run across or dreamed up on his own. The setting sequence alone suggested all sorts of possibilities. . . .

Grease spat on his hand. He started to rub it, noticed the eggs he was holding, and cracked them into the pan, then added a third. Food first, and then—oh, then he'd settle into some serious study of his new acquisition.

He'd better not get too deep into it, though, or he'd forget to call Rule. Cullen sighed. Pity, but he couldn't just drop out of sight and work on this, not now. Who else could tease out the truth? In this benighted age, so few grasped even the basics about magic. They didn't burn to understand, the way he did. No, just as children afraid of the dark pull the covers over their heads, they burrowed into their ignorance—and cast out those who didn't want to live trapped beneath their stifling restrictions.

As the clan that should have been his had cast him out.

Cullen drew a shaky breath. Enough. Rule had never shunned him for doing what he had to do. For that, Cullen owed him friendship. And a phone call.

When the eggs were done, he lifted them onto a plate, carrying it and the loaf of bread over to the table. He got a can of Coke from the ice chest and refueled quickly, hardly noticing what he ate, his mind teeming with symbols, structures, and relationships that had no direct physical analogue.

Thirty minutes later, the plate with its bits of congealed egg sat forgotten on the floor, where he'd moved it when he noticed it was in his way. The table was littered with scraps of paper, and he was frowning at a row of glowing symbols that hung in midair. After a moment, two of the symbols slid to the right, and another sequence took their place.

Yes, that was it. That's what he'd been missing. If the congruence between the object and the illusion was to hold, he had to—

A red energy ribbon snapped across his field of vision. He jolted. One of his wards had been breached. Not tampered with, not finessed. Something had powered right through as if the ward wasn't there.

Which should not have been possible.

Cullen lacked the usual lupus aversion for guns. With a quick wave of his hand, the glowing symbols vanished, even as he dashed for the corner where his shotgun waited, loaded and ready. He grabbed it, paused. A second's concentration, and the scraps of paper burst into flame. And he headed for the exit, moving fast.

Not the front door or the impromptu exit he'd added when he went through the wall yesterday. A trapdoor at the back of the shack. It opened on a cramped tunnel that led to a cave— one he'd long ago explored thoroughly. Cullen didn't like small, enclosed spaces any better than the next wolf, but he liked even the less the prospect of meeting whoever or whatever could brush through his wards that way.

Call him paranoid. Friendly visitors knocked, dammit.

He tossed back the throw rug, grabbed the edge of the trapdoor, and yanked. It was heavier than it looked, being made of solid steel.

And was hit by pure, burning agony. His back arched as his fingers released the shotgun. His knees buckled. He fell to the floor.

Cullen had a high tolerance for pain. Most lupi did. But this was like nothing he'd ever experienced, as if he were being burned alive from the inside out. He heard himself screaming and tried to clamp his jaws together, but his body twitched and spasmed and wouldn't obey. Instinctively, he tried to Change. And couldn't. Terror, as primitive and consuming as the physical agony, seized him.

Like flipping a switch, it ended.

As sex leaves an afterglow, so does intense pain. He lay there twitching and panting, his mind dimmed, his entire body aching like a bad tooth.

The gun.

It lay inches from his out-flung hand. He reached for it—or tried to. His arm didn't move. Frantic, he gathered his focus and tried again. His muscles gave a single obedient twitch— and sent a wave of fresh pain rolling through him.

He gritted his teeth, riding that wave. *Okay, so the attack was physical, not psychic. It did some damage. I can heal it. Lady, grant me time to—*

Several black-clad forms burst through the door. Three— four—and another two erupted from the hole in his wall. They wore what looked like black *gis* belted by long strips of red cloth tied with deliberate intricacy. Black scarves wrapped, Bedouin-like, around their heads hid the lower parts of their faces.

And they had rifles. Every damned one of them.

Ninja wanna-bes with guns?

"You," barked one of them—short guy, pale skin, smelled of seru—excited and aggressive. "Where are the others?"

"He can't answer, Second." Whisper-soft, that voice came from behind the knot of black-clad bodies near the hole in his wall. It sounded childish . . . if you could imagine a computer having a childhood, for there was no life, no feeling in that voice. "I'm surprised he's conscious. Speech will be beyond him for several hours."

The black-clad forms parted. A woman in a long red robe picked her way daintily through the bits of broken boards.

She was small, not much over five feet, and looked barely adolescent. Her hair was long, jet black, and hanging loose. A narrow silver band circled her head. The opal it held was large and black, and covered the brow chakra. She carried a staff of black wood banded in silver that was as tall as she was. It reeked of magic.

He wanted to find her ridiculous, a child dressed up like a B-movie extra. Instead, the hair on the back of his neck lifted. A wave of hatred—instinctive, unreasoning—curled his lips back from his teeth.

The tiny movement hurt like blazes. Damn, damn, damn, there were tears in his eyes as she sauntered over to him. "Look for them," she said crisply, a queen addressing her minions.

Them? Michael and Molly, he realized. These escapees from a costume drama wanted the other sorcerer, not him.

All this, and they aren't even after me. That's a pisser.

"Madonna," the man who'd spoken before said hesitantly. "Stay back, please. Let us protect you."

"Fool," she said in that baby-computer voice. "He can't move. See where that—" she gestured with her staff at the tunnel—"leads. And who might be in it."

The short ninja barked out orders. Three of them hurried to obey, lowering themselves one at a time into Cullen's escape route. Shortie moved closer to Cullen, watching him suspiciously.

She paid him no attention, her gaze fixed on Cullen. Her eyes were uncannily dark, so black he couldn't separate pupils from irises. There was something odd about her scent, too, but the smell of magic from her staff was so strong he couldn't tease out much else.

Her staff . . .

"I wonder why you're conscious," she said.

The staff. That's where his hatred focused. The need to destroy it rose fiercely in him. He wanted to Change, to take it in his teeth and splinter it, but—wait a minute. He hadn't been able to Change earlier, but the assault had ended. He'd been damaged, but maybe—

"All right," she whispered, "let's see what you're thinking. Where are they?"

He met her eyes—and crossed his own as her probe slid harmlessly off. He'd have stuck out his tongue if his jaws had cooperated.

"You're shielded!" she cried, high and astonished. Her face puckered, and she jabbed him in the ribs with her staff.

I will not be touched by that abomination. The power of hatred sent him surging to his feet, aware of pain but consumed by the need to crush the unclean thing.

But pain disregarded isn't pain defeated. He was slow, clumsy. He staggered and missed when he grabbed for the staff. And when the rifle butt descended, he caught a glimpse of it—too late to keep it from slamming into his skull.

ELEVEN

TWENTY minutes outside the city and climbing, Lily looked out the window at chaparral, scrub oak, and rock. The road was steep, the sky overhead so clear and intense it seemed she had only to put the window down to be able to breathe in the blue as well as see it. Compared to the Rockies to the northeast, they were runts, these mountains, but she loved them. They made her think of old cowboys, worn down to spit and sinew by hard living.

Rule's father owned a fair slice of these mountains.

That wasn't all Isen Turner owned, according to the dossier the FBI had given her. There were vineyards in Napa Valley. Chunks of real estate in San Diego and L.A. Stocks, bonds, and more land in a remote part of Canada. The FBI estimated his holdings at three hundred million, and Rule managed them.

Not that the Feds knew everything. They didn't know who Rule's mother had been, or how old his father was. They weren't even sure how old Rule was.

In his thirties, she thought. Though he could have passed for a twenty-something, his bearing spoke of someone older. Of course, being semiroyal might have that effect, too.

She glanced at him, then looked out the window again. The view was more interesting than a pouting werewolf.

His car, however, woke lust in her heart. A shiny new

Mercedes convertible—silver outside, dark leather inside, on-board navigation system. She hadn't wanted to suggest he put the top down, given the prevailing atmosphere of snit, but it was easier to hear the incredible stereo with the top up . . . not that there was much worth listening to.

He'd been playing Dvořák when he picked her up.

Mostly she tolerated classical music pretty well. But not that one, not one of the quartets. Maybe she should have gritted her teeth until it ended, but she hadn't. She'd asked politely if he could play something else. Equally polite, he'd switched at once to an oldies station. Which may have been a backhanded slap at her musical taste. She didn't care.

She'd apologized last night. What more did he want? And dammit, was she really wishing he'd go back to flirting with her? She couldn't be that dumb.

All right, she admitted silently. Maybe she could be. She'd work on it. But he didn't have to be so—so blasted *polite*. She'd tried. Hadn't she tried to start a civil conversation? Amazing how quelling a simple yes or no could be. He'd managed to freeze her courteously into silence, too.

He reminded her of her mother.

That thought was absurd enough to make her smile. She was taking herself—and him—far too seriously. And this was an investigation, not a pleasure drive.

She'd cleared it with the captain this morning. He'd agreed to her omitting all irrelevant details from her official report; he liked the idea of keeping the Feds in the dark. Then she'd gone to talk to Fuentes's neighbors, and caught two of them at home.

The one on the floor below hadn't known the couple at all. No help there. She'd struck pay dirt with 41-C, though. Erica Jensen was a young single woman who was Rachel's friend. She'd agreed that Carlos had had a wandering eye—also wandering hands and other body parts. He'd persuaded Rachel to try the scene at Club Hell and had been pleased when she attracted the attention of a lupus prince.

"Whole thing's weird, you know?" Erica had shrugged. "Carlos talked about how possessiveness is wrong, but I dunno. If you ask me, he liked it that other men wanted his wife. Made him feel important, because she was his. Just a different way of making like he owned her. But she seemed okay with it."

"Did Rachel tell you this, or did you talk to Carlos about it?" Lily had asked.

"Mostly Rachel, but Carlos talked about that weird church of his to anyone who'd listen." She'd looked sad. "I'm making it sound like he was a real lowlife, and he wasn't. He worked hard, and he was sweet with Rachel most of the time. You ask me, he had some wires crossed, was all. Rachel loved him like crazy. The deal with Turner . . . well, she loved that, too. She says the sex was incredible, but I think he made her feel special, too. And it made Carlos appreciate her more."

All in all, she'd made it sound as if Rule Turner was being a Good Samaritan by diddling Rachel Fuentes. Lily didn't buy that, but lupus mores *were* different. They didn't believe in marriage, for one thing.

Lily glanced at the Good Samaritan behind the wheel.

He'd forgotten to mention that this was casual day. He was wearing his usual black, but the jeans were worn at the stress points and his T-shirt was old and faded. He wore tennis shoes, no socks, and mirrored sunglasses. And he hadn't shaved.

So why did he look so blasted elegant? She broke the silence. "Clanhome is owned by your father, I understand."

"Technically, yes," he said in that cool, polite voice he'd used ever since picking her up. "He holds it in trust for the clan."

"A corporation could do the same thing."

"There's been some discussion of that, now that it's legal to be lupi. But corporate law and lupus custom don't mesh well."

"I suppose not. Stockholders are allowed to vote."

The mirrored lenses tipped her way briefly, then faced the road again. "No doubt you believe clan members are being deprived of their rights and would be happier if they were allowed to vote."

"Wouldn't they?"

"No."

Just that, no explanation. Lily clamped down on her irritation. He was hardly the first uncooperative witness she'd dealt with. "Tell me about your father. Will I meet him today?"

"He's a canny old bastard. I mean that literally, of course."

Now there was something other than courtesy in his voice. Mockery. "We're all bastards, by your standards."

"You don't know what my standards are. Is there anything I should know about today's ceremony?"

"No. You won't be attending."

Temper was bubbling up under the lid she'd put on it. "So that business of requiring my word was, what—window dressing?"

"All visitors to Clanhome are asked to promise not to talk about what they see. You can't attend the alliance ceremony because another clan is involved, and their Rho didn't want an outsider present."

Another clan—a new ally? Lupus politics, Grandmother had said, were played according to the rules— lupus rules. Which included ritual combat, sometimes to the death. "Which one? What's going on?"

"This isn't part of your investigation, Detective."

"It's wonderful how you can make 'Detective' sound like an insult."

"I'm doing what you wanted. Keeping things impersonal."

"Are you?" She turned to study him, then shook her head. "I don't think so. If things weren't personal, you wouldn't be pouting."

His eyebrows lifted. "Pouting. That's certainly in line with your other notions of my character. But you're right, of course." The car slowed. "Things are personal between us. I'm not the one in denial about that."

"I meant that you keep *making* things personal. Or trying to. Which your present snit proves is a big—what are you doing?"

"Behaving like a fool, most likely." He'd pulled to a stop, dead center in the road.

"You aren't going to suggest I get out and walk."

"I wouldn't dream of it." He tossed his sunglasses on the dash, then unfastened his seat belt.

The sudden jump in her heartbeat said she knew what he intended. She refused to listen to it. He wouldn't. Not when there was so much at stake, not while he thought he was still a suspect—not in the middle of the road, for heaven's sake. "There's a blind corner just ahead. You'd better move this car, unless you want to get hit."

"You may hit me," he said, and seized her left arm. "In a moment."

Her right hand flew out—not to slap, but to punch. He snagged it in midblow and struck back. Not with his hands, but with his mouth. On hers.

She bit him.

His breath sucked in, but he didn't pull back. No, the bastard chuckled. He rubbed his bloody lip over hers, slowly. Gently. Then he licked her lower lip.

And she . . . didn't move. Couldn't move. As if he'd shot a bolt of some strange metal through her body, she was pinned and quivering, her entire being vibrating to a new, soundless music.

He let go of her hand to cradle her head, deepening the kiss. And once freed, she didn't push him away. She touched him. His ear, and the hair that curled over it. His shoulder, firm and flawlessly male. His fingers stirred the hair at her nape, and God help her, but the music took on a familiar beat, the pounding rhythm of need. She made a small noise and chased his mouth with hers.

He answered with a masculine purr of approval. His hand settled over her breast, teasing the nipple. His mouth stopped coaxing and took.

She met his greed with her own. His shirt was thin, yet still in her way. She needed his body, needed it bare so she could touch and claim every plane and hollow. She knew him—no, she needed to know him, would know him, now, always, every part of him—

Lily heard herself moaning. The sound shocked her back into her right mind—or whatever was left of it. She jerked her head back.

He bent to her exposed throat, kissing, sucking.

"No—no, you can't. We can't—" The frantic sound of her voice frightened her. She pushed at him.

He lifted his head and looked at her out of eyes gone blind with desire, the pupils so large they nearly swallowed the irises. "No, of course . . . not here. I shouldn't have . . . come here, *querida,* you need to be held. Come, I need this, too," he said, and unfastened her seat belt.

His hand was shaking.

Like her. As if she'd been plunged into an icy pool, tiny shudders chased up her spine and shivered along her thighs. Her jaw tightened, and it was hard to get words out. "Don't touch me. You can't help. You did this. You did this to me."

"I kissed you. The rest is not my choice, either. This console is damnably in the way," he added, but it didn't seem to be giving him much trouble.

Nor was she. She let him arrange her, her mind overturned by confusion . . . her body still craving his.

His arm around her shoulders urged her as close as the console would allow. His chest heaved with breath as ragged as hers. "I'm sorry, *nadia*. I was angry, but I'd no right to be. You didn't know why you upset me. It's hard for you. So much you don't understand."

She understood that this was wrong. She told herself that, but didn't move. "You're using some kind of spell. You must be, even though I can't feel it."

"I'm not. You and I . . . you're right that this is no ordinary attraction. We are bound. Neither of us chose it, neither controls it."

"No!" She forced herself to straighten, pulling away. "There's always choice. Sometimes limited by—by circumstance . . ." Such as developing an incredible case of the hots for a man she had no business getting involved with. A man who lacked even a nodding acquaintance with fidelity. A man who wasn't entirely human.

"We can't always control our emotions," she finished more quietly. "But we choose whether to act on them."

"Why do I think I know what your choice will be?" He rubbed his neck, sighed. "Lily, it won't work. No amount of common sense or willpower will cut the connection between us. You can't turn your back on this as you might an infatuation."

"Amazing. We agree on something. I am not infatuated with you. I'm not altogether sure I like you."

"I'm aware of that. At the moment, I'm not too thrilled with you, either. You're stubborn, infuriating, prejudiced—"

"I am not prejudiced!"

"Then you have no problem with my nature?"

"It's your sexual habits I'm not crazy about."

His crooked smile was less than happy. "You'll be pleased to know that you've changed my habits. Permanently."

"Sure, and you've got a bridge you'd like to sell me, too." She looked straight ahead, tucked her hair behind her ears, and hoped she didn't look as all-to-pieces as she felt. Dammit, she was still shaky. "Don't you have a ceremony to attend?"

He just sat there, looking at her. She refused to look at him, but his gaze seemed to have weight. And heat. Her heartbeat wouldn't behave.

Finally he put the car back in gear. "There's a great deal you need to know, and no point in telling you any of it. Not when you're determined to disbelieve me. When you're ready to listen, let me know."

For the rest of the drive, she was as silent as he.

CLANHOME was a long, winding strip of land that bordered BLM land in places, and a wilderness preserve elsewhere. Maps indicated it was accessible by only two roads—this one, and a private road to the north that led to the tiny community of Rio Bravo. The stretch of Clanhome that met this road was fenced and gated.

Rule pulled to a stop at the closed gate. A young man in shorts—and nothing else—was waiting to open it for them. He looked fit and friendly, barefoot and freckled, a regular Jimmy Olsen of a werewolf. There was a walkie-talkie clipped to his belt.

After opening the gate, he didn't move aside for them to pass, but came up to the window. Rule put it down. "Sammy."

"Hey, Rule. Benedict says for you to take your guest to the Rho's house before you go to the Grounds."

Rule flicked a glance at her. "You can tell him you gave me his message."

The young man grimaced. "I said it wrong. It's the Rho who wants to see her, not Benedict." He peered into the car, obviously curious about Rule's passenger.

Rule didn't introduce her. His fingers drummed once on the steering wheel, then he nodded. The young man stepped back, and they drove through the gate.

"Apparently," Rule said, "you'll be meeting my father after all."

"Good."

"You're speaking as the detective with a murder to solve, I assume. Not as the woman I'm involved with."

She wanted to tell him they weren't involved, but the words stuck in her throat. She'd all but inhaled him a few minutes ago. Whatever they were, *uninvolved* didn't fit. So she said nothing.

Past the gate, the gravel road wound around the rocky shoulder of an aging mountain, then headed down into a long, shallow valley. Nestled in that valley was what amounted to a village. Two dogs—a terrier of some sort and a shaggy collie mix—raced along the shoulder with them as they neared the village.

She hadn't expected dogs. It didn't seem to fit with the wolf thing.

There was no clear line between wilderness and town. No tidy blocks or fences. The modest stucco, timber-frame, or adobe houses seemed to have been plopped down at random, with some on the main street, others peering out from the pines and oaks covering the slopes on each side. They passed a gas station, a small produce market, a café, a laundry, and a general store.

There were people, too. The road split to circle a grassy area a little larger than a football field where several dozen people were gathered. The location for the ceremony she wouldn't see? Like the guard at the gate, the men she saw mostly wore shorts, period. The women—why hadn't she expected to see women?—wore shorts, too, though they added shoes and a T-shirt or halter. A couple of them waved; several others simply stared as they drove past.

Farther up the street, a teenage girl sat on the porch steps of a small stucco home, drinking a canned soda. She wore a gauzy dress . . . and had one arm looped casually over the huge, silver-coated wolf panting cheerfully in the heat beside her.

The wolf turned his head to watch as the Mercedes went by.

The Rho's home was set partway up the slope at the end of the street. It was a sprawling stucco home with a red tile roof— lovely, but hardly a mansion. Not what she expected of a man worth three hundred million. Rule pulled into the curving drive, and she saw the man standing at one corner of the house. He was middle-aged and as nearly naked as everyone else she'd seen.

The blade in his hand was entirely naked. All two or three feet of it. "Good God. What's he, the palace guard?"

"Something like that."

Rule pulled to a stop in front of the house. The guard watched them. He didn't look nearly as friendly as the one at the gate had. "This doesn't say much for your claim that everyone's happy not having a vote."

"You're unacquainted with the situation."

"You could fill me in."

"I don't know what the Rho wants you to know."

"And you don't make decisions like that without consulting him?"

"Not when I'm speaking to the police." He opened his door.

She started to reach for him. She had no idea what she was going to say, and didn't have the chance to learn. The door of the house flew open, and a young boy burst out. "Dad! Dad!"

Rule shot out of the car almost as precipitously. He was rounding the hood before Lily got her seat belt undone, his face filled with such a fierce joy that she felt embarrassed, as if she'd intruded.

She climbed out slowly as the two connected, the man grabbing the boy and lifting him off his feet to swing him in a dizzy circle, then settling him on one shoulder as easily as she might sling her purse on a shoulder. The boy had short, straight hair a shade darker than Rule's, a softer chin, and no beard, but otherwise was a miniature of his father.

Though maybe the resemblance was exaggerated by their identical, beaming expressions.

"So what are you doing out here?" Rule demanded. "What about your lessons?"

"It's lunch!" he cried, indignant. "Anyway, I finished the spelling, and I know all the states, and Nettie says we'll do math after." He grimaced. "I am not looking forward to math, you know."

"I know. But you're doing better with division all the time, and you've got multiplication dicked. What's seven times seven?"

"Forty-nine! And you're *not* supposed to say dicked."

"I forgot. There's someone I'd like you to meet, *ma animi.*"

"Yeah?" He looked away from his father's face, ignoring the guard, and saw Lily. "It's a girl." He was surprised.

"A lady," Rule corrected. "Lily, this is my son, Toby Asteglio. Toby, this is Lily Yu."

"You?"

"It's a Chinese name," she said. "It sounds like the English pronoun, as if I'm always talking about someone else, doesn't it? But in Chinese it can mean lots of things, depending on how it's written."

"Do you talk in Chinese?"

"Sometimes, when I'm with my grandmother."

"Cool. My friend Manny, he's teaching me Spanish. His folks talk in it all the time, and I can't tell what they're saying, but I know a little. I can count to twenty. *¿Como está usted?*"

"Muy bien, gracias," she replied gravely. *"¿Y usted?"*

"You talk Spanish, too! Hey, Dad!" He patted his father's cheek. "She talks Spanish. Maybe she can teach me so's I don't forget, since I have to be here a while. Gammy says you're nuts for dragging me clear across the country," he added. "Or if you aren't, then you'd better get your act together. I don't think I was supposed to hear that part."

"Probably not," Rule said. "However, I'm working at getting my act together."

"She didn't mean it bad. She says that a lot. If I forget my homework, she says I'd better get my act together. But I'm glad you haven't gotten it together, 'cause I get to be here awhile."

A tall woman with a cloud of frizzy gray hair hanging nearly to her waist stepped out of the house. "Toby, you need to finish your lunch, or Henry will be convinced you're coming down with something."

"I'm not sick!"

"You know that, and I know that, but will Henry believe us?" The woman wore running shorts and an athletic bra. Her skin was coppery from heritage as well as sun, and her muscle tone was excellent, making it hard to guess her age. "Hello, Rule. Toby certainly knows the sound of your car. He shot out of the kitchen like we'd lit a fire under him."

"It's just sandwiches," Toby informed his father. "But with

Henry's bread, so they're good." He addressed the next to Lily. "He makes it himself. Gammy just buys hers, but Henry makes it. He lets me help sometimes." Back to Rule. "Are you going to have lunch with me?"

"Ms. Yu might, after speaking with your grandfather," Rule said. "I can't, not this time."

Toby made a face. "Oh, yeah. I forgot. You can't come in. But after the ritual . . . ?"

"I'll come see you," Rule said gently. "Work hard on your division, and you and I will go to the creek." He swung the boy off his shoulder, kissed his forehead, then set him on the ground and swatted his backside lightly. "Go eat."

Toby didn't move. The stubborn look on his face reminded her of Rule. "I would *like* to go with you."

"Yes, you would. But children are not allowed, which you know very well. Now go tend to your duties, and I'll take care of mine."

The boy heaved a huge sigh. "Nice to meet you, Ms. Yu. Maybe we can talk Spanish later."

"Maybe so," she said, charmed. And feeling guilty. This was not the distant relationship she'd been picturing. "Though I don't know very much."

"That's okay. I don't, either. Bye!" And he raced into the house at what she suspected was his usual pace: headlong.

Lily flicked a glance at the guard. The others acted like he wasn't there, but she found it difficult to ignore a man with a sword. Well, a machete, she amended. It was closer to two feet than three. She spoke quietly to Rule. "Your son's a charmer."

"I think so, too." He watched the door Toby had vanished through a moment longer, then turned to her. "I won't be going in with you, I'm afraid."

"What's that about?"

He just shook his head and gestured at the tall woman standing silently nearby. "This is Nettie Two Horses. I imagine she'll take you to meet the Rho. Nettie, this is Detective Lily Yu. You're expecting her?"

"I am." She held out a hand. Lily took it, and received a tingle of magic along with a firm, no-nonsense handshake. Native magic—she'd encountered its like before.

"Rule left off part of the introduction," the woman went on.

"I'm Dr. Two Horses. Not that you're obliged to call me that. Heaven knows no one around here does." She had a quick, wide smile. "I don't suppose I look like a doctor to you."

"Most doctors don't wear white lab coats at home."

"And you're wondering whether this is home for me. Well, Clanhome is. This house isn't, but I've a patient here." She grimaced. "A bloody difficult patient."

Rule smiled wryly. "He's awake, obviously."

"And doing well, under the circumstances. But I want him back in Sleep as soon as possible, which means I'd better take Lily to see him right away."

Rule nodded. "I'll see you later, then." He gave Lily a glance she couldn't read—then touched her cheek. "Be safe."

She lifted her brows. "Don't you mean, 'Be safe, *Detective?*'"

He chuckled. Then, instead of getting back into his car, he loped off, moving at an easy run that was pure pleasure to watch.

"He's beautiful in motion, isn't he?" the woman beside her said. "They all are. I've never tired of watching them."

Lily made a noncommittal noise, embarrassed that she'd been caught staring. "I didn't realize Isen Turner was ill. I hope it's nothing serious?"

"Serious enough, but he's not ill. Come, let's go inside. I'll explain some of it, but you'll need to save most of your questions for Isen." She started for the house.

Lily spared one last glance at the man with the oversize knife, then followed. "I didn't realize Rule's son was visiting."

"Mmm. Tell me, should I call you Detective? Or Lily?"

Meaning she wanted to know what it meant that Rule had touched Lily's cheek. Well, so did Lily. "I'm here as part of an investigation."

"I'm sorry to hear that. Would it make you uncomfortable to remove your shoes when you step inside? It's custom here."

"Not at all." Though in fact it made her feel a little weird, mirroring as it did the practice at Grandmother's.

Just inside the door Lily paused, taking a quick look around as she bent to slip off the flats she'd worn with her linen suit. The entry hall was large, tiled, with a skylight. It ended in French doors, left open, that led to an atrium. Doorways opened off both sides; one led into a dining room, the other a hall.

There was a shoe rack next to the door. *Déjà vu all over again,* Lily thought, straightening. The tiles were cool to her bare feet. Magic brushed her soles faintly, a fuzzy hum similar to what she'd felt at the murder scene.

Lupus magic. Which Rule seemed to lack. She faced her guide. "If Mr. Turner isn't ill, then he's been injured."

"That's right. Since you're a police officer, I'm hoping you aren't squeamish."

"Traffic patrol generally cures any tendency toward squeamishness."

"I can see that it might. Like working the ER, perhaps. But you're a detective now?"

"I am. Homicide."

Her eyebrows commented on that, but she didn't ask the questions Lily expected. Instead, she started for the hallway on the right. "Lupi heal better when their wounds are left uncovered, and, as you may have noticed, they lack body modesty. Isen isn't bandaged or clothed, and he isn't pretty to look at right now. He's regrown the skin and some of the muscle over the abdominal injury, but—"

"Wait a minute. He's got a gut wound, and he isn't in the hospital?"

Nettie paused, glancing over her shoulder. "Lupi generally hate hospitals. There are reasons for the Rho to remain here, and he's well cared for, though shock remains a danger. Which is why I keep him in Sleep as much as possible."

"When and how was he attacked?"

That sudden smile flashed over the other woman's face. "You're quick. Save your questions for Isen, though."

"All right. But this one's for you. You've used that phrase, 'in Sleep,' a couple times now. What does it mean?"

"A healing trance. It aids healing in almost anyone, but lupi benefit from it to an extreme degree, since they naturally heal so quickly. It virtually eliminates the possibility of shock." She started walking again, heading for the paneled wooden door at the end of the hall.

"You're a touch healer of some sort, I take it."

"I took my degree in conventional medicine in Boston, and trained in shamanic practices under my uncle."

Lily nodded. Shamanic practices meant earth magic, which fit with what she'd picked up when they shook hands. She was surprised to find a trained shaman here, though. Native healers were hot these days, especially with the Hollywood crowd, but not many of them left the reservations. Even fewer cross-trained in Western medicine. "You practice here at Clanhome?"

"Here and in Rio Bravo. I consult elsewhere sometimes. This is it," she said, and rapped on the door, then pushed it open.

Over six feet of solid male muscle blocked the doorway. This one wore cutoffs and had one of the most impressive chests she'd ever seen. That chest was smooth and hairless, and crossed by a leather strap.

Equally impressive was the machete he held as if he might want to skewer the next person to walk through the door.

TWELVE

"**BENEDICT**," Nettie Two Horses said, exasperated. "Move."

"She has a gun," the man said calmly. "She's not allowed to bring it into the Rho's room."

Lily had had about enough. "Put away the blade."

He didn't move. His eyes were dark, his skin coppery, like Nettie's. There was another, smaller scabbard at his waist, a scattering of silver in his black hair, and no expression at all on his face.

"Put it up," Lily repeated. "Or I'll arrest you for drawing a weapon on a police officer."

From behind him came a low chuckle. "It would be interesting to see how you went about doing that, but we're short of time. Benedict, stand down. She may keep her gun."

That voice was even lower than the guard's, seeming to rumble up from the bottom of a well. In one smooth motion the impassive hunk stepped back, sheathing his blade in the scabbard on his back. Nettie Two Horses moved into the room, and Lily followed.

It was a large bedroom, woodsy and masculine, with a beamed ceiling and what looked like a medieval tapestry on one of the forest-green walls. A cello sat in one corner. The furniture was dark and lovingly polished; it had been shifted to accommodate the hospital bed at the room's center. In that bed was a bear of a man with an IV in one arm. He looked nothing like Rule. His face was craggy with a prominent Roman nose, his age hard to guess. Fifty? Sixty? And yes, he was entirely naked, except for a patch over one eye.

He was also a bloody mess.

The wound running from his cheek up under the eye patch was bumpy with a heavy scab. New pink skin had formed at its edges, trailing into what was left of a grizzled, rust-colored beard. The gouges on his torso started in the furry chest just beneath the left nipple and ran all the way down his belly, stopping just short of his genitals . . . which didn't seem to be damaged. His abdomen dipped in oddly, as if not all of the usual pieces were in place beneath the skin. She couldn't see his left arm, but his right hand had only two fingers. The rest were marked by tiny, pink nubs.

"What," she asked, "was that all about?"

"Please excuse my son," the Nokolai Rho said. "He is responsible for my safety and diligent in his duty. Our customs require that no one enters my presence armed."

His son? Lily resisted the impulse to check Benedict for any resemblance to Rule and walked up to the bed, looking down at its mutilated occupant. She'd interviewed people in bad shape before, but usually they had more clothes on. This was . . . distracting.

But maybe that was the idea. "You wanted me here. I'm a cop, cops carry guns, and I'm guessing you aren't an idiot. You could have settled the gun business before I walked in. So why the dramatic welcome? Did you want me too irritated to feel sorry for you? Or was it just another way of putting me off balance?"

The single visible eye was set deep . . . and amused. "If my goal was to irritate you, I succeeded. Won't you have a seat?"

Since there wasn't a chair near the bed, she started to make another smart comment. But Benedict was good for something other than looking menacing. He brought up an upholstered armchair, carrying it one-handed as easily as if it had been a plastic lawn chair, then retreated to his post near the door.

Leaving her forced to put her back to him or refuse to sit. All right, she told herself as she sat down. Isen Turner liked to play games. She could handle that. She'd been dealing with

Grandmother all her life. "You were attacked, nearly killed. Who did it?"

"I don't remember an attack," he said blandly. "Perhaps there was a head injury, and it affected my memory. You smell of my son. The youngest one," he added.

"You're beginning to piss me off."

He made a muffled sound, and the lumpy skin on his abdomen shivered. "Ah . . ." he said after a moment. "That hurt. I can't laugh yet. Nettie, I need you to check on Toby. Or you could brew me one of your possets."

"You don't have enough duodenum at the moment to digest a posset, but I can take a hint. I'll go, but say whatever you have to say quickly. I'm giving you fifteen minutes."

"Thirty."

"Fifteen, and you're going back in Sleep when I return."

"The woman doesn't understand bargaining," he muttered, watching as Nettie Two Horses closed the door behind her.

Lily thought Nettie understood just fine—you only bargained when you had to. Apparently she didn't, which was interesting. It was also interesting that the Rho didn't dismiss the blade-toting Benedict. "Fifteen minutes isn't much time," she said. "You've got an agenda. So do I. Maybe we should quit fencing."

"Why not? You haven't rattled, despite my efforts. You don't even smell of fear. I wonder why that is?"

"Your son—the one standing behind me with that big people-opener—won't take a stab without your say-so. And you didn't bring me here to cut me up."

One bushy eyebrow lifted, and she suddenly saw a resemblance to Rule—not the features, but the expression. "And yet, even reasonable people fear us, at least at first. Logic can restrain fear but doesn't eliminate it."

"Curiosity works against fear, too. And I'm very curious. For example, I'm wondering about your attackers. You don't remember them." She nodded as if that made perfect sense. "But if you were to speculate, who would you suspect?"

"Well, now." That single eye was warm with amusement. "I might wonder if Leidolf was involved. I heard a rumor that three of their clan members suffered unfortunate accidents while in wolf form. As if they'd been in some sort of brawl."

"Did you hear the names of these brawlers?"

"I'm afraid not, but it hardly matters. They're dead."

And it was no crime to kill lupi in wolf form, leaving her without an investigative leg to stand on. "I wonder who the leader of the Leidolf clan might be."

"I can see why you might be curious about that." He smiled and said nothing more.

It was a trick Lily had used herself often enough. Let a gap fall in the conversation, and most people were compelled to fill it—and in their haste and discomfort, said more than they'd intended. She smiled back at him.

He chuckled. "I like you, Lily Yu. Not that you care, but I thought I'd mention it. As you say, let's stop fencing before my keeper returns. You mentioned agendas. Yours, I assume, involves your murder investigation."

"I've got a killer to catch, yes. To do that, I need to be free to talk to your people. They'll not give me much help without your approval."

"And yet I'd rather not see any of my clan behind bars. Particularly my heir."

She shook her head. "No, you'll want to help, because whoever did it tried to frame your son. The other one, not the one standing behind me." That startled him. Good. She was taking a risk, gambling that what she learned here would be important enough to justify spilling a little information.

"You have decided this? Or proved it?"

"I have certain evidence. I also have instincts, and they tell me that Nokolai is connected somehow. Perhaps as a target. First, it's your prince someone wanted accused. Second, there's that ceremony today. You're making a new alliance, and I have to wonder why. Then there's you, and the attack you don't remember. Someone seems to have it in for your family. I want to know who and why."

"I can't tell you who," he said slowly. "But I know why. Nokolai supports the Species Citizenship Bill. There are many who would do almost anything to keep it from passing."

She could believe that, but . . . "It was one or more lupi who attacked you, and a lupus who killed Carlos Fuentes."

"It isn't only humans who fear the consequences if the Citizenship Bill passes."

She digested that. The Species Citizenship Bill had two thrusts. First, it officially defined those of the Blood as nonhuman—which was pretty much a given to a lot of people, but had never been codified. Second, it granted certain of them, including lupi, full citizenship.

Lily brought up the part that bothered her. "Because they don't want to be legally nonhuman?"

He waved that aside with the hand that had pink nubs instead of fingers. "Human, nonhuman—what's the dividing line? Genetics? We make babies with you, but that doesn't make us the same as you. Names don't matter. We know what we are. No, what the shortsighted among us fear is the effect of such a law on our culture, our governance and customs."

"It would make it illegal for people to shoot you when you're furry, for one thing. That has to be a plus. But you couldn't kill each other anymore, either."

"Which will change us more than you can understand. But there is little wilderness left, and hiding becomes increasingly difficult in a crowded, computerized world. We must adapt to survive. Some can't see that. All they see is that the Challenge will be changed."

Lily's hip thrummed—not with magic, but from her cell phone, which she'd set to vibrate. "What's the Challenge?" she asked as she pulled her phone out of her pocket. Then she saw the Caller ID. "Just a minute. I have to take this."

A minute later, face grim, she stood and slipped the phone back in her pocket. "I have to get back to the city right away. There's been another murder."

RULE smelled his oldest brother before he saw him. Benedict didn't smell of any special alarm, however, so Rule continued with the ceremony, even as part of his mind wondered what had brought Benedict here, away from the Rho. It was unlikely to be good news.

But only part of his mind. The man part. Most of him was rapt in the sheer immediacy of the world—the feel of grass and dirt beneath the pads of his feet. The ruffled texture of sounds made by the people surrounding him and the Kyffin Rho. Though those attending stood quietly, there was a shifted foot now and then, the breeze hushing through bodies, hair. The breaths of those nearest him. And the air itself, so rich with scent it was like drawing the world inside every time he inhaled, then exhaling himself back into the waiting world. If vision was flatter, colors fewer and less vivid, the loss passed ungrieved amid such wealth.

He wanted to run—run for the sheer joy of running. But the man part wasn't gone or eclipsed. The terms of the alliance had been announced while he and Jasper were two-footed, but their agreement was meaningless without the submission. Rule waited, motionless, as the Kyffin Rho approached.

Jasper was a handsome wolf, slighter and sleeker than Rule, with a brownish dun coat and yellow eyes that reminded Rule of Cullen's wolf form. He was faster than greased lightning, from what Rule remembered from youthful tussles, and every bit as alpha as a Rho must be. Submission did not come easily for him.

He also had an unfortunate tendency to lose himself in the wolf. Which was why, when he reached Rule, his hackles were raised, and the scent of *seru* was strong. And why he immediately flopped down, belly up, like a puppy waiting for a rub.

There were a few muffled laughs. Decidedly anticlimactic, Rule thought, lowering his head to sniff the offered belly. Usually there was some growling, a brief combat before submission. Not with the intent to do real harm, but to demonstrate the strength of each and lend authority to the eventual submission. Jasper had told Rule ruefully that he didn't think even a mock combat was a good idea. He was likely to get caught up in it. Rule didn't think less of him for it. A good leader understands his weaknesses as well as his strengths.

He found a little fear-scent amid the *seru,* the wolf smell, and Jasper's individual scent, but not the mingled stink that spoke of guilt.

Having accepted the submission, Rule stepped back, and the ritual was complete. By not ripping out that offered belly, he'd accepted that Jasper had played no part in the attack on his father, restoring Jasper's honor in the eyes of the clans. In return, Kyffin would subordinate itself to Nokolai for a year and a day.

Usually at this point there'd be a general shifting, as some members of both clans—mostly the younger ones—took the opportunity to socialize in wolf form. Rule had expected to stay in this form to act as host and make sure the play didn't turn rough. But he sought the source of his brother's scent and found Benedict standing at the front of the circle of watchers, next to Rule's clothes.

Benedict made the small, circular gesture that said, *Change.*

Regretfully, Rule opened himself, reached for the order the earth required of him, and let the wildness sort him. It was easy, almost painless, with his paws on the earth of the ritual grounds. In seconds, he stood naked on two feet, with his head higher off the ground than before, and the world blunted to all senses except vision.

Jasper had sprung to his feet and was regarding Rule with his head tipped quizzically.

"I'm sorry. Benedict has need of me, but please—enjoy the friendship of Nokolai in whichever form pleases you." Rule glanced around, caught the eye of one of the older Councilors, and made the same gesture Benedict had. The man's eyes widened slightly, but he shifted obediently. Seth could serve as four-footed host—a necessity as well as a courtesy. Seth could keep the younger Nokolai in line. They were accustomed to obeying him.

Jasper glanced at the Councilor wolf, at Benedict, and back at Rule. He nodded and sat, waiting for Seth to trot over. Rule hurried to Benedict.

"What?" he said, catching the clothes his brother tossed him.

"Your detective needs to go back to the city right away." A hint of a smile ghosted across Benedict's blunt features. "She wasn't happy at being told she had to wait for your return."

Rule stepped into his jeans. "What happened?"

"A phone call. There's been another murder."

Rule cursed, zipped the jeans, and stamped one foot into a shoe. "Who? Where?"

"She didn't say, but of course I heard. She isn't aware of that, I think. Therese Martin, 1012 Humstead Avenue, Apartment Twelve."

"A woman?" Rule asked, his voice sharp with disbelief. "Attacked by a lupus?"

"The cops think so. You know her?"

"I don't . . ." But the name was vaguely familiar. "Humstead is near the club. I may have met her. Dammit all to hell." He was supposed to take Toby to the creek. He'd counted on that. Toby was counting on it, too. This sudden departure was a bitter disappointment.

But unavoidable. He started for the house at a trot. Bystanders, both two- and four-legged, saw him coming and moved out of the way, watching with startled curiosity as Rule and Benedict moved into an easy run.

"Toby?" Rule made the name a question.

"Our father said he would explain to the boy. He won't let Nettie put him in Sleep until he's spoken with him. You have your own explanations to make. To your Chosen."

There was nothing he could say to that, so Rule kept silent. Lily wasn't going to accept the truth easily.

"Isen told her about the connection between the Citizenship Bill, the attack on him, and the murder she's investigating—after she told him you aren't a suspect anymore. She has evidence."

"She *what?*" Rule should have been relieved, but the first flush of feeling that hit was anger. She'd told his father, but not him. A second later, he understood, though it didn't make him feel any better. She hadn't told him because she wanted walls between them—the higher the better.

The good news, he told himself, was that by speaking of the conspiracy to her, Isen had lifted his ban on revealing anything to the police. He'd be free to decide how much to tell her now.

"Would she lie about the evidence?" Benedict asked.

"I don't know. I don't think so, but how can I be sure? I'm learning her as quickly as I can, but I don't know her yet."

"I suppose not." Benedict was silent for several footfalls, then said, "Our father likes her."

That lifted Rule's heart slightly. He'd known why Isen sent for Lily, of course. Benedict would have told him about her, and his father had wanted to meet Rule's Chosen. And the Rho had needed to assess one who—little though she knew it—would soon be part of his clan.

Or so Rule prayed.

Lily was waiting by the car with Toby. Either she really

liked suits, or she found them convenient for hiding her shoulder holster. This one was black—a comment, perhaps, on the limited palette he employed. Her hair was pulled into a French braid, giving him a clear view of the smooth line of her jaw and cheek and the grave expression on her face.

Hunger hit and hit hard, clenching the muscles of his stomach. His cock stirred. By the time he reached them, Lily would be able to tell how glad he was to see her.

She was intent on whatever Toby was telling her. Rule slowed to a walk and caught a few of their words, and a smile eased some of the tightness. Though she must have been seriously impatient, Lily was "talking Spanish" to Toby.

Then Mick walked out of the house, and Rule's smile slipped.

Benedict spoke his name sharply.

"I know, I know." Rule sighed, stopping. "Control. It wasn't hard to find at the proving grounds just now."

"You like Jasper."

And that was the sorry truth. He liked Jasper, and he didn't much like Mick these days. "You haven't told him about Lily."

"Only Isen. I suspect he told Nettie."

"Probably. She won't say anything." Mick would have scented Rule by now, given the direction of the wind, but he didn't glance their way as he joined Lily and Toby. He was smiling. He said something flattering about Lily's hair, then laughed when she gave him her cop look.

Rule knew women wanted him. They always had, and giving them pleasure was his delight. But that pleasure was based on sensual excitement, with a *soupçon* of celebrity sweetening the mix for some. Mick didn't attract that sort of instant feminine notice, but women enjoyed him. They liked his teasing, his playfulness.

It was an adolescent's dream to be lusted after by every woman you met, Rule thought. He was an adult. He'd rather be liked. He wanted . . . no, needed for Lily to like him, and he was afraid she'd like Mick better.

And that was just pathetic. He dragged his attention back where it needed to be. "The next time the Rho is awake, let him know that I took his speaking of the conspiracy as permission to speak of it also."

"I will." Benedict held out his hand. "And, when the time comes, I will welcome the one chosen for you."

"Thank you." He gripped Benedict's forearm. He hadn't doubted that his family would accept Lily, but the gap between acceptance and true welcome can be painful.

Benedict returned Rule's grip briefly, then loped off toward the house. Rule walked the rest of the way, making sure his body wasn't putting out aggressive signals. He might not enjoy watching Mick flirt with Lily, but he didn't want to get into a pissing contest with his brother right now. Not with Toby watching.

Not to mention Lily. "You didn't have to rush," she said, frostbite chilly, when he reached them. "Mick said he'd take me back."

"You'll return with me." Rule swung Toby up into his arms, cherishing the feel of his son's body.

"That's not necessary." She glanced in his general direction, then away.

"I'm afraid it is."

"I don't want you to go," Toby announced. "You came back early for her, and now you're leaving, and I don't like it. Uncle Mick can take Lily back."

Rule leaned his forehead against Toby's. "We'll miss our trip to the creek. That sucks."

Toby nodded.

"And neither you nor Lily understands why. But your grandfather is staying awake, postponing his healing, so he can explain to you."

"You really have to go?"

Rule nodded.

The jut of Toby's bottom lip suggested he didn't think an explanation was a fair trade for his father's presence. He sighed hugely and wiggled, ready to be put down. Every time Rule saw him, he was less willing to be held—a passage Rule knew was necessary but still grieved over. He set the boy on his feet.

"I'll have to go talk to Grandfather so he can sleep and get better. He's all messed up right now," Toby told Lily. "Did you see him? But he's growing things back. He'll be okay soon."

"I'm sure he will. Ms. Two Horses will see to it."

"Yeah. Nettie can fix most anything. Bye, Lily."

"Hasta la vista," she said. "That means 'see you later.' I like it better than good-bye."

"Yeah." He turned to Rule, his face solemn. *"Hasta la vista.* You'll call me tonight?"

Rule ruffled Toby's hair. "I will." He called every night, but Toby needed to hear the promise often. Not for the first time, Rule cursed the mother who hadn't been able to deal with her son's nature. Such rejection cracked the soul in ways a father couldn't wholly repair.

Who would know that better than he? But he, at least, had had Clanhome. "Math," he reminded Toby, who grimaced, then headed for the house at less than his usual headlong pace.

"He's disappointed," Mick said, watching the door close on Toby. "I know I'm a poor substitute, but I can take him to the creek. I don't have to drive back until tonight."

"Thanks." Mick had always been crazy about Toby. But then, Rule didn't doubt that Mick was basically a good man. And what lupus didn't rejoice in children?

"Though I'd like that explanation, too." Mick's expression wasn't that different from Toby's, Rule thought—mulish, with a hint of hurt feelings. "I'd like to know why you don't trust me with the lovely detective."

"Good God, Mick, it's nothing to do with you."

"And you don't intend to tell me."

"Not now. And the plain fact is, I owe Lily an explanation, not you."

Mick stared at him a moment longer, then gave a quick shrug. "I guess you'd better leave so Lily can go solve crime. At least this time they can't pin it on you. You're alibied by a cop."

Lily shook her head. "I don't yet know the time of death, so we have no idea who's alibied. But I do have to go."

"Then I'll tell you *hasta la vista,* too," Mick said, the warmth in his voice matched by his smile. "This surely won't be the only time we meet. The Lady wouldn't be so unkind."

"Hasta la vista, Mick. Rule—*now* would be good."

It wasn't her voice that gave Rule the idea, though the way it changed between speaking to Mick and speaking to him irked him. Nor was it Mick's flirting. It was simple courtesy, after all, to let a woman know you appreciated her.

No, it was the way Lily refused to see him, as if she could pretend she didn't feel the pull as long as she didn't look directly at him. He took two steps closer, stopping near enough that her scent welcomed him, even if the rest of her did not. The jump of his heartbeat warned him to make this quick.

"Yes, we'll go," he said. "But first . . ." And he leaned in to plant a kiss on her frowning mouth.

He expected a punch, and not just from the kiss. He'd already decided to let her connect. But he didn't expect to land on his butt in the dirt.

Mick hooted with laughter. Rule stared up at her, astonished. She'd hooked her leg behind his knee, pulled—and down he went, before his mouth even touched hers.

"Ask, don't assume." She opened the car door. "Oh, and you can give me that explanation," she said, climbing in, "on the way back." And she slammed the door shut.

THIRTEEN

Ms. *Tough Guy,* Lily jeered at herself silently as she pulled the seat belt in place. She'd overreacted . . . but it had sure been satisfying to see the look on his face.

That satisfaction flickered and went out all too quickly. Beneath it she was shaky, like the time when, still a rookie, she'd been first on scene for a five-vehicle pileup. There'd been some reason, then, for her insides to squeeze and quiver and morph into jittery Jell-O. Now . . .

She'd dumped him on the ground because she'd been scared. Not because she didn't want his kiss, but because she did. Badly.

Lily inhaled slowly. She felt like an engine revving and revving but stuck in park. As if she were hitting some dangerous pitch and had to find a way to either shut off the engine or throw herself into drive.

The driver's door opened. He got in.

She stared straight ahead. "I hope you don't expect an apology."

"Not at all." He started the car and put it through a quick three-point turn. "I'm amazed, not angry. It's been a long time since I was taken so completely by surprise. On the other hand, I'm not planning to offer you an apology, either. Not for the kiss I didn't get. I do regret making you wait."

Lily thought of the kiss he *had* taken and shifted slightly. "If you're going to tell me there's some kind of weird lupus rule—"

"Not in the way you mean. But you'll consider my reason weird. And unwelcome." His words came out clipped, as if he were pushing them out through a tightening channel.

Never had she felt so hot just sitting next to a man. Or so unsettled. Automatically she switched mental channels, pushing the button sure to get her back on track. "Never mind that right now. Do you know a woman named Therese Martin?"

"You're avoiding the subject."

"I don't recall giving you permission to choose the subject."

He made a small sound, somewhere between exasperation and amusement. "All right. I don't remember her. She's the one who was killed?"

She gave him a hard look. "Why do you think that?"

"Benedict heard both sides of the call you took."

"That's . . ." She wanted to say impossible. "Can you do that, too?"

"My hearing isn't as good as his."

"Which doesn't answer my question."

"Vanity insists I retain some mystery." His voice turned grim. "If a lupus killed her—"

"If?"

"We don't harm women. I'm not saying it's impossible, but a lupus who would kill a woman . . . we'd call him insane."

She frowned, trying to remember the lupus kills she'd read about. Surely some of the victims had been female?

"I've been assuming Fuentes was killed as part of a larger scheme against Nokolai," Rule said. "My father spoke to you about that."

"Some. I have questions."

"Why does that not surprise me? But this newest killing— it doesn't fit. I wasn't involved with Therese Martin. I didn't even know her."

He'd spoken to her at some point, though, and been "real respectful." "She was a working girl. Had a corner on Proctor." And about a hundred dolls, all with yellow hair. Did she have a mother or sister who'd want those dolls now? "She was almost certainly the last party to see Carlos Fuentes alive, other than the killer. Her testimony narrowed the time of death enough to get you off the hook."

"Shit."

"Pretty much so, yeah." O'Brien was handling the scene, and Mech was there. She knew they'd do a good job, but she needed to *be* there. She needed to see the place, get a sense of what had happened. She needed to touch things, while they still held the buzz of magic.

Pity she couldn't smell the way that . . . wait a minute. "Could you sniff out her killer? If I got you to the body quickly enough, could you tell who did it?"

That surprised him. He didn't say anything for several moments. "In this form, probably not."

"You'd have to Change."

"Yes. I can't guarantee anything, but it might work."

How much grief would she get if she gave him access to the body? Plenty, she thought, scowling. Because of what he was. If he'd been any other sort of expert consultant, no one would bat an eye over her asking for his opinion now that he wasn't a suspect himself. And that was just wrong. Someone had ended all Therese's possibilities, stamping out the stubborn spark that had made the girl surround herself with yellow-haired dolls. It was Lily's job to find out who.

Damn those torpedoes and all that, she thought. *I'm not going to get anywhere with this one by playing it safe on half throttle.* "All right, then. Will you, um, need privacy to Change?"

"I'd like to have earth beneath my feet, if possible. Privacy might keep your associates from freaking. Lily—"

"What?" They'd left the valley behind and were drawing near the gate. The same redheaded guard opened it for them. "We don't want the press to guess why you're there, but I can't get you into the scene itself. Aside from the risk of contaminating it, a defense attorney would have entirely too much fun coming up with scenarios about that. So . . . the coroner's people will be ready to transport the body by the time we get there. Once I've looked things over, I'll have them bring her into the stairwell, and you can do it there."

"I can Change there if I have to. You're avoiding the subject."

"You know, I don't think you get to choose the subject. Were you at Club Hell last night?"

His fingers drummed once on the steering wheel. "I ate with friends at my apartment. They left about eight-thirty. I spent the rest of the evening at home alone. Why? I thought I wasn't a suspect."

"Dot those *i*'s, cross those *t*'s," she said absently. Something about this second murder didn't add up, but she couldn't put her finger on it. "I guess someone could have watched to see that you were alone. Who knew you'd be at the club the night of Fuentes's murder?"

He shrugged. "Any number of people. Thursday was my usual night to meet Rachel there."

"Did you have a usual time, too?"

"It varied."

"Did you tell anyone other than Rachel when you'd be there that night?"

"Why does it matter?"

"Humor me."

"All right. I told Max when to expect me. I believe he told Cullen. But Rachel could have mentioned it to any number of people."

"True." She chewed her lip. If only she knew how the killer lured Fuentes to the playground . . . Fuentes's two main interests seemed to have been women and the Church of the Faithful.

The playground wasn't a likely spot for a romantic tryst. "Have you ever heard of the Church of the Faithful? They're also called the Azá."

"You asked about them before. The name doesn't ring any bells. Lily, I've something to tell you. It's important."

"So's murder. Give me a minute. I'm onto something." She thought hard for a moment. "Okay, working hypothesis. Let's say that Fuentes was killed to implicate you. Naturally, the killer wanted to do it when you weren't alibied, but that's tricky. He also wanted to do it on your date night so us dumb cops didn't miss spotting you as a suspect. He knows it's hard to pin down time of death, though, without a witness. Anyone who reads mysteries or watches crime shows knows that. So

what he needs is a window when we don't know where
Fuentes is."

"I'm with you so far. How did he go about creating that
window?"

"Maybe he made it, maybe he found it. Either way, his main
concern would be witnesses. He picks the playground because
it's near the club and should be deserted. If he's smart, he wants
to get there before Fuentes does and make sure no one else is
around. But Therese didn't see anyone on the street or at the
playground. She talked to Fuentes just before ten, and she
didn't see anyone else nearby."

"If he was in wolf form, it wouldn't be hard for him to
hide."

"Maybe, but then why did he go ahead and kill Fuentes? If
he was there, if he saw Therese talking to Fuentes, he knew
there was a witness for when Fuentes arrived." She shook her
head. "Doesn't fit."

"Okay, then, he didn't arrive before Fuentes, so he didn't
know about Therese. When he found out . . ." Rule's voice
trailed off.

"Yeah." A hard knot of nausea lodged in her throat. She
swallowed. "That's the question, isn't it? How did he find out?"

"She might have talked to others about seeing Fuentes."

"She swore she hadn't, and I warned her. I warned her not
to talk about it. Maybe she did anyway. Or maybe someone
saw us go to her place, but they wouldn't have known what
she told us. The killer might have panicked—but why? We
didn't arrest him." The nausea was growing. "He had no reason to think she ID'd him. He shouldn't have known what she
told us. Unless . . ."

Rule finished it for her. "Unless a cop told him."

A sick sort of vacuum claimed her gut. Her mouth was
bone dry. *Follow it through,* she ordered herself. Who had
known about Therese? Phillips . . . but if he'd been bent, he
wouldn't have brought her to Lily's notice.

Who else? Who all had she told, who would have read the
report about Therese?

Mech. Captain Randall. The chief. Those two FBI agents.

God. She ran a hand through her hair. Not the captain.
Surely not. Mech? She couldn't believe it, but he was already

at the scene. And the two FBI agents could show up there. No one would think a thing of it.

"How fast will this thing go?" she asked.

"A hundred and twenty."

"Open it up."

Rule took her at her word. He didn't hit top speed—even with his reflexes, there were limits imposed by physics and a winding mountain road. But he pushed those limits pretty hard.

It was wonderful.

"You're enjoying this," his passenger said.

"Guilty as charged." He didn't glance at her. At this speed, that would be a bad move. "You're not throwing up," he observed.

"Yet."

She sounded more tense than frightened, though. "Maybe you're enjoying it, too, just a little."

"Trust me on this. I'm not." She paused. "Tell me something. You have two brothers, and at least one of them is older than you. Yet you're the heir. Why is that?"

"Lupi don't follow primogeniture."

"So what do you follow?"

Rule hesitated. He'd decided to hold off on telling her what it meant to be chosen. She'd just had a blow, one he understood all too well. Realizing there might be a crooked cop involved must have been a lot like hearing there was a traitor in Nokolai. But she needed to learn about the clan. "Custom. This varies from one clan to the next, but essentially the Lu Nuncio—"

"What does that mean?"

"Roughly, the acknowledged heir. The Lu Nuncio must prove himself through blood, combat, and fertility."

"You have a child," she said slowly.

"Yes. Benedict does, too, but not a son."

"But . . ." Her voice drifted off, then she said, "All right. I guess I've made some dumb assumptions. Lupi are always male, so I thought you only had male offspring. Some of the women I saw at Clanhome would be related to clan members, then?"

"Rather than being our sex slaves, you mean?"

"Actually," she said dryly, "I was thinking more in terms of domestic slaves. Men have a tendency to keep women around to do the dishes and the laundry."

"I think everyone at Clanhome today was of one of the clans." He had to slow then, as they were approaching the turn onto 67. He glanced at her briefly. "Did you think we drowned our female children at birth? Our daughters and sisters are Nokolai, too, though they aren't lupi."

"I admitted that some of my assumptions are showing. I'm working on it. What about your mothers, aunts, and grandmothers? Are they clan?"

"That's rare." How rare, and why, he couldn't tell her. Not yet.

"Hmm."

Traffic was light this far from the city. Rule slowed but didn't stop, accelerating strongly into the turn.

"Hey!" Lily cried, grabbing the dash as she lurched to the side. "We are not in hot pursuit."

"I love it when you talk cop," he murmured, and floored it. "Do you get to do this often?"

"No. And the purpose here is not for you to live out your fantasies."

"Newly developed fantasies. I didn't play cop as a kid. You folks were the bad guys."

"Times change. I—hey!" She grabbed the dash again.

He'd zigzagged around a couple of semis that were dawdling along at eighty or less. "You did want me to hurry."

"Try to remember that I don't heal the way you do. Or you could distract me from my imminent death by explaining the parts about blood and combat."

He chuckled. "Blood means I'm of the correct bloodline. Combat means exactly what you think it does."

"You fought your brothers?"

"I fought Mick and two others who challenged my fitness." One combat had been largely ceremonial, because no heir could be accepted without having proven himself in formal combat. The other had been deadly serious. But it was the battle with Mick that had troubled Rule's sleep for a long time afterward. Not the challenge itself—that had been inevitable, given his brother's nature. Even Mick's attempt to kill rather than merely defeat could be forgiven; some were more taken by the wolf than others.

What Rule couldn't put behind him was the suspicion that Mick's man part had been willing to kill, too.

"But not Benedict?' Lily persisted. "Your oldest brother didn't challenge you?"

"Benedict supported our father's decision." Had he not, Rule wouldn't be Lu Nuncio. He couldn't have defeated Benedict.

She shook her head. "Voting would be better."

"Voting works for humans. We are not a democratic people, but neither are we passive enough to be ruled autocratically. Custom provides some checks on the Rho's power. The Challenge supplies the rest."

"Your father said something about a challenge before we were interrupted. How does it work?"

"Challenges are common, both within the clan and between clans, especially among the hot-blooded young. Think of them as duels fought with teeth instead of swords or pistols. When we say *the* Challenge, however, we're referring to a clan member challenging his Rho."

"Your father's not young anymore."

"There are cases where a Rho must fight his own battles. Usually, though, if the Rho is challenged, the Lu Nuncio defends."

"That's you."

He nodded.

"This kind of challenge— is it to the death?"

"It can be. Don't worry, Detective. We fight in wolf form, so it's quite legal."

"That was certainly my only concern. If you—Rule, for God's sake, watch where you're going!"

"I am," he said, passing the tanker truck that worried her. He cut it a trifle close, perhaps, but the Datsun in the other lane gave him little choice.

Lily was cursing under her breath. He glanced at her, and his pleasure fled. "I'll slow down. You're pale."

"I turn Caucasian at ninety miles an hour and up. Pay no attention."

He gave a quick bark of laughter and stole another quick

glance. She was frowning slightly, that quick mind turning over what she'd learned.

"Your challenges won't be legal if the Citizenship Bill passes," she said.

"My father believes that only challenges to the death will be affected. Those involving lesser woundings simply won't be reported."

"And you? What do you believe?"

"The Lu Nuncio doesn't express opinions. It would be like an army general publicly approving or disputing the policies of his commander in chief."

"Do you express opinions to your father?"

"To my father, yes. To the Rho—no."

"Tricky, when they're the same person."

"He lets me know which one I'm addressing." They'd reached the city limits, and traffic was too congested for real speed. He did the best he could. "We should reach your scene in fifteen to twenty minutes."

"Good. What do you think of the conspiracy angle your father brought up? He seems to consider Nokolai's support vital enough to the bill's passage that someone might kill him to stop it."

"Without Nokolai, the other clans are unlikely to support the bill."

"The clans don't have that much political clout."

"Mmm. Not all lupi are as open about their nature as I am."

Her eyebrows lifted. "Are you saying you've got people in high places? People with a furry secret?"

He smiled.

"The mystery bit is getting old," she observed. "So you think that taking out you and your father could affect the way things go in Washington?"

"The idea wasn't just to remove me, was it? They wanted me arrested, imprisoned. If the, ah, poster boy for lupi is proved to be a murderer, will the public support a bill making us full citizens?"

"Citizens kill each other all the time, unfortunately. But I get your meaning."

She fell silent then, which was just as well. He needed to

give his driving most of his attention. But driving, even in this traffic, didn't require his entire mind.

She'd called him Rule.

Such a small thing, a name. But she'd never said his. Yet it had come out in a moment of stress, as if she were beginning to think of him that way. Personally. Warmth spread through him. She was beginning to open up with him about her investigation, too. Discuss the possibilities.

Such as the chance there was a dirty cop involved. Someone she knew, worked with, trusted. Someone who'd sold out the law she upheld, either for money or some twisted ideal that endorsed murder in the right cause. The warmth evaporated.

A dirty cop could plant evidence or hide it. Not a happy thought, considering he seemed to be someone's favorite pick for suspect. But if one cop was working against him, another one was on his side. At least, he amended mentally, on the side of justice.

How was she going to react when he told her the truth about them?

He'd never expected this to happen to him. Never wanted it, to tell the truth, even as an adolescent. But he'd had Benedict's example and Nettie's warnings, so he knew the dangers. And being chosen was so rare . . . he'd felt safe. But he had at least known it was possible, had been taught what it meant. Lily didn't even know such a condition existed.

She was not going to take it well.

He wanted time to court her. Time for her to begin to know him, for trust to send down its first roots. But his body was urgent for her, insistent in a way that denied delay. She thought she could choose whether or not to act on what she felt; he knew better. And he knew he had to tell her the truth before they lay together.

That's what young lupi were advised—if the Lady blesses you with a Chosen, be honest with her about what is happening. And be patient. *"It would be your responsibility,"* Nettie had told him once, *"to make it as easy on her as possible. But don't gloss over the difficulties If she's young and idealistic, she may romanticize it, see it as some sort of perfect union, a merging of soul."* She'd snorted. *"Don't let her get away with that."*

Rule crept along behind a bus occupying more than its fair share of the road, and glanced at Lily. She was young, yes, and possessed very high ideals, from what he'd seen. But she was not going to romanticize her situation. He'd give odds she would fight it, and him, like crazy—and the Lady only knew how much damage she'd do them both.

Tonight, he promised himself. He would tell her tonight.

FOURTEEN

THE street outside Therese's walk-up was cluttered with cars: two black and whites, the ambulance and the coroner's car, Mech's blue sedan, and O'Brien's battered Chevy. Lily had Rule drop her at the corner.

"I'll leave word to let you into the building," she said as she climbed out.

"Good enough. I'll park at the club. Max's reputation discourages local entrepreneurs from treating his parking lot as a parts supply warehouse."

He spoke lightly, but he looked grim. She felt the same. She didn't throw up anymore when the scene was messy, but her stomach wasn't happy. It was always worse if she'd known the victim, even slightly. "Are you okay with this?" she asked abruptly.

"I've seen death. Go. Do what you have to."

She nodded, closed the door, and headed down the street.

Lily recognized the uniform stationed at the entrance to the dingy lobby—the rookie from West Texas. She nodded at him. "Gonzales, right? Detective Yu. Is Sergeant Meckle in there?"

"Yes, ma'am. He has a witness. He's using the manager's quarters for interviews. It's behind the stairs."

"I understand she was found just before noon. Who found her?"

"A juvenile name of Abel Martinez. Fourteen years old. Your sergeant took his statement and let his mother have him. She lives in number ten, same floor. No father in residence. Two sisters, both younger."

"Number ten's right next to twelve," Lily said, remembering from her previous visit. "The walls are thin. No one heard anything?"

"I don't know, ma'am. Phillips talked to a couple people before Sergeant Meckle arrived and took over, but I've been handling access."

"Any Feds shown up? There's a couple that have taken an interest in the case."

"No, ma'am."

Her mouth tightened. This didn't eliminate Croft and Karonski, but it suggested she'd better look hard at Mech and the captain.

Oh, Lord, she didn't want it to be the captain. "I've got someone coming who will act as an expert consultant. Rule Turner. When he arrives, let him into the building to wait for me. He's not to go up the stairs. Just into the building."

His eyebrows went up, but he nodded. Lily started up the stairs. The sour smell of vomit hit her about halfway up. Might be Abel Martinez's contribution, she thought. She'd have to make sure a social worker talked to him.

Phillips had the door to apartment twelve. He was talking with the ambulance attendants. She could hear the hum of a vacuum cleaner inside the apartment. "Damned if this isn't getting to be a habit, seeing you around here," he drawled.

"I could break it, given a chance. You were first on scene again. Tell me what happened."

"I got the call from Dispatch at twelve-oh-seven, checked the scene from the door. No question she was dead, so I called it in. While I waited, I talked to the kid who found her. Seems Abel stayed home from school today with an upset stomach but had an amazing recovery and decided to shoot hoops. When he left his apartment, he noticed that the door to number twelve wasn't closed. He says he went inside to check on her." Phillips shrugged. "Probably thought he could lift something. Poor kid. He found more than he bargained for."

"O'Brien's inside?"

"Yeah. Detective—she didn't deserve what that damned were did. I want to know how he found out about her."

"So do I." This was going to be bad. Lily could smell the blood from here, and something nastier. She opened her purse and took out disposable gloves and booties. "Gut wound?"

"Smells like one." That was from one of the ambulance attendants. "Haven't seen her yet."

"Gut wound," Phillips confirmed. "Among others. Bastard ripped her up."

Lily pulled on the last glove. The door was open a few inches. She pushed it wider.

Therese was on the love seat. The one that used to be blue.

"Bag your feet," O'Brien told her. He was crouched on the floor near the body, his back to the door. An evidence tech was on her knees in the tiny kitchen area, using a handheld vacuum.

"I did."

"Oh, it's Yu." He glanced over his shoulder. "Get it? You—Yu."

"I get it." O'Brien's humor was even lamer than usual, but that may have been because his heart wasn't in it.

The bastard had ripped her up, all right. She'd been dead awhile—ten, twelve hours, at a guess. Most of the blood had dried . . . but there was a lot of blood.

She lay on her back, her head propped up on two pillows and turned slightly to her left. Her throat had been torn open. One arm hung off the side of the love seat, the fingers touching the floor. Some of her guts touched the floor, too. They had the look of hamburger left uncovered in the refrigerator— crusty brown on top with glimpses of moist red underneath. He'd slashed her repeatedly, opening the bowel, among other things.

The ripe smell made Lily's stomach churn, but it was the doll that got to her. Therese was still hugging a baby doll with one arm. The doll's hair wasn't blonde anymore.

Lily started toward O'Brien, watching where she put her feet. And stopped, frowning at the thin beige carpet. "There's no blood here."

"That would be because she was killed here, not over there."

"But he would have been drenched in it. He played with her enough. He should have been dripping when he walked away from her."

O'Brien glanced at her over his shoulder, frowning. "You're right. Damn, I'm getting old. Should've spotted that. He cleaned up afterward. Mona found some blood by the kitchen sink. But he should've left spots or tracks of some sort on the way there." His face wrinkled in puzzlement. "Maybe blood doesn't stick to them when they Change."

"Then why did he wash up?" She moved closer. No defensive wounds on the arm hanging off the love seat. Looked like he'd taken out her throat first, which explained why no one had heard screams or a struggle. "What have you got?"

He was tweezing something from the blood-soaked carpet. "Hair. I'd say wolf hair, but we'll let the lab make sure. There's some stuck to her hand, too, but the biggest clump fell on the floor. Looks like she pulled a hunk out of him."

Lily frowned. "She managed to rip out a handful of his fur while he was ripping out her throat?"

O'Brien shrugged. "She let him in. No sign of forced entry or a struggle, so he was probably a customer. Maybe she was petting him or something while they warmed up. You hear about that, about women who want to make it with them when they're wolves. Maybe some of the wolves like it that way, too."

"She wasn't working."

"Why'd you say that?"

"There's not much left of of the T-shirt she was wearing, but I'm pretty sure it's what she had on when I talked to her. That's her at-home clothes, not what she wore to attract trade."

"So he wasn't a customer. Just a close personal friend."

"Could be." Lily moved closer. The carpet squished. "What's that stuck to her side? Paper?" Lily tilted her head. "It looks like part of an ad. Glossy, like in a magazine."

"Bingo. She was a *Cosmo* girl." O'Brien's grin was brief. "I bagged the rest of it already."

"So she was lying on the couch reading *Cosmo,* petting her friend the wolf. Who suddenly decided to rip out her throat, her guts, pretty much everything but her face. Without getting any blood on himself."

"Don't ask me. My job's to find stuff and log it. You're the one who explains it."

She couldn't. "Those don't look like knife wounds."

"You wondering if someone tried to fake a wolf attack?" O'Brien put his tweezers down and carefully sealed the plastic bag. "Doesn't look like it. Skin's ripped, not sliced."

"But why did he keep ripping her up after he killed her? That didn't happen with Fuentes."

"Fuentes was killed out in the open. He had privacy here, time to do what he liked."

Lily shook her head. "This looks like hate. He didn't just want her dead, he wanted to shred her. Her body, not her arms or legs or face."

"Maybe he hates women."

Rule had said any lupus who killed a woman would be considered insane. Was that what they were dealing with, then? Not some big conspiracy but a single crazy lupus?

Who just happened to pick Lily's witness for his next kill. She scowled. The evidence tech had moved to the tiny bathroom, leaving her and O'Brien alone for the moment. "I need to check something."

"Right." O'Brien pushed to his feet. "I'll just get this labeled."

With O'Brien ostentatiously looking the other way, Lily tugged off one glove, took a quick breath through her mouth, and touched Therese's shoulder.

Magic shuddered up her arm. She snatched her hand back, startled by the strength of it . . . and by another sensation. An alien one. She bit her lip. Maybe it was just that this was so much stronger than what she'd touched of lupus magic before, but it didn't feel right. She had to try again, and was oddly reluctant.

Lily crouched and pressed her hand to a place on Josefa's hip where the blood was dry and the skin intact. And it hit again, harsh and discordant, like running her hand over nettles. She forced herself to remain still and pay attention, though she wanted to turn away, mentally and physically.

There was a vague overtone of lupus to the sensation . . . and something else beneath. Something strong and jarring and *wrong*.

Her breath shuddered out. She removed her hand and shook it, trying to dispel the sense of wrongness. What was this? Magic was neutral, a force like electricity or fire. It came in different flavors and could be used for good or ill, but Lily didn't pick up purpose or some kind of ethical charge when she touched magic. Only the power itself.

At least, she never had before.

Was that what evil felt like?

She stood, tugged her glove back on, and tried not to sound as shaken as she felt. "Guess I'll let them take her away now."

"Works for me." O'Brien looked up from messing with his samples. His eyes narrowed. "You okay?"

She shook her head, dismissing the question rather than answering it. "I've got someone waiting to have a look at her. I need to get her moved so he can." Lily headed for the door, wondering what Rule's sense of smell would tell him. Would it be anything like what she'd touched?

She paused to tell the attendants they could have her now and looked at Phillips. "With me," she said, and started down the stairs.

She'd have to make sure that once Rule Changed he didn't stand where he might get hair on her. Not that the lab would be able to tell one lupus's hair from another's, not with the way magic screwed up tests. But this was an unconventional procedure. If the defense attorney screamed contamination of evidence, she had to be able to refute that.

Which meant witnesses, at least two. Phillips, for one. He wasn't implicated in Therese's death, and his background with the X-Squad would make him look good on the stand. The defense couldn't accuse him of being soft on lupi. For the other . . .

"Holy Mother, what's he—" That was Mech's voice, from below. "Get back. Everyone get back. You! Hold it! Don't move or I'll shoot!"

Instinct and the rush of adrenaline said, *Run, get down there quick.* Lily knew better; racing into the middle of a possible shoot-out was a good way to get dead or block another cop's line of fire.

She couldn't see what was going on. The stairwell framed an empty stretch of wall at the bottom, so she pulled her gun and eased down the last of the stairs, quick but quiet, trusting her ears to fill her in. Behind her, she heard Phillips doing the same.

"I thought I was expected."

Rule's voice. Lily's heart rate shot up another notch. She lowered her gun and took the last steps even quicker, rounded the wall enclosing the stairwell—and saw Rule standing just inside the door, his arms held away from his sides, his face turned toward someone to her right.

Mech. Who held his Glock in regulation posture, two-handed, aimed at Rule. The uniform at the door had drawn on Rule, too—he stood ahead of him and to his left. And behind Mech—Ginger Harris? What the hell was she doing here?

Lily holstered her gun. Phillips, she noticed, stayed in the stairwell, weapon still held ready. "I told you to expect Turner," she said to the uniformed officer.

"I let him in. When your sergeant drew, I backed him up." Gonzales looked uncertain. Two other cops, including his partner, still had their weapons out, but the one with rank didn't.

Lily turned. "Sergeant Meckle? You have a reason for this? Turner was threatening someone?"

"I've got a warrant for him." Mech's eyes glittered. "Or will soon. It's on the way. So is special transport."

"You've got a warrant coming." She couldn't believe it. "Before I even got to the scene, you applied for an arrest warrant?"

"You were unavailable." Mech didn't take his eyes away from Rule.

"I had my phone with me. I had my goddamn cell phone with me."

"You were with *him*."

"So?" She stalked right in front of him. "Put it up. Put it up *now*."

He moved, trying to keep Rule in his sights. "You should never have been put in charge. You're not responsible for that. But you'll be responsible if he gets away."

Phillips spoke from the stairwell. "Might be a good idea to get out of the line of fire, Detective. Take a look at his eyes."

Lily turned.

Rule hadn't moved. His face was calm, expressionless. But his eyes were black. Black all over, with little triangles of white left in the corners . . . like an animal's. She swallowed. "You okay?"

"I'm in control." His mild voice was at odds with those beast-swallowed eyes. "But it would be a good idea if your men put their weapons away. I don't like having guns pointed at me, but I'm not going to Change. That's what he wants. But it upsets me," he said, his voice dropping to a low growl. "It does upset me to see guns pointed at me."

Before she could repeat her order, Phillips slid his gun back in the holster. After a second's pause, his partner did the same.

"What are you doing?" Mech cried. "You're taking orders from one of them?"

Phillips glanced at him. "Hate to tell you this, but this spot's too small for shootin' to do much good. We're too close. If he wants to take us out, we're meat."

"I've got special rounds loaded. One of those in the brain—"

"Might stop him, if you hit him with the first shot. Might not. They don't all react the same, and he's their prince, so I'd guess he's one of the tough ones. I'd just as soon not get him twitchy."

Lily looked at Mech. She didn't say anything. Just looked.

Slowly his hands lowered. Even more slowly, he holstered his gun. "You're making a mistake," he told her. "A big one."

"I already made it. Jesus." She shook her head, disgusted. "I *asked* to have you on the case. Consider yourself on report." She glanced at Phillips. "You drew on him, even though you knew you were too close?"

He sighed, gloomy. "You know how it is. You see someone pull a gun, you just got to pull yours, too."

No, Lily decided. He'd done it to give Rule multiple targets if he attacked, giving the rest of them more of a chance. Lily wasn't sure she liked Phillips, but she was beginning to respect him.

All at once she felt shaky. This could have been a bloodbath. *Unused adrenaline,* she told herself. *Ignore it.*

A glance around the little vestibule told her Ginger had vanished. The rookie looked worried, Mech stubborn, and Rule . . . his eyes weren't back to normal yet, but they were headed that way. He gave her a crooked smile, as if he were trying to reassure her.

She wasn't the one about to be hauled away on a murder charge—a murder she knew he hadn't committed. Lily walked up to Mech, tight with anger. "Now, Sergeant, maybe you can take a minute to explain why you've violated procedure up, down, and sideways, and nearly filled this place with bodies. Or is that your usual technique for interrogating a suspect? You draw on them just in case, never mind who's in the line of fire?"

"Normal procedures are ineffective against one of *them*. I couldn't let him get away."

"Yeah? So you see him running now that no one's holding a gun on him?"

Mech's eyes flickered. "I . . . maybe I misjudged."

"You think?" Lily let all her scorn show. "There's a few more holes you've punched in procedure, too. Like applying for an arrest warrant before you even spoke to the lead on the case."

"I spoke to the captain. Ma'am." The *ma'am* was tacked on with barely veiled sarcasm.

"No kidding? And I'm sure you told him I wasn't aware you'd decided to play Lone Ranger and round up the bad guys all by yourself."

"Yes, 'ma'am." That was satisfaction in his voice now. "I did, though not in those words. He agreed that the evidence justified applying for a warrant."

Without telling her? Lily felt cold. Was it the captain, then? Was Randall the one who'd set Therese Martin up to die? Or were they both in on it?

Getting paranoid here, she told herself. Conspiracies can do that to a person. "You're going to fill me in on this evidence now, I guess. Seeing as I'm the lead and all. Be sure to explain why Turner killed the witness who stood between him and possible arrest for Fuentes's murder."

"He paid her for that. I've got the deposit slip where she put ten thousand in her account, cash, right after she talked to you. She must have threatened him or gotten greedy, become a liability in some way. I've also got a witness who places him at the scene at the right time. That's motive and opportunity. For means—he's lupus. He *is* the means."

"You've been amazingly busy. Lucky, too, considering she was found only an hour and a half ago. Would that witness be Ginger Harris?"

His gaze flicked toward Rule, then back to Lily. "I need to see if she's all right."

"You do that."

"I'm going to execute that warrant when it arrives."

"I'm sure you are." She turned away, sick to her soul. This whole thing was a setup, and Mech was part of it. Either he was dirty or he was so warped by his prejudices it had the same result.

And the captain? Was he bent, too? How could she proceed if she couldn't trust the captain?

She turned slowly, feeling eyes on her. Rule stood where he'd been throughout, motionless as the predator he was, watching her. When their eyes met, her heart jolted in her chest. Even here, even now, she felt him pulling at her, as if he had a hook in her gut . . . or her groin.

For a second, she hated him.

And that didn't matter either, she thought, looking away as the steel box on wheels they called special transport pulled up outside. As far as the investigation went, it didn't matter whether she hated Rule or fucked him. Because it would soon be out of her hands.

Therese Martin had been killed by sorcery, not a werewolf. Murder by magical means was a federal crime. She was going to have to let the Feds have this one.

FIFTEEN

"**WHAT** do you mean, we aren't going to tell them?"

Randall clasped his hands on the desk in front of him. "What do we have? Your *feeling.* Which isn't evidence, isn't anything you can even put in a report."

"I realize we'd have to level with them about my abilities," Lily said stiffly. "I don't like that, but there's no other way."

"We aren't obligated to give them a thing that isn't in your reports. Particularly such subjective information. Wait." He held up a hand. "You're convinced of the accuracy of your, uh, impressions. But you said yourself you've never experienced sorcery. You don't know that's what you picked up."

"It fits," she insisted. "All 'subjective information' aside, it fits. It's such an obvious frame! There's no trace of blood anywhere except by the body and at the sink, so we'd think he washed up. The deposit slip Mech found—we don't have a thing tying it to Turner. Anyone could have put that money in. Then there's the wolf hair. She couldn't have pulled it out herself. They left it there."

"Listen to yourself for a minute." He was plainly exasperated. "Mech said you'd become biased, entranced by this lupus prince. I didn't believe him, but—"

"Mech's got a hate thing going about lupi. I didn't realize that before, but it was obvious at the scene."

He slapped his desk. "And *you* would rather decide that a fellow officer is guilty than that werewolf! You're postulating a conspiracy, and not just that, but one involving this department. *And* a murder committed at a distance through sorcery. That just isn't possible."

"It's been done. The historical record—"

"Before the Purge! That's four hundred years ago!" He leaned forward. "Let me make myself clear. I am not going to subject this department to a witch hunt by a pair of glory-seeking federal agents. And that's what would happen. They'd be looking at us—even at me—for a suspect. Or had that escaped your conspiracy-ridden mind?"

"No, sir," she said woodenly. "That hadn't escaped me. Though it's possible one of the FBI agents did it, it's more likely someone in this department tipped off Therese's killer."

His mouth tightened. "Get out."

"Sir—"

"Out!" He glared at her. "I'm not removing you from the case, but I'm close to it. Go on. Go get your head straight."

She left. She stopped at her office long enough to jam the FBI file and a couple more reports in her tote, then headed for the elevator.

"Hey!" Brady called as she passed through the bullpen. "What's with you and Mech? You got it in for him?"

She didn't slow down. "My report's on file. You want to know what happened, read it."

Brady scowled at her. "Why are you making trouble for him? He didn't make a pass. Not Mech."

T.J. shook his head. "Try to think about something other than sex, boy. It'll be hard, but try. Lily . . ."

She paused, met his eyes.

"You take care now."

Her smile flickered. "Right."

At least T.J. didn't hate her, she thought as she slung her tote in the backseat of her car. Yet. If she kept pushing, though, against the captain's orders . . . but Captain Randall was *wrong*.

Either that, or he was dirty. She couldn't make herself believe that, but she couldn't dismiss it, either. He'd had reasons for what he'd done—not good ones, in her opinion. But plausible.

She sent her car shooting backward out of her space, yanked the wheel, shifted, and hit the accelerator hard enough to burn rubber. The captain was right about one thing. She needed to get her head straight.

Fifteen minutes later she slammed the car door shut and started up the path to Grandmother's house. She rang the bell.

"Lily." Li Qin smiled. "How lovely to see you again. Please come in."

Lily shook her head. "Not today, thank you. I just wanted to let you know I was here and would be working in the garden awhile."

"Of course," Li Qin said, as if Lily often dropped by in the middle of a workday to pull weeds. "I hope you will allow me to bring you some refreshment. Tea or a cool drink?"

"Perhaps later? I'm not fit company right now." She managed to take her leave politely, then hurried along the flagstone path to the back of the house where the toolshed waited.

Five minutes later, she was in the native plants area west of the house, destroying invaders. The blue oak that anchored the space made salt-and-pepper shade, a shifting, dappled world. A strong breeze blew from the west. Lily knelt in the dirt in her linen slacks, uncaring of the damage she did them. She dug her trowel into the dry ground, loosened the roots beneath a clump of grass, and yanked it out with her other hand.

Twenty years ago, after Sarah Harris died and Lily didn't, Grandmother had taken Lily to a section of her yard and told her to get rid of all the grass. She'd had so much fear and hate in her then. Therapy hadn't done much good. How could a therapist help a child who won't talk?

Earth and sun and weeds had reached what words couldn't. Lily had pulled and dug, pulled and dug. Eventually, the grass had been gone and she'd planted. Eventually, her garden had bloomed. And she'd learned that life persists. Some live, some die, but life persists.

Lily had gone on to create other gardens, like this one. Planning a bed was fun. Planting was satisfying, and watching the garden come to life filled her in a way nothing else did.

But sometimes she just needed to dig and pull, dig and pull.

Captain Randall claimed he'd left her out of the loop because she was with Rule. He'd been afraid she would inadvertently tip Rule off that something was up, putting both her and the planned arrest at risk. Mech was supposed to have told her as soon as she arrived at the scene, but he'd been with his witness. With Ginger Harris.

Who must have lied. Why?

Lily shook her head. She'd tackle those questions later.

Randall's assumptions would have been less insulting, she thought, jamming her trowel in the earth, if the captain had known that lupi could hear both sides of a phone conversation. He didn't. He'd been worried that Rule would smell her fear. He'd assumed she wasn't clever enough to explain away a sudden attack of jitters.

Or he'd lied.

Maybe she was afraid of being with Rule, she thought, ripping out a greedy patch of star thistle. But she didn't fear him for the reason the captain assumed. Rule hadn't killed Therese—though so far, she'd had zero luck persuading anyone of that. Her word sure hadn't been enough.

The captain had given Mech a disciplinary slap on the wrist. Not for the way he'd rushed to an arrest, though. Because he'd handled the arrest badly.

Most officers had no experience arresting a lupus. Here in California, lupi hadn't been arrested; they'd been hunted, then captured or killed by the X-Squads. But everyone had been briefed on correct procedure for a lupus apprehension, and Mech hadn't followed those procedures. It could so easily have ended in officers down.

Instead, it had ended in Rule being taken away in shackles.

Lily's eyes burned, though whether from fury or tears, she didn't know. He was in a cage now—that's what it amounted to. Cities the size of San Diego had separate facilities for those of the Blood. They were too dangerous to mix with the general jail population, not to mention hard to hold on to.

By now Rule was locked up in one of the eight-foot-square, steel-lined boxes reserved for lupi and other, rarer preternaturals. Grandmother said lupi were claustrophobic.

That they went a little nuts if you locked them up. And those cells were so small. . . .

Lily shuddered and destroyed another clump of grass. She understood the horror of being trapped in a tiny space.

No judge would grant bail to a lupus who was up on a murder charge. Rule would sit in a tiny metal cage until she could prove someone else killed Therese.

She would prove it. Somehow.

All right, she thought, sitting back on her heels and surveying her battlefield, strewn with the corpses of grass and weeds. *Enough emoting. Look at the facts and the possibilities. Consider what's right, what's at risk. Then make a decision.*

She began digging more carefully. Weed seedlings had set up housekeeping next to the monkey flower plants. She loosened the dirt with her trowel and began plucking them out

Fact: Captain Randall didn't want to tell the FBI they had a murder by sorcery. The possibilities, she thought, were three. First, he simply didn't believe her. Maybe he thought she was lying, maybe he thought she was mistaken. Maybe he couldn't bring himself to trust in something he couldn't sense himself.

That could be, she admitted, shifting position so she could tackle the section near the manzanita. People knew that were-wolves, brownies, and such operated in part on magic, but there were some who insisted that Wicca was strictly a religion, no magic involved. Like flat-earthers, they majored in denial, explaining away the disorderliness of magic and denying what they couldn't explain.

The captain kept insisting that sorcery no longer existed. Admittedly, some experts agreed with him, but his attitude seemed more emotional than rational. Maybe he just couldn't admit real magic into his world.

Okay. Possibility number two: Randall knew she was right, but he didn't want his department to get a black eye. He was willing to cover up for Mech.

She didn't like that idea. It went against what she knew of the man, but it was possible. Randall was ambitious. He didn't like Croft and Karonski, didn't want them taking over, and most of all didn't want anyone finding evidence that one of his officers was dirty.

Well, dammit, neither did she. Lily began pulling out weeds that had hidden beneath the shrub's leaves. But covering up was not an option.

Possibility three: Randall himself was bent. He knew she was right about the sorcery, knew who had killed Therese and why. And if that were true, she was in danger. He'd have to discredit her . . . or kill her.

Which could also be true if Mech was the crooked one.

Sweat beaded on her forehead, but she felt cold. It wasn't the possibility of danger. It was the idea of being in danger from another cop.

It hadn't always been easy, being a female police officer. And it hadn't helped that she was short, slight, and Chinese. But she'd made a place for herself. She belonged.

But the cost of belonging had just gone up. To remain one of the boys, she'd have to continue to play by the rules, both written and unwritten.

Hadn't she always been good at following rules? But this time, she thought as she savaged another cluster of star thistle, to play one set of rules meant ignoring others. She *knew* Therese had been killed by sorcery and that they had locked up the wrong man. But she couldn't report what she knew to the FBI, and she'd better not talk about it elsewhere, either. To stay on the case, she'd have to pretend there wasn't a traitor in the department. Look as if she were toeing the line the captain had drawn.

Didn't that make sense, though? She wiped the back of her hand across her forehead, smearing dirt in with the sweat. She could do more for Rule by staying where she was than if she went haring off on some solo truth-and-justice crusade. How far could she get if she didn't have the power of the law behind her?

How far could she get if the power of the law was used against her?

At least one of the people sworn to uphold the law was subverting it. Mech. Captain Randall. The FBI agents, Croft and Karonski. She didn't know who her enemy was . . . but he knew her.

Rule was in a box, framed for murder. Framed by a cop.

Lily stood. The wind whipped a strand of her hair across

her cheek, and she turned her face into it. Clouds were piling up to the west, out to sea. Maybe they'd get some rain soon. The land could use it.

Slowly she pulled off her gloves. Normally she tidied up all the unwanted plants and grasses she'd removed. Today she glanced at the mess and didn't care. Let the wind clean it up.

She headed for her car. Her phone was there. She had a call to make. Then she had to go back to headquarters.

SIXTEEN

THEY never turned the lights off.

There were many things to hate about the metal hole they'd stuck him in, and some that weren't so bad. Rule didn't mind the lack of a bed. He couldn't stop moving, so a bunk would only have been in the way. The sanitary facilities were sparse but decent; both sink and toilet folded up into the wall. The walls themselves, though, insulated everything. Rule could barely sense the moon through all the steel, but he'd developed a tolerance for that. Humans used a lot of metal when they built cities. The silence was harder to bear—he couldn't hear a thing from outside his tiny cell.

But it was the unfaltering light that was making him crazy.

If he could have closed the darkness around him, he wouldn't have been able to see the walls. He could have fooled himself that they were farther away. Darkness wouldn't have kept him from pacing. He'd tried it for awhile with his eyes closed to see if that helped. It hadn't.

Things could have been worse. Because lupi healed so well, they made prime targets for a certain type of cop. Any damage wouldn't show for long. If someone did notice that the prisoner had a broken bone or two, it was easy to argue that he'd been unruly. It can take a lot of force to discourage an unruly lupus. And if some of the other cops suspected the truth, they didn't tell.

Rule understood that. The police were like a clan, though an ill-run one, in his opinion. So much was expected of them, yet they were denied the status their work merited. It was no wonder some of them went off track.

He'd been spared the indignity of being struck when he couldn't fight back, he reminded himself.

He would rather have been beaten.

Rule snarled at the metal wall and turned. Three steps one way, turn, three steps back. He'd been pacing since they locked him in here. Maybe in a day or two he'd tire himself out enough to sleep.

He'd used his one phone call to let Benedict know what had happened. His brother would arrange for a lawyer, and sooner or later they'd have to let that lawyer in to see him. Whether anyone else would be allowed to visit, he didn't know. He didn't know if anyone else would try.

His lip pulled back in disgust. No point in fooling himself; he wasn't worried about "anyone else" trying to see him. He wanted Lily to come. He wanted her to care at least that much.

She'd looked at him as if she couldn't stand him.

Three steps. Turn.

She'd kept her man from shooting him, though. No question in Rule's mind that's what the sergeant had meant to do— provoke Rule into Changing if he could. If not, force Rule to move, to make any action that could be interpreted as threatening. He'd wanted an excuse to kill. The others would probably have let him get away with it. Lupi had been fair game for a long time.

She'd walked *in front* of the damned gun.

What in God's name had she been thinking? She'd cautioned him earlier that she didn't heal the way he did. It wasn't something he was likely to overlook, but she seemed to have forgotten that fact. If her sergeant had pulled the trigger on Rule, Rule would almost certainly have lived long enough to take the bastard with him. The other cop had been right about that. He might have survived beyond that, too, depending on how many others shot him and where their bullets hit.

Lily wouldn't have. If that cop had pulled the trigger after she stepped in front of his gun . . . *Think of something else.*

Three steps and turn.

What would happen to Nokolai if he were found guilty? What would happen to his son?

Not the best choice of alternate subject.

How long had he been in here, anyway? Usually he could tell time by the dance between earth and moon, but her pull was muffled by all the steel. It must be night by now, though.

They'd taken his watch, his shoes, pocket knife, phone, keys—all those dangerous objects that were nothing compared to what he could do with his bare hands. Fools.

He stopped and looked up at the bedamned lights.

Two fluorescent tubes were set in a recess in the ceiling protected by steel bars. The floor-to-ceiling measurement was the largest dimension of his cell, perhaps ten feet. He could jump that high. Jump up, grab one of the bars, get his other hand between the bars, and smash the bloody glowing tubes to bits. He'd cut his hand, but what of it?

They would come running, of course, with guns drawn, ready for him to make God knew what devious escape attempt. He was watched. He knew that. The round black eye of a camera perched high in one corner.

Had it been lower, he could have pissed on it. A childish but understandable desire, he thought. Barring that, the camera would also be easy to smash, if he chose to do so.

It would be a break in the pacing, wouldn't it?

He bent his knees and launched himself straight up. Closed his fingers around one of the bars and hung there . . . and heard the snick of the lock.

He dropped to the floor, spun to face the door.

It swung open. "You okay?" a voice called. No one was visible in the doorway. "Door's going to stay open. No need to trample anyone."

He blinked. "Karonski? Abel Karonski?"

"Your memory's working, anyway." A bulky figure moved into view—rumpled suit, sour expression, stinking of those cigars he snuck. Definitely Abel Karonski, though it had been awhile since Rule last saw him.

"You weren't on my list."

"Would that be the good people list or the bad people list?"

"Of people I might see. I thought a lawyer might show up soon, or . . . but I wasn't expecting MCD."

"Well, you got us. Good news for you that you did. You're free."

Free. He took a step toward the door, hesitated.

Karonski stood back. Rule moved fast then. He shouldn't have. When you move too fast it scares humans, and scared humans with guns were likely to put holes in things.

But . . . he stood outside his cell, looking around. The short corridor was empty except for Karonski and another man, one Rule didn't know. Neither had their guns out. "Am I in your custody?"

"Nope. You're free, like I said, thanks to your girlfriend. I'd like you to come with us, though. You might want to do that, considering there's a dozen reporters salivating out front. They'll pounce when you come out. We've got a car waiting."

Rule nodded at the other man. "And this is—?"

"Martin Croft," the other man said. He was taller and darker-skinned than Karonski, and much better dressed. He held out his hand.

Karonski elbowed him. "Not yet. He needs to settle more." He scanned Rule. "You're jittery but holding. Can you make it through the piranhas with microphones without biting off someone's hand?"

"Of course." Reporters. He should have expected that. He wasn't thinking clearly. Rule ran a hand through his hair and wished for a mirror. He would perform for the cameras, but it had better be brief. "I trust someone plans to return my shoes. What time is it?"

"About ten. This way to checkout." Karonski started down the short hall. The door at the end was blank metal, no way to open it from the inside. Rule concentrated on keeping his breathing steady. He was almost out. It wouldn't do to crack up now.

The other man—Croft—smiled as he fell into step beside Rule. "If you're wondering why we had the honor of letting you out of your cell, you can thank Abel's descriptive abilities. He explained what happened once when a couple of cops released a lupus who'd been locked up too long."

"For Chrissake, Martin, you trying to get me jumped?" Karonski growled. "Turner, I didn't tell them why being locked up makes you folks twitchy. Let 'em think you just get put out at the injustice of it all."

Obviously he'd told Croft, however. "You two are partners?"

"For my sins, yes," Croft said.

Unexpectedly, Karonski chuckled. "He means that literally," he said as he punched the button by the door.

A few minutes later Rule slid his feet into his shoes and his wallet into his pocket, having signed for his belongings. Two more cops were waiting to escort him; the authorities didn't want him stopping for a press conference on his way home from jail, it seemed.

Lily wasn't there. He hadn't realized how much he'd wanted her to be until the disappointment hit.

It did his human side good to have his things restored, though. He wondered if humans experienced the same lessening of their civilized selves when they were stripped of the bits they normally carried on their bodies. "You said I was out 'thanks to my girlfriend,'" he said to Karonski. "What did you mean?"

Karonski gave him a quick glance. "Explanations later. Let's get through the media mob and go somewhere we can talk."

"Damn," Croft said as they reached the door. "It's raining again. I guess reporters don't have the sense to come in out of it."

"You won't melt. Come on."

Rule walked out into a damp night with Karonski on one side, Croft on the other, and a cop in front and one behind to clear a path.

Lightbulbs flashed. Microphones were thrust at him. Voices called out questions. They crowded him—people, sounds, lights, all pressed in on him until it was hard to breathe. With darkness backing them, rain drizzling down, and lights held high for the TV cameras, they became a wall of people and sound, lacking individual faces or voices.

Easy, he told himself. *You can get out, so you don't have to.* He paused, formed a smile for them, and put on one of the best performances of his life. "Gentlemen. Ladies. I'm far too vain to allow you to interview me like this." He gestured at his

T-shirt and jeans, which were certainly more casual than he usually wore for a session with the press.

A couple of them laughed. Someone gave a wolf whistle.

"Thank you." He hoped he got the grin right. "Allow me to get a night's sleep and groom myself properly. I'll give you a statement and take questions in the morning."

They didn't exactly give up, but, with the promise of an interview, they weren't as insistent. Rule's escort managed to get him to the dark sedan that waited. Croft got in behind the wheel; Karonski sat beside him, leaving the backseat to Rule.

He concentrated on breathing.

"You okay?" Karonski turned to look over the seat as they pulled away.

Rule hated the way he reacted. Lupi uniformly disliked small, enclosed spaces, but not all were as bloody sensitive as he was. But it couldn't be helped. He was scrambled. "There's a park a few blocks away. I'd like to go there."

"In the rain?" Croft asked.

"Would you get over your thing about the weather?" Karonski turned back around. "My mama always said, don't crowd a jumpy werewolf. No walls at the park. Tell him where to go," he added to Rule, and chuckled. "I do."

"All the time," Croft murmured.

A few red lights later, they pulled up at the park. Rule got out. It wasn't much of a rain, but the wind whipped it around, making a fuss. He tilted his face toward the sky and let the Lady clean him.

It helped. When the other two got out, he was able to say politely, "Excuse me a moment. I'll be back." And he ran.

Twelve minutes later he returned to the car. He'd kept to an easy lope, no faster than most humans could manage, and had seen two others out for a run, unwilling to let a little rain keep them inside. It was a good reminder. Not all humans closed themselves away from nature.

The FBI agents, however, had gotten back into the car to stay dry. When they climbed out, he apologized for having kept them waiting. "I wasn't in good shape to ask questions or hear the answers. Now I am. Why am I not in jail anymore?"

"Just as well you ran off your jumpiness," Karonski said.

"Normally you wouldn't shoot the messenger, but I'd rather you heard this with your head clear. You aren't going to like it."

CROFT and Karonski had Lily's address. They dropped him off.

She lived on the second floor of a small, overwhelmingly pink complex that might have begun life fifty years ago as a motel. A cement walkway on each floor connected the outside stairwells and gave access to the units.

The scent of the sea was strong and sweet in Rule's nostrils when he got out of the car. Water and decay, salt and sand . . . he was encouraged by her choice. Surely a woman who picked a spot so close to the ocean didn't automatically hide from the rain.

Which didn't mean she wouldn't hide from other things. "Go away," she said through the door after he knocked.

"No."

"Suit yourself. I'm not opening the door."

"And I'm not leaving." He settled himself on the damp cement, leaning his back against her door. No comment came through the door, but he knew she was still there. The door was too thin to hide her movements from him. "Do you go to the ocean often? You live close."

Another pause. He imagined her shaking her head, perplexed by his subject. "I run on the beach. It's good for the calf muscles."

"And the soul. We don't go to the ocean for anything as simple as happiness, do we? We go there to feel alive. Like life, the ocean holds chance and change, grief and terror and beauty. It promises mortality, not peace."

"I'm not in the mood for poetry tonight."

"I suppose not. You've had your life jerked out from under you. Hitting, screaming, and throwing things might be better. You can't hit me through the door, though."

A long pause, then: "You're not going away, are you?"

"No."

A second later the lock snicked. He rose to his feet and faced the door as it opened.

She wore old black sweatpants and a gray T-shirt that read,

San Diego Police Dept. No bra, he thought. Her hair was pulled back in an untidy ponytail. Framed by the soft light from inside, she looked stark and untouchable.

It didn't keep him from wanting to touch.

She shook her head. "I ought to call you in as a prowler and let them lock you up again."

"I'm fortunate that you're too kind to do that."

"I'm not kind at all." She stepped back. "Come in so we can get this settled."

He stepped inside and looked around, breathing in the scents—plants and spaghetti and Lily. Everywhere Lily. Her scent had sunk into the pillows and carpet and walls of her space, and it made him happy.

But there was another scent. "You have a cat."

Her lips quirked. "He's outside. You have a problem with cats?"

"They often have a problem with me." He moved farther into the room, touching a leaf, the drapes, looking at the single print on the wall, a black-and-white shot of the ocean. Her living area was small, scrupulously neat, and almost bare, except for . . . "You prefer plants to furniture?"

"I like to garden. Lacking a yard, I do it in pots." She crossed her arms, locking him away from her body. "You didn't come here to inspect my apartment, I hope."

They were such pretty arms, round and firm, the skin smooth. He wanted to lick his way up one arm and down the other. To give his hands something else to do, he ran one through his hair, shaking out some of the dampness. "No, but I was curious about your space. It smells good."

"Ah—thanks. Look, I'm glad you're out of jail, but I don't want company right now. If you came to thank me, let's consider it said."

"Gratitude is a flimsy word when I owe you more than I can repay. Why did they take your badge?"

She flinched. "It's temporary. And how do you know about it, anyway?"

"The FBI agents you spoke to. They released me from the metal hole where I'd been placed."

"I suppose they talked to the captain." She shrugged, but the movement was jerky. "It's none of your business."

"Isn't it?" Without thinking he took a step toward her, then forced himself to stop. He was already too close, his heart beating too fast. This was a damnably intimate space. "Were you suspended for going to the FBI?"

"Technically, no. Can't punish a cop for following the rules. Though I broke them, too . . . but it was the unwritten ones I violated."

"Then why?"

She grinned mirthlessly. "For having an affair with you."

That sucked the air right out of him. "Your captain is prescient?"

"Confident, aren't you? No, he's pissed." She started to pace, but the small room didn't give her much space for it. She reached the wall, turned, started back. "I'd been told to leave it out, you see. But that was wrong. Maybe I didn't have evidence, but I *knew* it was sorcery that killed her. The captain didn't want to believe me, and you were so handy. As long as he could believe you'd done it, he didn't have to look for a dirty cop in his department. In the end, I forced him to."

She passed within arm's reach of him on her circuit of the room. He didn't reach. Instead, he lowered himself to the floor and sat, to discourage himself from grabbing her. "How?"

"I went to Internal Affairs." She reached the other wall, turned. "You wouldn't know what that means."

"They're the cops who watch the other cops."

"Roughly, yes. But you don't go to them. You don't rat on your supervisor or your brother cops, because no one will trust you if you do. I can't explain it. That's just how it is."

"I think I understand. Internal Affairs are cops, but they aren't part of your clan of cops."

"What?" She stopped, gave a nervous laugh, and resumed her circuit of the room. "This is not like lupus clans."

"It seems very similar. The captain is your Rho. You knew he was wrong, but your rules don't allow you to challenge him directly. Instead you had to go out of the clan for a champion— which the rules allow, even encourage, but of course this behavior troubles you and your cop clan." He shook his head. "A strange system."

"I must be losing it," she muttered. "That made sense."

"In a true clan, you'd be punished through the Challenge

itself. Your rules make it seem as if you can go out of the clan without paying a price, but that feels wrong. So the other cops find a punishment for you, even if it means lying. You and I aren't lovers yet."

"Yet. Yet. Would you stop talking that way?" She dragged a hand over her hair, caught her fingers in the band holding the ponytail, and jerked the bit of cloth out, throwing it on the floor.

"Who told the lie about you?"

"Mech fed the captain a bunch of bullshit. Randall knew it was bullshit—I think he did, anyway. But then there I was, telling him he had to release you. I did that after ratting to the FBI and to Internal Affairs. I needed to be punished, all right." She slowed. "It should be temporary. They can't prove something that isn't true."

She couldn't believe that. He'd just been put in a cell because they'd been able to "prove" an untruth. But she wanted to believe it, needed to. She didn't want to lose her clan—that's what it amounted to. "*Querida.* You make me ache."

Her glance hit him and skittered away, like a stone skipped over water. "I didn't do it for you. You should know that. I did it because I have to live with myself, and it was wrong to cover things up. Even temporarily." Her feet took her into motion again. "I wanted to handle the investigation myself. I tried to persuade myself I could, but in the end I decided that would be risking too much. More than I had a right to risk."

She reminded him of himself earlier, pacing out his cell, unable to stop. What walls put her in motion this way? "What would that have risked?"

"You, for one. You were in a cage. I know what those cells are like—tiny. Probably smelled bad to you, too. You might not have been able to stand that for long enough for me to fix things."

"*Merde!* Did Karonski tell everyone?"

"What?"

"Never mind. You said you didn't do it for me."

"You were one consideration." She passed him again, achingly close. "The biggest one, though, was that they might succeed in taking me out. If I was the only one who knew for certain Therese's murder was sorcery, I was a big liability for them. If they killed me and no one else knew—"

He shot to his feet. "I didn't even think of that. I was so busy being crazy in that cell—"

"Why should you have? Took me awhile to see it, too. I'm not used to thinking of other cops as dangerous to me. I didn't want to see that, but once I did, I knew I had to make sure I wasn't the only one looking at things from that angle. Telling the FBI was good, but it wasn't enough. They could have been part of it, part of the conspiracy. I didn't know."

He dragged a shaky hand over his face. "Not Karonski."

She was startled. "You know him?"

"It's been awhile, but yes. I'd swear he's honest. Irritating as hell sometimes, but honest."

"What did he tell you, then?" She faced him, still for the moment.

"That you had called him because your captain wouldn't. That you knew the Martin woman had been killed by sorcery, not a lupus. He didn't say how you knew that. When I asked, he said I should ask you."

"Well." She chewed on her lip. "I guess he knows how to keep his mouth shut."

"You don't want me to know?"

"I don't want him deciding who should know. But you . . ." She looked unhappy, but shrugged. "Why not? The captain's planning to out me anyway, so it won't be a secret much longer. I knew she'd been killed by sorcery because I touched the magic the killer left behind. I'm a sensitive."

SEVENTEEN

HE had the funniest look on his face. Lily frowned and rubbed her arms. She felt weird herself—cold and hot at the same time. Jittery as hell. Aroused . . . well, that wasn't strange. Rule's presence flooded her tiny living room. He seemed to be pressing himself on her, though he wasn't moving.

She had to get away from him. That thought, barely formed but imperative, started her moving again. "What is it? You aren't spooked about sensitives, surely."

"No . . ." He looked distant, shocked.

"Sometimes it helps in my work, knowing who is of the Blood or Gifted. Like your friend Max—that was a surprise. I've never met a gnome. But I didn't mention what he was in my report. I don't out people."

He shook his head the way a dog shakes itself dry, seeming to return from some interior space. "No, of course not. This explains . . . much."

Explains what? Had she given herself away somehow? *It doesn't matter,* she told herself, impatient. Her secret would soon be no secret at all. Randall planned to put it in his report. He claimed he had to in order to explain why he'd put her in charge of the investigation.

She reached the wall, turned. Maybe he did. It would be easy to think of him as wrong about everything now, when they stood on opposite sides of such a chasm. But that would be a mistake.

Did the captain really believe Mech's accusations? Or had he seized on them as a means to punish her for going out of the clan?

God. She was thinking like Rule, as if she and the captain were lupi. Had to stop that. She'd really get herself confused that way.

She needed to figure out what Randall believed. If he'd gone after her from vindictiveness, he'd proceed differently than if he truly believed she'd stepped outside the lines herself. He was her opponent now. She hated that, but he was bringing charges against her. She'd have to defend against those charges.

Lily paused, glanced at Rule—and away—and back. She couldn't seem to look straight at him for more than a second. She couldn't stop looking, either. "Your presence here tonight will not make it easier for me to refute Mech's accusations."

"I'm sorry." There was a haunted look about his eyes. "I can't put it off any longer, *nadia*. You have to know."

"Know?" Her heartbeat spiked. She didn't know why. Her mouth went dry, and she felt oddly aware of her fingers, her throat, her skin—the sort of supercharged awareness she'd had sometimes when danger turned the world crisp.

Without even noticing, she stopped moving. "Know what?"

"You and I are chosen for each other."

There wasn't enough air. She tried to laugh anyway. "What's that? Some sort of lupus pickup line?"

"It means we are mates, chosen for each other by the Lady. Bonded for life. There is no breaking this bond short of death."

"That's crazy. That's just crazy." She had to move. She couldn't take her eyes off him. "You can't expect me to believe that."

"It's easily proved. If I reached for you right now, put my hand on you, you would be mine. In spite of all you have to lose, you wouldn't be able to refuse me. Your need is too great."

"That—that—" She managed to tear her eyes away and was able to move again. To pace. "You've gone beyond arrogance to ugly."

"You can't settle. Something's eating you from the inside. I can smell your arousal each time you walk past me."

She went pale, then flushed. "Then breathe through your mouth, dammit. That's just—it's intrusive. You have no business—"

"I can't help it. No more than you can. To be chosen is to have many choices taken away. They say that other choices arrive, some sweet, some terrible. It's a rare thing, to be chosen." He was bitter, not seductive. "You don't want to believe, but you must."

"I *don't* believe. I don't worship your Lady, and I don't think you're in love with me."

"That's as well. The primary bond is between our bodies, not our minds and hearts. Though I like you very much, Lily," he said with a smile as sad as it was breathtaking. "I admire and respect you as well. We have much to build on."

She couldn't say those things back to him. Not because they were untrue. Because she didn't dare. "I don't think God hands out a sexual *geas*. That's what you're talking about, isn't it? Not a romantic bond, but some sort of divine *geas*."

"Tell me to leave."

Her feet faltered.

"If I'm wrong, if you are free to choose, tell me to go."

She couldn't speak. Couldn't move.

"Two days ago, you had a dizzy spell you didn't understand."

Her head was whirling *now*.

"It passed within moments, fortunately. Because I realized what was happening and moved closer to you. There are limits to how far we can be separated. I'd surpassed those limits, and we both suffered."

Her heart beat frantically. "I'm bespelled," she whispered.

"Can a sensitive be bespelled?"

She shook her head. "But I must be."

"You aren't thinking straight right now," he said gently, stepping closer, "but that isn't your fault. I've the advantage of having had time to absorb the change in my condition. You haven't. You feel you're spinning wildly, coming apart while standing still. It will eat you alive, Lily. It's eating me alive. We have to touch." And he did.

His hands were large, smooth for a man's—did he heal any calluses before they formed? He fanned his fingers out along along the sides of her face. She felt each finger clearly. She didn't move. Her mind was washed white of thought, of possibilities, of anything other than the rightness of his touch.

He moved closer, bringing his head down as if he would kiss her. He didn't. Instead, his breath washed over her mouth. "Breath to breath," he whispered. "Sweet, so sweet to breathe you in."

The air itself had turned rich. Breathing was heady, intoxicating. Her skin was alive and her body ached. But one thing remained missing. "Why can't I feel you? When we touch, why don't I touch your magic?"

"Ah. That must have confused you. I would guess that our magics mesh so smoothly you can't touch the difference."

She jolted. "I don't have magic."

"Sweetheart." He abandoned her face to gather her close. His clothes were damp, his body hard and hot. "What do you think it means to be a sensitive, except that you're Gifted? A very rare Gift, but still a Gift."

Later. She'd think about what he'd said later. How could she think with his body touching hers? Her skin seemed to vibrate like the skin of a drum. And his face, so near hers, the sheer fascination of it . . . She traced his eyebrow with one finger. "I'm pretty much scared shitless, you know."

He answered with the sudden flash of a grin, so much less seductive than his smile. So much more dangerous. He was real when he grinned. "You do delight me."

"That's great. I'm scared, and you're delighted."

He shook his head, his grin fading. "We have so much to learn about each other." He ran his hands up her sides. "Later. I need you now, my *nadia,* my only one." He crushed his mouth down on hers.

Everything in her leaped to meet him. His taste—yes, she'd tasted him before, and she needed that, needed him—

A terrible, unearthly howl filled the air. She jerked back, eyes wide. He jolted and tilted his head up, eyes closed, his chest heaving. "Mother help me. Your cat wants in."

Oh. Oh, yes, of course, she thought, leaning her head on

his chest, trying to capture her breath. That was definitely Harry, howling his challenge. "He smells you."

"Yes." He sounded grim. "You love this cat?"

"Of course."

"Of course." He sighed. "A dog would have been so much easier. And he's male, too. You had better let him in."

"But—" *But I can't let go, can't just stop, I hurt with wanting. Couldn't you—couldn't we . . .* She shook her head, denying the image that had flashed through it. Her body mocked her, telling her clearly what she needed. Him. In her. Now. "I'm losing my mind."

"You'll regain it, but not until we join. First, though—" He grimaced, dropping his arms as he stepped back. "I must meet your cat."

She swallowed. She had to let Harry in. The neighbors would complain, maybe throw things at him. She didn't want him hurt. He was still howling, that rising and falling combat song of his. "I don't think meeting him is a good idea. I'll put him in the bedroom."

"No." Rule shook his head. "He needs to defend you. Let him in."

"You won't—"

"I won't hurt him."

He might hurt you, she thought, and grimaced. That was ridiculous. Rule fought other werewolves, for crying out loud. He could handle a cat. Even a seventeen-pounder with major attitude problems. Couldn't he?

She glanced over her shoulder at Rule as she reached the door. He crouched in the center of the room, knees flexed, arms ready. He was taking Harry's challenge seriously.

Maybe he should. "Um—his name's Dirty Harry."

Rule's eyebrows rose. "You named your cat for a fictional cop who blasts the bad guys?"

"It fits. Though his definition of bad guys is pretty inclusive." She turned the lock and opened the door.

Harry shot in—straight at Rule.

They moved too fast, cat and man both, for Lily's eyes to track them properly. She did see Harry leap. Rule seemed to translate from one spot to another without touching all the places between—something she'd seen Harry do at times. Then Harry was crouched a couple feet away, ears flat and tail lashing.

"That's right," Rule murmured, not taking his eyes off the cat. "You've the right to protect, but I won't hurt her. You don't wish to share, either, but that you will have to do."

Harry leaped again. Rule ducked—and had a cat on his back. There was another blur of motion, this one ending with Rule rolling on the floor, Harry separated and spitting.

Blood dripped down Rule's face. Lily took a quick step forward.

"Stay back," Rule snapped without looking at her.

She halted. Man and cat stared at each other out of narrowed eyes while she tried to figure out why she was following Rule's orders. And what, exactly, was going on.

Abruptly Harry gave one last growl and sat back on his haunches, looking away from Rule.

Rule straightened and turned his head, as if fascinated by the wall.

Harry stood, twitched his tail once, and stalked over to her, his fur still bristled. He stropped her leg once, meowed, and headed for the kitchen.

"He . . ." She swallowed what might have been laughter. "He wants me to feed him."

"He needs to assert his place with you," Rule said, still studying the wall.

"This is weird." But she followed Harry into the kitchen, where he waited by his dish, glaring at her. She fed him and went back in the living room, shaking her head. "I'm obeying a cat and a sometimes-wolf. I don't know what I'm doing. Obviously I've lost my mind. You're still bleeding." There were two crimson tracks along his cheek. One had bled down his neck. The other stopped just below his eye. She swallowed. "Did you let him do that? He barely missed your eye."

"Don't belittle your champion's skills," he said wryly. "I let him do nothing."

"You knew he would attack you when I opened the door."

He shrugged. "I allowed him to set the terms of our negotiation. The claws in my face were entirely his idea, however."

She started laughing. "That's a negotiation?"

"Cats negotiate differently than humans."

"I should get something for that cut. Some antibiotic ointment." But she moved toward him, not the medicine cabinet in the bathroom. The pull was so strong. "I didn't expect you to like cats."

"I respect them."

She stopped in front of him.

He touched her hair. His eyes were hot and dark with need. "*Nadia*. I can't wait any longer."

She swallowed. "I'm going to do this, aren't I?"

"We," he said, and wrapped his hand in her hair. "*We* are going to do this; yes."

"Then do it," she said, suddenly fierce. "Quit talking and do it. Put yourself in me."

As if she'd hit him, he gasped. Then his mouth came down on hers, hard.

She clutched him with both hands, digging her fingers into the flesh beneath the damp T-shirt, and hung on. He ran his hands up her back, then down, cupping her butt and holding her hard against him. She moaned.

He had a scent, too, she realized—one even her human nose could find when she nuzzled his neck. A wild scent, mingling man and damp cloth and something else, something indefinably Rule. It made her crazy. She bit him on the column of his throat. "Now."

He groaned. One of his hands moved. He unzipped his jeans and sprang free, then tugged at her sweatpants and panties. She stepped out of them, dizzy with need. Shaking.

"It's all right," he told her, and put his hands beneath her butt and lifted her off the ground. "Put your legs around me, Lily. Yes, like that." He shuddered when she obeyed, opening herself to him. "It will be all right," he repeated. Still standing, he slid inside.

She made a noise, the sound of something breaking open— something private inside her being breached. "Ahh," she said then, clutching him, squeezing her eyes closed and seeing white, not dark behind her lids—swirling white.

He was thick. Long and hot and thick inside her.

Then he began walking, still lodged inside her. The sensation was incredible. Her eyes flew open. "What, you do it walking?"

He may have meant the stretch of his mouth for a grin, but strain made it a grimace. "The chair. I can't make it to your bed."

I love you. She almost said it and was appalled. Where had that come from? Because he was inside her? Because she was a fool, an idiot, unable to tell the difference between—

"This will be crowded," he said, looking at her chair and a half. "It's made for snuggling, not fucking."

And he ought to know. He'd probably fucked more women than she'd shaken hands with men.

"What is it?" His eyes were suddenly fierce. "Where did you go? You aren't with me anymore."

She stared back. "If I were an inch more *with* you, you'd be inside my uterus instead of rubbing up against it."

He groaned. And sank to his knees with her riding him, causing his cock to move inside her, rubbing places that had never felt quite that sensation before. "Hold on. Hold onto me," he said, and eased her onto her back. And began to move.

Driven by the flexing rhythm of his hips, she flung her head back, dug her fingers into his shoulders, and met his thrusts with her own. It was a wild ride. Her need, and his, made it a short one. Climax ripped through her, bucking her body and blanking her mind. He cried out.

When she drifted back to herself moments later, her face was wet. Her name, she realized. It had been her name he'd called when he came.

Why would that make her cry?

Rule was sprawled on top of her, his head next to hers, his breath stirring her hair. He'd caught himself on his forearms as he collapsed, so not all of his weight was on her. He was still inside her . . . and still hard.

"Lily?" He propped himself up on one elbow. "Ah, *cara,* don't. What is this?" He pressed his mouth to the corner of her eye, then licked at the tears. He kissed her mouth, his tongue soft, persuasive. His lips said to trust him. To let him inside, all the way inside. "Don't cry. Please don't."

"I don't . . ." Her breath caught as he shifted his hips. "I don't cry. I don't know what's happening to me. Is that"—she pushed up with her hips, demonstrating—"normal for you?"

"Very little is normal for me right now. Or for you, which is why the tears, perhaps."

"I guess." She wanted him still. She'd just hit a home run for the record books, and the need was already building. "If this was supposed to clear my mind, it didn't work."

His eyes crinkled at the corners. "Then we'd better try again. See if we can get it right."

"I know the male answer to everything is sex, but—oh!"

He'd bent and was suckling her through her T-shirt. After a moment he looked up. "Naked would be better."

"Yes." She ran her hands up his back. "Yes, it would."

Thirty minutes later she was flat on her back in her bed. Rule lay beside her on his back. They were both breathing hard, which gave her some satisfaction, considering the advantage his nature conferred. "I think . . . I can safely say"—she had to stop and drag in air—"that yes, naked is better."

He chuckled and rolled onto his side, propping himself up to look at her. "Mmm." He drew his hand along her ribs, down her hip. "You are as close to perfection as it's possible to get without boredom."

She turned her head to look at him. "You couldn't possibly."

"No?" He quirked a brow at her. "I've heard that the first month for a Chosen pair can be . . . strenuous."

"I'm not sure I buy all this Chosen stuff. There's a bond, a pull, something. I don't deny that. But you might have some of it wrong."

"Perhaps. I believe that everything I've told you is fact, but this . . . what's happened to us . . . it's rare. I don't know all there is to know about it."

She fell silent. She ought to ask questions, and part of her wanted to do that. To interrogate him, break down his story— or find out the truth of her condition.

She didn't want to know. Lily closed her eyes, tried to close off her thoughts. She was in bed with a man who was still a stranger to her in many ways. But worse was that she was a stranger to herself.

She needed to finish what she'd begun, find the answers to Carlos Fuentes's death. To Therese's. She was a cop. It wasn't just what she did; it was what she was. But a cop without a badge—What did that make her? "All in all, it's been a hell of a day."

"For both of us. These charges against you . . . we weren't lovers before, as they claim, but we are now. How will that affect you?"

She turned her head. The pillows were on the floor, as were most of the covers, so she looked straight at his face with nothing between them. "I'm probably sunk."

His face twisted. "I'm truly sorry."

If he was being straight with her, he'd had no choice, either. He was as trapped as she was, as unable to undo any of it. All she could do was go forward from where she was now. And now . . . it felt so right to lie here with him. Necessary.

And if that bothered her, she'd deal with it tomorrow.

"Distract me," she said and pressed a kiss to his shoulder, running her hand down his belly.

His breath sucked in.

Already the pleasure was rising in her again, drawn from her as easily as the sun draws mist from water. "You can't make any of it go away," she said, "but maybe, for awhile, I can forget." She nipped the side of his throat. "Maybe we both can."

EIGHTEEN

THEY were coming for him again.

Cullen lay on his back on the hard floor, picking up the vibrations from their footsteps with his body. He didn't get up. They thought he couldn't sense anything outside his cage, which was damned near true. Glass was miserable to work through, being all but impermeable to magic, and the walls and ceiling of his cage were heavy, tempered glass in a steel frame. The floor was rock, but with a mesh of power beneath it that resisted his seeking with painful efficiency. That mesh was tied to the nearby node, and the node was keyed to Her. The Old One these crazies worshiped.

Desperation can be a real mother, though. His had given birth to patience bordering on obsession. And he'd know about obsessions, wouldn't he?

They'd kept him alive at first for the novelty factor. A werewolf sorcerer? It wasn't supposed to be possible. He'd performed for her holiness three times now—the first time while in a great deal of pain.

The pain wasn't so bad now, but her staff kept her safe, damn it and her, while he did his tricks. It held more raw power than he'd ever seen, more than enough to control him. But she wasn't herself a sorcerer. She had power, vast power—and little more idea of how to use it than a child playing in the cockpit of a 747.

They needed him. They didn't trust him but wanted badly to use him. He'd had little trouble convincing them of his essential venality. "Ask anyone who knows me," he'd told her. "I'm a selfish sod. I can be bought—but money isn't my price."

There were disadvantages to having lived a thoroughly selfish life, though. No one would look for him. Max would grumble when he didn't show up to dance, but he wouldn't be alarmed. Rule—

The creak of the door had him sitting up. "She'll talk to you now."

That was the guard he'd dubbed the Hulk. He was big and stupid, and he had a temper . . . which, unfortunately, Cullen sometimes couldn't resist tweaking. It was so damnably boring here.

"But of course. I'd be delighted." He rose fluidly—that hadn't been taken from him, at least. His body and mind remained his own, much to his captors' frustration. "Am I presentable?" he asked. "I do so hate to look unkempt when I'm to spend time with a lady."

The blow to the side of his head from a wooden staff staggered him. "No talking. Put these on."

The handcuffs landed with a clink on the floor. He went still. The rage was getting harder to master, but he managed. It helped to picture her lithe body writhing in agony as fire consumed her.

He was good with fire.

The only outward sign he gave of his reaction was a single, shuddering breath. Then he bent, picked up the handcuffs, and slid his hands through the bracelets, locking them in place. "And my lovely necklace?"

He got another blow, of course, for speaking. "Come here."

He wanted to refuse, dearly wanted that. But the only way out of this cage—for now—lay in obeying. He stepped forward.

This was the part he hated most. Hard hands slid the silver choke chain over his head, snugging it around his neck.

Someone tugged on the other end of his leash. "Heel." Someone else laughed.

Such a simple sense of humor his guards possessed. The

same joke over and over, and it never failed to amuse them. Putting a leash and collar on the wolf-man was only part of the fun, though. The rest of the joke lay in teasing a blind man. Tripping him was always good for a laugh.

Cullen took a single step. He knew the contours of his glass cage very well, and his guards never entered it, so he was safe from their humor until he left it. He felt with his foot for the steel doorsill. . . .

A sharp tug on the collar almost overbalanced him. "I said heel, boy. Hurry up."

This time the rage won. He launched himself into space toward the one holding his chain.

The guards were only human. They couldn't react in time. He slammed into a big, hard body and managed to loop his cuffed hands over the man's head as they crashed to the floor. He landed on top and pushed up on one knee, using his forearms as a vise on the man's head. One good twist—

The pain hit, crippling him body and mind, making his arms spasm. Along with the rest of him. It was brief, though. An instant's overwhelming agony, then someone's foot rolled him off his tormentor and temporary victim.

Who was moaning, Cullen noted as he lay on his back, twitching like a dreaming dog, each little spasm sending shards of pain through his muscles. Apparently she'd zapped the Hulk, too. And that smell . . . the Hulk had pissed himself.

Cullen's mouth contorted painfully as the impulse to grin got tangled up by his scrambled nerves.

"Did you think I wasn't here?" A thin ghost of amusement brought a rare touch of life to that high, hated voice. She stood near his feet. "You must learn to master your impulses, Cullen. I can't allow you to damage my servants. Second . . ." The slight shift in sound told Cullen she'd turned. "I asked you to tell the men not to tease Cullen. It causes problems."

"I told them, Madonna."

"Then John disobeyed." That high, cool voice sounded so like a child's . . . and not childish at all.

"Madonna, please . . ." That was the Hulk. He was panting. "Please, make it stop."

"I have stopped, John. You're only feeling the echoes now. I advise you to stop trying to move; that makes it so much worse. But I do require an answer. You forced me to use power to keep him from killing you. Did I waste that power? Are you going to continue to disobey?"

"No, Madonna." He was sobbing now. "No, I obey you in everything."

"Try to remember that. Second, have him removed. He smells bad."

Cullen lay there recovering while they hauled John the Hulk away, whimpering. It was one of the best moments he'd had since a horde of ninja wanna-bes came crashing into his shack.

"I suspect you can stand up now," computer-girl said to him. "You're more durable than John, and it was such a brief punishment."

Was there any advantage in pretending weakness? Not enough, he decided. She was unpredictable. He inched his head around, able to "see" her by the power bound up in her staff, which wasn't a staff at all to his sorcerous vision, but a rent in reality outlined by pulsing red and purple energies. The reek of it made him want to snarl.

He smiled instead. His muscles were obeying him again, though it hurt like hell. "Shall I stand, then? You see how tractable I am, asking permission."

"Not tractable at all. But you are clever and supremely self-interested. You'll behave for now. Yes, stand. Second, take his leash and bring him to my quarters."

The slight swish of cloth told him she'd walked away.

Moving was a bitch. Cullen managed it without wetting himself or whimpering, a small triumph that helped him endure the walk to her quarters, directed by tugs on his collar and an occasional word.

His world wasn't completely dark. He was blind to the material world, yes, but he had other senses. He knew they were well belowground, for example; he even knew the approximate area from reading the ley lines that radiated from the node. Once they left the large main room that held his cage—he knew the room was big by the way sound behaved there—the air smelled of damp stone. It was some sort of tunnel, the walls and floor hacked out of the rock.

Sorcéri danced here, shifting auroras shed by the node that

was so close and so unavailable. But sorcéri weren't much help when it came to avoiding walls or crossing an uneven rock floor.

They'd put out his eyes while he was still unconscious. To keep him from escaping, he'd been told. He didn't buy it.

True, that was a time-honored means of discouraging sorcerers. During the Purge the authorities had blinded and maimed those they hadn't killed outright, cutting off their hands and removing their tongues. Couldn't cast a spell then, poor bastards. Couldn't wipe their own asses, either, so Cullen was glad he'd kept his hands. But he thought spite, not practicality, was the real reason for his blinding. Her holiness turned pettish when thwarted.

The sorcéri grew thicker as they neared the Madonna's rooms, which were very close to the node. There were tales of adepts in the old days who'd been able to use the dancing lines of energy with their minds alone, with no spoken or physical components to the spells. Cullen sighed. He was far from being an adept.

But so was she. She couldn't see the sorcéri and wouldn't miss what he harvested. He wasn't sure she knew they existed. Sorcéri weren't like ley lines; they were more of an energy leakage. Low in power compared to a node, but they *were* power.

Cullen couldn't call them to him by mind alone like an adept, but if he brushed against one, it was his. He stumbled for the fourth or fifth time—and collected a green line.

The chain tightened around his neck. "Two feet and turn left," the one she called Second told him. Cullen had noticed that names were low status for these people. Once they reached a certain level, they were always called by their titles.

Or maybe they still believed you gained power over a person through his name. Which was theoretically possible, but the spells for that had been lost long ago with the vanished Codex Arcanum—the Book of All Magic.

He made the two steps, turned, and didn't walk into a wall, which was a relief. The stink from her staff told him he'd arrived. The jerk on his collar confirmed it. He turned toward the staff and gave a little bow.

"He's a bit of a mess," a man's voice said, amused. "Can't you get him to wash?"

"You are so tidy, Patrick." That was *her*. The staff was, as usual, right beside her. "He might be able to make use of water if I allowed him enough to wash with. I'm not sure of the extent of his skill with magic. And having him washed by others could result in some of my servants being damaged. Cullen, this is the Most Reverend Patrick Harlowe. You will address him as Most Reverend."

"My pleasure, Most Reverend." Cullen offered another little bow in the general direction of the man's scent—easy to find, since he was wearing one of those musky men's colognes. "I apologize for my disheveled state."

"Quite understandable." The amusement deepened. It was a rich, mellow voice, the kind people consider charismatic. *A touch of a Gift there,* Cullen thought. "Won't you be seated? Ah—there's a chair to your left."

"Thank you." Cullen slid his foot to the side until he'd located the chair, identified which way it faced, and seated himself.

"You'll find a cup of tea on the table to your left," her frigid holiness said. "I believe it's still hot."

"Tea. How lovely." He found the cup—an awkward business with his hands cuffed in front of him, but he managed to pick it up and take a sip.

Nasty stuff. They could have offered him whiskey.

"How long will it take to grow your eyes back?" the Most Reverend person asked. "They don't seem to have done much healing yet."

"The lids have to regrow first." A lie, but worth trying. "Can't have bare eyeballs, can I? That should take about a week. It would go quicker if you let me have a blindfold. Given some protection, the eyeballs could get started. But faster may not be better, from my point of view. I'm wondering if I'll be allowed to keep them this time."

"You would be allowed much," said that light, dead voice, "if you were more reasonable."

"Ah, well. We have differing ideas of what's reasonable, don't we?" He set the cup back on its saucer, pleased that he managed it without fumbling. "I don't consider it reasonable to allow you to meddle with my mind."

"I'm not requiring you to remove your shields entirely. Just long enough for me to confirm what you say."

"And yet—forgive my distrustful nature—once I lower my shields, you could do pretty much whatever you wanted, couldn't you?" No sorcerer, this woman, which was why she was talking with him instead of killing him. They needed him. But she was a telepath, quite a strong one. And she had that thrice-cursed staff. She could stir his mind into a puddle of goo in short order. Or plant a compulsion to obey her, which was more likely.

"Where did you get these shields of yours?" Patrick asked. There was a clink of china, as if he were sharing in the little tea party. "Helen tells me she's never encountered any quite so complete."

Helen. The bitch's name was Helen. He closed his mind around the name greedily. "I traded for the spell that created them shortly before her holiness paid me that little visit."

"Oh, yes." Leather creaked as the man leaned forward. "The other sorcerer, the one we'd hoped to find. You said his name was Michael?"

"That's the name he used. I doubt it's his real name."

"And you have no idea where he went."

"None whatsoever." Though he'd give his eyes all over again to find out. The man owed him. "Nor any reason to lie to you about it. I don't care what happens to him."

"Yet if we found him, would we need you?" That was her again.

"Madonna, I couldn't say. You've told me so little about your plans." Though he knew a good deal more than they'd told him, having overheard things while in his cage. Maybe they thought glass stopped sound as well as magic. "But you have me, and you don't have him."

"*Do* we have you?" That was His Reverendness. "Your body, yes. But you won't let us into your mind, and you aren't committed to our cause. You don't worship Her."

Cullen shrugged. "I worship knowledge, and I'm very fond of power. The Madonna can give me both. I see no reason we can't deal."

She spoke. "You proposed some ways to test your sincerity the last time we spoke."

She seemed to be musing aloud, as if turning things over in her mind, but it rang false to Cullen. Her Bitchiness—Helen—never spoke without thinking first.

She'd decided how to use him. His heatbeat picked up, and it was all he could do to keep his face and posture easy. He had a chance.

"Most of your little tests involved killing you if you failed us." There was a rare touch of feeling in her voice—faint, but discernable. Killing him held some appeal for her. "But none of them involved killing others. Will you kill for me, Cullen?"

"Yes." It was like being back in school. Feed the teacher the answers she was looking for, win an A+.

"Just yes? You have no questions about who or how or why?"

"My questions involve payment. If I pass your test, what do I get?"

"Madonna." Patrick shifted in his chair, perhaps turning toward her. "He's entirely amoral. Is this the type of person we want working for us?"

"*With* us," she corrected gently. "We can't afford to have him work for us. He's too dangerous, too capable of turning on us. We must enlist him entirely."

"But if he won't give himself over to Her, how can we do that?"

Oh, yes, Cullen thought. The Patrick person was better at it than she was, but this conversation had been choreographed. They were leading him somewhere.

"We make sure he has every reason to please us. First, by giving him some of what he wants. Second, by making it impossible for him to survive without us. Cullen, you said you would kill for me."

"That's right."

"You would kill strangers? People you've never met?"

"If the price was right." His stomach knotted as he thought of one conversation he'd overheard.

"You would be paid in knowledge. I don't share power."

No kidding. "And perhaps better quarters."

"Perhaps." She was amused again. "What if I asked you to

kill in wolf form? In such a way that it would be obvious a lupus had done it?"

That surprised him. He let it show. "You don't want me to work magic for you?"

"Perhaps later, when you are bound more fully to us. Which you will be, once you have killed in wolf form. We will use you to destroy—"

"Helen!"

Patrick's protest sounded genuine, not planned. Interesting.

"We must tell him our goal, Patrick. He's bright enough to figure things out on his own. Better he knows now what he's agreeing to."

A pause. "You're right, as usual, Madonna."

"Cullen, you are aware of what I am."

He nodded. "A telepath, very strong. One of the rarest of the Gifts." Because of its tendency to drive its possessor crazy.

"Yes. My Gift allows Her to use me. To speak to me and sometimes to act through me." There was actual feeling in her voice now—a burning undercurrent, the throbbing passion of fanaticism. "She has rewarded me richly, far beyond my deserving, for my service, but the true reward is that contact with Her. I know what She wants, what She dreams of. It is my joy and delight to work to give that to Her, Cullen. But—" the amusement was back— "Her dream may not delight you."

Sometimes Teacher wants her students to ask questions. "And what is Her dream?"

"The first step is keeping the Species Citizenship Bill from passing, and we are well on the way to achieving that. But that is only the beginning. We will kill a number of people, Cullen. A great number, quite violently, all over the country. They will be lupus kills, and there will be no more talk of tolerance or legal standing for lupi. The American people will demand the extermination of *your* people, Cullen, because that is Her dream. The destruction of the lupi."

One good thing about lacking eyes. People were used to looking for reactions there, reading your feelings by what they saw in your eyes. Couldn't do that with him, could they?

"I have no people," Cullen said.

NINETEEN

MORNING sun striped the bed, falling in thin slices through the vertical blinds of the single window. Lily's bedroom wasn't that much bigger than the cell Rule had paced yesterday, and was almost as empty. Aside from the bed, there was a chest of drawers placed so she could watch the television on top of it. That was it for furnishings, though there was a large, unframed print over the bed—something Oriental, Rule remembered. He couldn't see it from where he lay.

It wasn't the light that had woken him, though. It was the seventeen-pound cat sitting on his chest.

"You don't approve, do you?" Rule murmured. He didn't make the mistake of moving so much as a finger. Harry was enjoying his dominant position too much. He'd be sure to punish any suggestion of independence on Rule's part. "You'll adjust," he told the cat.

As Rule would have to do, too. There would be huge changes in his life, the shape of which he couldn't yet see clearly. But there were some perks involved for him. He doubted that Harry saw a brighter side to Rule's intrusion.

Lily made a sleepy sound and nestled closer.

As a boy, Rule had heard tales of Chosen who'd killed or died for each other. Thrilling tales, heroic and satisfying to a child. But there were cautionary tales, too, of Chosen who couldn't accept the bond or adapt to the other. Tales of suicide and insanity.

Then there had been Benedict's example. Rule didn't know the whole story, but he knew its outcome. He'd seen the shadows cast by wounds that couldn't heal.

In spite of the grim tales, the Chosen state was celebrated. Rule hadn't understood that. To be chosen was to be set apart from other lupi. Already, because of his birth and his position in the clan, there was distance between him and the rest. He hadn't wanted anything that would further separate him. Nor had he wanted any one person to mean so much. What could possibly be worth such a risk?

Lily rolled onto her stomach, poking him in the ribs with her elbow. And his heart turned over.

He understood now. "Lily," he murmured, "I think Dirty Harry wants to be fed. I'm hoping he has cat food, not fresh meat, in mind."

"What?" She lifted her head and frowned at him from behind a curtain of tangled hair. "Good Lord. It wasn't a dream."

"No." He started to reach for her, to smooth the hair out of her face. Harry growled. "Ah . . . does he usually sleep with you?"

"He?" She shoved her hair back herself and twisted her head. "Oh." A smile tugged at her mouth. "Looks particularly evil this morning, doesn't he?"

"I suspect he's hoping I'd take the hint and leave."

"Mmm."

"Were you," he asked carefully, "hoping the same thing?"

Her eyes met his. She shook her head but didn't speak.

"Or wishing last night hadn't happened?

She took her time responding. "Can't put the genie back in the bottle. And it would be hard"—at last, slowly, a smile—"if not impossible, to wish away last night. But this morning is complicated."

Harry decided he'd been left out of the conversation long enough. He stood, stretched, and planted his front feet on Lily's shoulder, staring at her intently.

She shoved him aside. "All right, Harry. Move it, and I'll get up."

The cat jumped down, and Rule thought wistfully about

delaying her for thirty minutes or so. But she was right. This morning was indeed complicated.

Lily rolled over and got out of bed. "Come on, Harry. Food for you, a shower for me. And for you"—she looked at Rule— "questions. Some of which I should have asked last night."

He sighed. "Of course. You always have questions."

"That's my approach to most things. The trick is finding the right questions." She turned, opened the closet, and took out a robe. It was pretty, a bright blue silk, but not as pretty as her skin.

"You have coffee beans?" he asked hopefully, swinging his feet to the floor. "A grinder? I could put some coffee on."

She disappointed him. "There's some already ground," she told him as she stepped into the tiny bathroom. "Coffeepot's by the stove. Feed Harry, will you?" The door closed. The cat stopped next to it, offended.

He looked at the cat. "I think she wants us to bond, Harry." Harry glared and twitched his tail.

"True. But I'll feed you anyway."

LILY took her time in the shower, hoping to wash some clarity into her head. Nothing was right this morning. She ought to concentrate on how to defend herself, she thought as she lathered her hair. But she hadn't seen the charges against her yet. She was suspended pending charges, but didn't know exactly what she was up against.

She'd worry about that later, she decided, and rinsed.

Damn Randall, anyway. The sense of betrayal went deep. She ought to be getting ready for work right now. She had leads. She needed to talk to the Azá's Most Reverend guy. Then there were Ginger and Mech. Ginger had lied about seeing Rule. Mech had been all too eager to frame Rule. They were part of it.

And she wasn't. The Feds would follow up with Ginger and Mech, not her. At least, she wasn't supposed to. . . .

When she emerged, she knew Rule had found her coffee. The aroma drew her out of the bedroom as soon as she'd pulled some clothes on. He'd also found her stereo, which she kept on the shelf in the coat closet. And her CDs. Several of them were scattered on the floor.

But he wasn't playing her music. He was listening to opera on the radio. Standing there totally naked in her living room, listening to a soprano warble through some aria.

"Rule," Lily said, appalled. "It's seven-thirty in the morning."

He cast her an amused glance and turned the volume down. "Not an opera fan, I take it."

"No." She frowned at the mess. "Don't you think you should put some clothes on?"

"If it makes you more comfortable." He turned to face her. His body expressed its interest at seeing her, and he smiled.

"I need coffee," she said and retreated to the kitchen. "Where's Harry?"

"He ate and ran. I hope it was okay to let him out."

"Can't keep him in. He lived on the streets too long to be happy with walls twenty-four/seven." She noticed Harry's food dish was nearly full. Rule had given him way more than he was supposed to have.

Lily filled a mug with coffee and stayed where she was, sipping. Given the size of her apartment, the kitchen afforded only a semblance of privacy. But she needed that semblance.

It had been a long time since she'd woken up beside a man. Even longer since that man had been here, in her space. She couldn't decide how she felt about it. Confused, mostly. She liked having him here . . . or maybe that wasn't her, but the mate bond thing, screwing with her mind.

She'd figure out how she felt later. For now . . . how did this Chosen business work? How could she find out? Even if Rule was being completely honest with her, he might have some of it wrong. It seemed to have religious connotations for him, and religion sometimes kept people from asking the right questions. If you think you already have all the answers, you stop asking.

All Lily had were questions. It was time to go ask some of them. She took a last swallow of coffee went back into the living room.

He'd pulled on his jeans and was replacing the CDs he'd

hauled out. Which was good, but— "They're organized by type, and alphabetical by artist within each type."

He glanced at her, eyebrows lifted. "Tell me you don't alphabetize your spices, too."

"I might, if I cooked."

He went back to replacing the CDs. "This is going to be a challenge for both of us."

"What do you mean?"

"You'll understand when you see my apartment."

She rubbed her chest, where the skin felt oddly tight. That jumpy feeling was back. "You're making assumptions based on your beliefs. I'm more into evidence than belief."

"I suppose a cop would be." He slid the final CD back in place and turned. "I thought you might like opera. You have a lot of classical music."

"Instrumentals. I played violin at one time." She caught herself moving toward him, stopped, and scowled. "It's pulling me, isn't it? Making me want to touch you."

"We need to touch, yes." He came to her and put his hands on her arms. "Is that so terrible?"

"I don't like being forced. I don't like having something make me need this." But when he pulled her to him, she leaned into his embrace, laying her head on his chest.

He was too tall. She'd never liked men who were this much taller than her . . . but his heartbeat steadied her, wiping away the jumpiness, leaving her both calm and revved, ready to go. "It isn't even sex. I mean—that's there, but sex isn't all of it."

"No." He ran a hand down her back. "For the first few weeks, especially, we'll both need the feel of the other, the physical contact."

"Like an addict needs a fix." She pulled away. "Well, I've had mine for the time being."

He wasn't happy. "Have you noticed that there are two of us involved? What if I didn't get my fix yet?"

"I . . ." What was she supposed to do? Make him suffer— make both of them suffer? But if she gave in, allowed her craving to win, she wouldn't be *her* anymore. Something else would be driving. "I'm scared."

"I know. But this isn't a habit you can kick with some

twelve-step program. The sooner you accept that, the easier it will be."

"We'll see." God, the jitters were back. As soon as she stopped touching him, they came back. "How far can we be away from each other without having dizzy spells?"

"It varies, but . . . not far," he admitted. "We won't always be pulled this hard. Sometimes a Chosen pair can be many miles apart for a time. Not with comfort, but it becomes possible for some. Mating will have tightened the bond for us, though, so for the next few weeks we'll need to stay close. After that—"

"Wait a minute. You didn't say anything about sex tightening the bond." She felt panicky. "You mean it's worse now?"

"It will be, for a time. Lily, we had no choice. We're free to choose how we deal with the bond. We aren't free to refuse it."

"That's your belief."

"It is fact." He looked as if he wanted to shake her. "If you fight the need too long, you go crazy."

"*This* is crazy." She gave in to one need and started pacing. "But I'll sort it out later." Her list of things to deal with later was getting longer. "For now," she added with grim humor, "it looks like you're going to be a big part of my investigation."

"I thought you'd been taken off the investigation."

"That's going to make it tricky."

"Lily—" He stopped, glanced at the door. Two seconds later, the doorbell rang.

She hadn't heard anything. Obviously, he had. "You take some getting used to," she muttered and went to the door.

The peephole showed her Croft's chocolate face. Great. Should she ask Rule to hide? No, dumb idea. It would be too easy to prove he'd been here all night. It went against the grain to play cover-up, anyway.

She sighed and unlocked the door. "You're out early."

"We need to talk to you," Croft said. Karonski stood behind him, scowling. "May we come in?"

"Why not? There's coffee."

Karonski brightened marginally. "With creamer?"

"I've got milk." She stepped aside and let them in.

TWENTY

NEITHER of the federal agents looked surprised at finding Rule in her living room, half-dressed. Karonski nodded at him. Croft did seem discomfited when he realized there was only one chair.

"You can wrestle for who gets the chair. The yellow pillow's mine," Lily told them, retreating to her tiny kitchen. "Let me know who wins."

No one took the chair. When she came back with four mugs, sugar, and a little glass of milk on a tray, they were sitting around the square coffee table she used as a dining table.

The pair from the FBI looked funny sitting on the floor in their suits. Rule looked bare and quite unbothered by it. He was talking to Karonski. "Surely you can do something."

Karonski shook his head. "Doesn't work that way. Not only would the locals resent the hell out of it if we tried to interfere, we don't—hey, here's the coffee."

Lily put the tray on the table. "Help yourselves." She looked at Rule. "Were you asking them to intervene with the captain for me?"

He shrugged. "Yes."

"Like he said, it doesn't work that way." She went to her oversize chair and retrieved the folders she'd brought home. She brought them with her to the table.

The yellow pillow was next to Rule. She hesitated. Better if she had the table between them. The need to touch him was strong and sneaky. It would be embarrassing if she started groping him or something.

Embarrassing, too, if she asked everyone to move so she didn't have to sit next to the man she'd woken up beside. She'd just have to watch herself.

She sat tailor-fashion on the pillow. "I assume you want to ask me some questions about the Fuentes investigation, since it relates to yours. This has copies of my reports to date." She handed Croft a folder. "And this is yours." The second folder she held out was the one he'd given her. The one about Rule.

Croft and Karonski exchanged a glance. Croft spoke. "We do have some questions, but that isn't our priority."

Karonski snorted. "Skip the fancy lead-in. We're here because we want to recruit you."

Her jaw dropped.

"We believe your captain made a serious misjudgment," Croft said with that pleasant smile. "One we hope to take advantage of."

She shook her head. "Wait a minute. The FBI doesn't go around recruiting police officers who are neck deep in disciplinary shit. You don't recruit individuals at all."

"The FBI as a whole doesn't, no. We're MCD. We operate less bureaucratically."

Karonski had already turned his coffee pale with milk and was busy loading it with sugar. "What the hell. Let's go ahead and brag. Turner already knows, and she'll have to." He leaned forward. "We're not just Magical Crimes Division, we're part of a hotshot unit within it. Hush-hush stuff. We've got the authority to hire on the spot, and we want you. You're not an idiot. You know why."

"Because I'm a sensitive." It left a sour taste in her mouth. "A touch sensitive."

"Which makes you one in a million. We need you."

"Forget it. I don't out people."

"We don't do that," Croft said. "True, MCD has been responsible for identifying lupi and others in the past, but that's never been the unit's job. We're sent on the unusual cases, the ones where special knowledge or abilities may be needed."

She glanced at Karonski.

He grinned and added another spoonful of sugar. "Like witchcraft, yeah. With some prep I was able to confirm what you told us about Martin's murder." He took a sip of the noxious brew he'd made of his coffee and sighed with contentment. "Sorcery, all right. Nasty business."

"And you?" She looked at Croft, curious in spite of herself. "I didn't pick up anything when we shook hands."

"Not everyone in the unit is Gifted. I'm just an experienced field agent with an unusual hobby. I've a rather broad knowledge of magical systems, persons, and creatures."

Karonski chuckled. "He's an egghead with a weird obsession. Useful, but weird."

Rule spoke coldly. "Is that why you won't help her clear her name? You wish to recruit her. It's to your advantage if she's off the force."

"We can't help. We could put in a word for her, sure, but Randall has a thing about Feds, and he can't stand Croft. They bumped heads on another case a few years back. If either of us speaks up for her, it's likely to backfire."

"*You* could do more than speak up for her."

Karonski looked pained. "Persuasion spells are illegal."

Lily slapped the table. "Hold it. Just hold on, both of you. I do not need anyone fighting my battles for me, and I'm not off the force. Suspended for now, and I may get demoted for unprofessional conduct. But it isn't likely I'll be kicked off."

Croft looked worried. "You may be underestimating your risk. If Captain Randall did tip the killer off about Therese Martin, you're a major threat to him."

"I don't think it's him. I don't have any evidence, but I can't buy it. He's a *cop*." She looked at the two skeptical cops listening to her. "Randall doesn't just do the job, he *is* the job. He couldn't step outside it enough to set up a murder and a frame. Not for any reason."

Karonski nodded. "I hear you. But sometimes a cop starts thinking the job is justice. They break rules because their idea of justice is more important than the law."

"Not Randall."

He and Croft exchanged one of those looks. Croft spoke. "You've worked with the man. Your opinion is part of the picture. But we want more than your opinions. We want you to continue with your investigation—only for us."

"You mean . . ." Her mouth was suddenly dry. She licked her lips. "You want to recruit me right this minute. Sign me up, and I can keep the investigation. Both of them, really—Fuentes and Martin—since they're linked."

"That's right. You'd be working with Abel and me."

"Don't you have to run me? A security check, deep background . . . oh," she said, reading their faces. "You already have."

"We haven't got the deep background check yet," Croft said. "Just the basics."

The basics would be enough. Twenty years was a long time, but it had been in the papers. She looked at the two men—one dark, urbane, and smiling, the other rumpled and pushy. They knew, and they weren't asking questions. That was a mark in their favor.

Karonski was leaning toward her again. She could almost feel him pushing at her, willing her to agree. "We don't just want you because you're a sensitive, though God knows that's important. We need someone who can't be fooled by magic. Lately there's been—"

"Abel," Croft said, giving him a warning look.

Surprisingly, it was Rule who finished Karonski's sentence. "An increase in the number of magical crimes committed?" he suggested. "More odd reports coming in. Reports of unlikely or inexplicable events."

Croft gave him a hard look. "What do you know about it?"

"Not enough. *Was* a banshee sighted in Texas?"

The two agents exchanged a glance. "I'll need to know your source, Turner," Croft said. "But we can discuss that later."

Karonski turned back to Lily. "We need you because you're a sensitive, yeah. But you're also a cop, a good one. Not many Gifted go into law enforcement. There are still laws on the books in several states prohibiting it, for one thing."

"Not to mention federal regulations," Lily said dryly. "Yet here you are."

"We don't operate under the same regs as the rest of the Bureau," Croft said. "That's one reason we don't advertise our existence."

"The point is," Karonski said, "you're already trained. We need you on this one because you know the case, the city, the people involved. And you've got one hell of an in with the lupus community." He glanced at Rule and waggled his eyebrows.

"And you don't have a problem with that?" she demanded. "You come here, find Rule running tame in my place, and you don't question my involvement with him? My judgment?"

Croft spread his hands. "As I understand it, you had little choice. Which is another reason to consider our offer. You might have some difficulty explaining a necessary association with Turner to your superiors on the police force. We'll be glad to work around whatever, um, special requirements are necessary."

Her head swung toward Rule. "You *told* them?"

But he was looking at Croft with that peculiar, threatening stillness. "The existence of the Chosen isn't known outside the clans."

Croft met Rule's eyes, unfazed. "I know people in the clans."

"Okay, fine." She pushed to her feet. "You two go ahead and duke it out. I need to think." She started to pace but reached the wall and stopped, hugging her elbows. She needed space, time, and privacy to consider her options. She wasn't likely to get any of them.

Lily didn't hear Rule stand and come toward her; she *felt* him draw near. He stopped behind her and put his arms around her . . . and, with a sigh, she leaned into his body.

"You're used to dividing your life into tidy compartments marked Professional and Personal," he murmured. "It's uncomfortable for you when they slop over into each other."

She grimaced. "Uncomfortable isn't the word I'd use." Almost everything had fallen in the Professional pile the past few years, but he was right. She hated having the job invaded by her personal life. She hated needing his touch, and she hated the FBI agents for being there, because she was beginning to need more than a touch. Yet as the warmth of his body seeped into her, her thoughts began to settle.

Their offer was tempting. Terribly tempting. She could work with people who valued her more unusual abilities instead of having to hide them. She could finish what she'd started with this investigation, and do it wearing a badge. But she'd have to turn her back on Homicide. For years, that had been her one goal: to be good enough to work Homicide.

When she turned back to face the two FBI agents, Rule kept one arm around her waist. She didn't pull away. "I'd have to resign from the department to accept your offer."

Croft's eyebrows rose slightly. "Well, yes."

"I'm not willing to do that. I'm not sure what I'll decide, long term, but I don't want to leave the force right now. Wait," she said when Karonski started to speak. "I've got an offer of my own. I want to stay on the case, and you want me there. Why don't I give this deal you're offering a test drive? I could serve as your expert consultant."

Karonski's mouth snapped shut. He looked at Croft, the two of them wearing identically surprised expressions. Beside her, Rule chuckled.

"What do you think?" she said. "You'd have to clear it with the department, of course. I'd suggest going up the ladder for that. The captain isn't likely to approve it."

A smile spread over Croft's face. "I think something could be arranged. And it won't do you any harm to be requested by us while you're on suspension, will it?"

Karonski nudged his partner. "We'll get Brooks to call the chief. He's got the pull, and he talks almost as slick as you do. Time he made himself useful."

"Brooks?" she said.

"The boss. He runs the unit."

A flicker of panic touched Lily. She didn't know anything about this unit of theirs, and she'd just agreed to work for them. No, she corrected—*with* them. Temporarily. It was all temporary.

Rule's thumb stirred little circles on her waist through the silk of her T-shirt. "It's getting confusing, isn't it?" he murmured. "I think I'm now an expert consultant to an expert consultant."

Heat was pooling in her stomach. Touching him was more distraction than comfort now. She moved away and ran a hand through her hair—still damp from her shower, she noted. She always blew it dry right away, but this morning she hadn't.

Nothing was the way it was supposed to be. "Why am I

doing this? I'm a color-inside-the-lines sort of person. This is so far outside the lines I—" Over by the chair, her purse chimed. Or, rather, the phone in it did. She glanced that way. "Damn."

"You're doing it because you want to stop a killer," Rule said quietly. "And the lines keep moving."

"Yes." She met his eyes. "I guess they do."

Her phone chimed again. "I'd better get that. What do you think?" she asked the others as she crossed the room. "Have we got a deal?"

Croft nodded. "We do."

"Good." It was good, wasn't it? She pulled out her phone and touched the Talk button without looking at it. "Yu here."

"Have you heard from your Grandmother?" her mother asked. "She's disappeared."

"Disappeared?" Alarm shot through her. "What do you mean? How long has she been gone?"

"Well, not disappeared, exactly. But she is gone. Li Qin tells me not to worry, but how can I not worry with the wedding only three weeks away?"

Lily sat on the edge of the chair. "Li Qin knows where she went?"

"Not that she'll tell me. Grandmother asked her not to discuss it." Julia sniffed. "I suppose it's too much to expect that your grandmother would tell her own daughter-in-law when she leaves town. But why did she leave? This is not like her. She never travels, and to take off like this, just before the wedding, without a word to me . . ." Her voice lowered. "Do you think she could be getting . . . well, you know. She *is* old."

Lily swallowed a bubble of hysteria. "I don't think Grandmother is going senile."

"I didn't say that. I just wondered . . . ah, well. You haven't heard from her?"

"I spoke to her a couple days ago," Lily said carefully. "She said something about getting in touch with an old friend. I thought she meant by phone, but maybe she intended to travel to see this friend." To collect on that favor she was owed . . . by someone.

Her mother grumbled a bit more about Grandmother's odd behavior. Lily didn't really listen. She'd have to tell her family she was suspended. God, she hated that. She could just imagine what her mother would say.

Maybe she could get everything cleared up quickly, before she had to tell them. "Sorry. What did you say?" she asked when she noticed that a pause had fallen. "My mind drifted for a moment."

"I reminded you to get your dress fitted, and I asked if you'd found a date yet."

A date?

"For the rehearsal dinner," Julia said, reading her mind in the uncanny way mothers have. "You've been putting me off. Have you even tried to find a date?"

"No, but—"

"This is a formal dinner, Lily. You simply can't attend without an escort. Your father and I would lose face."

The face argument was impossible to counter. "All right. No problem. I'll bring a date."

"Who? Have you found someone?"

Lily's gaze went to Rule. That bubble of hysteria was back. "As a matter of fact, I have."

RULE was supposed to give a press conference. He also needed clothes. After discussion, it was decided that Croft would handle both chores. He needed to issue a statement anyway, informing the press about the FBI's new role in the investigation. Otherwise, as Croft said dryly, they'd just make up stuff. He could tell them that Rule was "assisting the investigation" and had been asked not to talk to them at this time.

Rule couldn't even go get his own clothes. Not unless Lily went with him. They didn't know how far they could stretch the mate bond, but his apartment was almost certainly too far away.

Lily was making a second pot of coffee. Rule lounged in the doorway—there really wasn't room in her kitchen for both of them—finishing an apple. Apples were the closest she'd been able to come to actual breakfast food, since the bread had turned out to be moldy.

She filled the pot and slid back in place. "Is this joined-at-the-hip business as weird to you as it is to me?"

"It's disconcerting. I never expected it to happen to me."

"You said it was rare."

"Yes, and . . ." He hesitated. "The Lady has never gifted a Lu Nuncio with a Chosen. Not since the days of the old tales, at least, and those are as much myth as history. This is unprecedented."

"I guess the odds caught up with you. You were pretty much blindsided, too."

"I did at least know such things were possible, but yes." Another pause. "My brother had a Chosen."

Had? She faced him. "Which brother?"

"Benedict. It worked out badly for him."

She studied a face turned suddenly impenetrable. "You don't want to talk about it."

"I'm averse to turning my brother's tragedy into a cautionary tale. Though it makes a good one." Obviously ready to change the subject, he moved forward. "Where's your trash?"

Her skin prickled as he drew near. Her heart beat faster, and she wanted to touch him, to lay her hand on that firm chest and see if his heartbeat had quickened, too.

She stepped back. "Organic wastes go in the little ceramic container under the sink, for composting."

He found it and deposited his apple core. "You care for the environment?"

"I'm a gardener. We're greedy about organics."

He smiled slowly. "You're greedy about other things, too, as I recall."

Heat climbed in her face—and throbbed lower down. It infuriated her. She turned away. "We need to get to work. Karonski's waiting."

"Lily." He stopped her when she tried to go past. "Don't fight it too hard. Animals who gnaw their legs off to escape a trap bleed to death."

"How do you expect me to react? I've known you five days, and we're supposedly bound for life. How am I supposed to deal with that?" She pulled her arm away. "Don't crowd me."

Karonski had spread papers and files all over her coffee table. "If you two lovebirds have finished billing and cooing, we need—okay, okay," he said hastily when he saw Lily's face. "No lovebird jokes. Got it."

"I have a couple questions," Lily began.

"Naturally," Rule murmured, entering the room behind her and crossing to the table, where he made himself comfortable. He picked up one of the folders—the one containing copies of her official reports, she noted. Karonski didn't object. Apparently they were letting the civilian in on everything.

Which might be okay if the civilian was equally forthcoming with them. She was fairly sure he hadn't been. She frowned at Rule's bent head.

"You had questions?" Karonski prompted her.

"Right. First, you only found out yesterday that I'm a sensitive, yet you've already got a background check on me. Even for you people, that's quick. You had me checked out before, didn't you?"

"We ran backgrounds on several of the players involved in this," Karonski agreed. "Didn't know which way things would shake down, but we wanted to be ready."

"Ready for what? That's what doesn't make sense. Why are you two here in the first place?"

"The boss is a precog. He says go, we go."

Startled, she stared for a moment. "I thought the government didn't use them because they weren't reliable."

"Brooks tests at about seventy percent. I figure that's low; the tests are pretty boring, and precognition picks up the juicy bits better. Stuff with some emotion attached."

"I've never heard of a precog hitting seventy percent. Not consistently."

"He doesn't pick up on everything, but when he does get something, he's right. Croft thinks Brooks has a touch of elf in him. Be interesting to see how you read him when you two meet."

"*If* we meet. I haven't agreed to join your unit. One more question. How do you know Rule?"

Karonski grinned. "He consulted on another case of mine, back before I teamed up with Martin here. Had ourselves a pretty good time after we wrapped things up."

She glanced at the ring on his finger.

He caught it. "Hey, I wasn't married then. But my party days are over now, and this one's far from being wrapped up, so we'd better get busy. We need to bring you up to speed on what we've got," he said, sorting through the debris on her table. "Mostly background, like I said. But some of it makes for interesting reading. Now where . . . oh, here it is." He handed her a folder.

Her eyebrows lifted. "You have a whole folder on the Azá?" Rule looked up.

"That's just the recent stuff. We've been watching them since they set up shop in L.A. three years ago."

"So who or what are they?" Rule asked.

"They originated in Great Britain but claim to go back to ancient Egypt. Cults go for that sort of thing—ancient heritage, knowledge passed down in secret. Makes 'em more interesting. We watch them because they've been tied to death magic."

"Death magic!"

"Animal, not human, and nothing's been proven against them since they crossed the big puddle. But yeah, they source some of their rites on animal sacrifice."

"Ugly." She began skimming the file. "I never heard of this goddess of theirs. Ani—"

"Uh—don't say it, okay?"

"Why not?" She looked up, caught his sheepish expression. "Oh, come on. Name magic has been obsolete since the Purge."

"I know, I know. But Brooks told me not to say the name. Not to let anyone with any magic in them say it, either." He shrugged. "He doesn't know why. But when he warns me specific like that, I listen."

"Let me see that." Rule reached for the page she'd been reading.

Lily handed it to him, frowning. His voice sounded odd.

He glanced at it, his eyes scanning quickly—then stopping. He sat motionless for a long moment.

"What is it?" she asked. "You said you hadn't heard of the Azá."

"Them, no. But Her . . ." At last he looked up. "Have you ever had a legend jump up and bite you on your ass?"

"Quite recently," she said without thinking.

Surprised pleasure flashed across his face. "Thank you."

Karonski cleared his throat. "So you've heard of this goddess of theirs? She's part of your legends?"

"Legend, history . . . the two become tangled after a few thousand years. But yes, I've heard of Her. She is the reason my people exist."

"She's your Lady?" Lily asked, finding the idea distasteful. "The female version of Deity that you worship?"

"You misunderstand." He met her gaze, his eyes hooded and dark. "My Lady is Her enemy. We were created to destroy Her."

TWENTY-ONE

CULLEN lay on his side with his hands carefully disposed. As a token of his slightly improved status, they'd given him a mattress and a lightweight blanket. He was still very much a prisoner, but they wanted him to believe he would be treated well once he'd proven himself.

Right. He sneered at the blackness surrounding him. And he believed in Santa, too.

No question that the mattress was more comfortable, but otherwise it was a damned nuisance. The power grid beneath his cell had been hard enough to trace when he was lying directly on the floor. Now he had a mattress between him and it.

But the blanket was pure blessing. A blind man in a glass cage never knows when he's being watched, but the blanket provided a smidgeon of privacy. If one of them saw the slight movements of his hands beneath it, they'd probably think he was playing with himself.

Lord knows there wasn't much else to do . . . aside from what he was really doing, that is. Weaving sorcéri.

Spells were normally woven with words, material objects, or a combination of the two, and could be powered various ways. Working directly with sorcéri was about half-mad, he supposed, for anyone short of an adept. But in theory, it could be done. The idea was to make his own spell bits match the fluid patterns of the grid closely enough to slip them into it. Once enough of them were in place, he could take control of the grid. Theoretically.

In practice, he might succeed in blowing himself and his glass cage into teensy-weensy pieces. If that happened, he hoped Helen was standing very close by.

Funny. He'd never believed those stories about the Great Wars and how his people had been created to serve as warriors for one side. The side of truth and justice, of course. The good guys.

Oh, he'd believed there had been a conflict—a tremendous, realms-wide conflict—in the remote past. Before the Codex Arcanum was lost, that much had been accepted as fact, so it was probably true. But the tales handed down among lupi were of heros and villains, gods and goddesses. Those he'd dismissed as myths. No oral history could have held onto so much detail over such vast amounts of time. Besides, the good guys were the ones who lived to pass on their version. Obviously his side had survived.

It had taken one whiff of that staff to change his mind.

Maybe he didn't know how to spot the good guys, Cullen thought as he painstakingly urged a crimson sorcéri into the proper pattern. But he knew who the bad guys were now.

He studied the pattern he'd made. It looked right . . . only one way to find out. He let one hand slip off the mattress, his fingertips touching the floor, and began easing his spell into the grid beneath.

At first the voices were an annoyance, a distraction to close out. Then he realized that one of them was familiar—and not from his stay here. Startled, he let go of the spelled line. It vanished into the grid.

". . . not happy with . . . Turner is still . . . must be stopped."

That was Her Frigidness, too far away for him to catch all the words. He spared a second's focus to check on his spell. It seemed to have integrated smoothly. . . .

". . . not exactly thrilled, either, Madonna. Removing him is . . . joined you. Which is why . . . came here today."

And *that* was the voice he'd recognized. Mick Roberts. Rule's brother.

"Not looking as pretty as usual, is he?" That was Mick again, amused, standing right outside Cullen's cage.

No point in pretending he didn't hear. Mick would know better. Cullen swung his legs around and sat up, facing in the general direction of the voices. "Hello, Mick. Fancy meeting you here."

"He knows you're here," she said, shocked.

"Of course he does. You didn't remove his ears along with his eyes. Hello, Cullen. I hear you're trying to talk your way out of that cage."

"We do what we can," he said mildly. The nausea came as a surprise. He hadn't thought he possessed enough ideals for betrayal to affect him so viscerally, but talking to Mick made him ill. "You don't seem to be in one."

Mick laughed. "Same old Cullen. But there's more to you than I'd realized, isn't there? The Madonna here tells me you tinker with sorcery. For shame."

"Speaking of shame, why are you out there, chatting up the Madonna? I expect that kind of behavior from me, but you're supposed to be a cut above a lowly clanless type."

"Don't be comparing yourself to me." Mick's voice throbbed with a sudden influx of emotion. Anger, mostly, with a healthy serving of contempt. "I'm fighting to save my clan. You're just trying to save your own sorry hide."

"Forgive me for being dense, but I'm not quite following you. You've allied yourself with our hereditary enemy and are doing your best to kill your father and destroy your brother . . . for the good of the clan?"

"You always were a fool. The Rho would destroy us all with his political pipe dreams. He'll destroy the Challenge and turn us into imitation humans, pale copies of those who have never heard the Lady's call. I won't let that happen."

Mick's voice was hard now. Determined. It reminded Cullen of Rule . . . a sad, twisted version of Rule. "Well, to each his own. Um . . . I can't help wondering. My lamentable curiosity, you know. You *are* aware she can read your mind, aren't you?" At the very least. It was supposed to be impossible to actually take over another person's mind, but she had a lot of power in that staff . . . though he couldn't imagine any lupus allowing such an abomination to touch him.

Mick laughed. "Not mine, or any other lupus's. You really are a fool, aren't you? She whom the Madonna serves can't affect us that way."

But She didn't have to. The cold bitch who was Her priestess had her own Gift—possibly augmented by power from the goddess, but not originating with Her. Cullen suspected this wasn't the time for a lecture on the differences between sorcery and the Gifts, however. "Did you stop by to buck up my spirits? How considerate. I'm feeling better already."

"I wanted to see you in your cage. I thought I'd enjoy that—and I was right."

The Madonna spoke. Her high voice came through the glass softly but quite clearly. "Mick has a notion about how to use you. I had planned another means for you to prove yourself, but I rather like his idea. It allows me to make sure of you and advances our cause at the same time, and we wouldn't have to wait until your eyes finish regrowing."

"Beguiled by efficiency, are you?" Cullen spoke lightly, but his heartbeat accelerated. He wasn't ready. The grid wasn't under his control yet. Though he was close—

"It all depends on how flexible your sense of loyalty is," she went on. "Mick assures me it's extremely flexible. But you consider yourself a friend of Rule Turner, don't you?"

"Sure. Rule's a female magnet. Not that I have any problems attracting women, but they fall over him in such numbers, he couldn't possibly service them all. I take care of the overflow."

"I don't care to hear about your sexual habits." Distaste thickened her voice. He'd noticed that the lovely Helen hated any reference to sex. "Are you willing to lure him to us?"

He smiled. "What do I get in return?"

"Aninnas wishes to eat him. If She doesn't get to, she might settle for a werewolf sorcerer."

"You do know how to motivate a guy."

AT eleven-thirty, Rule was on his way to see Ginger. With Lily, of course. He'd won the toss for who would drive, so they were in his car.

Croft was pulling more data on the Church of the Faithful.

Karonski was going to pay a visit to Internal Affairs and see what they'd learned about Mech and Randall. Lily had wanted a shot at Ginger.

It would have been practical to split into a different set of pairs—Lily with Croft, Rule with Karonski—but the mate bond made that impossible. Even if it hadn't, Rule had no intention of letting her out of his sight. Lily was a threat to the killers and to the rogue cop working with them. He wasn't taking any chances with her.

They'd gone looking for Cullen first. He still wasn't home, and a call to Max confirmed that he hadn't seen or heard from Cullen, either. Rule was annoyed with himself for worrying. Cullen went off for weeks sometimes, playing with some snippet of a spell he'd uncovered. He was always rooting around in old manuscripts and journals looking for that sort of thing.

"You're sure Seabourne's a sorcerer?" Lily asked for the third time. "Not just someone with a bit of a Gift who wants to sound interesting?"

"Lupi don't have Gifts."

"You aren't supposed to be sorcerers, either."

True. "He casts spells that are sourced outside himself. That's the definition of sorcery, isn't it?"

"How do you know where they're sourced? You can't see or sense magic."

Out of patience, he snapped, "He was stripped of his clan because he wouldn't give up sorcery, which suggests his motives go a little deeper than wanting to sound interesting. They must have thought he was the real thing. And that," he added with a sigh, "is more than I should have told you."

"I'll keep it private, unless—"

"Unless you can't. Understood." He was beginning to regret telling her about Cullen. But when he'd realized the identity of the Old One that was stirring this pot, he'd felt she and the two Feds needed to know everything he did.

Cullen had been studying what he called disturbances in the flow that made him think the relationships between the realms were shifting. He'd sensed a connection to Nokolai, some kind of conspiracy, and come to Rule. Using Rule as the focus for a more complex spell, he'd discovered a plan to kill the Rho—slightly too late.

She touched his arm. "I won't out him, Rule. Not unless he's guilty of more than practicing an illegal art. Though I have to say, this is the first time my privacy policy has protected a sorcerer."

"Cullen says sorcery has gotten a bad rep. That it's not inherently good or evil, no more than electricity is."

"That's what I always thought, too. Magic doesn't carry a moral charge; it's how it's used that matters. But what I touched in Therese's room . . ." She shook her head as if trying to throw off a bad memory.

When he reached for her hand, it was already waiting. The bond was working, he thought. It would continue to work—if only she'd let it. "So what does it feel like to touch magic?" he asked, glancing at her.

She smiled wryly. "Tell me how it feels to Change."

"Wild. Painful. Right."

"Okay, you're better at finding words than I am. Magic feels like . . . texture. Sand or glass, wood or stone or leaf . . . when I touch something or someone that holds magic, it has this extra texture."

"Not always the same one?" he asked curiously.

"Oh, no. For example, lupus magic feels a little like fur, a little like teeth."

That made sense. Sort of. If he could imagine something feeling furry as well as hard and pointed at the same time.

"Which is why I don't understand what I felt in Therese's room. Texture isn't good or evil—it just is. I suppose you could have a texture that hurt, like ground glass. But pain and evil aren't the same thing."

"Not once we pass the age of three or four," he agreed, signaling a turn.

"I guess . . ." She seemed to notice that she was holding his hand and pulled hers back. "Hey, didn't you just drive past Ginger's place?"

Patience, he reminded himself. "I didn't see any parking spots."

"Oh. Good. I mean, it's good to know you're only human— oh, that didn't come out right. Mortal like the rest of us, I should say. I never find a parking place when I need one."

His humanity, or the lack of it, bothered her. He didn't

know what to do about that. Did she find his nature hard to deal with because she felt ambiguous about her own? "What's the hardest thing about being a sensitive?"

"Being neither one thing nor the other, I suppose."

"I'm not sure what you mean." He pulled into a parking place. "You're certainly human."

"What does that mean? Where do you draw the line and say, everyone on this side is human—the rest of you are something else? You're comfortable being outside that line. I just want to know where it is." She opened her door and got out.

Why did she need lines? he wondered, climbing out. Maybe it was a consequence of being clanless. He'd always known who he was.

But in some ways, her family was her clan. That reminded him. . . . He spoke as he joined her on the sidewalk. "Wasn't there something you needed to ask me?"

"Frequently, but not right this minute."

"You were going to ask me for a date."

"Oh." She shot him an annoyed glance. "I gather you heard both sides of my conversation with my mother."

He smiled.

"All right. Would you go to the blasted rehearsal dinner with me?"

"I'd be delighted. I was beginning to wonder if you meant to ask Karonski."

"I thought about it."

Her surly tone amused him. "How formal is this dinner? I have a tux."

"You would. No, a suit will be fine. It's being held at my Uncle Chan's restaurant. Maybe you've seen it? The Golden Dragon in the Gaslamp Quarter."

"I've been there. Excellent moo shoo pork." He glanced at her. "You're less than enthused. Am I an embarassment?"

"No. No, it isn't that. Actually," she said, a small smile starting, "I'm looking forward to seeing Mother's reaction to you."

"So you invited me to irritate your mother."

She nodded thoughtfully. "Pretty much. Mother insists she isn't prejudiced, but of course she is. Not against lupi in particular, but let's face it. You aren't Chinese."

He let out a laugh. "No, I'm not."

"It would help if you were a surgeon. Or a lawyer, as long as you worked for a prestigious firm. She's big on personal achievement. But a playboy . . ." She shook her head. "Though she'll like the part about you being rich."

"I'm not rich."

She glanced back at his car, then at him, her eyebrows raised.

"A prop for the image."

"Which you enjoy very much."

He grinned. "I do."

"You'll also be meeting my father, but he's pretty easygoing. My sister Susan—the one who's getting married—is perfect, so she won't be a problem. My younger sister, Beth, will probably flirt with you. Um . . . then there's Grandmother."

"You have just the one?"

"No, but Grandmother is one of a kind. She . . ." Lily sighed. "There's no explaining Grandmother. You have to experience her."

"I'm looking forward to it."

"Shows what you know," she muttered.

They'd reached their destination—La Jolie Vie, an upscale salon owned by Ginger Harris. "Lily." He put a hand on her shoulder, stopping her from opening the door. "What's wrong?"

Her eyebrows expressed polite surprise. "You mean, aside from being bound for life to a man I barely know? Or finding out that the perp behind the killings just might be an immortal goddess?"

His lips twitched at hearing Her described as a perp. "An Old One. I prefer not to honor Her with the other term. You'll have trouble making an arrest, I'm afraid, since She can't enter this realm."

"You said something about that earlier, but how can you be sure? Your knowledge is based on legends so old there's no telling when they originated."

"If She were here," he said grimly, "you wouldn't have to worry about our mate bond. I'd already be dead. So would most of my clan, along with the majority of lupi on the planet. Not to mention any humans she considered a threat—the president, Congress, some portion of the military."

"Okay, you're starting to scare me."

"Good." But she'd been scared before. The closer they got to the salon, the more fear scent he'd picked up from her. "You aren't going to tell me why seeing Ginger upsets you, are you?"

She looked away, her face closing down. "Memory's a bitch sometimes. Sure you don't want to get your hair or nails done while I talk to her? No one's going to jump me between the hair dryers and the mud room."

"My nails are in fine shape, thank you." He wondered if she knew she'd put her hand on his waist. "I won't interfere, Lily."

She looked up at him, grimaced, and pulled her hand back. "Don't stand so close. It doesn't make the right impression if I'm rubbing on you while conducting an interview."

TWENTY-TWO

GINGER had done well for herself, Lily thought as she stepped inside the salon. Venetian plaster on the walls, slate tiles on the floor, a crystal chandelier overhead, and a receptionist who looked like a blonde Julia Roberts seated at an antique desk.

"May I help you?" the woman asked with a warm smile. Amazingly, she barely glanced at Rule.

There were disadvantages to being an expert consultant. Lily's hand started to reach for her ID before she remembered. "I'd like to speak with Ms. Harris. I'm sure she's busy, but I'm an old friend." Lily smiled. "Tell her Lily Yu is here to see her."

"An old friend?" Rule said, very low, while the woman spoke into an in-house phone.

"Later."

The receptionist had already finished and was standing. "Come with me, please."

Lily followed six feet of fashionable blonde skinny into the main part of the salon—a trendy place with eight-foot potted palms, decorative tile, chemical smells, and women. Lots of women. Every one of them stared at Rule as they passed.

Maybe the receptionist was gay.

They passed through a door at the rear into a more utilitarian zone—a brief, carpeted hall with doors at either end. Lily made a halfhearted effort to persuade herself it was relief making her heart pound. She hadn't been at all sure Ginger would see her.

But relief doesn't make your palms damp.

They stopped at the door on the east end. The Julia clone gave it a quick rap, then opened it and stood back, still smiling.

Ginger's office was furnished in expensive kitsch: a neon palm in one corner, pink fuzzy chairs for visitors, a chrome and glass desk. Ginger wasn't behind the desk but stood at the window as if she'd been looking out. She wore a brief, stretchy top in fuchsia and snug cropped pants that showed off her belly button ring.

She turned as the door closed—and her eyebrows climbed. "Rule. I wasn't expecting you. Since you're here . . ." She glanced at Lily, and her lips curled up at the corners. "We could try a threesome. The love seat's too small, but there's always the floor."

To her intense aggravation, Lily felt herself blush. "Does that mean you don't mind having sex with a murderer? Or that it doesn't worry you to get naked with a man you tried to frame for murder?"

"Ooh, you talk tough these days." She shook her head, and for a second Lily thought hurt flashed through those big eyes. "I guess you're not here to talk about old times, after all."

"Good guess. I should mention that I'm not here as a cop, either. I'm assisting the FBI in their investigation."

"The FBI?" Ginger ran a hand through her cropped red hair, fluffing it. "How scary. Have I mentioned that I swing both ways?" She gave Lily an up-and-down look, that cat smile curving her lips. "Nice jacket."

"Thanks. Who persuaded you to lie about seeing Turner last night?"

"I didn't lie." She glanced at Rule, shrugged. "Didn't mean to get you in trouble, sweetie."

"As you see, the trouble was of short duration." His smile was sharp enough to cut glass. "I understand that lying to federal officers creates more lasting problems."

"Could be I made a mistake, but it sure looked like you." She waved at the fuzzy pink chairs. "Let's do sit down. Can I offer you anything? We've a nice Chardonnay, or you could have some fizzy lemon water, if you're being all prim and proper and on duty."

Letting Ginger set the dial to chat wasn't going to help. The other woman would keep control that way, flirt with one or both of them, and tell them nothing.

Lily walked up to her. "These people—the ones you're protecting—are killers. Do you know what they did to Therese Martin? Ripped out her guts. Made a real mess of her, right there in her home, where she thought she was safe."

Ginger's tongue darted out, touched her upper lip. "That's awful, I'm sure, but nothing to do with me. Maybe I made a mistake about who I saw come out of that building, maybe not. Either way, I'm not guilty of anything."

"What were you doing there? Not that night—I understand you'd been at the club. The next day, when you just happened to see the cop cars outside Therese's place and wandered over to see what had happened."

"My, it does sound odd, the way you put it." Ginger tilted her head to one side, then brushed Lily's cheek with her fingers. "You know, sugar, your skin's good, but I don't think that shade of foundation is working for you. Makes you look sallow. I could work you up a personal palette with the brand we carry. You'd love it."

Lily wasn't wearing foundation. "You didn't answer the question."

"For someone who isn't here as a cop, you're sure sounding like one." She shrugged. "Why not? I told the other officer about it. I'd left my purse at the club, which I didn't realize until I tried to pay the cabbie." She grimaced. "He was *not* very understanding, let me tell you. I had to wake up my neighbors and borrow some money, and they weren't understanding, either. I went back to get it the next day."

"Why did you take a cab home?"

Ginger rolled her eyes. "Just between you and me, sugar, I've had a little trouble with my license. I take cabs everywhere these days."

"Club Hell is two blocks away from Therese Martin's apartment. How could you see Turner clearly enough to identify him from that distance?"

"We drove past it, sugar. I don't know if the cabbie saw him or not, but I always notice Rule." She slanted him a smile.

Lily nodded slowly, wondering if they—whoever they were—had arranged for a man to leave Therese's building at the right time for the cabbie to see him. "It's a good story, Ginger. Tight."

"Story?" Those thin eyebrows lifted in outsized surprise. "Sweetie, I'm not the one who makes up stories about where she's been or where she's going. That was you and Sarah."

The air was sucked right out of Lily's chest. *Was it my fault? Have you blamed me all these years? I could have said no, could have talked Sarah out of it. . . .* She got her breath back. "Good one. That connected. But I'm not eight years old anymore, and I hit back. You might want to remember that, because you really need me to be your friend. You're in a world of shit, even if you are too dumb to know it."

Anger flashed through Ginger's eyes. "Now, now. Mustn't call names."

"Think it through. If you saw the killer, you're in danger from him. If you didn't—if you agreed to lie for some reason—you're in even more danger."

"How sweet of you to worry about me." Her voice lowered to a purr. "Poor little Lily. You think highly of safety, don't you? After what happened, I'm sure I can't blame you. Did you go into police work because you felt safer with a gun and a uniform between you and the bad guys?"

Another good one, Lily thought. But Ginger had always known how to jab below the belt. "The thing is, Ginger, I know you didn't see the killer. Because the killer wasn't there."

The thin eyebrows lifted. "Now, that's quite a trick. He killed her without showing up?"

"Yes. You see, Therese wasn't killed by a lupus. She was killed through sorcery."

For a second, fear flickered in those expressive, too-familiar eyes. Ginger gave a nervous little laugh. "You've been watching too many trash movies."

"I said I was assisting the FBI, remember? They've got the case now. Murder by magical means is a federal crime . . . the only one with an automatic death penalty."

For a second, Ginger didn't say anything. Then she jerked one shoulder in a dismissive shrug and turned away. "I've really got to get back to work, sugar. I do appreciate you filling me in on all these fascinating little details, but—"

Lily took her by the shoulder, stopping her. "Listen to me. They don't need you anymore. We know Turner didn't do it, so you're a loose end. You think they won't hurt you as long as you keep your mouth shut, but that isn't how they'll see it. You could change your mind. As long as you're alive, you could decide to talk. And the person who killed Therese can reach out and stop your heart any time he wants."

"Wow." She was trying for smart-ass but couldn't quite pull it off. "That's some imagination you've got."

Lily said nothing, letting Ginger's own imagination work.

She looked away, fiddled with one earring, looked back. "So what happens if I tell you someone asked me to say what I did? Will I get in trouble?"

"I think I can see that you aren't charged with obstructing justice."

"Well." Ginger bit her lip. Her gaze darted around again, as if she were seeking some reassurance. It landed on Rule, who'd stayed back near the door. "All right." She heaved a sigh. "It was Cullen. He asked me to say that."

"Cullen Seabourne?"

She nodded. Her lower lip jutted out like a sulky child's. "He and I have had an on-again, off-again thing for awhile. That's the way it is with lupi. But when they're on . . . oh, my." Her smile returned briefly, smug, then faded. "We've been more off than on lately, and I was hoping to change that. I didn't know what he was going to do to that poor woman, but I guess I knew he wanted to make trouble for Rule. I didn't realize how much. Truly I didn't."

"SHE'S lying," Rule said. He slammed his door shut.

"Maybe." Lily pulled her seat belt across and fastened it. "When I looked for Seabourne the other day, I couldn't find him." She glanced at Rule. "You did well. Didn't butt in."

"It wasn't easy," he said grimly. "Lily, I know Cullen. He's not part of this."

But it fit awfully neatly. They were looking for a sorcerer. He was the only one Lily knew about. "You're friends. Close friends?"

"Yes. I know it looks bad for him, but Ginger isn't the most reliable witness."

"Considering that she's already lied once, no. But what does she gain by lying about him?"

"It could be her way of protecting herself, but I'd vote for spite."

"Hmm. Are she and Seabourne involved, then, like she said?"

"Involved might be too large a word for it. Cullen doesn't indulge in relationships. Just sex." He pulled out into traffic. "Which won't make you think highly of him, but there's a difference between promiscuity and ripping out a woman's throat."

She turned it over in her mind. "Ginger lies easily, but she was genuinely frightened."

"You're scary when you get going."

"How long has she been coming to the club? Is she one of your groupies, or is it lupi in general she likes?"

"She likes having sex with lupi. She doesn't actually like us." He swept her with a quick glance, his expression unreadable, and returned his attention to the street. "I never had sex with Ginger."

"I didn't ask."

"You were thinking it loudly enough," he said dryly. "She's afraid of us. I found that a turnoff."

That startled her. "She hangs around lupi because she's scared of you?"

"She enjoys fear. It excites her."

Lily sorted that into what she knew of Ginger as she had been and as she was now. It fit. "I want to—hey. Why are you stopping here?" He'd pulled into the parking lot of a beach-front restaurant.

"For lunch." He shut off the motor and turned to look at

her. "And for questions. This time I'm asking them."

"I'm not hungry."

"I am, but it can wait. You said you'd explain later. This is later."

"Tonight will be. later, too." Seeing Ginger had been more than enough of a trip down memory lane. She didn't want to linger there. "Look, I was friends with Ginger's sister in grade school. Bad stuff happened. It was a long time ago, and I've got an investigation under way."

"You're hurting. I want to help."

Lily looked out the window. Beyond the parking lot, a slice of ocean showed between buildings. It was a deep blue today, sparkling back at a cloudless sky. Twenty years ago, sky and sea had been gray. Gray and stormy.

Deep inside, something tugged at her, urging her to tell him. To trust him.

She couldn't. She unfastened her seat belt. "I can't talk about it. I've never been able to talk about it."

"Never?" He laid his hand on her shoulder.

She felt the warmth immediately. The connection. She shook her head.

"All right. It's up to you, but the mate bond can be good for more than sex, if you let it."

Lily looked out the window again, at gulls wheeling overhead and a sky as clean and shiny as polished glass. At first they'd all wanted her to talk about it—the cops, her mother, the therapist. She hadn't been able to. Parts of it, yes, but never the whole story. Never the worst part.

But it had been a long time since she tried. A long time since anyone urged her to try.

Maybe, she thought, she could do it now. Maybe she was tired of silence.

She bent and pulled off her shoes. "Let's walk on the beach."

IT was surprisingly uncrowded near the water. Families mostly came on weekends, of course, at this time of year.

"All we need is a sunset," Lily said, "and we could be in an ad. We must look like the perfect California couple, walking barefoot and hand in hand on the beach. Lord knows you're photogenic enough."

"Someone's usually smiling in those pictures."

"I'm fresh out right now." She wasn't sure she could do this, or that she wanted to. "We need to keep this short."

"All right. You knew Ginger several years ago."

"Twenty. Twenty years ago last month." Was it sick to know to the day how much time had passed? No, she decided. Sad, maybe, but inevitible. "Her sister was my best friend in grade school. I spent the night with her often enough, played with her after school. So I saw a lot of Ginger."

"Did you like her any better then?"

She smiled without humor. "No. But she was the older sister, so naturally she was contemptuous of us little kids. Back then, Ginger was the obedient child, believe it or not. Sarah . . ." Her breath caught. She so seldom said that name out loud. "Sarah was the one who got into mischief."

"I've a hard time picturing you getting into much mischief."

"I was pretty much a Goody Two-Shoes. I did my homework, didn't cut in line, didn't talk in class. But Sarah loosened me up some. She could talk me into things. We played hooky one day," she said abruptly.

His hand remained warm and easy, holding hers. "Not a large rebellion."

"You wouldn't think so." She walked on in silence a moment. Her blood seemed to pulse through her body at a new tempo, quick and insistent. *Keep going.* "We didn't like our teacher, and somehow it made perfect sense to punish her by skipping school. We had it all worked out—how to slip away before class started, which bus to take. We hadn't planned on the weather, though. It was working itself up to storm, so hardly anyone was at the beach. At first we were bummed, but then we decided it was cool. We had it almost to ourselves."

"What happened, Lily?"

"We were abducted."

His breath sucked in. For a moment, his fingers tightened hard enough to hurt.

"He was a friendly man." It was like presenting a report, wasn't it? She'd written up cases every bit as bad, and worse.

"He reminded me of Santa Claus, only without the beard. Grandfatherly. He just started talking to us, teasing us about not being in school. At first I wouldn't answer. I told Sarah we weren't supposed to talk to strangers. So she asked him his name, then she introduced him and me and said we weren't strangers anymore. She thought that was terribly clever."

Her feet stopped. She stared out at the gulls swooping low over the shifting blues of the water. This was where she always stopped, the point she couldn't go beyond, not out loud. There was pressure in her chest, as if all the words were backed up there, pressing, all but cutting off her breath.

Rule moved behind her and began to rub her arms gently. Up and down, up and down. The repetitive touch soothed her physically. She grew aware of him standing there, just behind her. Not touching, not asking questions or making her deal with his shock, his feelings. Just there.

He had her back. And the words came tumbling out. "He got us to go with him to his car. He didn't try to talk us into getting in. That would have scared us. He said he needed help getting his picnic stuff to the beach, and we were helpful little girls. We went with him. We didn't think about the trunk, that it could be dangerous.

"He hit her. I saw that and tried to get away. I don't remember him hitting me. I don't remember that, but I woke up in his trunk. My head hurt, and I'd thrown up. I tasted it in my mouth. Sarah was crying. The car would turn, and we'd bump into each other, but we couldn't see each other. It was so dark. You felt like you couldn't breathe, like all that dark was sucking the air right out of you—" Her breath caught now, remembering.

"Breathe now." He wrapped his arms around her. "Breathe now, Lily. You're safe."

He was wrong. There was no safety. But his arms felt good. She leaned back against him and, after a moment, continued quietly. "He drove around until night, when he took us to his house. Sarah was a pink-and-white little girl with pretty blonde hair. Her bad luck. He tied me up, saved me for later. But I was there. I was in the room when he raped her."

A shudder went through Rule's body.

"I don't think he meant to kill her. He looked so surprised." That was one of the worst parts, for some reason. The surprise on his face when Sarah stopped moving, when her legs stopped kicking and her eyes bulged open, unblinking. He'd choked her, but he couldn't seem to connect what he'd done with her being dead. "It scared him. He wanted me to agree it had been an accident. I did. I agreed with everything he said."

Rule rested his chin on the top of her head. He was wrapped all around her now, and it helped. It helped. He didn't speak, and that helped, too. For a few moments she stood there and let comfort seep into her body from his. "I was lucky," she said at last. "I didn't know it then, but some-one had seen him put us in his trunk. A jogger. She got the li-cense plate number. The police had been looking for his car for hours. They found it just in time . . . for me. Not for Sarah."

She swallowed. "He didn't rape me. The officer who spot-ted the plates called it in, but he didn't wait. He broke the door down. He came in alone, against regs. He said later he'd had a feeling that he couldn't wait for backup. He was a patrolman, only a few years on the force. His name was Frederick Ran-dall."

"Hell."

"Yeah." Her voice wobbled. She got it steady again. "That's why I had to go to Internal Affairs. I couldn't be sure I was seeing him clearly, because of our history. But he feels betrayed. I hurt him."

"You said he's a cop all the way down. That means putting the job first. That's what you did. He'll see that, sooner or later."

"Maybe." She wasn't sure. Maybe because she wasn't sure she could forgive Randall for having doubted her. "Ginger was right, you know. I did join the police to feel safer. When you know in your blood and bones that there really are mon-sters, you want to do what you can to get them locked up. And you want as many others on your side fighting those monsters as you can get."

He was so close she heard it when he swallowed. "You chose to work homicide."

"Murder doesn't just destroy one person. It sends out

shock waves that hurt so many. . . . It broke something inside Ginger. She was a pain when she was eleven, but lots of girls that age are a pain. Especially to their little sisters and their sisters' friends. But she wasn't all twisted up the way she is now."

"You warned her. You offered as much help as you could."

She didn't speak. A jogger thudded past between them and the sea. His dog, a big black Lab, loped alongside him in violation of the No Pets signs. The dog's tongue lolled happily.

"What's it like?" she asked quietly, watching the dog. "To be a wolf, I mean. Do you think and feel as a wolf?" *Do you feel safe then? Knowing you're stronger, faster, able to heal almost anything that's done to you?*

"The wolf is always with the human, and the human is always with the wolf. I'm myself in both forms, though not exactly the same self. Are you still yourself when you sleep? When you dream?"

"I see what you mean." She turned her head slightly so she could breathe him in. His scent settled her.

He hadn't answered her unspoken question, but it was a stupid question. No one was safe. All too often, though, the monsters who had hurt his people had worn badges. "Is it a problem for you, me being a cop?"

"A complication." His voice was wry. "Lily?"

"Yes?"

"What happened to him?"

It was the only question he'd asked. She took a slow breath. The pressure in her chest was gone. "He was on death row for thirteen years. Lots of appeals. They finally executed him."

"We handle things differently in the clans, but I guess your system worked. Eventually."

"There are reasons for appeals. The law doesn't always get it right. But he was locked up all that time. He didn't grab any more little girls."

He was silent. She let herself rest against him a little longer. It hadn't been so bad, telling him. He'd made it go easier than she'd expected . . . or maybe that had been the mate bond, tricking her into trusting him.

At the moment, it didn't seem to matter. She felt . . .

clearer. As if telling her story had let it settle into the past a bit more. Lily turned her head, looking up into his eyes. "Ready to go chase monsters?"

"What did you have in mind?"

"The Most Reverend Patrick Harlowe."

TWENTY-THREE

BUT Harlowe wasn't at the church. Lily had hoped the same helpful little man would be there—and would remember her as a police detective, so she didn't have to make any unnecessary explanations. But he wasn't, and the secretary regarded her request to speak with the church's leader with deep suspicion. They didn't learn much from her.

They tried his house with an equal lack of success. Frustrated, Lily glared at the door—Spanish style, hand-carved, and very old. It suited the four-thousand-foot stucco home. "The Rev lives well, doesn't he?"

"Religion has been good to him," Rule agreed. "What now?"

"The neighbors. Then lunch."

Two of Harlowe's neighbors were home. They spoke of a man who fit the house—urbane, upper middle-class, at ease in social gatherings. The first woman didn't like him much, though she didn't say so; the older couple both thought highly of him.

She and Rule were eating seafood tacos when her cell phone rang. "Yu here."

"Lily?" It was Ginger's voice, high and frightened. "Could you come over here? I'm at home and I—I think someone's watching me."

"Have you called it in?"

"You mean the police? No! No, I can't—some of them are in it. *You* know who I mean. I need you to come right away."

"We'll be right there."

"Hurry." She hung up.

Lily explained quickly to Rule, grabbed her purse, and headed for the car.

Ginger's apartment was on the other side of the city. They were halfway there when her cell phone rang again. This time it was Karonski.

"I turned up some interesting connections between the Church of the Faithful and the little church your Sergeant Meckle attends. We're leaving now to have a chat with Harlowe."

"Good luck. I struck out at the church and his home." There was a moment's silence. "Right," she said, rubbing her neck. "I should have checked in with you first. I'm still thinking this one's mine. Sorry. We're headed for Ginger Harris's apartment," she said, conscientiously filling him in this time. "She thinks someone's watching her."

"I was going to ask you to join us for the meet with Harlowe."

"You mean you got hold of him?"

"Reached him on his cell phone. He's driving back from L.A. We're meeting him in Oceanside in twenty minutes."

"Damn." Lily wanted in on that interview, but Ginger might be in real trouble—or spooked enough to cough up a few more facts. "Guess I'll have to read your report."

He chuckled. "I'll fill you in. I've left a key for you at the front desk here. If you finish up before we do, let yourselves in, get comfortable. Order anything you like, as long as it's coffee." He disconnected.

IT was nearly five when they left Ginger's. She'd been drinking. It didn't bring out her best side. She'd alternated between abusing them for putting her in danger and begging them to stay there and protect her.

They hadn't found any sign of a watcher.

"What do you think?" Lily said as she climbed back in the car. "Was she for real, or was she playing us?"

"I don't know. Ginger is a good liar, but I don't think she

can make herself smell scared." He started the car. "She's frightened, but her watcher could be the product of guilt and alcohol."

Lily was uneasy. "I wish she'd agreed to a safe house. Not that I have the authority to arrange one, but Croft could. Maybe we should stick around, keep an eye on her place."

"Neither of us can protect her from sorcery. As she pointed out, a safe house wouldn't, either."

"Yes, but . . ." She shook her head. "I don't know. Something's not adding up." She couldn't put her finger on what was bothering her, though.

"You want to give Karonski a call and see if it's too late to join them?"

Oh, yeah. But . . . "If they're still talking, it could throw things off for us to show up this far into things. I'm going to pretend I'm a grown-up and know how to let someone else run with the ball once in awhile."

"Where, then?"

"Karonski mentioned coffee. Let's head to their hotel and see if caffeine will wake up a few of my brain cells. I need to think."

RULE decided he'd had too many unpalatable cups of coffee in the last few days. He stopped at a small speciality food store and bought coffee beans, a grinder, and a French press. Lily seemed torn between amusement and exasperation until he pointed out that he wanted to have decent coffee at her place, too. Then she fell silent, no doubt brooding over the way he'd been forced on her.

Between that stop and the traffic, the other two beat them there. Croft and Karonski were on the tenth floor of a hotel that specialized in suites for business travelers. The small sitting room was pleasant enough in its generic fashion, with the usual amenities, including a round table with four chairs. An improvement over the conferencing arrangements at Lily's apartment, he thought with a smile.

The hotel's housekeeping services left something to be desired, however. As soon as he stepped inside he noticed a faint, unwholesome odor. Nothing the humans with him would be aware of, he thought. A dead mouse in the closet, perhaps.

"How'd it go?" Lily asked. "And what's the connection between Mech's church and the Church of the Faithful?"

"There isn't one," Karonski said gloomily. "We had it wrong."

Rule went to the table and began taking out his purchases. "Who wants a decent cup of coffee?"

"Ah—none for me." Karonski had an odd look on his face. Sheepish.

Croft frowned at Karonski. "What my partner is avoiding saying is that we've been barking up the wrong tree. There's no connection between the Azá and the killings."

Lily stopped dead. "What do you mean, we're barking up the wrong tree? You talked with this Most Reverend guy for a few minutes, and he persuaded you that he and his entire organization are lily pure?"

Croft looked annoyed. "A certain degree of coincidence *does* occur, you know. I'm afraid we jumped to conclusions."

"Coincidence!" Lily looked ready to bust something. Maybe Croft's nose. "Of course they're connected. Finding out how is what police work's all about."

Croft just shook his head. "We've come at this all wrong."

Rule spoke before Lily could incur charges for slugging a federal agent. "Harlowe was the last one to speak with Fuentes, I understand. What did he say about that?"

"He cooperated fully."

Rule stared. "That's all you have to say? He cooperated fully?"

"Look." Karonski ran a hand over his head, making a bad haircut worse. "Like Martin said, we jumped to some conclusions. Got a little carried away. We don't have evidence that Therese Martin was killed by sorcery, much less that the Church of the Faithful is implicated. A few old legends, a similar name . . ." He shrugged. "It's not much, when you get right down to it."

Rule couldn't believe what he was hearing. "Abel," he said quietly, "how did they get to you?"

Karonski scowled. "I'm going to pretend I didn't hear that."

"Just a minute," Lily said. "Hold on a minute. We don't want to let our tempers take over."

He glanced at her, puzzled by the sudden change.

She looked calm. She didn't smell calm. And he heard, muffled, *"Get ready. They may go for their guns."*

She'd subvocalized it. A trick used often among lupi—not one he'd expected her to be aware of.

She smiled at the other two. "Rule and I were taken aback, that's all. I thought we were all on the same page, but it looks like you've skipped to a different chapter and don't want to fill us in on the details. Am I right?"

"That's about it." Croft was apologetic.

"Okay. I don't agree with your assessment, but you're the ones with the badges. I take it you don't want me on the case anymore."

"We'll be leaving ourselves in the morning. There's no case here for us."

"Well." She shrugged. "Guess we'll take our coffee and go, then. No hard feelings?" She held out her hand—and finally Rule caught on. He eased closer to the two agents. And stood ready.

"Of course not." Obviously relieved, Croft stood and shook her hand.

Rule heard the slight catch in her breath.

"Karonski?" She turned and held her hand out to him. "No hard feelings?"

Karonski seemed more confused than relieved. "You don't have to . . ." He shook his head and looked at her hand, still outstretched, then took it and gave it a brisk shake. "Sorry. I'm not sure what I was going to say."

Lily pulled her hand back, holding it slightly away from her body. Her eyes cut to Rule, making sure he was with her. He nodded. She backed up a step, putting space between herself and the agents.

Then she spoke. "You're bespelled. Both of you."

"What?" Karonski laughed. "You're joking."

"It's the same feel. The same ugly feel as the magic used to kill Therese Martin is all over you."

"Can't be." Karonski was humoring her. "I know my protection spells. Martin and I can't be tampered with that way."

"Think about it. Think about what you believed before you spoke to this man. Compare that to what you think now."

Croft frowned.

Karonski looked puzzled. "I changed my mind."

"Abel," Rule said softly, "you performed your own tests at the murder scene. Why would you say there's no evidence that it was done by sorcery?"

"Because . . ." Karonski's face screwed up as if he'd bitten into bad meat. "My spells aren't admissible as evidence except in certain rare and strictly defined instances."

"But they did show that the woman was murdered by sorcery, didn't they?"

"Definitely. The traces were strong, unquestionably the result of sorcery, and . . ." His voice drifted away. "I forgot what I was going to say."

Lily looked at Rule. "A persuasion spell, maybe? What do you know about persuasion spells?"

"Not much."

Karonski answered. "They're pretty weak stuff, generally, even when used by someone with a Gift of charisma . . . huh. That's funny. I remember thinking when I met Harlowe that I wouldn't be surprised if he had a touch of that Gift."

"We were there too long," Croft said suddenly. Beads of sweat stood on his forehead, as if he'd been exerting himself. "We arrived at three-thirty. We got back here at five-thirty. But I don't remember enough. I can't account for enough of the time."

"Shit," Karonski said. "You're right. We interviewed him for about ten minutes, then . . . I can't remember. Was someone else there?" He looked at Croft. "Did someone come in while we were talking to Harlowe?"

"I don't know. I don't remember." Croft looked at Lily. "You're right. We've been tampered with. You can't trust us."

WHAT do you do with a pair of special agents who've lost their minds—or parts of them?

Lily tried to determine the extent of the tampering. The two agents were willing, and they tried to cooperate, but it was soon obvious they couldn't reason their way past what had been done to them.

Twenty minutes later, Rule put a hand on Lily's shoulder.

"I think we'd better stop. Pushing them any further might do permanent damage to their minds."

Croft was staring at his hands, clasped on the table. His face was chalky with strain. Karonski was muttering to himself, reciting a litany of reminders about why he couldn't trust his own mind. Every time he stopped, he reverted to the programmed thoughts.

"They need medical help," she said. "Or some kind of help. I'm out of my depth here. If only we could get them to call their boss, he could—"

Croft looked up. "Brooks, you mean? I already called him. He knows we're pulling out."

"Right." Lily nodded. "That's good. You know, you aren't looking so hot. Maybe you should lie down."

"I'm not . . ." Croft rubbed his forehead. "Have we been drinking? I can't seem to think straight."

"Not pulling out," Karonski said suddenly. "Need to be out, though. Sedate us."

"I can arrange that," Rule said.

Karonski met his eyes. "Do it. Do it while I still remember why."

Rule took out his phone. "While I arrange things, Lily, talk to them about anything other than the case. Karonski likes basketball."

KARONSKI had no trouble talking about basketball. Croft wasn't interested, though, and was in worse shape than his partner, his short-term memory scrambled. They needed to engage both men's minds as completely as possible, so once Rule got off the phone, they played poker.

Croft was deadly at poker. Whatever had been done to him hadn't affected his ability to think and plan—as long as he wasn't trying to think about the case. The strain didn't disappear from his face, but it eased when he had something else to focus on.

By the time help arrived, he'd fleeced Lily for thirty bucks and taken more than that off Rule and Karonski.

"I hope you know what you're doing," Nettie Two Horses said as she came inside. "Where are my patients?"

"Right here," Lily said. She hoped they knew what they were doing, too.

Two muscular young men followed Nettie into the room. Lily recognized one—the redheaded lupus who'd been at the gate when she visited Clanhome. The two of them looked at Rule for a moment, then fanned out.

Croft had risen to his feet when they entered. He had a tense, ready-for-trouble look. "What's going on?"

"You weren't feeling well, remember?" Lily said. "This is Dr. Two Horses. She's going to examine you."

"I'm feeling better. No need for a doctor."

Nettie set her bag on the table. "Why don't I check you out, just to be sure, since I'm here?

Croft moved closer to Karonski. "I don't think so."

"It's all right, Martin," Karonski said. "We asked them to come."

"I don't remember that." His forehead glistened. The strain was back.

"Yeah, well, we're having a little trouble with our memories, aren't we? That's why they're here."

"I don't know . . ." His eyes darted around the room. Nettie and Lily stood closest to him, at the table; Rule was walking their way. The two young men were working slowly closer, coming from the sides. "We weren't having any problems until *they* showed up."

He went for his gun.

"Martin, no!" Karonski cried, hitting his arm—and the other three men turned into blurs of speed.

Two seconds later, Lily had her weapon out, but it wasn't needed. One of the two young lupi held Croft's arms; he sagged, dazed. Lily thought the other one had hit him, but it had happened so fast. . . .

"All over?" Nettie Two Horses said. She was on the floor, where she'd dropped with admirable alacrity.

"Pretty much," Rule said. He stood next to Karonski. "You okay, Abel?"

"No." He was white and shaking. "Hell, no. Hanging on by my teeth . . . can't remember why we're letting you do this. It's like swimming in butter to try to think, dammit."

"You get the first dose," Nettie said briskly, standing and

taking a syringe from her bag. "Don't worry—your partner will be fine. Sammy didn't hit him too hard. Sammy, you can get the trunks now. Lily, you can put that up."

Lily glanced at the gun still in her hand, shrugged, and holstered it. The redhead went out the door and came back in with a large, empty trunk. Then he brought in a second one.

They put the agents in the trunks. Sammy and the other young man each carried one out, handling it as easily as if it were empty—which is what they hoped anyone watching would assume. Once they reached the panel van they'd arrived in, the agents could be removed from their cramped quarters.

Lily began gathering up the papers and folders on the table. "Your men are alarmingly well-versed at getting bodies out of hotel rooms."

"They watch television," Rule said. "I take it we aren't leaving things for whoever comes to see why Kronski and Croft don't return to headquarters?"

"We're taking temporary custody of everything. We'll turn it over when the time comes. Get the laptop, will you?"

He moved to help her. "Are we going to tell anyone about this?"

"When someone comes asking, yes. Not now. I'd rather not spend the next twenty-four hours or so locked up. We know at least one SDPD officer is with the bad guys, so they're out. And the local Feds would pretty much have to take us into custody and holler for someone from MCD to come sort things out."

"I have a few questions before I go," Nettie said. "I understand you're a sensitive, Lily."

She glanced quickly at Rule, then away. "Yes."

"What can you tell me about the feel of the spell on these two?"

"Ugly. Raspy and sort of rotten-mushy. Like . . . like touching fresh shit with ground glass in it. Will you be able to help them?"

"I don't know. I can keep them sedated, but I'll need to know more about the spell before I try removing it."

Rule spoke quietly. "I smelled it."

"What?" Lily turned. "You didn't tell me."

"At first I didn't know what I was smelling. It was faint,

and I'd never encountered its like before. Later I didn't have a chance. Unfortunately, subvocalizing only works one way between us."

"That was weird, by the way," Lily said. "Handy, but weird. That's how you told those two men of yours what to do? Subvocalizing?"

He nodded.

"So what does the spell smell like?"

"Putrefaction."

Nettie looked at him sharply.

"Yes. I'm told that death magic has the same reek."

TWENTY-FOUR

THEY left the hotel at twilight. The air itself seemed gray, as if all the color had bled out of it. Everywhere buildings were opening yellow eyes on the approaching night, and the dash lights stood out crisply against the muffled charcoal inside Rule's car. Lily rubbed her temple and tried to organize her thoughts.

"One thing I don't understand," Rule said as he pulled out into traffic. "Why did Harlowe tamper with them? He should know by now that you're sensitive. He took quite a risk."

She frowned. That hadn't occurred to her. "There might be a communications problem in their camp, and he didn't know. More likely, though, he didn't realize I'd be able to tell. I'm . . . well, I'm a lot more sensitive than most."

"I don't know much about it," Rule admitted.

"Most sensitives don't pick up secondary magic unless it's really strong. They'd be able to shake your hand and know you were a lupus, but they wouldn't feel the lingering magic on the floors of your father's house, left by the feet of many lupi."

"You felt that?"

She nodded, her mind on the question he'd raised. "Harlowe might have thought that even if I picked up on the spell, no one would listen. I'm off the force, discredited. Croft and

Karonski were the only ones who'd believe me—and they're the ones bespelled."

"Not a comfortable thought, considering we're likely to be visited by someone looking for them."

"We have to hope MCD has witches on the payroll who can confirm the existence of the spell. A coven would be good. Solo practitioners can't summon as much power or perform the more intricate spells."

"I'd assume they don't have a sorcerer," he said wryly, "given that sorcery's illegal. Dammit, I wish we could find Cullen."

"So do I." Though not, she suspected, for the same reasons. "Um . . . I hate to sound ignorant, but why would a sorcerer be better than a coven? A first-rate coven can draw a lot of power."

"According to Cullen, sorcerers see magic. That's how they're able to work directly with the forces involved, unlike shamans and witches. I'm guessing that a sorcerer would be able to look at Karonski and Croft and see the spell binding them—a great aid in removing it, I would think."

"That would be handy," she admitted. If they could trust the sorcerer in question. Rule had a great deal of confidence in his friend. Lily didn't.

"I can think of one more reason Harlowe took the risk of bespelling Karonski and Croft," Rule said slowly.

"What?"

"They've got something big planned for the very near future, and it was more important to get the Feds out of the way than to maintain his cover."

A chill ghosted up her spine, the ripple of possibilities she'd rather not contemplate. What would a group like this consider big?

They lapsed into silence. Outside, the city was waking to its nighttime self, stringing lights along its streets and spires like a lady donning a gaudy abundance of jewelry.

Was it the growing darkness that made her so aware of Rule? Not that she'd been unaware of him before. All day she'd felt him near, known where he was without needing to see him. But the nature of it had shifted. Now it prickled along her skin, gathered in a hot ball in her belly. She could almost feel his breath, as if some part of her was leaning toward him, even though she sat perfectly still.

She shook her head. This was not the time, dammit. She needed a clear head, not the fog of lust. She was missing something. Something important.

All at once she had it. "Shit. Ginger."

"You think they did to her what they did to Karonski and Croft?"

Lily shook her head. "She touched my face when she made that dig about my makeup, and all I felt was annoyed. No, what hit me right now is that she decoyed us. Kept me from going to the meet with Harlowe, didn't she? They didn't want me there. I couldn't be spelled and would have tumbled to them."

He checked the mirror—and made a sudden left turn across two lanes.

Lily grabbed the dash. "What the—"

"They've used her twice," he said grimly. "First to implicate me, then to draw you away from the meeting with Harlowe. But we know about her. She's pure liability to them now."

Fifteen minutes later they were back at Ginger's apartment. She didn't answer her door. "What do you know," Rule said as he reached for the knob. "I don't think it's locked."

"Wait a minute." She grabbed his arm with both hands—and wouldn't have been able to stop him if he hadn't let her. "Breaking in will make enough noise to get the neighbors all excited, and it won't help her. If they've killed her, she's just as dead with you on this side of the door as on the other. If she's there and not answering, she'll call the cops on you. Don't think she wouldn't."

He nodded. "You're right. It's the back door she forgot to lock."

"Hey! That isn't what I . . ." Too late. The door to the stairwell was already closing behind him.

The only back door to the apartment was to Ginger's balcony, three floors off the ground. Lily didn't suppose that would stop him. Muttering under her breath about stupid, stubborn, arrogant werewolves, she drew her weapon and waited.

Seven sweaty minutes later, the door opened. "She's not here," Rule said.

Neither, it turned out, were some of her clothes. "Either she packed in a hurry and cleared out, or they want us to think that," Lily said as they got back in his car.

"Is police work always this frustrating?"

"Sometimes it's worse. At least we have some leads. You want to pick up a pizza? Lunch was a long time ago."

"If we went to my place instead of yours, I could fix you a real meal."

"You cook?" she said, astonished.

"I eat, therefore I cook. Quite well, too. How can you not cook?"

"Takeout. And my uncle owns a restaurant." She considered the offer, then shook her head. "I have to let Harry in. Besides, so far the reporters haven't linked the two of us. It would only take one busybody hanging around your place to change that."

"Your place, then."

Lily lapsed into silence, thinking about their list of suspects, some of them certainly involved, some with a big, fat question mark after their names.

Ginger. The Most Reverend Patrick Harlowe. Mech. Captain Randall. Cullen Seabourne, though he was only on her list, not Rule's. Someone in Nokolai, from what he'd told her of his father's attack, who might or might not be the lupus who'd killed Carlos Fuentes . . .

"You know what's missing?" she said suddenly. "Motive. There are a lot of people involved. Can they all really be nuts about stopping the Citizenship Bill? There are a lot of ways to keep a bill from passing that don't involve murder."

"The Old One the Azá worship doesn't think as a human would."

"And lupi don't either, I guess. But it's mostly humans we're dealing with, humans who are either carrying out Her instructions or making things up themselves. Western, twenty-first-century humans. Why? What do they get out of it?"

"I see your point, but fanaticism isn't reserved to certain portions of the globe."

"So you think it's religious fervor? It's more fun to kill the nonbelievers than just to defeat a bill they don't like?"

"Fanatics have been known to see things that way."

"But they're risking so much. This church of theirs is just getting started here, but according to the FBI, they're picking up members at a fair clip. Donations, too. They cultivate a mainstream look, as if they plan to settle in for the long haul. Look at that house of Harlowe's. Money and position matter to him. Why would he risk everything this way?"

"Maybe he has no choice. We saw what they could do to federal agents who believed themselves protected." He turned off on her street. "I'm not suggesting everyone involved is under a compulsion spell. But some of the bad guys may have been influenced in ways they couldn't guard against."

"Mech," she said, startled by the thought. "Or Randall, or whoever it was . . . that's possible. I don't pick up anything through clothing usually, and I don't go around touching other officers. But compulsion spells are supposed to be very limited. The victim is compelled to one particular act, and it has to happen quickly, or the spell loses its power."

"That's the problem with dealing with an Old One, even at one remove. We don't know what's possible and what isn't."

"What if it wasn't a spell? There are mind Gifts that, being innate, don't rely on spells. Karonski said something about Howell being charismatic."

"Hmm." He considered that a moment, then shook his head. "A charisma Gift boosted by power from Her might be irresistibly persuasive, but it wouldn't wipe out memory. Croft and Karonski lost more than an hour."

"Drugs could do that. But why did they need to wipe out that hour?" She brooded over that as he pulled up in front of her apartment. Dammit, she was missing something. "Speaking of that lost hour—at least we know it takes them awhile to do whatever they did. It isn't just, zap! You're possessed."

"Or it took an hour to question them and learn everything they know about the case."

"You're not lifting my spirits."

They got out and were met by an irritated cat. Harry led the way upstairs, tail twitching, reproving them loudly for having made him wait. "He's not attacking you," Lily observed, fitting her key in the door.

"Harry and I understand each other. He'll tolerate my

presence in your bed as long as I recognize his right to be there, too."

She swung the door open and flipped on the single light, a floor lamp by her chair. Harry streaked past her, heading for the kitchen and the food dish Rule had filled that morning. "You make it sound kinky. Two males in my bed at the same time."

"You could have that, you know."

"What?" She turned. His expression was closed as solidly as the door behind him. Her mouth twisted as something inside her soured. "If you're offering to get together a threesome, don't."

"I'm saying that you aren't bound only to me. Not sexually. If you choose to have others in your bed, you can."

She turned her back on him, setting Croft's briefcase on the table. "Maybe by your standards that's a polite offer. By mine, it rates about a nine on the yuck scale. And I'm not extending the same privilege to you."

"You don't have to. I will never be with another woman again."

She stiffened. "Lupi don't believe in fidelity."

"It has nothing to do with beliefs. You're my Chosen."

Slowly she faced him again, feeling so tense a sudden move might shatter something. "You mean that you can't be with another woman? It isn't possible?"

He grimaced. "Physically, it might be possible. But to the lupus half of a bonded pair it would feel filthy, a violation. Like rape or incest."

Lily realized her hands were clenched and forced them to relax. Her palms felt clammy. "What about the human half?"

"The woman, being human, reacts as a human. She behaves as her nature and beliefs dictate."

"You mean I could be unfaithful, and you couldn't?"

"I wouldn't put it in those terms, but yes."

Her heart was pounding. "Why are you telling me this?"

He didn't respond right away. The shadows cast by the single lamp made a mystery of his expression, and his body was utterly still. Finally he said, "Earlier you trusted me with a very tender place inside you. I wished to return the gift."

She took a step toward him. He was making himself

vulnerable to her, but she didn't understand. What did he fear—or hope? "How would you feel if I took another lover?"

"I . . . wouldn't like it."

Another step. "Rule, what's the difference between the mate bond and falling in love? Aside from the fact that the bond is imposed on us, I mean."

"I don't know. Lupi don't fall in love. I . . . don't know if you experience the bond the same way I do."

One last step, and she stood close to him, looking up at that beautiful, exotic face—the slashes of eyebrows, sculpted cheeks and eyes so dark. . . . "How do you experience it?"

His mouth crooked up on one side. He lifted his hand and laid the tips of his fingers on her cheek. "As bliss. And pain."

Her breathing wasn't working right. "To a human, that sounds a lot like love."

"Does it?" He skimmed his knuckles down her cheek, her throat, leaving a tingling wake. "For me, love is what I feel for my brothers, my father, my son."

"Not your mother?" she asked softly.

He shook his head. "That's a story for another time. You and I don't know each other well enough to love yet, do we? I hope . . ." His voice trailed off wistfully. "It would be good if we grew to be friends."

Lily swallowed. "Yes. That would be good." Then she went up on tiptoe and kissed him. Not the hungry kiss she'd thought of, off and on, all day. A gentle kiss. One that spoke of . . . hope.

Almost hesitantly, his lips answered hers.

Slowly she eased up against him, lifting her hands to his face, cradling it as she deepened the kiss. His cheeks were rough with beard stubble, his body firm and angular. His mouth tasted of last night's passion and today's discoveries, of coffee and man. But it was his skin that fascinated her. The texture of it, the warmth . . . the sheer intimacy of pressing her hand along the skin of his throat made her breath catch.

He rested his hands on her shoulders. Just rested them there, neither urging nor seducing, though his heart beat fast, like hers. Letting her set the pace.

She ran her hands along his sides. The man liked silk. Feeling his shirt slide over his flesh beneath the stroke of her hands, she decided she did, too. He was lean enough that she could find the jut of ribs beneath the muscle, tall enough that her nose didn't quite reach the hollow of his throat.

Too tall, standing up. In bed he was very much the right size.

"Am I supposed to want you this much?" she whispered. "I should be working. I need to . . ." Something. There was undoubtedly something she ought to be doing instead of playing with the dip of his spine.

He bent his head. *"Nadia."* His voice was low, the word a warm breath against her cheek. "You are supposed to have me anytime, anywhere, any way you wish. Work will still be there afterward."

Could she take a few minutes for herself? Would it be right? She eased back slightly and looked in his eyes. Yes, she decided. And she could give those minutes to him, too.

She took his hand. "In that case, I want you slowly. Very slowly."

They didn't turn on the bedroom light. In dusk and shadows they undressed each other, pausing to kiss, to touch.

Naked, he pulled back the covers and pulled her down with him onto the bed. Skin brushed skin as lips met, tested, parted. Need mounted, sweetened by delay. They played with each other, but it was serious play: light touches, indrawn breaths, the air turning thick as hearts pounded, pounded.

His hands were fisted loosely in her hair when he pulled back from a thorough kiss. He leaned his forehead against hers. "Your breath makes me dizzy."

Yes, that's how it was—a sublime vertigo she inhaled with every breath, as if she were falling, every second falling toward a steady, burning center. She rubbed her cheek against his, then urged him onto his back. For a moment she just looked at him—at an elegant body, lean and powerful. Long legs, strong shoulders. His penis, hard and ready. And his face, watching her. Waiting for her to tell him what she wanted. What she needed.

"Now?" she whispered, and he smiled.

She slid on top, using her hand to guide him inside as she sank down, filling herself with him. He gripped her hips and began to move—adagio, not fortissimo. She gripped his shoulders and matched him.

The slow, aching tempo let her catch and hold each sensation, glut herself on them, pay attention to the shift of muscles beneath his skin and the subtleties of shadow on his face. She drifted ever closer to that burning center, reluctant to reach it, willing herself to stay *here*—here with the delicious fullness, the friction. Here with his eyes on her, watching her, strain cutting grooves in his cheeks as he prolonged their pleasure, thrusting slowly. Slowly.

Climax, when it hit, was a surprise. She bucked and cried out—and it hit again. And again. Dimly she heard him call out something and felt his seed pump into her. Her world whited out.

She came back to find herself sprawled over him, with his chest heaving and tears in her eyes. And knew herself changed. Quietly and forever changed.

He ran a hand down her back. "You're trembling."

"Sensory overload," she muttered into his chest. Which could bring on strange fancies . . . that's all it was, the odd fancy of an overwhelmed nervous system. People don't change in any fundamental way between one blink of the eye and the next. She was still herself.

But her arm shook slightly when she propped herself up to look at him. "Hey. Something wrong?"

He shook his head slightly, his expression bemused. "You pack a punch."

Had he felt it, too? *Stop that,* she told herself. Nothing had happened—nothing except incredible sex, that is. "So do you. And now that I've had my way with you, we'd better—"

The weight that landed on the bed made them both jump. Lily looked over her shoulder into a pair of glaring yellow eyes.

"Feed the cat?" Rule suggested.

"Right. And *then* we'd better get back to work."

BUT they accomplished very little more that evening. They were going through the papers in Croft's briefcase and recent files on the laptop they'd brought from the agents' room when Nettie called. Her patients were installed in her guest bedroom, still asleep and under guard. It would take time to discover what had been done to them—if she could do it at all.

They did at least find the connection Karonski had mentioned so briefly when he called Lily. The elders of Mech's church—a fundamentalist Christian denomination—had secretly raised and donated a substantial amount to the Church of the Faithful.

"Strange bedfellows," Rule murmured.

"You'd think. But they found a common cause." Lily passed him a printout.

It seemed that both churches believed fervently in the need to safeguard "the purity of the human race." Both opposed the Citizenship Bill and spoke of the destruction of decency and civilization. Though they defined decency very differently, they agreed that the lupi were creatures of the devil who should be exterminated, not enfranchised.

Lily shook her head. "How could an African American buy into this drivel after what's been done to his people?"

"How does anyone buy into it? No one is racially exempt from bigotry."

"What about lupi?"

"Certainly not us." He grimaced. "Not all of the tales of lupus savagery are fabrications. There have been those of us who preyed on humans. For some, lupi or humans, honor extends only as far as the line they've drawn between 'us' and 'them.' What's done to 'them' doesn't count."

It was late when they gave up and went to bed. Rule was tired, but not so weary he wouldn't have welcomed another loving. But Lily was distracted, her eyes shadowed, her body language saying plainly she wanted sleep, not sex.

But she did cuddle into him, and that was good, too. To fall asleep with her in his arms . . .

Not so good being woken up by her moans, with the stink of fear-sweat thick in his nostrils. "Lily?"

She was still in bed, but no longer cuddled up to him. In the darkness he found her by touch and smell. He spoke her name again, laying a hand on her shoulder. "Wake up, sweetheart."

He heard her gasp. She went rigid, then a shudder passed through her. "Oh, God."

He eased closer, murmuring love words, endearments. All of a sudden she rolled over and all but burrowed into him.

She was shaking. He wrapped her up tightly in his arms

and held on, just held on, until the trembling stopped. "A nightmare?"

Her head moved against his shoulder in a nod. "I haven't had it in awhile. It's . . . from the abduction. I guess I should have expected it to pay me a visit after seeing Ginger today."

He stroked her hair. "Do you want to get up? When I have a nightmare, I don't go back to sleep easily."

She pulled back to look into his face. There was just enough light for him to see her wobbly smile. "What does a werewolf have nightmares about?"

"The usual things. Fire, hatred, being lost or threatened, losing someone I love. Being locked up . . . trapped."

The tremor that went through her answered the question he hadn't asked.

He made hot chocolate. That had been Nettic's all-purpose remedy when he was a boy, and he still found comfort in it at times. They sat together in her single oversize chair, sipping and speaking very little, giving her world a chance to turn normal again.

And he wondered bleakly if the nightmare had been triggered by seeing Ginger—or by him. Because Lily's demons were all about being tricked and trapped . . . and that was how she felt about the mate bond. Tricked into caring. Trapped for life.

TWENTY-FIVE

LILY woke disoriented. She wasn't in her bed, she was . . . she blinked, then smiled. Curled up with Rule in her chair and a half.

She turned her head to look at him. He was bristly with morning beard, his head tilted back, eyes closed, mouth slightly open. So much less elegant than the man she'd seen in Club Hell.

So much more real.

And hers. For better or for worse . . . not that lupi believed in marriage, but what else was this mate bond but a marriage that no court could dissolve?

Of course, marriage used to be pretty permanent, too. A few generations back, women often found themselves bound for life to men they knew little or not at all. In her own family, Lily had only to go back two generations. Grandmother's first husband had been a stranger to her on their wedding night. That didn't make what had been done to Lily right, but, as the T-shirt said, Shit Happens.

And when it did, it was Lily's job to clean it up, put things right. Police work was a lot like housework, she thought. An endless and mostly thankless task that people only noticed when the dust bunnies or the criminals got out of control.

It was all she'd ever wanted to do.

The phone rang. She sat up carefully, but the phone had already woken Rule. "I can't feel my left hand," he muttered.

"Sorry." She'd been sleeping on that arm. She stood, looking around. Where was her phone? In her purse, which was . . . not ringing, she realized as she reached it.

"I think it's mine." He stood, shaking his left hand and frowning.

She grinned as he headed for the bedroom and his jacket, where he'd left his phone. There was something silly about a werewolf's hand going to sleep. Silly and kind of endearing.

A moment later he was back, all sleepiness wiped away. "That was Max. He's says Cullen left me a message at the club. He wants me to come see it."

LILY stared at the message written in sloppy cursive above the bar at Club Hell: "Rule—Don't believe me. Don't come. And don't mention this."

The letters were still smoking. Beside them was a crude map—at least, that's what she thought it was supposed to be.

"It's Cullen's handwriting," Rule said.

"Does he often leave you notes burned into walls?"

He wasn't amused. "No."

Max was perched on top of the bar, glowering at Lily. "I know she's got great knockers, but did you have to bring her with you?"

He'd been grouching about Lily's presence ever since they arrived. She'd had about enough. "Are all gnomes obnoxious little perverts, or is it just you?"

"What the hell are you talking about? Just because I'm on the short side doesn't mean you can—"

"Save it, Max." Rule pulled his attention away from the smoldering writing. "She's a sensitive."

His squinty little eyes opened as wide as they were able. "No shit?"

Exasperated, Lily said, "You want to just put a notice in the paper and save yourself the trouble of telling people one at a time?"

"Max will no more tattle on you than you would him. Will you, Max?"

"Haven't I taught you better than that? If you have to ask if you can trust someone, you can't."

"I trust you. I also trust Lily."

"Yeah?" He sighed heavily. "Well, you're young. So what do you make of the vandalism to my place?"

"I don't know. He says not to come, but he drew a map. That upside down V must be a mountain, and SD would stand for San Diego, but the rest of it . . ."

"The squiggles might be water." Lily moved closer. "And that's the number five, isn't it? Five miles, maybe. I'd better make a copy."

"Don't bother, Knockers. I already did." Max held out a sheet of paper.

Her eyebrows rose. It wasn't a sketch. It was an exact replica, done in blue ink.

Rule spoke. "He's in trouble."

Max snorted. "More likely he was test-driving a new spell. And picked my wall to do it on, dammit! I'm gonna have a word or two with him when he finally shows up."

Max reminded Lily of a parent with a kid in trouble—mad on top, worried underneath. "You think he's in trouble, too."

His long drip of a nose quivered. "Who knows, with a jerk-off like him."

"Breakfast," Rule said suddenly. "Max, I know you've got mushrooms. If you can find some eggs, too, we'll eat. We need fuel and coffee . . . and then, I think, we need to talk."

THEY adjourned to Max's private quarters above the club, a crowded hodgepodge of kitsch and art. One crowded end table, for example, held a beautiful Victorian lamp, a plastic hula dancer, three undistinguished rocks, a cheap candy dish shaped like a skull, six paperbacks, and a small stone replica of Michelangelo's *David* that was, quite simply, perfection.

Max saw her studying the little statue and smirked. "Mike copied me, but what the hell. He did a good job. Let him take the credit."

She shook her head and followed Rule into the kitchen.

They'd argued downstairs. Rule wanted to tell Max everything. Lily agreed that they needed help, but a lewd gnome with a bad attitude wasn't the source she'd have picked.

"Max has been around a very long time," Rule had said. "He's seen things that are myth or history to us, and he can't be corrupted by our enemies."

"You have a lot of faith in your friends," she'd said noncommittally.

He'd been irritated. "Don't they teach you anything these days about those of the Blood? Gnomes can't be corrupted by spell or by Gift. They're too bloody stubborn. Max has no loyalty to ideals as you or I think of them, but he would literally stop breathing before he betrayed a friend."

He'd persuaded her. So, over mushroom omelets—Rule really did know how to cook—they filled Max in.

Rule got as far as mentioning, without naming, the One the Azá worshiped when Max interrupted.

"She? Who's she? Don't talk in riddles."

Instead of answering, Rule asked for a pencil and paper, then in three swift stokes drew what looked like an advertising logo—a line drawing of an egg lying on its side with a slash through it. Max started cursing. Fluently. In several languages, for longer than Lily had ever heard anyone curse before.

Eventually he stopped, wiped his forehead, and said, "Tell me the rest."

He didn't speak again until Lily described what had been done to the two agents. Then he asked a number of precise questions. Finally he nodded. "Okay. First, your federal cops weren't bespelled. There's a fucking *difference* between spell casting and mind Gifts, which no one these days—"

"Skip the diatribe on our degenerate times," Rule said. "How do we tell the difference?"

Max scowled. "Sorcery ain't like Wicca. If you work with power directly, you gotta shape it, which means you gotta get the pattern of the spell inside you. Mind Gifts you're born with, they're already part of you, like feet. You don't have to understand how your feet are made to walk on 'em. Which is one reason sorcerers are so blasted stuck on themselves, thinking they know so much more than anyone else—hell, never mind that. The point is, the results come out different. Your two Feds had these thoughts they couldn't get away from, set up like a loop. That means someone put those thoughts there and tied 'em in place with a good jolt of power."

"Thoughts can't be put in place with a spell?" Lily asked.

"Yeah, if you're an adept." He snorted. "Which no one in this realm *is,* or any of the nearby realms, either, never mind what his Hoity-Toitiness in Faerie thinks."

She blinked. Was he talking about the King of Faerie? "This, uh, goddess of theirs couldn't make someone into an adept?"

"Nope. Not that She would if She could, but She can't work here directly. Has to work through her tools—people native to this realm. Can't just hand someone the words and gestures to a spell and have it work, can She? No more than I could hand you a stone and chisel and you'd chip out a bust of Rule, here. But she can give them power."

He leaned back in his chair—a barstool with arms and a footrest—and laced his hands over his belly. "Now, the way it works is, the new thoughts have to blend natural with the old ones. If you give someone who dotes on pretty little birdies a bunch of bird-hating thoughts, they're more likely to go crazy than to do whatever it is you wanted 'em to. So your telepath gets into someone's mind and—"

"Telepath?" Rule's eyebrows went up. "Speaking of crazy, aren't telepaths driven insane by their Gift?"

"Yeah, unless they're cats. So? You have any reason to think you're dealing with sanity here?"

Unless they're cats? Lily was still chewing on that when Rule said, "Are we dealing with two threats? One is a telepath, the other a sorcerer. Or could both skills belong to the same person?"

"You ain't listening to me! You don't have one bloody reason to think a sorcerer's involved!"

"Hold on a minute," Lily said. "I felt the magic used to kill Martin."

"Yeah, but you're as ignorant of sorcery as most fools these days. What you felt was power, power generated by death magic. Which your U.S. law calls sorcery, but that law was written by ignoramuses. Power is not the same as sorcery. A sorcerer *could* use raw power for a slice and dice, yeah, but so could anybody if they had a tool that stored enough juice."

"Okay," Rule said. "So we may or may not have a sorcerer, but we know we have a crazy telepath who practices death magic and has access to a great deal of power."

"Plus this telepath is under Her thumb, and She wants you dead or otherwise inconvenienced. Your best bet is to leave the country."

"You know that's not possible."

Max sighed. "I knew it. I just knew you wouldn't be sensible. Second choice would be her." He nodded at Lily.

This time it was Rule who scowled. "What do you mean?"

"Send Knockers after your loony-tunes. Can't bespell her, can't get inside her mind—sensitives are immune, period. She's the only one could get close enough to do much. Anyone else gets blasted."

LILY asked a few more questions before they left, but Max didn't have much more he could tell them—a few guesses, a couple of shrugs. Rule was silent until they got to his car. "It was a damned stupid idea, talking to Max," he said, slamming his car door. "Just don't let him give you any damned stupid ideas."

Lily buckled up. "Such as?"

"You are not going after Harlowe alone."

"I can't, can I? You'd have to be nearby." How near, they didn't know. They hadn't tested the boundaries of the bond. "Do you think Harlowe's the telepath?" she asked thoughtfully.

"I'm not sure."

"Who, then?" He jammed down on the accelerator.

The man was in a seriously bad mood. "Well, if we accept Max's opinion as a working hypothesis, the telepath in question is nuts. Yesterday we talked to several people who know Harlowe and didn't get a hint of anything like that."

"Crazy doesn't always show."

"True." Rule was scared for her. That's why he was so angry. It made her feel odd, disoriented.

It wasn't as if no one cared if she put herself in jeopardy. Her family worried, though she took care to keep most of the scary stuff from them. But the risk inherent in her job was one reason they disliked it. Why did Rule's reaction make her feel so funny?

"Lily." He'd forced more calm into his voice. "You aren't thinking of going after him alone, are you?"

"He has to be questioned, and backup won't help if Harlowe—or whoever—can screw around with their minds." With a jolt she understood why Rule's reaction left her feeling all turned around. She *liked* it. She liked being important to him, but it was the mate bond making him feel this way. It messed with his feelings just like their hypothetical telepath had messed with the minds of the two FBI agents.

In a tight voice he said, "If he can't screw around with your mind, he might settle for killing you."

"What do you think I've been doing the last few years— going to tea parties? I've arrested plenty of people who would've been glad of a chance to kill me. They didn't get it."

"Dammit, Lily, you can't arrest him anyway. You don't have a badge."

She shrugged. "Even if I did, we don't have enough evidence yet for an arrest. I wish that I'd accepted the position with the Feds, though. Aside from the problem with making an arrest, the two of us aren't enough."

"I can call on roughly two thousand clan members. What do you need?"

Her eyes widened. "Just like that? I thought your father had all the authority."

"Technically, I have no authority. But if the Lu Nuncio tells someone the clan needs him urgently, he'll come. Or she will," he added. "Some of our sisters and daughters marry out, but many remain within the clan."

A sudden thought made her grin. "I see. You're like Grand-mother—no technical authority, but if she says come, we come."

"I really need to meet your grandmother."

"Be careful what you ask for." She felt a little steadier. "We need to figure out what Seabourne's map represents, even if we aren't sure why he sent it. We need to finish the financials. Croft ran the ones on the church, but we should look at Har-lowe, too. A few trained law enforcement personnel would be nice, but I don't suppose you have any of those."

He was silent a moment. "Crystal and I should be able to handle the financial aspects, if you tell us what to look for."

Lily raised her eyebrows. "Crystal?"

"My assistant. I don't think you've met her. The map has me puzzled, but Walker knows the wilderness areas around here intimately. He might be able to identify some of the features. I can't get you any law enforcement personnel, but I can summon some security. I should have done it earlier."

"If you mean bodyguards—"

"I do. Has it occurred to you that if Max is right, Harlowe and company know everything that Croft and Karonski did? Which includes the mate bond. You're the only one immune to their tampering. You're also the key to controlling me. The only real question in my mind is whether they'll try to grab you or just kill you."

THEY went to Rule's apartment. Hers was simply too small. He'd made several phone calls en route, and they'd soon be joined by a number of Nokolai.

Rule lived on the tenth floor of a high-rise. It struck Lily as they waited for the elevator that this was odd. "Why would a claustrophobe want to ride up and down in an elevator every day?"

"I'm not phobic. And Nokolai owns the building, so it's practical for me to live here."

Testy, she thought. *Don't call the man a claustrophobe just because small spaces scare him. Right.*

The elevator arrived, and they stepped inside. She had Croft's briefcase; Rule was carrying Karonski's laptop. She eased close to him, just in case the big, tough werewolf wasn't as comfortable as he pretended.

He pushed the button for his floor, stuck his hands in his pockets, and said, "Besides, it's a fast elevator."

She smiled.

"What about you?" he asked quietly. "You okay in small spaces?"

"Mostly. I don't do saunas." The trunk had been swelteringly hot.

"When I moved here I thought it might desensitize me to ride the elevator every day."

"Did it help?"

His smile was wry. "Not noticeably."

The elevator opened onto a small shared hall—only one other unit on this floor, she noticed. Must be large apartments. Rule's door was at the west end. He opened it. "I'm going to make some coffee."

"Why am I not surprised?" She followed him inside, closed the door, and turned. "Where should I . . ." Her voice drifted off as she stared. The apartment had an open floor plan, and almost the entire west wall was window. It overlooked the ocean.

"That's the other reason I live here," he said. Apparently the coffee craving wasn't too strong yet, because he stayed beside her.

"That has to be one of the best views in the city."

"I think so."

She tore her gaze from the sea and skyscape and looked around the apartment itself. There was a long, sleek couch covered in a beautiful pale leather . . . and in newspapers, magazines, and books. The dining table was some rich, dark wood. What she could see of it, that is. Everywhere she looked she saw beautiful things. And clutter.

"It's not as tidy as you're used to."

She glanced at him. That wasn't a hint of a flush riding those elegant cheekbones, was it? "Who would have guessed? You're a slob."

He scowled. "It's not that bad."

"It's a mess." She turned and put her arms around his waist, smiling as she laid her head on his shoulder. "But that's okay. Under the mess it's a beautiful place."

He pressed a kiss to her hair. The arms he slid around her were hard with tension as well as muscle. He cleared his throat. "So what do you think—could Harry be happy here? There's lots of room."

Oh, shit. He wasn't really talking about Harry. She swallowed. "I don't know. He couldn't get outside from here. He's been on his own a long time. I'm not sure he could adapt to being penned up inside all the time."

He didn't say anything, but his body remained tense. Unhappy? Hurt? She tilted her head back to look at his face and found his eyes, dark and grave, waiting to meet hers. "Maybe we could try him here for a little while," she said. "See how it goes."

"Good idea." He used both hands to smooth her hair back from her face and dropped a kiss on her mouth, lingering long enough to make it more of a promise than a peck. "You ready for coffee?"

Her laugh was a trifle shaky. "Sure, why not? Uh—mind if I clear a space on the table?"

"My piles are organized, even if they don't look like it. Scoot them to the other end, but keep them separate."

She saw what he meant when she started moving the stacks of papers. This wasn't the random mess of advertising and charitable solicitations; it was quarterly reports, correspondence, and other business-type debris. "Looks like you need an office," she said, sitting down and opening Croft's briefcase.

"I've got one. I prefer to work out here." He set a mug by her elbow and sat across from her. "I do work, you know," he said dryly. "I manage the Rho's investments for the clan."

"You oversee everything?"

"Not all by myself." He was amused. "I have an excellent assistant, whom you'll be meeting soon. Also two secretaries and managers for the individual properties. We keep a very expensive accounting firm busy and have a legal firm on retainer."

"So where is this staff of yours?"

"They're clan, so they live and work at Clanhome. The last few days haven't exactly been normal. Usually I spend about half my time there."

Okay, that made sense. It also underlined how little she really knew about him. *Never mind,* she told herself. That could wait. It would have to. "Here's the material on Harlowe," she said, taking a file from Croft's briefcase. "We have his social security number, checking account number, that sort of thing. Can you do something with that?"

"Something, yes. What am I looking for?"

"Connections, things that don't add up, properties he owns. Does he have a house or business in Oceanside, for example, where he met Croft and Karonski? Anything else up that way? We've only his word for it that he was coming back from L.A. yesterday."

"It will take awhile. What will you be doing?"

"Calling a friend to ask a favor. Then I'm going to ride the elevator, maybe take a little walk." She met his eyes squarely. "We have to know, Rule. We have to find out what the limits of the bond are."

He took a deep breath, exhaled sharply through his nose. "Of course. And I have to get over the idea that something will happen to you if I let you out of my sight. But wait until my people arrive. If you go too far and keel over, it would be nice if someone was there to catch you."

TWENTY-SIX

LILY called O'Brien. She thought he might be willing to pass on what he'd learned from Therese's murder scene, and he was, though first he gave her a hard time about having "gone over to the dark side." Apparently the whole department knew she was in trouble with the captain but was working with the Feds. Cops were terrible gossips.

He agreed to fax her a copy of his report. She gave him Rule's fax number, disconnected, and headed for Rule's home office to wait for the fax. It was every bit as messy as the great room. For some reason that made her smile.

According to Max, if Therese had been killed by a telepath rather than a sorcerer, the killer had probably been on the scene. Eyeball range, he said. Without a spell guiding the power, the killer would have needed to see his victim. He could have stood in the doorway and slashed her up without getting blood on himself.

Lily was hoping to find something to back that up. It would be good to know for sure if they were dealing with a rogue sorcerer as well as a mad telepath. Cullen Seabourne, maybe. He could have had his mind messed with. Hadn't he told Rule not to believe him in that odd message?

But nothing in the crime scene evidence gave her any new ideas. She'd gone over it twice by the time Rule's people arrived—two brawny young men, including the redhead Lily had encountered twice before. The older man with watchful eyes was Walker. And Crystal, Rule's assistant, a short, squat, sixtyish woman who looked disconcertingly like a bulldog—heavy jaw, square head, thick lips.

Lily hoped her astonishment didn't show.

"Glad to meet you," Crystal said in a gruff voice that suited her face if not her name. She didn't sound glad. She spared Lily the briefest of glances before returning her attention to Rule. "Nettie wanted me to tell you that she's making progress with Croft, but Karonski will need to be treated by a coven. Something about the degree of trust involved. Can't say I understood, but that's what she said."

Rule nodded. "I expect we'll be hearing from their superiors soon. Hopefully they can arrange something with a coven."

"What do you need me for?" she said briskly, dropping her purse on a chair.

"I'll show you in a moment, Crystal. First I need to make everyone aware of something. Lily is my Chosen."

That bulldog face just lit up. She threw her arms around Rule's waist and hugged him hard. Walker was suddenly at Rule's side, hugging him around the shoulders. Both young men wore wide grins. "Son of a *bitch!*" Sammy cried. "When's the ceremony?"

"Not for awhile yet," Rule said dryly. "We've a few things to attend to first."

"Oh, sweetie," Crystal said. "Oh, sweetie." She sniffed, patted Rule's cheek, and turned to Lily, beaming. "Welcome to Nokolai."

Welcome to—? Stunned, Lily met Rule's eyes over the woman's head.

He shook his head slightly and mouthed *later.* Aloud he said, "You all know about the attack on the Rho. You may also be aware that Nettie is treating two FBI agents whose minds were tampered with. These things are connected. There is a group of people, both human and lupi, who are trying to destroy Nokolai." That wiped away the grins. "Lily is a target. She's also the best hope we have for stopping them."

"They'd target a Chosen?" Sammy said, incredulous.

"The lupi involved may not know she's a Chosen. The humans would use it against us."

"What do we need to do?" Walker asked quietly.

"I've a map for you to look at. Sammy and Pat, you'll go with Lily. Crystal is going to help me dig into the finances of one of our enemies."

LILY had never had bodyguards before. She didn't like it. "I'm testing the limits of the mate bond," she said stiffly, pushing the elevator button. "We need to know how much distance we have."

Sammy nodded. The other one—Pat—smiled shyly. "I've never met a Chosen before."

"I've never been one before," she said dryly. The elevator doors opened, and she got in, followed by her troops, who took positions between her and the doors.

"I saw a Chosen once," Pat said as the doors closed. "At the last All-Clans."

Sammy jabbed Pat with his elbow. "Excuse me, Lily, but we aren't supposed to talk. It could distract us."

"Then listen. The people we're investigating use death magic. Rule says it has a definite smell."

She couldn't see their faces, but the sudden stiffness in their bodies suggested shock. Sammy's voice was steady, though. "It's supposed to. I've never smelled it."

"I hope you never do. But if you should smell anything rotten—putrefaction, Rule called it—let me know immediately. Don't—" The dizziness hit so fast she couldn't finish the sentence. It was worse this time, a sucking vertigo that made her stagger and brace one hand on the wall, bent over. "Dammit. Dammit. What floor was that?"

"Second." Sammy's hand was under her elbow, steadying her. "Are you all right?"

"Wobbly."

The elevator stopped. Sammy turned to face front again, keeping his hand on her arm, as the doors opened . . . on three men in dark suits. Two of them stood with professional readiness.

The third wasn't standing at all. He was in a wheelchair. He was thin—wasted, really—with a narrow face and hooked nose. "Ah—Detective Yu," he said in a light, clear tenor voice. "Excellent. I'm Ruben Brooks. I believe you have my men."

"Ah . . . not with me." She tried to straighten but had to lean on Sammy when the world grayed out. She tried the sub-vocalizing thing. *"Sammy, you smell anything nasty?"*

He paused, then shook his head.

All right, then.

"Are you ill?" Brooks asked.

"I'll be fine in a few minutes. I have to head back up, though. Not trying to get away or anything," she assured him. "Just have to get back."

"I think you've misunderstood. I'm not arresting you. I'm here to place my unit at your disposal."

THERE were a few moments of confusion. Brooks's body-guards didn't want to leave him, Lily's pair didn't want to leave her, and they wouldn't all fit in the elevator at the same time.

Lily wasn't much help, since she was fading in and out. She ended up riding with Brooks, Sammy, and one of the FBI types, a tall, blond man. By the time they passed the third floor, she was fine.

"Fascinating," Brooks said. "There's quite a sharp boundary, isn't there?"

She glanced at the silent blond man, frowning. "It seems your men filled you in thoroughly."

"Were you not in the habit of keeping your superior officer fully informed?"

"Not about some things, no. Unverifiable evidence didn't go in my reports, and I didn't include anything orally that wasn't pertinent. I don't out people."

He nodded. "Understandable. After we've worked together awhile, I believe you'll trust me with such information."

"I haven't agreed—"

"Ah, here we are," he said as the elevator stopped. "After you."

His motorized chair followed her down the short hall. When

she reached Rule's door, she didn't have to use the key he'd given her—he opened it. She walked straight into his arms.

It wasn't professional, but it was necessary. She needed to feel his heart beating, needed the pressure of his body against hers. After a moment, though, self-consciousness had her pulling away. "This is Ruben Brooks," she said. "I don't know the other one's name. Gentlemen, Rule Turner."

Rule glanced at her, eyebrows raised. She nodded slightly.

"Come in, won't you?" he said, smiling as he stepped back. "Would you care for coffee?"

"CROFT called you from Clanhome?" Lily said a few minutes later, surprised. "I didn't realize he was—well, awake."

"Dr. Two Horses allowed him out of Sleep long enough to—ah, thank you." Brooks accepted the mug Rule handed him. "Long enough to report, so I am reasonably up to date on your situation."

"How is he?"

"Doing well, though Dr. Two Horses wishes his mind to be at complete rest for a few days, which means being in Sleep most of the time. Karonski is being kept sedated until a coven can be flown out here. His Gift and religious beliefs make treating him more complicated."

"You arrived very quickly," Rule said quietly, sitting on the back of Lily's chair and stroking her hair. After their brief test of the mate bond's boundary, they needed physical contact.

"I was already en route when he called. When Croft and Karonski didn't return on time, I had a feeling I would be needed."

Lily's eyebrows rose. "Karonski said you were a precog."

"Yes." He sipped his coffee. "This is excellent. Precognition is the least reliable of the Gifts, of course, but this was an exceptionally strong feeling. It didn't carry much in the way of information with it, unfortunately, but Croft's call from Clanhome remedied that. So now you see why I need to place the unit in your hands for the time being."

"Actually—no, I don't. I lack the experience, the training. . . . I'm a good detective. I am not qualified to run a top-secret FBI unit I hadn't even heard about until a few days ago."

"But you're the only one who can," he said gently. "Though I fully expect to contribute my skills and knowledge, the person in charge must be one whom we know, at all times, has not been interfered with."

"The lupi," she said desperately. "They can smell the presence of death magic, so they'll be able to tell us if someone's head has been messed with."

"Can they? That will be handy. But it will only work in person. Orders must sometimes be given over the telephone."

Lily wasn't sure how it happened, except that Ruben Brooks was the most soft-spoken, polite steamroller she'd ever met. Fifteen minutes after meeting him, she took an oath to "support and defend the Constitution of the United States against all enemies, foreign and domestic."

"Are you sure this is legit?" she asked afterward. "I thought agents had to go through training."

"You will have to go to Quantico at some point, but this is quite legal. The President has granted me the authority to swear in agents at my discretion, waiving the usual requirements."

The President? Lily felt dizzy, and it wasn't the mate bond this time.

"Now," he said, glancing around at the lot of them, "I would appreciate a report, if you don't mind."

Lily nodded. "All right, and when I'm finished, I'd like you to contribute your skills and knowledge. And maybe a map expert and the authority to look into a few bank accounts."

THINGS picked up speed after that. Brooks detailed one of his men to handle the paperwork for obtaining any court orders Rule and Crystal needed. A top-of-the-line computer mapping system was on its way, along with an expert to work with Walker on identifying Cullen's crude drawing.

You might even say he took charge, Lily thought, amused. Not that he issued any orders, but everyone pretty much hopped to implement his polite suggestions.

With the immediate needs taken care of, Lily called a conference of two. She sat on the end of the couch nearest Brooks's chair and leaned forward. "I don't know enough about federal laws. Now that Croft's going to able to testify, we've got enough on Harlowe to pick him up for questioning. But I'm damned if I know what to charge him with. Obstructing justice?"

He nodded thoughtfully. "Legislators seldom pass laws covering impossible crimes, and no one knew investigators' minds could be altered this way. I conferred briefly with the U.S. attorney for this region on my way here. He's not eager to prosecute any charge short of murder by magical means or conspiracy to commit murder by magical means."

Lily suspected "not eager" was a euphemism. "Okay, so my question is, do we get anything from arresting him now? Or do we get enough to outweigh the risks?"

"Why don't you go over your reasoning with me?"

"The way I see it, we don't know enough yet. If he's our hypothetical telepath, arresting him on a lesser charge might be worth it. But if he isn't and we pick him up, the rest of his crowd is likely to go into hiding. Including the telepath or sorcerer or whatever, and that's who we have to get."

"I thought you were fairly confident of your informant's information. You believe a sorcerer might be involved?"

"My . . . oh, yeah." She'd described Max as someone with wide experience and knowledge of magical systems who preferred to remain anonymous. Pushing to her feet, she began to pace back and forth. "I don't know. Simplest is often right, and simplest would be if there's just one big bad guy, a telepath with some kind of tool like my consult suggested. But it's still possible that a sorcerer's involved. Not as likely, maybe, but possible."

He nodded. "It's reasonable to plan for various possibilities."

"Right. But it has me spooked," she admitted. "I don't know the procedures for safely apprehending and neutralizing a sorcerer. If there are any." To her knowledge, it hadn't been tried since the Purge—and that had been a bloody and terrible business. Mostly they'd just killed those suspected of sorcery.

"As far as I know, there aren't," he said calmly. "Some theories hold that truly holy men and women cannot be affected by sorcery because spiritual energies are of a higher order than temporal or magical energies. Even if that is true, however, I don't believe the FBI employs any holy persons."

It took her a moment to see past the deadpan delivery to the twinkle in his eyes. She stopped pacing and said dryly, "I don't think the SDPD does, either."

"The historical record indicates that all sorcerers are not created equal. There are degrees of mastery. However, I think we must assume that if a sorcerer is involved—even one with a relatively minor ability in those arts—arresting him or her is likely to involve casualties on our part. The use of deadly force may be necessary."

In other words, things hadn't changed that much since the Purge. It was still easier to kill a sorcerer than to contain one.

"One more thing. I told you I had a feeling I would be needed here. Connected to that was a strong—very strong— feeling of urgency. I offer this as information," he said in his calm, slightly pedantic way. "I don't wish to influence you unduly, but I am very seldom wrong about such things. It may be as important to act quickly as it is to act correctly."

She scowled at the floor, thinking hard—felt a tug, and looked up to see Rule drawing near.

If there was a sorcerer involved, it was likely to be his friend Cullen. Willingly or not.

He slid into a chair near Brooks. "I'm superfluous over there at the moment. Crystal and your man are deep in the county records, which I know little about. I couldn't help overhearing your discussion."

Lily raised her eyebrows at that. "Couldn't help overhearing?"

"I eavesdropped shamelessly," he admitted cheerfully. "I have a suggestion. Use my people."

"I don't follow you."

"You're trying to decide what to do if it turns out you have to go up against a sorcerer. It would be foolish to send humans in. Lupi can absorb a good deal of damage and continue to function, and we have a large stake in this."

Brooks steepled his fingers. "An interesting proposition."

She glanced at him, startled. "You do realize what the press would do with this? Sending werewolves after the leader of a minority religious group?"

"If we can prove sorcery was involved, all will be forgiven.

If not"—he shrugged—"we'll need to be sure of our evidence."

Which, at the moment, they didn't have. Lily began pacing again. "What we need is that damned tool. The one storing the power." If there was such a thing. Max had seemed pretty sure of it. "We don't know what it looks like, but I could identify it by touch. If we could find that, we'd have proof of sorcery as the law defines it. We'd also have stripped our perp of most of his power."

She stopped, looked at Brooks. "I want search warrants for the church and for all Harlowe's properties, once we know what they are."

"We'll have to word them carefully, and it may be tricky getting a judge to agree," he said slowly, "but I believe I can handle that."

She looked at Rule. "Get me those people of yours. I want a trained team who knows how to follow orders. They'll be on standby. We'd all better pray we don't have to use them."

RULE contributed very little over the next couple of hours. He did call the Rho, who agreed to send a squad right away. Then he put on a huge pot of chili and tried not to think about Cullen or the danger Lily would be in. But thoughts are less obedient than arms and legs.

He was in the kitchen stirring up batter for cornbread when she slipped up behind him and put her arms around his waist. The comfort was immediate.

So was the arousal. He turned, tipped her face up, and kissed her thoroughly.

"Well." Her face was flushed, her hair tousled, her pretty mouth damp and smiling. "Hello to you, too. It smells wonderful in here. You really do cook."

"My father's houseman taught me years ago." He thought he could stand here for a day or so, just holding her, breathing in her scent.

"Houseman? Is that like a housekeeper?"

"Pretty much. Any news?"

"Walker thinks he's identified the general area covered

by Cullen's map. It's a remote portion of the mountains northeast of the city." A worried frown pleated her brow. "He says there are caves in the area. It's not easy to find a suspect underground."

"That's what lupus noses are for. But it might be a good idea to call Max. Gnomes and caves go together. Now, if only we knew what the map signified."

"One step at a time. I need to ask you something."

"All right." He toyed with her hair. He loved the silkiness of it, the sheen. It reminded him of the night sky—so dark, yet full of light.

He couldn't lose her. He'd just found her. Somehow he had to keep her safe.

"This is important."

That meant he wasn't supposed to play with her hair. With a sigh, he dropped his hands to her waist. "I'm listening."

"Why did Crystal welcome me to Nokolai?"

Uh-oh. "As my Chosen," he said carefully, "you are considered part of the clan."

She was quiet. Dangerously so, for several heartbeats. "And the ceremony Sammy mentioned?"

"There's a ritual to welcome you. It's intended to honor you, and . . . it's when you accept the clan as yours. If you so choose."

Relief flooded her face. "Then I get a choice. This isn't just one more thing being *done* to me, whether I want it or not."

"You get to choose."

"Rule?" She frowned. "What is it? I'm sure you like the idea of me being in your clan, but it feels like one more thing I'm not qualified for. Not to mention the commitment. I can't swear fealty to your father."

"That's not part of the ceremony."

"There's something you aren't telling me."

A great many things, most of which there simply wasn't time for now. His mouth twisted wryly. "There's one problem, from my point of view. If you refuse to be Nokolai, then neither can I."

She stared, shocked.

"As my Chosen, you will learn much about us that outsiders aren't allowed to know. You must either become Nokolai, or I must leave the clan." When she continued to stare, saying nothing, he smoothed his hands down her arms. *"Nadia,* I know this feels like one more chain around you, but—"

"You don't know." She pulled out of his arms, putting space between them. "When were you going to tell me?"

"After we were no longer chasing mad telepaths and their murderous friends."

"Okay, that's reasonable." She took a shaky breath and used both hands to push her hair back. "I'm going to have to think about this, and I can't right now."

"I know. I wasn't going to—" The doorbell chimed, drawing his attention. Sammy was stationed there, so after a brief exchange, he opened it. Benedict entered with five others—his personal squad.

"Smells good in here," Benedict said, looking around until he spotted Rule. "I hope you made a lot of chili."

Rule was moving toward him. "There's plenty. I knew a squad was coming. I did *not* know you would be leading it."

"Rho's orders. He wanted to be sure nothing goes wrong if we do fight. I left Houston in charge at Clanhome. He's competent."

Houston was a good deal more than competent in anyone else's terms, but Benedict was in a class by himself. "Lily . . ." He turned, knowing she was behind him. And saw every human in the room on his feet. One had his hand inside his jacket, reaching for a gun. "Ah—have a word with your men, would you?"

"Stand down," she said sharply. "Now!"

They did. The one who'd reached for his gun looked sheepish.

Rule shook his head. "I wasn't thinking. I should have prepared your people."

Lily said dryly, "Your squad isn't exactly what we're used to."

Two of the squad, like Benedict, had multiple blades—scabbarded, but he could see that the humans would find them unsettling. One had a machine gun; all but one of the others had automatics holstered at their waists. And, of course, none were wearing much in the way of clothing, as they were dressed for combat. Denim cutoffs were the usual choice.

"Devin has Pat's and Sammy's gear," Benedict said. "I'll want a word with them. They haven't worked with my squad before."

"I believe," Brooks said placidly, "I will put a call in to the local police department. Mr. Turner's neighbors are likely to call them, and we don't want them getting excited."

Crystal's voice came from the dining table, filled with satisfaction. "I've got it."

Rule turned. Crystal had, of course, kept working. He liked to think she would have moved under the table to continue her task if a gun battle had broken out, but he wasn't sure. "What have you got?"

"Harlowe's property. He owns a nice little section of land northeast of the city." She looked up from her laptop. "And it's right about where Walker places your friend's map."

THERE are fourteen men and two women in this room, Lily thought. Nine of them were at this table, trying to come up with a plan. And none of them agreed.

Good thing this wasn't a democracy. "All right," she said, standing. One by one, the others quieted down. "We've hashed out the possibilities pretty thoroughly. First, I like the idea of getting the Air Force to do a flyby of the area so we know what's there now. Walker hasn't been there in a few years, and the aerial shots we got off the Net are dated. We need to know if Harlowe's put up any structures.

"Second, I'm not sending a small group in to reconnoiter. We don't know this telepath's range. All the woodcraft in the world won't shield them if he or she can pick up their thoughts."

One of the FBI men spoke. "If we go in—"

"Or if we do," said a dark lupus whose name she couldn't remember.

"If anyone goes in," the FBI man said, "we'd need to make sure Harlowe wasn't at the property."

She shook her head. "We don't know for a fact that Harlowe's the telepath. I'm not sending people in to have their brains picked or pickled. Or to get sliced up. We'll do this the boring way—with a search warrant. Which I will execute . . . with two lupi and two humans as backup." She paused. "The lupi will be there mostly to smell—people or spells. The humans will be there to watch the lupi. If someone gets tapped by our telepath, I'm hoping one of the others will spot it or smell it."

Benedict—the only one at the table who hadn't offered an opinion—nodded slightly.

"This doesn't mean we're dropping the rest of the investigation. I still want search warrants for the other properties and the church, but this place is priority." She looked at Brooks. "What's your gut telling you?"

"The sense of urgency hasn't abated."

"All right. Get me that search warrant, and put in call to whoever can get us a flyby. Press them for speed. If—" Someone's cell phone rang. She paused, frowning. If that was her mother—

"It's mine," Rule said, standing. He moved away from the table to answer it.

She went on, "If we can't get the aerial photos in time, we'll go in without them. Benedict, I'm going to need a better understanding of what your people can do, but for now let's talk about contingencies. The first one involves chain of command. If I'm taken out or taken prisoner, that will devolve on Brooks—but he won't be in the field. I don't know everyone's capabilities. Suggestions for field command?"

"For combat, tactics, and strategy," Benedict said, "I'm the most qualified. Give me a target, and I'll reach it. But in a chaotic situation, when goals change—" He stopped suddenly, his head swiveling toward where Rule stood with his cell phone.

"Yes, I've got it, but don't hang—Cullen. Cullen! Dammit!" He looked up, his expression as grim as Lily had ever seen it.

Lily's heart beat in her throat, throbbing in the sudden silence. "What did he say? Where is he?"

"He says he was taken prisoner by the Azá, who want a tame sorcerer. He managed to escape, but he's badly injured. He doesn't know how long he can stay free. They're looking for him. He's holed up in a small shack in the mountains. I know the place."

Lily swallowed. The next words were among the most difficult she'd ever spoken. "Rule, it's a trap."

His eyes were hard as flint. "I know. He warned me, didn't he? 'Don't believe me. Don't come.' The shack is twenty miles from the spot he marked on his map."

TWENTY-SEVEN

"THE question, then," Benedict said, "is who do we send to meet Seabourne? Rule can't go because of the mate bond."

Surprise and gratitude flared in Rule. He met his brother's gaze and said simply, "Why?"

"The Rho extended the comfort of the clan to him for a moon. That time isn't up. We don't leave one of ours in the hands of Her creatures."

"Your friend may not be there," Brooks put in. "If their goal is to kill or capture you, his presence wouldn't be necessary."

"But some of *them* will be," Lily said suddenly. "Probably quite a few. Maybe the telepath." She looked around at the rest. "It's easy to bring charges against someone who's shooting at us."

Brooks tilted his head back to look at her. "And difficult to make the arrest if we start shooting each other. We do not know the capabilities of our telepath."

"At some point we'll have to do it." But she looked frustrated. She shook her head. "In judo, the idea is to use your opponent's moves and momentum against him. They've made a couple of moves we should be able to turn to our advantage— tampering with Croft and Karonski, and now this. The first tells us what they can do. The second tells us where some of them will be at a given time. We need to find a way to use that information."

The doorbell rang.

Rule glanced at Sammy, who was stationed near the door, where he could hear any movement in the hall. He had a funny look on his face. "Two people," he said. "Neither of them large. And . . . a cat."

It rang again.

"Who is it?" Sammy called through the door. He turned a puzzled face to Lily. "She says she's your grandmother. And that I'm to open the door this instant."

Lily closed her eyes and rubbed her forehead with both hands. "Of course. That's just what this night needs." She started for the door. "Let her in."

A tiny old woman in slim black slacks and a magnificent satin jacket, heavily embroidered, stepped into the room. Her skin was porcelain—pale, powdered, fragile with age. Her posture was perfect. Her eyes were black and imperious.

A slightly taller and much plainer woman entered behind her. Holding Harry. Who was growling.

"Well?" the old woman snapped, looking around the room. "Which one is he?"

Lily reached her. "Grandmother, I'm pleased you are well, but this is not a good time, and . . . You brought my cat?"

"He wished to come. There are too many people here. Which one is your wolf?" Her gaze flicked from one to the next, settling on Benedict. "The big one?" Unmistakable feminine approval lit her eyes.

"I regret to disappoint you," Rule said, coming forward, "but I . . ." He stopped. *What the hell—*?

Dark eyes shaped much like Lily's laughed at him. "Hmph. Not so big as the other one, but pretty."

"Grandmother, this is Rule Turner," Lily said. "Rule, I am honored to present to you my grandmother, Madame Li Lei Yu, and her companion, Li Qan. Grandmother, it pains me to be rude, but I cannot entertain you now."

"Bah." She glanced at her companion. "Find a place for Harry. He is not happy with so many people."

"The bedroom, I guess," Lily said helplessly, gesturing toward the hall.

"You smell that?" Benedict asked.

"Yes, but what is it?" Not human. Not anything he'd ever smelled before.

Sharp black eyes swung toward him. "You. Stop talking of me. I do not like your smell, either, but I am not rude enough to say this."

Rule's mouth fell open.

That amused her. "You wonder about me, eh? I don't tell you yet. Lily." She turned to her granddaughter. "I am old, I am tired from much traveling. You do not offer me to sit down?"

"Grandmother." Lily's voice was firm. "We are planning a major operation now. We cannot be interrupted."

Thin eyebrows lifted. She raised her hand and, with one red-nailed finger, drew a shape in the air—a shape like an egg lying on its side. Then she slashed through it. "You are here to defeat Her. So am I."

Shock held Rule still a moment. Then he moved to the old woman's side, holding out his arm. *"Treat her like royalty,"* Lily had told him earlier. He understood now. "Madame, be welcome to my home. Be seated. And please, be quick about whatever brings you here. My friend's life is at stake."

She laid one hand lightly on his arm, studying him with shrewd black eyes. "You worry for him. I forgive your rudeness. But many, many lives at stake."

Rule escorted Madame Yu to the couch. Lily followed and sat beside her grandmother—and most of the others followed, too. Brooks positioned his chair next to Rule.

"How did you find me?" Lily asked her.

"Silly question. You were not at your little place. Your wolf is in the phone book. You must be where he is, so I come here."

"But—you know about the mate bond, then?"

"Of course I know. Did I not go to ask that very question?"

"And Harry?" Rule asked, fascinated.

"He did not like to be alone. He did not like me, either, but all cats like Li Qan, so she bring him."

"I am sorry about the damage to your door, Lily," Li Qan said softly, reentering the room without Harry. "I think it will not cost too much to repair. Your Grandmother lacked a key."

"Never mind that. Grandmother." Lily's voice was urgent. "Who did you go see?"

The old woman looked down, frowning, and smoothed an imaginary crease out of her slacks. She said something to Lily in Chinese.

"You *what?*" Lily exclaimed—then she, too, switched to Chinese. For a few moments the two women held a fast-paced, musical, and wholly unintelligible dialogue. Lily put her hand on her grandmother's and asked something. The old woman patted it and replied firmly.

Lily faced the rest of them. "Grandmother does not think everyone should know who she spoke with, but he—he is one whose word we must accept. He sent her to us with information and . . . a gift."

Madame Yu looked over her audience, her small, neat head held regally. "You will all be quiet now. I have much to say, and time is short. You all know of Her whose sign I made. You fight Her, which is good. You do not know what She plans. I do."

She sought Rule's gaze and held it a moment. Then, one by one, she picked out every lupus in the room. "*You* know Her. In your blood and bones, you know. What She plans for your people is very bad, but is not all She plans. She wants to come here. To cross, to . . . bah. I don't know words." She shot another stream of Chinese at Lily.

Lily looked pale. "Grandmother says *She* isn't supposed to be able to enter our realm, but the realms are shifting. Things in the other realms are changing, and . . ." She glanced at her grandmother, asked a question, then went on. "And some of those who watch are very old now, and weary. Others are busy. Distracted by—she's not sure. Conflict of some kind. Scheming or politics or war."

Madame Yu picked up her tale again. "She make plans, can't cross yet. Needs much power. Needs also right conditions. To make ready, She gather believers to Her. They give Her power. They also ones to open . . . way, path. At place of power." She looked at Lily and spoke a single word.

"Node," Lily said. "They'll open a path for Her at a node?"

"Yes." She nodded once. "At a node. This node must be made different some way." She shrugged. "I don't know how. I tell you as I am told. Something to be changed at node. For this, humans here must open it to other realm. To Dis." She looked over her audience again, saw that they didn't understand, and muttered something Rule was sure wasn't complimentary. "You don't know Dis? Other name is Hell."

Two or three exclaimed. Most looked doubtful. They'd been caught up in the old woman's story until then, but this was farther than belief would stretch.

Lily had no doubt at all on her face, Rule noticed. And he found a sick, taut certainty inside himself. He believed. For whatever reasons, he believed this strange, imperious old woman who smelled like nothing he'd ever encountered before.

Brooks leaned forward. "Madame. You expect us to accept that the Azá are willing and able to open a gate to Hell?"

"Why not? Dis is close. Little openings happen all the time. Fabric between here and there not so strong. All know this."

"Yes, but nothing major. A fool in Memphis managed to summon a minor demon last year, but . . ." Brooks shook his head. "Nothing like you're talking about. There has not been a major incursion from Hell in over four hundred years."

"Four hundred years long time to you. Not so long to some. Things changing. You see other things leaking through, maybe? Little demon, maybe others?" The expression on Brooks's face seemed answer enough. She nodded firmly. "Odd things happening now. More will happen. Realms shift, we can't stop. Her, we must stop. She gather already one to Her with strong mind Gift, very strong. This one a female, lives belowground by node. This the one you must stop."

"The caves," Rule said suddenly. "The caves on Harlowe's property." He was definitely calling Max.

Alert eyes switched to him. "You know where this is? Good."

"How?" Lily leaned toward her grandmother urgently. "How do we stop Her?"

Some emotion tightened the muscles in that small, regal face. For the first time, briefly, she looked old. "He tell me much," she said softly, "but not that. He gave me gift for your wolf, though. Small spell. He is not supposed to, but he is great meddler." A smile touched her mouth—the sort of smile that softens a woman's face when she remembers a man who once pleased her very much. Rule's eyebrows went up.

"What kind of spell, Grandmother?"

"Protect—that part I understand. Also find spell—for finding wolf. This I don't understand."

Lily asked something in Chinese. The old woman answered in that language, then reached into a pocket in her jacket. She held out her hand to Lily. In the palm rested a large bead or marble, pearly gray and softly glowing.

Lily touched it. Surprise, pleasure, and a touch of wonder flitted across her face. "It feels . . . clean," she said hesitantly. "Strong and cool, like wind." She glanced at Rule. "It's a good gift."

"You keep it for him." Madame Yu folded Lily's fingers around the bead. "When time comes, you break it on him." She slapped the palm of one hand with the fingers of the other. "Like so. It lasts many hours, but less than one day. Do not use it until ready."

Lily looked at her closed hand. "It won't break?"

"It must touch his skin. Work only on him."

Lily slid it into the pocket of her slacks. "This is not a small spell."

"For him, it is small." She chuckled, a low, raspy sound, incongruous, coming from such a tiny body. "He hopes so small no one notices. Get him in trouble. But he cannot or does not tell me what you do, only . . ." Now she took Lily's hand again, looking at her intently. "Only what She plans. You are part of Her plan, Granddaughter. You and your wolf. It takes much power to open gate. Can gather power slowly, but She is greedy, wants to gobble down big bite of power."

She paused. "There is much power in mate bond. Power from Her enemy. She wants it. The one who serves Her will take you and your wolf, if she can. Sacrifice you to Her."

"No." Instinctively Rule moved to sit beside Lily, who was quiet. Too quiet. He touched her arm, reassuring himself as well as her. "That won't happen."

Dryly Madame Yu said, "It is good you think so, but Her handmaiden has much power already. How do you stop her?"

Lily spoke two words. "We don't."

* * *

IT was the dark of the moon. The night wasn't wholly dark, though. The road ahead was lit by their headlights, and the stars were brilliant overhead.

They were well outside the city. Not far to go now.

Lily had expected resistance from Rule, and she'd gotten it. Aside from the danger, he knew what being taken—captured—meant to her. But she was asking him to risk himself. If she could do that, he could accept the danger to her. The stakes were too high. They couldn't hold back from fear for each other.

Brooks had been more of a problem, since he could have taken back command. In the end he hadn't, for which he deserved a good deal of credit. After all, he didn't know Grandmother—or who had provided her information and that "little spell."

She'd gotten unexpected support from two quarters—Benedict, who had told Rule flatly that the plan was tactically excellent. And Grandmother.

Rare approval had shone in the old woman's eyes. She'd patted Lily's hand. "*Very* good idea. They think to swallow you, you make them choke. Heh. Yes, very good. And I," she'd announced, "will come after you. This time I will know where you are. Find spell is linked to me."

Needless to say, no one in that room had understood that. One poor fool had grinned. Lily had left Grandmother to sort them out. Time was short.

"Just who did your grandmother speak with?" Rule asked.

She looked at him. He'd been silent most of the way but was driving with one hand so he could hold hers with the other. "I wondered if you were going to ask."

"Am I allowed to know?"

"It should be okay, since she—damn, we have too many anonymous females. The telepath won't be able to read your mind. The, uh, person Grandmother spoke with shows up in a lot of stories. Some of the Native American tribes know him as Raven."

His breath sucked in. "Another Old One. Or god."

"Well, yes."

He slowed and turned off on a rough dirt road. The shack

should be up ahead about six miles. Her stomach felt queasy with fear. It was one thing to decide, logically, that the best way to succeed was to use your opponent's move against her. It was another to walk into a trap. To let yourself be captured.

And Rule. They would take him, too. She hoped he couldn't tell how frightened she was.

"Lily," he said, "how does your grandmother know Raven?"

"I don't know. One doesn't ask Grandmother questions like that. She said he owed her a favor."

"Must have been quite a favor," was all he said. Then, a few minutes later: "This is it. The shack should be just around the curve." He stopped the car.

They had to play this as straight as possible. Unless the Azá were idiots, they'd expect Rule to be wary, on the lookout for a possible trap. They'd make the last approach on foot.

Two feet for her. Four for Rule, because that was how he'd handle this if he were trying to avoid capture instead of snapping the trap shut on himself.

Lily opened her door. Rule had disconnected the interior lights, so no betraying light silhouetted her as she got out. She left the door open. No point in announcing their arrival.

The air was cool and fresh and still. Scrub oaks climbed the hill to her right; the ground was dry and hard beneath her feet. It was very dark, with the shoulder of the hill and the scattered trees cutting off most of the starlight. Automatically she checked that her SIG Sauer was ready in her shoulder holster, then felt her braid. The thin knife woven into it was secure.

Lily had flatly vetoed bringing anyone else along. The Azá wanted her and Rule alive and relatively undamaged. Anyone else was likely to be killed. Besides, they would all be needed later.

Her plan hinged on two things. First, the spell. That would allow the others to find them—and should confuse whatever arrangements Harlowe and company had made. They'd expect their telepath to able to control Rule. Second, she and Rule had to be alive and awake for the sacrifice. Unconscious victims didn't yield the energies the goddess craved.

Lily was fast. Much faster than they would be expecting. And it was very difficult to control a conscious and determined werewolf.

Rule moved around the back of the car to join her, so silently that she didn't hear him at all. He'd changed to the cutoffs the others favored for combat; his skin was pale enough for her to see him in the darkness.

She reached into her pocket and took out the spell bead and felt again the rush of wonder and pleasure, as if she held the wind in her hand. Then she slapped it against his chest, and the wind melted into him. For a moment she left her hand on his chest, feeling his heartbeat. Her mouth was dry.

He covered her hand with his, bent, and kissed her. With his mouth near hers he murmured, "I didn't agree to do this because you are in charge."

"No?" she whispered.

"I agreed because you were right. It's our best hope for stopping them."

A sudden surge of feeling for him made her dizzy. There was gratitude, yes, intense gratitude for the way he'd tried to shoulder some of her burden. But there was so much more. More than she had words for, more than they had time for.

She seized his head in her two hands, pulled it down—and instead of kissing him, pressed her cheek against his. Then, her heart pounding, she let him go and stood back.

And watched him Change.

It was as if reality itself flickered, time bending in and out of itself like a Möbius strip on speed. Impossible not to stare. Impossible to say what she saw in the darkness—a shoulder, furred, or was it bare? A muzzle that was also Rule's face—a stretching, snapping disfocus, magic strobing its fancy over reality.

Then there was a wolf beside her. An extremely large wolf. The top of his head reached her breasts. An atavistic thrill shot through her, not quite fear—the visceral recognition of power. She rested her hand on his back. *So this is how Rule's fur feels* . . . and there was as much wonder in this touch as in the earlier one, when she'd held Raven's spell.

Together they moved forward.

This was the one way Rule wasn't keeping to the program he would have followed had he meant to walk away from the trap. Normally he would have coursed ahead, using scent and hearing to mark the presence of any attackers. But he'd refused to leave Lily's side. They would be taken together.

Lily couldn't hear Rule at all; her own feet scuffed softly on the dry ground. They followed the road but kept to the cover at its side as they rounded the curve. Just ahead was a blacker shape that must be the shack. It, like the area around them, looked utterly deserted.

A large, furry head pressed against her legs, stopping her. She looked down. Rule tipped his muzzle to the left, pointing.

"They're in the trees?"

He nodded.

Okay. They'd go forward as if they didn't know that. She drew her weapon and nodded.

There was cover all the way up to the shack. The place might have been chosen for its accessibility to those who didn't want to be seen. Lily slipped from shadow to shadow, crouching now behind a bush, now behind a rusted barrel. Though she moved as quietly as she could, she wasn't as silent as Rule. He was a shadow himself, darkness wrapped in darkness.

They were as close as they could get without going in. Lily was on one knee behind a tangle of high weeds, her weapon ready but pointed at the ground. Rule was beside her. If it hadn't been for the bond, she wouldn't have known he was there.

He nudged her shoulder with his nose. Her heart was pounding hard—adrenaline as much as fear now. She hoped, burned for a fight. But that wasn't why they were here. She nodded at him.

He slunk, near to the ground, up to the gaping darkness where the door should be, then stood upright, looking over his shoulder.

That was a come-ahead look. She licked her lips, stood, and followed him.

The door was missing, though she had to put out a hand to tell. The interior was utterly black. Rule moved forward, vanishing into that darkness.

For a second she hesitated. *It's no worse than opening your mouth when the dentist is standing there with his drill,* she told herself. *Sure, it's going to hurt. So?*

She felt with her foot, found the place where dirt ended and floor began, and stepped inside.

No one hit her over the head. She couldn't hear or see

Rule, but she felt him nearby. Cautiously she eased forward, wondering if she should risk a light. But what was the risk? They were supposed to—

The hissing sound to her left made her spin that way—only her head kept spinning. Round and round, a sickening spin that flung her loose from consciousness as the blackness swallowed her.

TWENTY-EIGHT

LILY woke slowly. Her mouth felt fuzzy, and her head pounded. She was lying on something hard. And she was cold. Her eyes blinked open. A gray ceiling . . . rock. Rock overhead, and rock beneath her. She was . . .

Rule! Where was he?

She turned her head too fast. Nausea rose, and her throat burned. She swallowed and closed her eyes again.

"It should pass off quickly," a man's tenor voice said cheerfully. "Humans don't react as strongly to the stuff as lupi do. Rule's still out."

"They gassed us." Already the nausea was passing, though her head hurt.

"A derivative of fentanyl—crude, but effective. My suggestion, I'm afraid. I thought it would do less damage than a whack on the head if you two were stupid enough to show up for our little rendezvous."

She turned her head carefully. And stared. "Cullen Seabourne?"

"Live and in person."

The beautiful face was wrecked. Scar tissue covered his empty eye sockets. His skin was patchy—dried blood from the terrible wounds had flecked or rubbed off in places but still stained him in others. His beard was growing out. He was shirtless, and his jeans were stiff with old blood. "You're a mess."

"A sight to scare the kiddies, I'm sure. Itches like crazy."

He was lupus, she reminded herself. He could heal the wounds . . . if they all lived through this.

The fuzziness hadn't been confined to her mouth. As her head cleared, she stretched out her left hand and found Rule's arm. His skin was warm and comforting. He'd reverted to human form when the gas knocked him out.

Feeling steadier, she gave sitting up a try.

She didn't pass out. She did have to swallow a few times.

Rule lay beside her, eyes closed. His nakedness wasn't a surprise, as he'd warned her that clothes didn't travel through the Change. The handcuffs were, but they'd allowed for that possibility. They should fall away when he Changed again.

His breathing was reassuringly even. She put her hand on his shoulder and noticed that her arm was bare. She looked down. She was wearing a thin, white cotton shift and nothing else. Dammit, had they . . . she put a hand to her head and found that her hair was loose. The knife was gone.

Not good news. Instead of panic, though, a hard, cold knot of anger began to throb inside her. "How long was I out?"

"One loses track of time here, but I'd guess you were delivered about thirty minutes ago."

Thirty minutes. Not bad, depending on how long it had taken to bring them here. The others needed time to get in place.

"Tell me what the place looks like, won't you?" Cullen said. "I've made some guesses—they let me out now and then to do tricks or take tea with our hostess—but eyes pick up more detail than ears."

"We're in a glass cage—looks like pretty thick glass—in a cave or cavern—"

"I've got all that." He was impatient. "Get to the details."

Her heart was pounding hard, but steady. She was locked up, yes, but she was cold, not sweltering. She could see out. "We're at one end of a long, narrow cavern, maybe seventy feet from end to end. The ceiling's about ten feet here, rough gray stone. It rises at the other end. I can't see how high it is there—the light doesn't reach that far up. Two visible exits, but there could be more. The walls are uneven, and the shadows make it hard to tell."

"How's it lit?"

"Cables strung along the walls."

"Anyone watching us?"

God. He wouldn't know, would he? They'd blinded him and locked him in a glass cage. . . . Would they have done that if they'd taken over his mind? "There's a guard about five feet from the wall facing the main part of the cavern. Big fellow, over six feet, maybe two hundred pounds. He's watching us, but not closely. Looks bored. He has a rifle, looks like an M-16, and . . . I can't see what's holstered at his hip."

"Is he wearing black pajamas?"

"Something like that." She squinted at the other end of the cavern, trying to make out details. The light wasn't good. "Why?"

"Just wondered if they played dress-up all the time."

"There are three people at the other end of the cavern wearing robes. White robes. Ah . . . they're cleaning a big slab of rock. Maybe an altar." She couldn't make assumptions about Cullen. Maybe sorcerers were harder to control than others, and they'd used pain to weaken him.

"Getting ready for tonight's performance, are they?" He sighed. "Not to knock the company, sweetheart, but I was profoundly discouraged when they dumped you two in here with me. Seems to accord us all the same status, doesn't it? And I've worked so hard to persuade them of my willingness to sell out friends, family, whoever. I quite thought I'd succeeded." He paused. "Almost makes one doubt their sincerity."

She looked at him, frowning. "What in the world are you doing?"

He was sitting cross-legged, his back to the rest of the cavern, his hands busy—with nothing. He smiled. It was an odd sight in that ruined face. "Weaving. It helps to have a hobby. Would you like to meet my imaginary friend?"

"No, thanks." Only one way to know for sure. She leaned toward him and put her hand on his arm.

"Why, sweetheart." His smile turned suggestive—and that was just plain grotesque. "I'm not averse to an audience, but do you really think this is the time?"

Lily snatched her hand back. The buzz of magic had been strong and strange—lupus, but mixed with something else. It had not been slimy. He was clean. "You're annoying, but you aren't bespelled."

"Ah." He still had his eyebrows, though the hairs were rusty with flecks of dried blood. He lifted them. "So you know about Helen's habits? Interesting. No, I'm shielded, much to her frustration."

"Who's Helen? The telepath?"

He continued with his air-weaving. "That's all the name I have for her. *They* call her Madonna, and not after the rock star, which would certainly piss off a lot of . . . ah, he's waking up. Good."

How did Cullen know that, without eyes? But he was right. Lily turned and found Rule's eyes open. "Give it a minute before you try to move," she said softly. "Cullen says the stuff they gassed us with hits lupi harder than humans." Automatically she rested a hand on his shoulder. And froze.

He grimaced. "My mouth feels like I forgot to take out the garbage . . . what is it?"

"The spell. It's gone."

He didn't say anything for a long moment. "You're sure?"

"Yes." She should have noticed right away, the first time she touched him. She hadn't been thinking—the need to touch had overridden everything else. *Damn, damn, damn . . .*

"What spell?" Cullen asked sharply.

Rule's eyes flicked to hers, a question in them.

"He's clean," she said, "but . . ."

"If he's clean, we can trust him." Grimacing, he rolled onto his side and sat up. His eyes widened when he saw Cullen. "Holy Mother. They did a job on you, didn't they?"

Cullen spoke without looking up from his mysteriously busy hands. "Never mind that now. What are you *doing* here? I wasted a lot of time and energy getting you that message, dammit."

"We're supposed to be defeating the bad guys and rescuing you," Rule said dryly. "But my protection seems to have failed."

Cullen snorted. "No, it hasn't."

Lily shook her head impatiently. "It's gone. I'm a sensitive. I can tell."

"And I'm happy for you, I'm sure, but if Rule weren't protected, he'd stink of that damned staff of hers. He doesn't."

"I know the spell is gone. I couldn't be mistaken about that."

"Had a protection spell, did he?" Cullen looked up briefly. "You're right. I don't see anything like that. But there's some spooky things going on with the power flowing between you two.

"Uh—you see this?"

"I can't see your face, sweetheart, but I can see your colors."

"Apparently you're seeing the mate bond," Rule said. "But it doesn't confer any kind of protection."

"Well, it's doing something." He was back to playing with his fingers, frowning intently. "Which is not supposed to be possible, but a lot of odd things have been happening lately, haven't they?"

That's what Grandmother had said. "But what? What could the mate bond do?"

"I'd guess that Rule is somehow drawing on your immunity to magic. The downside is that the protection spell couldn't stick. But his borrowed immunity seems to have kept the lovely Helen from working her wiles on him, so it evens out."

"Not entirely even," Rule said. "The spell was also supposed to lead the others to us."

"Others?"

"Max, several federal agents, Benedict, and his squad."

Cullen sighed. "What I wouldn't give to see Benedict come howling to the rescue—if I could see at all, that is. But it sounds as if we'll have to handle things ourselves."

Lily thought dimly that she should have been terrified. But the knot of anger was growing, taking over her chest. It was cold, icy cold, and calm rather than roiling. She welcomed it. *I won't let them do it. I won't let them hurt him. I'm older now, stronger. I can fight back.*

Rule scooted close to her so that their hips and arms pressed together. He bent his head. "You all right?"

"Yes." Rage was better than fear. She leaned her head close to his and breathed in his scent. The richness of it flooded her, blending with the rage. "We're down to your teeth and my reflexes."

His smile was swift, the gleam in his eyes feral. "My teeth are sharp."

"And I have my grandmother's reflexes."

"There!" Cullen exclaimed, his voice thick with satisfaction. "That's the last one. Let's see how it works."

She turned to look.

He was lowering his hand, palm down, toward the stone floor, his head tilted as if he were staring intently at it. When his hand reached the floor, he waited a second, then exhaled gustily. "It didn't explode. Always a good sign, I think."

Lily was beginning to think that Cullen's head might not have been tampered with, but it wasn't screwed on too tightly.

"Can that guard hear us?" Rule asked.

"I don't think so, if we keep our voices down," Lily said, then, "What?" at his and Cullen's identical astonished expressions.

"I spoke under the tongue."

"Subvocalizing, you mean? You couldn't have. I can't hear that."

"Can you hear this?" Cullen asked.

His lips hadn't moved. Wide-eyed, she nodded. "Yes."

"Then I'd say you're getting a little something through the mate bond, too. Fascinating. But no time to dwell on your new trick. There are things you need to know. First . . ." He glanced at Rule, his voice for once free of mockery. "I'm sorry, Rule. Mick's with them."

Rule's face went blank. After a moment he said, "You're sure?"

Cullen nodded, his face twisted with pity. "He wandered over to exchange courtesies with me. Uh . . . your current predicament was mostly his idea, I'm afraid. His idea as prompted by Her Nastiness, that is. She has this bloody abomination of a staff that snap-crackle-pops with power. With it, she can plant thoughts, not just read 'em. It's not quite like mind control, but it comes close."

They'd taken Rule's brother. *His brother.* They'd turned him traitor, using his mind against him. Lily's hands clenched into fists. "We saw the results with two FBI agents."

"You have some idea, then," Cullen said. "From what I've seen, she finds thoughts that seem to head in the direction she wants, then twists them a few notches until she gets the results she's after." He looked at Rule, then away. "Mick, uh . . . the way she twisted him, he believes he's saving Nokolai by getting rid of you and Isen."

Rule's eyes were bleak. "I will kill them for what they did to him."

"You'll have to take a number," Cullen said grimly. "The good news is that these Azá don't know jack shit about sorcery. I've been collecting sorcéri, and—" He stopped, his head turning.

Lily heard it, too. Chanting. How far away? She couldn't make out words.

"I can blow this thing," Cullen continued quickly. "Our glass cage, that is. I've got control of the grid under the stone. At least, I think I do. My plan was to wait for the next time Her Holiness showed up, and when she was standing close enough—ka-boom!" His ruined face was fierce with joy for a moment. Then he shrugged. "But I'm not crazy about going ka-boom along with it. So the question is, do we all go up in glorious martyrdom together? Or do we try something when they come for us? Which I gather," he added, "they are about to do."

The chanting was closer. She could hear words now, but they weren't in a language she knew.

"An explosion." Lily licked her lips. "Yes. It would make a good distraction."

"If you can do it from a distance," Rule said. "Can you?"

"Probably . . . yes, I can take this . . ." He put his hand back on the stone. "I need a piece of it. Like a fuse."

Lily looked at Rule. "If Benedict and the others are anywhere close, they'll hear it."

"But they may not be. Cullen and I will have to keep the rest of them back while you get the staff away from her."

"Which means we need to be away from this cage but close to her before we act."

"Shouldn't be a problem." Cullen's cheer bordered on the manic. "She'll herd us around personally with that damned staff. You should know, though—"

"They're here," Lily said as the first cowled figures emerged from one of the exits. Their robes were white. They carried candles. *Yes,* she wanted to tell Cullen, *they do play dress-up. . . .*

"That staff of hers," Cullen said quickly. "She can paralyze you with it. The pain is . . . incredible. I don't know how close she has to be to use it that way."

"She can't paralyze me," Lily said. "And if Rule shares my immunity—"

"Maybe he shares it, or maybe it's halved, split between the two of you." Cullen grimaced. "Be good to make some tests, but—"

The white robes had given way to a group wearing black— ninja-style dress like the lone guard near their cage.

"—there's no time, is there?"

White robes headed for the other end of the cavern, chanting. "There are twelve guards, twice that many in robes," Lily said quickly. "The guards are armed—rifles and side arms. All male, I think. With them is a woman dressed in white."

"Headed this way," Rule added.

"Her Holiness. God, I can't wait. If the Lady is kind, I'll sink my teeth into her throat tonight."

"I'll make an arrest, if possible." But Lily's words were as much for herself as him, because the rage inside her understood. Agreed.

Cullen's lip lifted in a snarl. "You can arrest what's left of her, if you like."

The guards were forming up in two lines, leaving a passage for the woman.

"If you've got any sense," Rule snapped, "you'll help me with the others so Lily can tackle Helen."

"Get the damned staff away from her," Cullen said, low and fierce. "Get it away, and I'll burn it. It has to burn."

A high, chilly voice said, "Open it."

They were here.

The woman was tiny. Her body was concealed by her loose white robe, and the hand holding a tall, wooden staff was almost childishly small. She had a high, rounded forehead, very pale skin, and a small chin. She looked about fifty.

Lily felt her lip lifting in a snarl. This was the one who, through whatever intermediary, had killed Carlos Fuentes. She'd made a bloody pulp of Therese. She'd corrupted Rule's brother. She planned to kill Rule, to feed her goddess with his death and the mate bond.

The burly guard unlocked the door and swung it open.

"Madonna." Cullen was on his feet, smiling. "How nice of you to drop by. I'd ask you in, but my quarters have grown a bit crowded."

"I am going to remedy that, Cullen. The woman first," she said to the guard.

Lily had hoped they'd be careless with her—she was small, she was female, and they hadn't bothered to tie her hands. But the gun barrel in her back told her to wait. Wait a little longer.

Instead she looked in the eyes of her enemy and said, "You're under arrest."

That earned her a single peal of girlish laughter. Amusement lingered in the curve of her thin, pale lips. "With what am I charged?"

"Murder by magical means. Conspiracy to commit murder by magical means."

"You may have a little trouble bringing your case to trial, Detective. I don't think they allow dead people to testify." She looked at the guard behind Lily. The one with a gun in her back. "Use the knife—at her face, I think."

The flat of a blade was pressed against Lily's cheek.

"You will behave, won't you, Mr. Turner?" she said in that high, sweet voice. "Or my guard will remove your mate's eye. I prefer to deliver her undamaged, but it isn't necessary."

Rule's lips were white. His eyes were black. Completely black.

"Bend your neck and allow my man to slip the chain over."

He bent. One of the guards slid a choke chain around his neck, then backed away and tugged. "Come on."

Rule left the glass cage with three rifles trained on him. They led him to stand next to Lily.

"Now, Cullen, it's your turn."

"I think I'll sit this one out," he said amiably.

She shook her head. "If I have to punish you so that my men can carry you out, I will not be gentle."

Cullen heaved a huge sigh. "Persuasive as always."

They tossed a pair of handcuffs into the cage. Cullen groped for them and put them on. He moved to the doorway, ducked his head, and received a chain like Rule's.

They started down the cavern, with Helen bringing up the rear. Too far away. *Wait,* Lily told herself. The bitch was the priestess or something like that. She'd be part of the ceremony. She'd have to come close.

"How far should we get to be safe from the blast?" Rule asked.

"The farther the better, probably," Cullen replied.

"Probably?"

"You think I've done this before?"

The white robes stood in curved rows facing the altar stone, with a wide aisle left open. They were still chanting as Lily, Rule, Cullen, and guards processed down the aisle like a macabre wedding party. Chanting the same phrase over and over.

One man stood next to the altar, leading the chant. His hood was pushed back. He was an older man, with a pleasant but nondescript face. The kind you would forget two minutes after meeting him.

"Is that Harlowe?" Lily asked, surprised.

"Yes." That came from Cullen. *"He's a slimy bastard—not a true believer like Helen, but he likes power. He's not happy with her right now. She's pushing them faster than he likes."*

Lily nodded. Her mouth was too dry to spit. Her mind was clear, though, her heartbeat steady. Her rage burned cold and strong. *Not this time. You won't kill someone I love while I watch. Not this time.*

The chant stopped.

"Line up in front of Her altar," that clear, childish voice said.

Lily reached it first and turned to look out at a sea of anonymous, white-robed figures. Shadows danced from the candles they held.

Rule stopped. "Mick," he said, his voice hoarse. He was looking at one of the white robes.

One of the guards smashed a rifle butt into Rule's kidneys, staggering him. "Keep moving."

The white-robed figure stirred slightly.

"Mick," Rule said urgently, "never mind about me. Will you let them sacrifice my Chosen?"

The figure spoke, his voice thick, as if the words were

dragged up against resistance. "Your . . . Chosen?"

"He's lying to you, Mick," Helen said. "There is no Chosen here. Just one of your brother's whores."

"I am Rule's Chosen," Lily said quickly. "That's why she wants us. Because of the mate bond. She—" The blow from her guard came too fast for her to dodge, an openhanded slap to the side of her head that sent her to the ground.

"Rule." Mick's voice was suddenly clear and urgent. "On your honor. *Is* she your Chosen?"

"Yes."

Mick shifted, agitated. "That's wrong. That's wrong. You can't—"

"Mick." Helen moved closer to him. "They're lying. You know they're lying." She held out her staff—

"Now!" Rule said.

And the other end of the room exploded in a blistering, white-hot flash.

Lily was on the floor, so she rolled quickly two times to get out of the reach of her guard. She *felt* Rule Change as the room exploded again—with screams and gunfire this time— and she rolled up into a crouch, aimed herself at the small white figure who was turning toward Rule, staff extended. And leaped.

She crashed into Helen, bringing her to the ground. The woman landed fighting, hitting Lily with the staff, screaming, "Damn you, damn, you, *die!*"

Lily barely noticed the blows. She seized Helen's head in her hands and banged it against the stone floor. Once. Again. *Yes, smash her head, yes, she won't touch Rule, won't hurt him.* Helen was limp now, not moving—

Something struck her shoulder. She felt this blow; the shock of it flashed down her left arm, which went suddenly weak.

A bullet. She'd been shot.

Lily blinked, dazed, and looked down at Helen, who was . . . dead. Helen was dead.

The staff. Had to destroy the staff, too. But when she twisted, looking, she didn't see it. She did see Rule, his jaws clamped around the neck of one black-clad figure. He flung the man away, but there were others—others firing at him even as he launched himself at the next one.

A gun. She needed a gun, had to shoot them, stop them—yes, there was an automatic one of them had dropped. She started to crawl to it, but her left arm collapsed under her weight, so she rolled again, ending with the unfamiliar weapon in her hand.

The huge, full-throated roar of a tiger sounded over the din of gunshots and screams.

Oh, thank God. Thank God. Grandmother was here.

Lily sighted as best she could, one-handed, and started shooting.

TWENTY-NINE

HARRY butted his head against Lily's leg, complaining loudly.

"All right, all right. Not that I have time for this," she muttered, heading for the kitchen and Harry's food dish. Her *own* kitchen, in her own little apartment. Rule still wanted her to move in, but she wasn't ready for that.

"The ceremony's in . . ." She started to glance at her watch, winced, and remembered to look on her other wrist.

One hour and twenty minutes. She had time, she told herself. She was dressed, which was what took the longest right now. And it was ridiculous to be this nervous, only it took forever to fix her hair with this stupid sling.

Just getting the lid off the bin holding Harry's food was a chore. She managed, and was replacing the lid when her doorbell rang.

"Not a good time," she said under her breath as she went to the door. But when she looked through the peephole, she opened the door. "Well, look at you."

Karonski was as rumpled and fashion-challenged as ever, but for once he wasn't scowling. "Got any coffee?"

She shook her head, smiling. "There's probably some left in the pot. Come in. You'll have to get it yourself, though," she said, heading for the bathroom. "And talk while I finish getting ready. I'm, ah, due somewhere at noon."

"I know."

She glanced over her shoulder at him, surprised.

He smiled crookedly. "I'm your ride. Rule asked me."

"Oh. Well, that's great. How are you feeling?" she asked, picking up her brush and frowning at her reflection. There was no way she could braid her hair. It would have to be left loose.

"Good. I'm good. I was one of the lucky ones."

"Yes." She dragged the brush through her hair.

When Helen died, there'd been a sort of rebound effect on her victims. Most of them had gone crazy, though in different ways. The ones who'd been under her control the longest and the deepest—many of them in the cavern—had exploded in homicidal fury. But two of them had suicided.

So had Mech.

Lily's eyes filled. "Dammit." She flung the brush down. If she hadn't killed Helen, Mech would still be alive.

"It's okay," Karonski said quietly. "I've been there. You do fine when it's all going down, but afterward . . ." He shrugged awkwardly. "You get weepy all of a sudden."

She tried for a smile. "You, weepy?"

"Hey, us Poles are manly men. A few tears doesn't change that."

She nodded, took a deep breath, and picked up her mascara. Good. Her hand wasn't shaking. It was hard to apply mascara when you had the shakes. "So how's Croft?"

"Busy. He's the smart half of the team, you know, so I let him handle the paperwork." Karonski chuckled and went on to talk about his partner, idle talk that filled the moment, giving her time to get herself back together.

Lily did her best to take advantage of that. But her attention wasn't with him or the familiar task of applying makeup.

Karonski had been one of the lucky ones, all right. Still sedated when Lily killed Helen, his mind had been shielded from the worst of the rebound. And he'd had a trained shaman standing by. None of the others had been as fortunate.

There was a city councilman in a quiet, private room at a sanitarium. The wealthy widow of a congressman was catatonic. The doctors were optimistic about a few of them, though. The Air Force colonel who'd turned himself in, for example, once his mind cleared. He hadn't been under Helen's control long.

Captain Randall had been unaffected. He'd been clean all along. And he hadn't forgiven Lily for doubting him, though he had paid her a stiff courtesy visit before they discharged her from the hospital.

She'd apologized. And then she'd quietly resigned from the department.

As for Harlowe . . . Lily was trying not to worry about him. Not today, at least. They didn't know what the rebound had done to him because somehow, in all the confusion, he'd gotten away . . . apparently with the staff. They'd never found it, either. Or Ginger.

Then there was Mick.

Lily swallowed past the ache in her throat and dropped her lipstick in her purse. Rule had been down, bleeding. One of the Azà had been about to put a bullet in his head—a silver bullet.

Mick had leaped between them. The bullet had smashed his heart beyond the power of even a lupus to heal. Some might call what he'd done suicide. But since he'd died saving his brother's life, she prefered to think he'd gotten a sudden, overwhelming dose of sanity.

"I'm ready," she said. "Let's go."

"SO," Karonski said, sliding behind the wheel of his car, "you want to explain to me how you can be here when Rule is at Clanhome?"

"I would if I understood it. For some reason the mate bond suddenly loosened after the big fight. Rule said that happens sometimes." It was still very much present, though. She needed him, physically and every other way, and didn't want to be away too far or too long.

But she *could* be away now, for awhile. And she'd needed that, needed a bit of privacy. Time to herself. She had a lot to work through.

"Another thing I don't understand. How did the others

manage to arrive in the proverbial nick of time?"

She glanced at him, amused. "I don't know about nick of time. A few minutes earlier would have been nice."

He sighed. "You aren't going to tell me, are you?"

"Nope. Need-to-know only, Karonski. And you don't."

The answer she wouldn't give him was Max. When the spell failed, the others had been halfway to the spot marked on Cullen's map. They'd continued, of course. Walker knew where one cave was, though they had no idea if it connected to the place where she and Rule had been taken.

But they'd had Max. Gnomes know rocks and earth the way birds know air and wind. With his usual combination of insult and braggadocio, Max had assured them that he could find his way to any spot in any cave system blindfolded.

It hadn't been that easy, of course. They'd made a few wrong turns, and some of the passages had been hair-raisingly tight. But once they got close enough for the lupi's ears to pick up the chanting, they'd had a directional fix. Max had been able to lead them straight to the cavern.

Lily just wished she could have seen the confrontation between Benedict and Grandmother before they entered the caves. Lily had put Benedict in charge of the field team, and he had flatly refused to take an old woman into battle. He'd been ready to tie her up to make sure she didn't "tag along," as he'd put it.

But no one was in charge of Grandmother. She'd resolved the argument by Changing.

Lily shook her head, smiling. Trust Grandmother to pick the moment with the ripest drama to let the others know that lupi weren't the only ones with a second form.

"What's the joke?" Karonski said.

"Families. They can drive you crazy, but where would we be without them?"

"True enough. You're sort of picking up a lot more family today, aren't you?"

"I guess I am."

SOMEONE else was at the gate this time. Sammy, the redhead, was mending from the bullet he'd taken, but he wasn't fit for duty yet. They parked a little ways from the open field in the center of the village. It was filled with people.

Rule was waiting. He limped toward the car, smiling.

Rule had taken four bullets to her one. The guards had hesitated to shoot at her, since she was so close to Helen. One of the bullets had collapsed his lung, which hadn't slowed him much at the time but had made for some scary moments after it was over. But his wounds were nearly healed now, while her shoulder still hurt like blazes and kept her from using that arm.

The mate bond hadn't given her his ability to heal. They were still trying to figure out what, exactly, had changed in each of them.

In more ways than one. "Hi, there," she said, moving easily into his arms.

He hugged her, careful of her shoulder. "Ready?"

She nodded.

Lupus ceremonies were more casual affairs than most human rituals. People called greetings to Rule—and some to her—as they walked, hand in hand, to the center of the field, where the Rho sat on a large, flat stone.

Normally he would have stood for the ceremony, she'd been told. He wasn't well enough for that yet, but he had insisted on holding the ceremony today anyway. Lily didn't understand why, but for the lupi, the discovery of a Chosen—any Chosen— was cause for great celebration. It seemed to be tied to their religious beliefs.

Whatever the reason for their feeling about Chosen, it went deep. Deep enough to have jolted Mick out of Helen's control for a moment, giving them the chance they'd needed.

Someone else waited in the center of the field. A lean man with hair the color of cinnamon and the most stunningly perfect face she'd ever seen—though part of it was hidden by dark glasses. Cullen's eyes hadn't finished regrowing yet. He was nude.

Lily wasn't the only one joining Nokolai today.

While Lily was still in the hospital, the Rho had summoned Cullen. No one knew exactly what passed between the two of them, though Cullen had shared one part of it with Lily; even Benedict hadn't been present for that meeting. But Cullen had emerged dazed—and having accepted the

Rho's offer. The clanless one would be outcast no more.

Rule and Lily stopped a few feet back, leaving Cullen alone before the Rho. "Cullen Seabourne," Isen said in a deep, carrying voice. "You are called to Nokolai by blood, by earth, and by fire. How do you answer?"

Cullen dipped gracefully to his knees and bowed his head. "I submit, and answer with blood, to the earth, and through fire."

"Raise your head and your arm."

Cullen did, extending his right arm straight out.

The Rho lifted his own arm. He bought up a knife in his other hand—and slashed Cullen's arm. Blood welled and dripped.

Then he slashed his own arm. He turned it so the wound was facing the earth where Cullen's blood had spilled, and let his own blood drip into the same spot. "Our blood is joined," he announced. "We seal the union with fire."

A woman Lily hadn't seen before stepped forward. She had gold-rimmed glasses and short white hair. She wore a loose green dress and carried a wand.

She stopped three feet away from the two men, pointed her wand, and fire leaped from its tip to touch Cullen's wound, then the Rho's. Neither man's expression changed.

Lily winced. That had to hurt. *"Rule . . ."*

"Shh. Don't worry. You aren't called by blood, earth, and fire."

Okay. Good.

"By blood, to the earth, and through fire," the Rho boomed, "you are Nokolai."

There were a few cheers and a few who shouted "Welcome!" to the new clan member. Cullen rose gracefully to his feet and backed away. Someone tossed him a pair of cutoffs, and his grin flashed. He looked over at Rule.

Rule gave him a grin and a thumbs-up.

Then it was their turn. She walked with Rule to the stone where his father sat, and she knelt—less gracefully than Cullen, she feared. Rule knelt beside her.

"We have been given a Chosen," the Rho said, his voice even lower, a rumble like distant thunder. "The Lady has blessed Nokolai. When she calls on us, do we answer?"

A hundred voices shouted, "Yes!"

"But the Chosen also chooses. How do you choose, Lily Yu?"

Lily had been told what the traditional reply was. She gave it—with an addition of her own. "I choose to honor the mate bond. I choose Nokolai. And . . . I choose Rule."

Rule's hand tightened convulsively on hers.

Isen blinked, startled, but he recovered quickly. "Then, in token of the Lady's choice and yours, accept this token from the hand of your Chosen." He held out something that glittered, golden, in the sunlight.

Rule took it. Lily bent her head, his hands at her nape as he brushed her hair aside, and he settled the necklace in place.

She felt something else, too. Her hand went to the small gold shape suspended on the chain—a fluid shape, abstract, representing nothing that she recognized.

But it felt familiar. It felt like magic, just a tiny breath of it. Magic . . . and moonlight.

"Be welcome to Nokolai," the Rho said in a voice rough with emotion. He leaned forward, took Lily's face in his two hands, and kissed her on the mouth. Then he sat back, grinning broadly. "And now," he roared, "we party!"

IT was hours before Rule had a moment with Lily alone. Finally, sensing that she was overwhelmed by all the attention— and frankly wanting to have her to himself—he'd pled his wounds and hers, and escaped to the Rho's house.

"Thank God," Lily said, dropping onto the couch in the small parlor. "Everyone's been great, but it gets a little . . ."

"Overwhelming?" Rule sat beside her. Now that he had her alone, he didn't know how to lead up to the question that had been burning in him all afternoon.

She nodded. "I feel a little like a token myself." Her fingers brushed the little golden symbol that hung around her neck. "Everyone wanted to touch me."

"We're a touchy-feely bunch."

"But there's more to it than that. There's all this religious stuff attached to being a Chosen. It's hard to take."

"What you see as religion, we see as fact. Not undistorted," he admitted. "We've a long oral history, but the stories have undoubtedly lost pieces and gained others over the centuries." He took her hand. "Lily . . ."

She leaned back, resting her head on the soft back of the couch and smiling at him. "Yes?"

"You added something to the ritual. Words of your own. About me."

"It seemed right."

He swallowed. "Not long ago, you hated the bond, and you weren't too sure about me. What changed?"

"As Cullen says your father told him, I may be stubborn. I may be slow sometimes. But I'm not stupid." She leaned close and kissed him, gently but thoroughly, on the lips. "It took me awhile, but it finally dawned on me that the mate bond hadn't been done *to* me. How could it? I'm immune to magic. It had to come from inside me. I couldn't repudiate it without rejecting part of myself."

The slow seep of relief, deep and profound, loosened his muscles. He sank back like her, resting his head on the back of the couch. And smiling.

"Just think," she said dryly. "In a few days we get to go through another ceremony of sorts."

"Hmm?"

"The rehearsal dinner, remember? You'll meet the rest of my family. They may not be as welcoming as yours has been."

He'd deal with that when the time come. Right now it was enough—more than enough—to be here with her. Accepted. Chosen . . . by the Lady *and* by Lily.

After a moment she put her hand on his thigh. "Tired?"

"Exhausted," he admitted. And aching in a few places that hadn't finished healing . . . and beginning to ache somewhere that hadn't been damaged, as her hand eased farther up his thigh. He turned his head.

"Not *too* tired," he told her. And, a second later, he caught her laughter with his mouth.

Dear Reader,

The question writers hear most often is, "Where do you get your ideas?"

With *Tempting Danger*, the answer seems obvious. A little over a year ago I wrote a novella called "Only Human" that drove me distracted. It did not want to be a novella—the characters and their world begged to be made into a longer, richer book. I was blessed with an editor who agreed and asked that I expand it into a series. Look for more about Lily and Rule in *Mortal Danger*.

And yet, as those of you who've read both novel and novella have seen, the story told in *Tempting Danger* is very different from that in "Only Human." Though they explore some of the same ideas, they share only a single scene—the opening—and even that isn't identical.

What happened? Do I just like to make things hard on myself?

Well, yes, that's probably part of it. There's also the old adage about never stepping in the same stream twice. When I returned to the stream I'd forded in "Only Human," the water had moved on. I was in a different stream. The current was stronger and carried me farther, through different—and wilder—territory.

Then there's Dark Matter.

Scientists say that around 98 percent of our universe is composed of a mysterious substance they cannot see, measure, or identify. They've dubbed it Dark Matter—and that's where my ideas really come from. Like the mystery mass that makes up so much of reality, creativity can't be seen, measured, or identified. It's everywhere . . . and it's moving.

Happy traveling.

Eileen Wilks

Turn the page for a special preview of
Eileen Wilks's novel

Mortal Danger

Now available from Berkley Sensation!

ACCORDING to Lily, "budget" was a word dear to every Chinese mother's heart, but it lost all meaning when applied to a wedding. Looking around, Rule could see her point.

Wedding guests filled both banquet rooms at the Bali Hai and spilled out onto the the patio, where the ceremony had been held. Here, the curving walls framed a splendid view of the ocean, which lent its faint note to the medley of smells in the room—food, flowers, candles, and humanity.

Buffet tables were artfully piled with fruits and crudités, shrimp, smoked salmon, and other edibles. The remains of a towering wedding cake occupied a place of honor at a separate table. Beneath the babble of conversation drifted the hum of music from the other room where couples were dancing.

Rule had danced with Lily exactly once. He wanted another one. Several more. She could at least dance with him, dammit.

Lily wasn't pleased with him just now. The feeling was mutual. Rule hadn't liked her insistence on staying in her own apartment, but he'd accepted that she needed time to come to terms with the changes in her life. Then he'd learned that she was having nightmares—and she *still* wouldn't move in with him. And instead of talking to him, she'd pulled back inside her shell.

He wove through the crowd, looking for a small, slender woman with hair the color of night, skin like cream poured over apricots . . . and a dress the color of mold. A smile twitched at his mouth. Truer love hath no sister than to wear such a gown.

As it turned out, it was the mother, not the daughter, he found. Julia Yu was speaking with two women about her age—one Anglo, one Chinese—when she saw him. She motioned for him to join them.

Rule repressed a sigh. He'd been glad of the chance this wedding offered to become acquainted with Lily's people. They were part of her, after all, and he was endlessly curious about her. Last night he'd met her parents at the rehearsal dinner. Neither of them approved of him, but that was no surprise. Her father was at least reserving judgment. Her mother liked him, didn't want to, and was baffled by Madame Yu's approval of him.

But it was Lily he wanted now.

So, apparently, did her mother. After the briefest of introductions, she excused herself to the others and took Rule aside.

Julia Yu was a tall, elegant woman with beautiful hands, very little chin, and Lily's eyes set beneath eyebrows plucked to crispness. At the moment she'd tucked a frown between those eyebrows. "Have you seen Lily?"

His own brows lifted in surprise. "I was just looking for her, actually."

"Tch! I'm being silly." She shook her head. "It's Beth's fault, putting ideas in my head, and then I've been so busy . . . you have no idea what it is to put on a wedding like this."

He replied automatically, gripped by worry as sudden as it was formless. "You've done a magnificent job. The wedding was magnificent, as is the reception. But what ideas did Beth put in your head?"

"Such a silly story! Of course she was imagining things. Beth is very imaginative." It was impossible to tell if she meant that as a compliment or criticism of her youngest daughter. The frown hadn't budged. "I paid it no heed at all."

"What kind of story?"

"She said she saw Lily go into the ladies' room and followed her. They haven't had much opportunity to talk lately, you know, so I suppose . . . but Lily wasn't there." Julia's lips pursed. "Beth swears Lily could not have left without her seeing, but of course that's nonsense."

It had to be. Didn't it?

Rule stood stock still for a moment. Lily wasn't far. He *knew* that. But he hadn't been able to find her, and the world wasn't as sane and orderly a place as it appeared. The realms were shifting.

Then there was the fact that Lily had recently pissed off a goddess.

"I'll find her." He turned away, moving quickly, propelled by a wordless and possibly foolish urgency.

The last place she'd been seen was the ladies' room, so that's where he headed. The restrooms lay off the hall that connected the banquet rooms to the main dining room. A knot of unhappy women had collected outside the ladies' room. He picked up snatches of conversation.

". . . sent for the manager?"

"Is there another one?"

"Plenty of stalls, no need to lock the door."

". . . some kind of sadist, if you ask me!"

His heartbeat kicked up and his mouth went dry. He eased his way through them, using his size, his smile, and—after a moment—their recognition to part them. "Excuse me, ladies. Pardon me. No, I'm not the manager, but if you'll step aside . . ."

"Shannon," one of them whispered to another, "you dummy! That's the Nokolai prince!"

He pretended he didn't notice the sudden hush. "I think I can fix this, so if you'll . . . thank you," he said as the last one moved away and he reached the door.

Lily was on the other side. He felt her nearness as a slow stir beneath his breastbone. He tried the knob. Locked, and stoutly.

Something was very wrong.

Rule put his hand through the door.

A couple of the women cried out. He ignored them and the pain in his hand, reaching through to unlock the door. His blood made the mechanism slippery, but he managed it. He shoved the door open.

Lily lay on the floor by the sinks. She wasn't moving.

EILEEN WILKS

USA *Today* **Bestselling Author of**
Mortal Danger **and** *Blood Lines*

NIGHT SEASON

Pregnancy has turned FBI Agent Cynna Weaver's whole life upside down. Lupus sorcerer Cullen Seabourne is thrilled to be the father, but what does Cynna know about kids? Her mother was a drunk. Her father abandoned them. Or so she's always believed.

As Cynna is trying to wrap her head around this problem, a new one pops up, in the form of a delegation from another realm. They want to take Cynna and Cullen back with them—to meet her long-lost father and find a mysterious medallion. But when these two born cynics land in a world where magic is commonplace and night never ends, their only way home lies in tracking down the missing medallion—one also sought by powerful beings who will do anything to claim it...

M110T0907